PRAISE FOR *THE MOSTLY TRUE STO*

"You'll never be able to see what's coming ir

taining ride of a novel—which is a coming-of-age story, a contending-with-age story, and a surprising exploration of how womanhood is a matter of surprising others . . . and oneself."

—Jodi Picoult, *New York Times* bestselling author of *Wish You Were Here*

"Colleen Oakley is in a world of her own when it comes to creating lovable, quirky characters—and those in *The Mostly True Story of Tanner & Louise* are her best yet. With an abundance of charm and wit, a dose of adventure, and surprises around each corner, you'll be rooting for Tanner and Louise with every turn of the page. An absolute blast."

—Taylor Jenkins Reid, #1 *New York Times* bestselling author of *Malibu Rising*

"*The Mostly True Story of Tanner & Louise* is pure joy on paper. With wit, sass, and real emotion, Tanner and Louise, two unlikely fugitives, find connection, common ground, and true friendship across generations. A delightful reminder that there are meaningful second, third, and even fourth acts in life."

—Chandler Baker, *New York Times* bestselling author of *Whisper Network*

"Colleen Oakley's *The Mostly True Story of Tanner & Louise* is the ultimate road trip, featuring a pair of quirky, original characters on the lam from the law. A funny, fresh take on unlikely friendships and family. I'd ride shotgun with Tanner and Louise in a heartbeat!"

—Mary Kay Andrews, *New York Times* bestselling author of *The Newcomer*

"An absolute delight. A twenty-first century version of Bonnie and Clyde . . . if Bonnie were an octogenarian jewel thief on the run and Clyde her bitter twentysomething caretaker. It's also a story of lifelong friendships, the (often) extra work women are saddled with, and the value of second chances. You will laugh out loud, maybe cry; but you will definitely be rooting for these strong, powerful women. Tanner and Louise will live forever in your heart and (likely) be the ones whispering for you to take that chance and risk it all."

—Julie Clark, *New York Times* bestselling author of *The Last Flight* and *The Lies I Tell*

"Deliciously entertaining, this feminist caper of a novel has a little of everything, from a wild road trip, to quirky and lovable characters, to a "keep you on your toes" mystery. With great charm and wit, *The Mostly True Story of Tanner & Louise* offers a dazzling cornucopia of truths: the might of female friendship, that women only get better with age, and that the journey to self-discovery is a path worth taking. Colleen Oakley has done it again—I loved Tanner and Louise!"

—Karma Brown, *USA Today* bestselling author of *Recipe for a Perfect Wife*

"Absolutely delightful! I would follow Tanner and Louise anywhere."

—Elle Cosimano, *USA Today* bestselling author of *Finlay Donovan Is Killing It*

"I adored everything about this book. Sparkling writing, characters you root for, an unlikely partnership who may or may not be on the lam from the authorities, and twists you didn't see coming. Move over, Thelma and Louise, and make room for Louise and Tanner!"

—Allison Winn Scotch, *New York Times* bestselling author of *The Rewind*

PRAISE FOR *THE INVISIBLE HUSBAND OF FRICK ISLAND*

"Sweet, quirky, surprising, and altogether lovely, *The Invisible Husband of Frick Island* is everything I long for in a book. I fell in love with Oakley's sparkling prose, charming characters, and quaint island setting. This is a story I can't wait to revisit again and again. A must-read."

—Emily Henry, #1 *New York Times* bestselling author of *Beach Read*

"An utterly charming story brimming with heart and humanity. This is the hopeful book we all need right now. I loved it!"

—Emily Giffin, #1 *New York Times* bestselling author of *The Lies That Bind*

"What's a town to do when a recent widow keeps talking to her husband, who no one else can see? Follow along, of course. Colleen Oakley's captivating *The Invisible Husband of Frick Island* is populated with quirky characters that stole my heart. Make this your summer read and discover the joys of a delicious Frick Island cake, the sanctuary of a tight-knit community, and the hope of second chances."

—Amy E. Reichert, author of *The Kindred Spirits Supper Club*

"*The Invisible Husband of Frick Island* is a tender, surprising story of love and loss with a sprinkle of laughter, too. Colleen Oakley's writing is as fresh as the fish caught by the Frick islanders. Once you hop off the ferry to join them, you'll never want to leave. This was the most enjoyable book I've read in a long time."

—Phaedra Patrick, bestselling author of *The Curious Charms of Arthur Pepper* and *The Library of Lost and Found*

PRAISE FOR *YOU WERE THERE TOO*

"A beautifully woven story of love, grief, and the power we do and don't have to choose our fate, *You Were There Too* brought me to tears."

—Jill Santopolo, *New York Times* bestselling author of *The Light We Lost*

"Hypnotically beautiful, *You Were There Too* delves into the chasm between the life we have and the life we imagine for ourselves. Unique, lyrical, and thoughtful."

—Kristan Higgins, *New York Times* bestselling author of *A Little Ray of Sunshine*

"A rare gem of a novel. . . . I couldn't wait to find out what happened next, while at the same time hated for this lovely book to end. This is the kind of book we all long for, one to read and savor, and then read again."

—Karen White, *New York Times* bestselling author of *The House on Prytania*

TITLES BY COLLEEN OAKLEY

• • • • •

The Mostly True Story of Tanner & Louise

The Invisible Husband of Frick Island

You Were There Too

Close Enough to Touch

Before I Go

THE *Mostly* TRUE STORY OF TANNER & LOUISE

COLLEEN OAKLEY

BERKLEY
NEW YORK

BERKLEY
An imprint of Penguin Random House LLC
penguinrandomhouse.com

Copyright © 2023 by Colleen Oakley
Readers Guide copyright © 2023 by Penguin Random House LLC
Excerpt from *The Invisible Husband of Frick Island* copyright © 2021 by Colleen Oakley
Penguin Random House supports copyright. Copyright fuels creativity, encourages diverse voices, promotes free speech, and creates a vibrant culture. Thank you for buying an authorized edition of this book and for complying with copyright laws by not reproducing, scanning, or distributing any part of it in any form without permission. You are supporting writers and allowing Penguin Random House to continue to publish books for every reader.

BERKLEY and the BERKLEY & B colophon
are registered trademarks of Penguin Random House LLC.

ISBN: 9780593549094

The Library of Congress has cataloged the Berkley hardcover edition of this book as follows:

Names: Oakley, Colleen, author.
Title: The mostly true story of Tanner & Louise / Colleen Oakley.
Description: New York: Berkley, [2023]
Identifiers: LCCN 2022025790 (print) | LCCN 2022025791 (ebook) |
ISBN 9780593200803 (hardcover) | ISBN 9780593200810 (ebook)
Subjects: LCGFT: Novels.
Classification: LCC PS3615.A345 M67 2023 (print) |
LCC PS3615.A345 (ebook) | DDC 813/.6—dc23
LC record available at https://lccn.loc.gov/2022025790
LC ebook record available at https://lccn.loc.gov/2022025791

Berkley hardcover edition / March 2023
Berkley trade paperback edition / February 2024

Printed in the United States of America
1st Printing

Book design by Alison Cnockaert

This is a work of fiction. Names, characters, places, and incidents either are the product of the author's imagination or are used fictitiously, and any resemblance to actual persons, living or dead, business establishments, events, or locales is entirely coincidental.

For the women in my life who taught me how to be a woman in this world:
Marion, Penny, Kathy, and Megan

Louise: I just haven't seen you like this in a while. I'm used to seeing you more sedate.

Thelma: Well, I've had it up to my ass with sedate.

—*Thelma & Louise*

1

A PHONE CALL

"MY MOTHER IS missing."

"How old is your mother? How long has she been gone?" The cop's voice was monotone, unperturbed, as if he got reports of mothers gone missing ten times a day. *Who knows?* Jules thought. Maybe he did.

"Seventy-nine. No, wait, that's what she tells everyone." She paused. "Eighty-four. It's been three days since any of us have heard from her."

"Do you talk to her every day?"

"No, but she always picks up when I call, and she hasn't been answering her phone all afternoon. So I called her hair salon, and she missed her hair appointment this morning. She never misses her hair appointment."

"I see. Have you been to her house?"

Jules bristled. "Of course not! We all live, like, three, four hours away. Well, Charlie's the closest, but he coaches his son's baseball team, and there's a tournament thing this weekend. Anyway, I called one of her bridge friends. He hasn't seen her either. And she recently—" She stopped again. Her mother had always been quite a private person, and Jules didn't feel comfortable airing her business to a stranger, but she supposed desperate times and all.

"Recently what?"

"Well, she received some . . . upsetting news."

The cop grunted. "Is it possible she just wanted to be alone?"

"No—I'm telling you." Jules's voice went high-pitched. Frantic, to match the feeling creeping from her stomach up to her throat like a vine. "Something's not right."

"OK, OK," he said, and Jules pictured him holding his hands up as if to tell her to calm down in the same condescending manner her ex-husband used to. If there was anything worse in life than a man telling you to *calm down* when you were upset, she didn't know what it was. "I'll send someone to check it out."

"Thank you." She unclenched her jaw.

"Anything else we should know about—any history of unpredictable behavior or dementia?"

She blew out a long stream of air and muttered, "Oh, just her entire life."

The man paused. "Ma'am?"

"Nothing diagnosed. She's fine. I mean, except she's missing. I think she's been kidnapped. Adultnapped. Is that a thing? *Stolen.* Against her will."

Though she knew deep down that Louise Constance Wilt had never done anything against her will in her entire life.

2

TEN DAYS EARLIER

LOUISE WILT STARED at the letter.

Or rather, she stared at the envelope she had quickly stuffed the letter back into after reading it. It sat at militaristic attention on the sideboard, propped up by a Lladró figurine of a puppy peeking out the top of a woman's high-heeled boot. (Louise didn't collect Lladró or even like it, really—it was all a bit too precious for her taste, like a Hallmark Christmas movie—but she had found that the older she got, the fewer gifts she received that coincided with her actual interests.) The letter had arrived yesterday without fanfare, the way most letters do, in a plain white envelope; one of the long, rectangular ones that a bill might come in, shoved between a coupon for a $6.99 all-you-can-eat buffet at China King and the latest issue of *Southern Lady*—a magazine Louise felt certain someone must have subscribed her to in jest.

Thanks to a book she had read not too long ago, fittingly titled

Letters That Changed the World (also a gift, but from whom, she could not recall), Louise was familiar with the idea that one letter could indeed change everything.

Abraham Lincoln grew his infamous beard based on the advice of an eleven-year-old letter writer, Grace Bedell, who stated directly and to Louise's delight, "You would look a great deal better for your face is too thin."

Tennessee House of Representatives member Harry Thomas Burn cast the deciding vote for women's suffrage thanks to a letter from his mother, Febb Ensminger Burn, admonishing him, "Don't forget to be a good boy."

Harriet Beecher Stowe wrote *Uncle Tom's Cabin* after receiving a letter from her sister urging her to "write something to make this whole nation feel what an accursed thing slavery is."

And while she found the anecdotes interesting, Louise didn't actually think she would ever be on the receiving end of such a letter. A life-changing letter, that is. She, of course, was not suffering under the delusion that this letter had the power to do anything as bold or sweeping as help upend the institution of slavery, but nevertheless it was upending her life considerably.

She eyed the letter again from where she sat in the tufted armchair—the one she had reupholstered with a pretty hummingbird fabric, draping the headrest with a pillowcase so the greasy dandruff from what was left of Ken's balding hair wouldn't ruin the new material when he sat in it to listen to his favorite operas. Ken had died five years earlier, but the pillowcase remained.

Louise had recognized the handwriting immediately—the small cursive slanted to the right, the bottom of each letter flattened, as if the writer had used a ruler as a guide. Though she hadn't seen it in decades, she would recognize George Dixon's handwriting anywhere.

And in twenty-four hours the letter had morphed from a simple missive to an animate object, as if it were a feral cat stealthily watching her every move. Or maybe as if it had sprouted magical properties and George could actually see her, the letter acting as a conduit of sorts connecting the two of them. But then, letter or no, they would always be connected, wouldn't they? Had always been connected. By what they had done.

The doorbell rang, startling Louise even though she had been expecting it. She dragged her gaze from the letter to the front door and grasped the handle of her cane with her clawlike grip to begin the painful process of standing and greeting her guest. For now, the letter would have to wait.

THOUGH LOUISE WISHED it were not a universal truth, there were only a handful of women in this world who could pull off a bare face. The girl in front of her was not one of them.

No, Tanner Quimby was not technically a girl in that she was twenty-one. And yes, Louise was aware of the myriad ways society infantilized women by referring to them as girls—an entire spate of fiction was absurdly and indefatigably devoted to the practice. Yet, despite her age, Tanner was a girl.

A girl who was dressed in a way that suggested she hadn't planned on leaving her house today. (Sweatpants and a stained T-shirt. Mustard, perhaps?)

A girl who could have done with a little rouge on her sullen cheeks.

A girl who didn't want to be sitting in Louise's living room any more than Louise wanted her there.

And she wouldn't have been if that stupid Turkish rug that Ken *had* to have from Scott's Antiques hadn't curled up on the edge and caught Louise's toe, sending her sprawling on the hardwood, cracking her hip right in half. One surgery and two months of inpatient physical therapy later, and Louise's kids didn't think she was fit to live at home by herself any longer, even though she could walk just fine (with only minimal use of the tripod, rubber-tipped metal cane that resembled a medieval torture device). Louise had never much cared what they thought, but when Jules threatened to move in with her and Charlie started sending websites of home care workers, she chose the least of three evils: Tanner Quimby, a girl who needed a place to live, who was not a blood relation, nor did she wear orthopedic shoes. Thank God for Lucy—Louise nearly smiled thinking of her youngest—who always had been the most creative problem solver of the three, even if her executive functioning skills did leave something to be desired.

"My daughter tells me she went to high school with your mother?" Louise reached forward to pick up the dainty teacup from the coffee table, ignoring the twinge in her hip. The two had already been through all the typical pleasantries, though Louise thought it a stretch to call them pleasant, considering Tanner had thus far responded to all her inquiries with one word and as though she were sucking on a lemon.

"Apparently," Tanner replied.

Louise took a sip of the bitter brew and set the cup back on the table. She never much cared for tea but, seeing as it wasn't even noon, felt she couldn't very well offer Tanner the Finlandia on the buffet behind the sofa. "Well, would you like to see the room?"

"No. I'm sure it's fine."

"OK."

Silence overtook them once again. Louise focused on the sound of the familiar faint ticking of Ken's father's ancient grandfather clock in the hallway, startling only a bit as the first of twelve mournful rings of the bell heralded the top of the hour. Louise eyed the Finlandia bottle again.

"Why is it called a grandfather clock and not a grandmother clock?" her eldest granddaughter, Poppy, asked once.

"Because only a man would find the need to announce it every time he performed his job as required," Louise replied.

Poppy blinked, while Jules rolled her eyes in Louise's direction. "She's three, Mother. Perhaps we can wait to indoctrinate her against the patriarchy for a few years?"

"Never too early to start, dear."

Poppy was now twenty-four, and Louise had not the slightest clue whether she was indeed indoctrinated against the patriarchy, since she only heard from the girl once a year, on one of the days leading up to or away from her birthday—but never on the actual date.

Louise shivered, even though she was wearing her red Mister Rogers cardigan. She never imagined she'd own a Mister Rogers cardigan, much less six of them in various shades and fabric weights. But growing old, Louise found, was just one indignity after another.

Like how she was always cold. Even in houses where the thermostat was set to a sweltering seventy-eight degrees. (And to think—there was a time when she would flash so hot her blood would nearly boil, her skin felt as though it could melt as easily as Velveeta. Oh, the irony!)

Or how despite a near-habitual intake of calcium supplements, her bones betrayed her anyway, turning fragile as a butterfly wing, snapping in half at the slightest jarring bump.

Or how her children began talking to her as though they were degreed medical professionals and she had not passed the second grade.

Or how, one day, as an eighty-four-year-old woman, she found herself in her own living room, surrounded by Ken's mother's antique furniture, interviewing a morose twenty-one-year-old *girl* to be her new roommate.

She glanced at the vodka again. And then at the framed photo of her late husband, who'd died before he could suffer all of these late-in-life indignities. Lucky bastard.

"So, like . . . you just need me to drive you to your appointments and stuff, and the rest of the time I can spend in my room?"

Louise gaped at Tanner momentarily, surprised by the sudden verbosity. And then was relieved that they both had the exact same arrangement in mind. "Yes, that would be fine."

"Cool," Tanner said and slapped her hands on her sweatpants-clad thighs. "Can I move in tomorrow?"

"Oh! Um . . . well." Louise hadn't anticipated the arrangement would begin so soon. She'd only just returned to her house yesterday and had been reveling in the solitude after so many weeks spent shuffling around in the nursing facility with all those . . . old people. Louise knew she should say *other* old people, but honestly. That would suggest she was one of them.

She put her hand on the rubber grip of her cane and once again began the painful ritual of pushing herself up when Tanner stood. Or jumped to her feet, more like it, as easily as she blinked. Louise didn't envy much about twenty-one-year-olds, but this? She would give anything to have that agility back. She leaned heavily on the cane and braced herself for the shot of fire through her hip, waiting for Tanner to say something polite like *Oh, please don't get up. I can see myself out.* But she didn't. And Louise couldn't decide if she was pleased to have not been patronized or horrified that the girl was so rude. Regardless, Tanner was at the front door before Louise could even fully straighten her spine.

Tanner paused, her hand on the knob, and looked back at Louise as if she'd just remembered something. "Louise, is there a TV, like, in the room? I need one, and my mom's not letting me bring mine." She hesitated. "I guess, technically, *hers*."

"It's Mrs. Wilt," Louise said, clenching her teeth as the fire ripped through her hip. She closed her eyes against the pain and then opened them.

"I'm sorry?" The girl tilted her head like a cocker spaniel. Good grief, were they still teaching girls to apologize for nothing?

"My name. It's Mrs. Wilt." If Tanner was going to be here under professional circumstances, Louise saw no reason to do away with formality.

"Oh. Right."

"And this is the only TV I own." Louise nodded toward the large flat-screen on the far wall across from the couch. Another gift, this time from the children—who apparently expected her to ooh and aah over the size, when the thirty-two-inch television she'd had for fifteen years worked just fine. The benefit of having Justin Farmer's head on the five o'clock news the size of an inflated beach ball was unclear.

"As long as it has A/V input and output, it will be fine."

Louise stared at her blankly, having no idea what A/V input and output was or if her television was in want of it. "You're welcome to check."

Tanner pulled a face, as if the two minutes it would take to check would be two minutes longer than she wanted to be there. "I'm sure it's fine." And then she was gone, before Louise could even say a proper goodbye.

Louise glanced around the room as if searching for confirmation that she was not the only person to witness that abrupt and ill-mannered departure.

Her gaze landed on Ken once again.

"Oh, shut up," she said to his smug smile. He would find all of this uproariously funny were he alive to witness it. Well, not the letter, she thought, her eyes falling from her husband to George's missive. He wouldn't find that funny at all.

She wondered if he'd go pale with shock or red-faced with worry first. That was the thing about Ken—he was always so transparent with his emotions. Left nothing to mystery, which made him eminently trustworthy. But Louise had always found full transparency in a relationship to be a little overrated. Left no room for wonder. Speculation. Excitement. To be perfectly frank, it was a little boring. Anyway, Ken wasn't here. So, like everything else, she was going to have to figure this out alone.

The faint ticking of the grandfather clock wormed its way into her ears as she considered what to do next.

She had a plan, of course, for this exact moment. One that she had concocted decades ago, back when she was young and nimble and didn't have a bum hip, much less a cane. A way to drop everything at a moment's notice and disappear. But as the years dragged on, without even realizing it was happening, she had become . . . complacent. No longer spending her days looking over her shoulder or waking up in the dead of the night, heart thundering at an unexpected noise. In short, she had come to believe she had finally gotten away with it, once and for all. But having spent the formative years of her childhood on a farm, she of all people knew: Chickens always come home to roost.

And even in the grips of her waning shock and rising fear, she couldn't help but recognize the amusing irony: that now, when she could barely walk—she was going to have to run.

3

LOUISE WILT SMELLED like toilet water. And something floral. Not in an eau de toilette way—Tanner knew that's what all those fancy French perfumes were supposed to be made of—but literally like water out of a toilet bowl with its faint boiled egg odor, covered up by a hefty gardenia scent.

That's what Tanner wanted to say when she walked through the front door and her mom looked up and asked "How was she?" in her fake singsongy voice. As if Tanner had just seen Lizzo in concert, and not been forced to drink tea (*tea!* Like they were in some nineties romantic comedy starring Hugh Grant) with an octogenarian woman whose house temperature rivaled Death Valley, California, in the summertime, because her mother—her own flesh and blood—was kicking her out of the house.

"Fine," she said instead, sticking with the monosyllabic responses she'd perfected in the two weeks since her mother had accosted her with her out-of-left-field—and a little unnecessarily aggro—ultimatum.

It all started at lunch on a Monday, when Tanner was making a ham-and-turkey sandwich. She pulled out the brand-new jar of pickles, but when she saw the label, her blood ran so hot, it took everything in her not to smash the jar onto the linoleum floor.

"Mom!" she screamed, even though her mother was standing not ten feet away, studying the wall calendar hanging beside the microwave. "Fucking bread and butter?! *Again?*"

In retrospect, Tanner could see it was an overreaction. They were just . . . pickles. But in her defense, they weren't dill, which everyone knew was the only acceptable sandwich pickle, and her mom had done the exact same thing two weeks earlier, and how hard was it to *read a goddamned label*?

Regardless, if it was a contest of who overreacted the most, Tanner felt sure it was her mother Candace's response.

Typically when Tanner had one of her Hulk-outs, which was what she had taken to calling the explosions of fury that seemed to overcome her from out of nowhere the past few months, Candace would placidly look at her, sometimes even indulgently, as if her therapist had advised her that all Tanner needed right now was her love.

But this time her face looked different—her eyes went dark, her nostrils flared. "You need to move out."

Tanner wondered if perhaps her mother had gotten a new therapist.

"Is that what you wore?" Candace said to her now, her brows furrowing instantly into what Tanner viewed as their natural and most comfortable state of utter disappointment.

"Yep," Tanner replied, not without a little defiance, practically daring her mother to say something else—how sweatpants aren't "appropriate attire" outside of the house. Or that she could have at least "put on a little mascara." Tanner prepared to load her response like a bullet in the chamber of a gun, ready to fire at any second, but she had trouble deciding between flippant (*how delightfully sexist of you*) or droll sarcasm (*and here I've always thought it's what's on the* inside *that counts*).

"There's egg yolk on your shirt," her mother said, and then turned her attention back to the cat-and-mouse detective thriller on her e-reader.

Tanner looked down, and sure enough there was a yellow oblong stain right over her left breast. She shrugged, even though she was a little embarrassed to have worn a dirty shirt to Mrs. Wilt's house.

But then she thought, *Who cares? She smells like toilet water.*

Tanner stood in the center of the basement, surveying what had been her "room" for the past five months, since as soon as she'd left for college her mother had turned her bedroom, the one she grew up in, into a crafting space. She stared at the heap of clothes spread on the marred blue felt top of the pool table. Impossible to tell what was dirty and what was clean. She knew she should wash the whole lot and fold it all neatly for her move tomorrow, but that task felt insurmountable for several reasons, not least of which because her leg was in major throbbing mode.

She slunk over to the PS5, clicked both it and the TV on, and then fell into the couch, propping her knee up on two pillows. *Horizon Zero Dawn* filled the screen. Tanner knew she should be happy, or at least *relieved* that she had a place to live—considering she didn't think her mother cared if she ended up on the street in a cardboard box—but all she felt was the same familiar anger that, like a heartbeat, spiked and ebbed but never ceased.

Anger that this was her life.

Anger that she had done everything right. Gotten straight As, become vice president of the Beta Club, been captain of the soccer team (both club and high school), volunteered eight hours a week at Must Ministries organizing the food pantry, didn't drink, didn't smoke, hadn't even gone to one party at Matt Cleese's house or one bonfire in the clearing in the woods behind the Crescent Cliff subdivision. Every bit of it a means to the end of what it was all for: a full-ride athletic scholarship to play soccer at her dream school, Northwestern.

Only to lose it in the span of three seconds in March while trying to leave a party she didn't even want to go to in the first place.

And though she knew it was wildly illogical, she hated the person who'd thrown that party: Sonora Brewer. She hated Sonora's frat guy boyfriend who had—as it turned out—created the faulty railing on the balcony by loosening the posts so they could re-create some pulley system for beer they'd seen on TikTok. She hated her body for not falling on her arm or her shoulder, but on her leg. She hated the surgeon who told her it was the worst comminuted fracture he'd ever seen and that she may never run again—at least not at speeds that would make her an asset to a college soccer team, much less a professional one—even though he was the one who fixed it, placing the metal rod into her leg, allowing her to at least walk. She hated that she wasn't even the tiniest bit grateful that she could at least walk.

But mostly she hated that after nearly three years of hard work, instead of returning to her beloved Northwestern for her senior year, where she would currently be decorating her apartment with her best friend, Vee, and about to start fall-quarter classes, she was moving into a geriatric's home to become a glorified babysitter.

When she'd realized back in May that her parents couldn't afford the $10,690 it was going to cost *after* financial aid and student loans to attend her senior year, she hatched a plan. She would get a job, work overtime if she had to, save enough money to return—maybe even in time for second quarter—and just be a few months behind. What she didn't account for was that most of the jobs she found required long hours of standing on her feet, which she wasn't healed enough to do, and the few that didn't, like secretarial work, went to people more qualified than she was.

Now, after weeks of searching, she finally had a job—except could living in an old woman's guest room and making $100 a week really be considered a *job*? It certainly wasn't going to get her close to the $10,000 she needed anytime soon, and her dreams of returning to Northwestern were suddenly as dead as her soccer career. She felt another flare of anger and tried to tamp it down. She focused on the postapocalyptic setting of her video game, trying to get lost in it, instead of her rage-y thoughts. Her body had just started to relax when Candace's voice floated down the stairs. Tanner paused the game.

"What?"

This time her mother's words took form. "Chicken spaghetti for dinner?"

Tanner knew it was an olive branch, offering to make her favorite concoction of canned soup and cream cheese and Italian dressing mix all over angel-hair pasta, but it felt like a manipulation and just irritated her further.

Still, it was her favorite.

"Fine," she said and pressed play, turning her attention back to the battle at hand.

"YOU GOT A job!" her father boomed jovially when Tanner loped into the kitchen an hour later.

"You did?" Harley looked over from the fridge, wide-eyed and milk mustached due to his disgusting habit of chugging directly from the plastic jug.

"It's not a job," Tanner muttered, slipping into her seat and feeling like she could fall asleep right then and there. She didn't think anyone in her family appreciated how utterly exhausting it was to be so angry all the time.

"Your *first* job," Dad continued as if she hadn't spoken. "Reminds me of my first job. Working at the horseradish plant. Had burns up to my elbows. Probably be illegal now." He cocked his head. "Probably was illegal then, come to think of it. I was all of fourteen. But a little hard work never killed anybody."

"What's your job?" Harley asked, sliding into the chair across from her, while Tanner eyed her mom humming and spooning big globs of pasta onto each plate like she was June fucking Cleaver.

"It's not a job," Tanner repeated through clenched teeth at the same time Dad said, "She's moving in with Louise Wilt, Lucy's mom. To be her caregiver."

Harley's eyes widened. "That old lady? What's wrong with her?"

"She's old," Tanner said at the same time Dad said, "Broken hip."

Glee flashed in Harley's eyes. "And she picked *you* to take care of her? It's a bit like the blind leading the blind, isn't it? What, are you guys going to limp together to physical therapy?"

Tanner stabbed her fork into the pasta and twirled. She wished briefly that her younger sister, Marty, hadn't left for her sophomore year of college, if only to have someone on her side. And then she remembered how poorly she'd treated her sister all summer—and realized it was probably for the best she was gone.

"Get it? Because—"

"Yes, we're both crippled. I get it."

"Tanner!" her mother yelled.

Tanner gaped at her, though she wasn't at all surprised *she* was the one getting yelled at. She always thought Harley should have been named Jesus for how much her parents worshipped him. The "surprise" baby of the family, he was born with a heart defect, and though he'd survived four life-threatening surgeries as a toddler, her parents apparently still thought that causing him the tiniest bit of stress in life, like holding him accountable for his actions, for instance, would kill him.

"Both of you. C'mon now," her dad said. "And for goodness' sake, you're hardly . . . *disabled*, Tanner. You were running at your last physical therapy appointment."

"I was barely jogging." Tanner didn't bother to mention the excruciating pain that accompanied the movement.

"You showed them," he continued, grinning, as if he hadn't heard her.

After a few minutes of silence, save for the clank of forks on plates, her mother spoke up. "Sounds like you're going to have some spare time at Mrs. Wilt's house," she said.

Don't say it don't say it don't say it, Tanner chanted to herself, squeezing her eyes shut against what she knew was coming.

"Have you thought any more about community college?"

Tanner slowly exhaled, not wanting to rehash the numerous arguments she'd gotten into with her parents about this.

She didn't *want* to go to community college. She wanted to go back to Northwestern. To live in her off-campus apartment, be with her friends, get a slice of Fat Elvis at Hoosier Mama's, jingle her keys at football games, let out a Primal Scream with the rest of the students during finals. She wasn't angry at her parents for not being able to afford it—she was angry at them for not understanding that she couldn't just pick up and start over as if nothing had happened. As if her entire world hadn't gone up in flames.

"You have to move on, Tanner. Northwestern is not happening. You need to find a new pur—"

"I KNOW I'M NOT GOING BACK TO NORTHWESTERN!" Tanner shouted, her hands balling into fists. Her eyes welled, and she bit her lip to keep the tears from overflowing. She hated that she sometimes got so angry she cried.

Silence enveloped the room again, this time without any clanking forks. Finally her dad broke it, speaking calmly, as if nothing had happened. "I just hope you won't be too busy to come home once in a while to work on Bessie."

Bessie was the 1970 Fiat Racer Tanner and her father had been rebuilding for the past five years. He'd originally bought it for a song when she was a junior in high school—a neighbor had found it in his great-uncle's barn up in North Georgia—and planned for it to be her high school graduation gift. They had spent hours together under the hood, but he didn't count on how time intensive the restoration would be, much less how expensive. And with her father working as a midlevel manager at a Costco (the only job he could get after being laid off from his senior manager position at a car dealership during the pandemic recession a few years earlier) and her mother, a retired elementary school teacher, now working part-time as an administrative assistant at an optometry office—money was not something they had in spades.

"Mm," Tanner said, once she trusted her voice not to shake as she spoke. "I'll try." But considering they hadn't worked on it together once the entire five months she had been home, they both knew she was lying.

* * * * *

LATER, WITH A stomach full of congealed pasta, Tanner sat on the basement couch again, leg propped up on a pillow, folding her clothes and setting them in the suitcase open at her feet.

Her phone buzzed with a text message, and hope swelled in her belly that it was Vee (she hated that hope swelled in her belly). Or anyone from the team, really. From the time she'd met them at her first practice at Northwestern, she thought they were all going to be best friends forever like some Judy Blume novel, but it had been five months since she'd left, and while some of them (not Vee, not that Tanner could blame her) had texted and sent funny memes and videos during and after the surgery, the time between messages slowly grew longer until eventually Tanner stopped hearing from any of them at all.

Tanner glanced at the alert and tried to swallow the disappointment that it was not Vee but Grant.

Grant, with his Superman-tattooed bicep, carefully shaggy hair, and long typing fingers. The second Tanner spotted him the first day of her spring-quarter sophomore political science class, stretching back in his chair—just enough to reveal a thin strip of taut, tanned skin above the waistband of his jeans—and stifling a yawn, she became convinced (in the way only a girl who has never had a boyfriend can be) that he'd be her first real love. Passionate, all-consuming.

Tanner didn't date in high school, which she pretended was because she didn't want to—too busy with soccer practice and travel team and volunteering and schoolwork—and not because she didn't know how. It was as if her peers who coupled up were part of an underground club and no one had bothered to show her the secret handshake. She had hoped college would be different, that how to date would become not only suddenly obvious but easy. That she would have not just *a* boyfriend but a string of them, a conga line of relationships that in future years she would look back on individually with rose-colored nostalgia, at the hearts broken, lessons learned—material enough to write four or five albums' worth of Taylor Swift love songs (if she had the ability or desire). Alas, college had started much the way high school had ended, with nary a potential boyfriend in sight.

And then, Grant. He didn't notice her for the entire quarter, despite her plotting—doing her best to choose a seat within his eyeline when possible, studying harder for that class than any of her others so she could answer all of the professor's questions, forcing the spotlight on herself, and—to that end—getting up a full thirty minutes early to shower the Tuesday and Thursday mornings before those classes, instead of her Monday, Wednesday, Friday routine of rolling out of bed and pulling her hair up into a messy topknot.

Finally, on the last day of class before finals—like magic—it happened.

"Hey, genius," a voice said from behind her, close to her ear, and she didn't have to look up to know it was him. Her entire body alerted her to his proximity, the way a gazelle knows when a cheetah is near.

And instead of coquettishly denying her intelligence, giggling it away the way she'd seen girls do ad nauseam since middle school, she turned toward him with a full-body confidence she had only ever possessed on the soccer field when a ball was in play, looked him square in the eyes, arched an eyebrow, and said: "Yes?"

Theirs was a summer affair, played out on the shores of Lake Michigan, free movies in the park at nightfall in Evanston, evenings in his air-conditioned icebox of an apartment sharing bowls of pho and bingeing old episodes of *The Walking Dead*. And it was full of surprising revelations for Tanner.

Like how when he called her "kid," she didn't find it patronizing.

Or how sex was so much sweatier than she had anticipated.

Or how easy it was to have a boyfriend (and swoon when she thought of him as her "boyfriend," though she'd never considered herself a swooner), and how she couldn't remember what was possibly so difficult about it.

Until summer ended—and with it their relationship, as though a kitchen timer dinged announcing it was cooked through. Done. A timer that Tanner wasn't aware had been set, but apparently one Grant had been waiting for. As soon as students began pouring back onto campus for first quarter junior year, Grant became sporadically less available, spouting various excuses—Classes! Studying for an exam! Touch football with the boys!—and then he stopped offering excuses at all. Oh, she heard from him sometimes. Mostly when he was drunk and texting at 2:00 a.m. And Tanner analyzed each one, as though she were a detective searching for the Grant she had known that summer, each message a clue that needed to be deciphered. But *that* Grant had disappeared. Vanished. And the one she was left with was just so wildly disappointing.

Tanner swiped her phone open to read his newest missive.

R u wet?

She stared at the screen and sighed.

It wasn't like she hadn't been a willing participant in the sexting. At first, anyway. It felt forbidden, like she wasn't supposed to be doing it, which of course added to the . . . titillation. But she quickly discovered the universal problem with sexting that no one ever discussed—there were not enough hands. How were you supposed to hold the phone and tap out the play-by-play narration of what you're doing *and* actually *do* what you're dirty-narrating? That was why she'd dropped the *doing* part a few sexting sessions ago. Grant didn't seem to be any the wiser.

She couldn't explain why she continued to respond. Why she hadn't told him to stop contacting her already. Maybe it was boredom. Maybe it was the fact that he was the only person from Northwestern who seemed not to have forgotten her. Maybe it was the tiny flame of hope that the old Grant was still in there somewhere and would show himself eventually, like the bad guy at the end of *Scooby-Doo.*

She knew all of those reasons were pathetic. She also knew she would text him back.

She rolled her eyes and lifted her T-shirt until the lacy gray of her bra was showing—gray because she hadn't washed it in a few weeks, but she figured Grant would never know. Or care.

She held up her phone and tried to angle it to get the best view of her nearly nonexistent cleavage, using her upper arms to squish her breasts together. She frowned and snapped a picture just as thundering footsteps hurtled down the stairs.

"Harley!" she said, yanking her shirt down.

"What?" her brother said, standing at the foot of the stairs.

"You could knock."

"On what?" He glanced back up the stairs. "The wall? Door was open."

"I was changing!"

He cocked his head, studying her. "You don't look like you were changing."

"Well, I was," she said lamely.

"*Forza*?" he asked, coming over to plop next to Tanner on the couch.

"Yeah, fine."

Tanner tossed her phone onto a couch cushion while her brother picked up a controller and started adeptly pushing buttons. She stared at Harley's fingers—his nails covered in flecks of chipped blue polish. She remembered when they were chubby and thick, like little cocktail sausages, clutching on to Matchbox cars or grabbing her hand at Kroger on errands with their mom, and she was suddenly overcome with emotion for her little brother and all the good in him. Like how his entire face lit up when he finally learned the 50-50 grind on his skateboard or how he stuck his tongue between his teeth in concentration when trying to pick out that one Billie Eilish song by ear on the guitar or how he cried when they watched the Greta Gerwig remake of *Little Women* together.

"I'm gonna miss you," she said.

He didn't take his eyes off the screen, where his Audi was in the middle of a difficult-level street race, his tongue sticking out between the left side of his lips in the same concentration he used to play the guitar. He didn't respond, and Tanner thought at first he didn't hear her. But finally, when his car crossed the finish line, he glanced at Tanner with his kind eyes and little grin. Then he shrugged.

"Don't be gross."

4

TEXT EXCHANGE A FEW HOURS AFTER LOUISE WILT WAS REPORTED MISSING TO THE POLICE

JULES: The police said nothing looks unusual at her house.

CHARLIE: . . .

CHARLIE: You called the *police*?

JULES: Yes, of course.

LUCY: Mom hates the police.

CHARLIE: Good grief, Jules. It's not even been twenty-four hours.

JULES: It's been THREE DAYS.

CHARLIE: . . .

CHARLIE: It has?

LUCY: Did you try to call Tanner?

JULES: YES, I TRIED TANNER. She hasn't been answering her phone all day either. I swear to God, neither of you ever listen to me.

CHARLIE: Who's Tanner?

JULES: 🤯

LUCY: You know how busy mom is. She's probably at bridge.

JULES: At bridge. For three days.

CHARLIE: I think Lucy's just saying . . .

JULES: DO NOT SAY IT, CHARLIE.

CHARLIE: . . . that maybe you're overreacting a bit.

JULES: I DO NOT OVERREACT. If anything, you underreact.

LUCY: I don't know—remember when you made all the kids get out of the lake that time?

JULES: You both admitted that log looked exactly like an alligator.

LUCY: . . .

CHARLIE: . . .

JULES: I knew we should have hired a nurse and not some irresponsible college dropout.

CHARLIE: Wait—Tanner's not a nurse?

JULES: JESUS CHRIST, CHARLIE. Look, the reason I'm texting is the police cannot legally go into her house, so one of us is going to have to go down there.

CHARLIE: Not it.

LUCY: Charlie's closest.

CHARLIE: Jen has a spa appointment tomorrow. She'll kill me if I don't watch the kids.

JULES: I can only hope that that is not hyperbole.

LUCY: Jules! Be nice!

CHARLIE: So you think Mom's, like, dead? Wouldn't Tanner have called us?

JULES: No! I don't think she's dead. I just think something's not . . . right. Call it intuition.

CHARLIE: Like your intuition that the log was an alligator.

JULES: 🤬

JULES: Charlie, you're going.

CHARLIE: . . .

CHARLIE: . . .

CHARLIE: Fine. But you owe me.

5

FOUR DAYS AFTER her husband died, Louise boarded a bus headed for the mountains of southwest Virginia and went fly-fishing. The trip, a Road Scholar adventure for seniors, had been planned for months—and more importantly, *paid* for in full—and Louise didn't see why she should cancel. It wasn't as if sitting at home and missing him would raise Ken from the dead.

If she had been a normal widow, she may have worried over whether it was too soon, if people would think it meant she wasn't grieving properly (as if there were a manual with step-by-step instructions) or that she didn't love Ken (she did). But Louise Wilt had never given one rat's derriere about what other people thought.

Standing in waders with the cold river rushing around her legs, the fresh mountain air on her face, Louise had the brief thought that she might quite enjoy being a widow, were it not for the whole Ken-being-dead part. She had forgotten the freedom that came with being alone. Not that Ken had ever been overbearing or controlling in their forty-three years together—the opposite, really—but even in the most egalitarian marriage, one still had to consider the other person. And now, she had no one's feelings to consider but her own.

Of course, as much as she relished the benefits, widowhood was not without its downsides. Like how, five years out, she still sometimes woke in the early hours of dawn, fully expecting to open her eyes and find Ken snoring lightly beside her, the few nose hairs that he stubbornly refused to trim peeking out on the exhale and disappearing with each inhale. And how her breath caught in her throat when she found his side of the bed empty.

This was one such morning. She lay there in the dark and allowed the grief to flow through her veins, thick as mud. She'd learned long ago not to fight it, to make space for it, the way one might for a new tchotchke on the shelf, a souvenir from a trip you didn't want to forget. That was all grief was, really, Louise had determined—remembering.

She closed her eyes and focused on remembering Ken, his loud cackle when he was really tickled over something, growling *I know why tigers eat their young* when Charlie or Lucy (never Jules) did something disappointing, his stubborn nose hairs.

And then, she remembered the letter.

She sat up and gently stretched her tired bones. She had stayed up most of the night considering her options. She could run—she probably should run, of course. But then again, as much as she didn't like to dwell on the fact, she was eighty-four years old. Maybe it was time to take her licks, as it were. Face the consequences of her actions, the way she had once often admonished her children to.

She yawned and put her feet solidly on the floor. That girl Tanner would be arriving in a few hours, and Louise wanted to spend every minute she had left savoring the quiet of her own house, alone. Especially because either way—run or stay—she likely wouldn't be in this house for much longer.

She got dressed, fingering the buttons of her green cardigan, impatient and annoyed with her arthritic clumsiness, how it took multiple tries to thread each plastic circle through its corresponding slit, as though she were a toddler. She brewed a fresh pot of coffee (which she wouldn't drink now, but after lunch over ice with plenty of milk and sugar); ate a poached egg, a slice of rye toast, and half a grapefruit; and swallowed the seven pills of various sizes, shapes, and colors from the Sunday compartment of her plastic medication box.

After spitting toothpaste out into the bathroom sink and rinsing her mouth, she fit her partial dentures into the spaces between her teeth and swiped lipstick across her thin lips—Revlon's Cherries in the Snow, the same color she'd been wearing since 1972. She knew it was 1972 because as she was trying on the color at Filene's, the counter girl grabbed her hand, eyes bright, and said, "Did you hear? Shirley is running for president." First name only, as if Shirley Chisholm were someone they both knew, a mutual friend. The lipstick had also been George's favorite.

Her heart clenched for the second time that morning, the way it always did when she allowed herself to think of George—and all the time they had missed together. Forty-eight years. Not that she regretted it. She had had a good life with Ken, the kids. And of course the risk would have been too great. It wasn't so much a choice, a decision, as it was the only move that was possible in their game of chess. Sacrificing the queen to avoid a checkmate.

Until now.

The grandfather clock struck nine when she entered the living room and step-thump-stepped with her cane over to the sideboard to pluck George's letter up in her left hand. She took it into the kitchen, clicked on the front burner of the gas stove, and stuck the corner of the letter into the fire. As she stood and watched the orange flame lick its way up the paper, the doorbell rang. Louise, in no hurry to let that girl back into her house, calmly step-thump-stepped over to the sink with the burning letter and held it pinched between her thumb and forefinger until the very last possible second, ignoring the searing pain from the heat—and the ear-piercing blare of the fire alarm.

IRRITATED, TANNER SHIFTED her weight on the hard cement of Louise's—wait, no—*Mrs. Wilt's* front porch, clutching her suitcase in her left hand and her video game console under the same arm. She had rung the doorbell twice already—had the old woman somehow already forgotten she was coming today? She raised her free hand to knock, when a loud noise came from within—the high-pitched squeal of a smoke alarm, only slightly dulled by the thick wood of the door. She froze, not quite sure what to do. "Mrs. Wilt?" she said loudly, trying to peer into the window panels on either side of the door, but curtains blocked her view. She jiggled the door handle—locked. She banged on the wooden panel of the door with the side of her fist forcefully and in vain—there was no way the old bat would be able to hear the knocking above that racket. "Mrs. Wilt? Are you OK?"

Panic rose within her as images of the old woman lying helpless on the floor, struggling to breathe through smoke-congested air, filled her mind, along with an admittedly more selfish thought: if Mrs. Wilt croaked, Tanner could return to playing video games in her parents' basement and pretend none of this had ever happened. She quickly pushed the latter idea away, dropped her belongings, and rushed down the stairs from the porch to the first window, standing on her tiptoes trying to peer in. She rapped on a pane of glass before taking off again, past the garage and up the side yard, shuffling as fast as her bum leg would allow her toward a chain-link fence—its gate secured with a hefty metal padlock. Without thinking, she scaled the fence using her hands and good leg, and jumped over to the other side, a searing pain shooting through her shin as she landed in the grass. Ignoring it, she half walked, half hobbled past a large garden shed to a cement patio with a sliding glass door, the handle of which—of course—was locked. Sweating and out of breath, she quickly scanned her surroundings, her gaze landing on the wrought iron metal table and chairs on the patio. She grabbed the arms of one of the chairs, and in a gargantuan feat of strength—it was much heavier than she had anticipated—hefted it above her head and turned to throw it through the glass—

"Aaaaaaahh!" she screamed at the figure that had suddenly appeared where the closed door had just been. "Mrs. Wilt," she said, her brain catching up with real time.

The woman, in a cardigan—green today—and with perfectly coiffed hair, looked at her quizzically. "I'd rather hoped you would use the front door."

"What? I tried! It was locked, and the smoke alarm—" Although Tanner noticed the alarm was no longer blaring and wondered how long it had been off. She let the chair fall back to the ground with a thud and dropped into it, sudden exhaustion replacing the adrenaline, the pain in her leg screaming for attention.

"Just a piece of burnt toast," Mrs. Wilt said, waving her hand at the air. "Nothing to get all excited about. That alarm's always been sensitive."

"Right," Tanner said, attempting to tamp down the anger flaring up inside her. She was out of breath, out of shape, and sweaty, and had just put the healing of her leg in jeopardy by attempting to come to the aid of a woman who didn't need it.

"Chair wouldn't have worked, by the way."

"Huh?"

Mrs. Wilt thumped her knuckle on the clear sliding door panel. "It's Hammerglass."

Tanner had no idea what Hammerglass was and found that she didn't care.

"Come along, girlie," Mrs. Wilt said. "I'll show you the guest room."

Girlie? Tanner rolled her eyes and forced her feet to move forward.

CHINTZ. DAMASK. TOILE.

Tanner wasn't exactly sure what any of those terms meant, just that they were related to old-fashioned decor, and one of them likely described the horrific floral pattern papering the walls in the room in which she was now standing.

"You may use the top two drawers of the dresser," Louise said, gesturing to an ornate wooden chest that looked better suited to a sixteenth-century English country estate. Tanner set her suitcase down on the floor, placed her PlayStation gently on the queen-sized four-poster bed covered with a muted green quilt, and tried to ignore the faint musty odor that apparently permeated every room in Mrs. Wilt's house. "There are towels in the guest bath across the hall. And a shower."

Tanner narrowed her eyes, unsure if it was her imagination or if Mrs. Wilt had, in fact, looked at her pointedly when she said *shower.* Granted, Tanner couldn't exactly remember the last time she'd taken one. When Mrs. Wilt turned to straighten a figurine on the top of the dresser (a ridiculous sad clown statue clutching three primary-colored balloons), she bent her head down and surreptitiously sniffed her armpit, and then wrinkled her nose.

Apparently satisfied with the quarter-millimeter turn of the statue, the old woman turned back and let go of her cane, sticking her forefinger out and tapping it with her opposite forefinger. "Mondays and Wednesdays I have physical therapy at nine thirty. Tuesdays are my hair appointment at Elon Moore. Thursdays, my bridge group meets at ten. Fridays I reserve for lunch dates. Some Sunday mornings, I have church—not every Sunday, but I expect to go next week. And then there are the errands. Tuesdays I go to Aldi because it's right near the salon. Mondays are CVS and the post office, if necessary—"

"Wait," Tanner held up her hand, her senses swimming with the overload of information, the obscenely busy wallpaper, the musty odor, the days of the week. Granted, it was the reason she was here, but couldn't she sit down a minute before being bombarded with a schedule? "Could you maybe just share your Google Calendar?"

Mrs. Wilt blinked. "No. I cannot."

Great. Along with all her other old-people clichés, the woman didn't use technology either. Well, Tanner could fix that. "It's like an app. It's super easy; I can show you how—"

"I know what it is." Mrs. Wilt cut her off. "My calendar is on the wall in the kitchen should you need it for reference."

The two women stared at each other for a beat, taking measure. "OK," Tanner said. "Well, what about today—Sunday?"

"What about it?"

"Do you need to go anywhere?"

Louise paused, as if considering. "No. Not today."

Tanner exhaled, feeling her shoulders relax a bit as she did. "Great. So I can use the TV?"

"Yes." Mrs. Wilt gripped the handle of her cane tighter and straightened her spine. "As long as you're not watching *The Doctors*."

"The what?"

"Or any of those terrible housewife shows."

"Housewife shows?"

"Or *The Price Is Right*."

Tanner's eyebrows shot skyward. "What's wrong with *The Price Is Right*?"

"That new host."

"They replaced Drew Carey?"

"No. That one." Mrs. Wilt said sharply.

"What's wrong with him?"

"His voice is too nasally. It grates the nerves."

"Ohhh-kay," Tanner said, drawing out the *O*. She had been in this house no more than ten minutes, her leg was throbbing in earnest, and she was flat-out exhausted. The faster she could sit down and get lost in *Horizon Zero Dawn*, the better. "So other than those . . . rules . . . I can use the TV."

"Yes. Until 4:00 p.m."

Tanner nearly screamed with irritation. She clenched her teeth. "What happens at 4:00 p.m.?"

"Cocktails."

"Oh. You have like, people, friends over?"

"No."

Tanner waited for elaboration. The woman offered none. Instead, she said, "I'll leave you to your unpacking." And then she gripped her cane and step-thumped her way out of the room, leaving a trail of boiled egg–gardenia scent in her wake.

FIVE HOURS.

Five *hours*!

Louise tried to think of the last thing she'd done for five hours straight. She hadn't even slept for a full five hours in she didn't know how long, her bladder forcing her up at least once in the middle of each night.

And they said kids today lacked attention span. Louise had never seen attention like that in her life. Laser focused. A high school marching band could have paraded through the living room and Louise didn't think the girl would have so much as blinked.

Even now, after clearing her throat loudly three times, Tanner's eyes remained glued to the screen, her fingers moving quickly and confidently on the buttons of the video game controller. (Turned out she hadn't wanted to *watch* TV at all!) Holding a glass tumbler filled with ice in one hand, Louise resorted to letting go of her cane and pushing the power button on the television with her other. Then, and only then, did Tanner's face change—first in confusion, a flash of anger, even, and finally, when her eyes found Louise, a kind of clarity or realization. "Oh. Is it four?"

"It is."

Tanner nodded and stretched her arms overhead, making a little mewing sound in her throat.

She dropped her arms and tossed the video game controller onto the couch cushion beside her. Louise stared at the white plastic contraption. One of the many benefits of living alone (God rest

Ken's soul) was not having to pick up after anyone, and she'd be damned if that was going to change now. Fortunately, the girl was not as oblivious as Louise feared. Tanner followed her eyeline and picked up the controller and set it gingerly on the coffee table.

Tanner stood up and stretched once more, and Louise thought she saw a wince cross her face when the girl straightened her leg. She'd be lying if she said she didn't feel a small sense of glee to note that even twenty-one-year-old bodies sustained aches and pains from sitting in the same position for five hours.

Louise watched Tanner as she left the room and walked down the hall—presumably to unpack, since she had begun playing her video game within ten minutes of being inside the house—and then, when the girl was out of sight, she walked to the buffet and poured three fingers of Finlandia over the ice in her glass.

She typically allowed herself only two, but after the eventful weekend she'd had—what with a stranger moving into her house, and George's unfortunate letter—she felt she deserved an extra tipple. She had spent the afternoon as she did most Sundays, at her secretary writing correspondence: anniversary cards, birthday cards, condolences (it seemed people she and Ken had known throughout their life together had begun dying at alarming rates—so much so that she had bought a bulk pack of forty sympathy cards at the drugstore last year and was down to her last two). Now, as she settled into her sofa, she allowed herself to consider the matter at hand and outline a plan, should she need it. Not that she had decided anything, of course, but just in case. Louise Wilt was nothing if not practical.

She also knew that successful jobs—in which the definition of success was any job that one completed without getting caught—were all in the plotting.

Any crime caper movie would tell you that if you bothered to pay attention; ninety percent of the *Ocean's Eleven* remake was the setup. She had always liked that movie—and not just the Brad Pitt scenes, wherein he was always eating something (cliché or no, Louise enjoyed a firm jawline). It was clever, the misdirections and whatnot, and Louise had always appreciated cleverness.

Anyway, that was where most criminals failed. They didn't have the patience or, frankly, intelligence to plan for all contingencies; the what-ifs, like a barking German shepherd or an unexpected person walking through the front door.

Louise understood this, of course, but planning was not her strong suit. As smart as she was, George had been the brains behind their operation, the methodical schemer, balancing Louise's more impulsive nature. The yin to her yang. It was why they were the perfect team. George planned out each mission down to every last detail, and Louise executed, using her gut instincts to pivot where necessary.

And twenty years ago, maybe, she could have taken off like a thief in the night (ha!) in a matter of hours. But now, logistically, it wasn't quite so easy.

Flying was out of the question, of course. Never mind that she had a low-level fear of it, but it was entirely too traceable. That left the car. It was in good shape—August had seen to that—but it was old. How far could she realistically get before it broke down or left her stranded? And furthermore, since her hip surgery, she hadn't been cleared to drive. Not that rules had ever stopped Louise from doing anything, but she didn't even know if she could.

And then there was the girl. Louise couldn't exactly just leave the house for days and expect that Tanner wouldn't notice. (Although, the way Tanner lost herself in that video game, Louise felt sure she would have a good head start before Tanner even realized she was gone.)

But the biggest problem? Her kids. Jules, in particular. While Charlie and Lucy called fairly infrequently, ever since her divorce, Jules had been . . . clingy. Overbearing. More so than usual, anyway.

The doorbell rang, jerking Louise out of her thoughts. Who on earth—

"I've got it," Tanner yelled, and Louise suddenly wished she had laid down some more ground rules, starting with no visitors. It was bad enough having *one* stranger in her house. Before Louise could say anything, Tanner opened the front door, and Louise saw the flat cardboard box exchange hands.

Pizza.

Relieved, Louise sat back in her chair, while Tanner shut the door and turned, not toward the kitchen but back toward the hallway.

Louise straightened her spine again. "Excuse me," she barked, as if decades hadn't slipped by and she was a young mother once again admonishing her children not to eat anywhere but the kitchen—which was exactly one of the many reasons she didn't want this *girl* living in her house. It was exhausting, parenting. Hadn't she already done her part? And then she wondered why she cared anyway. She hated that guest room. Grease stains couldn't make it any uglier. Besides, she'd be leaving it all behind soon enough, one way or another—and she'd never have to see that wallpaper again.

"I'm sorry," Tanner said, stopping in her tracks. "Did you want some?"

"God, no," Louise said. Was there anything worse than chain restaurant pizza? Give her a slice of John's from New York any day (the real John's in the West Village, not that impostor in Times Square). Or a perfectly wood-fired margherita hot off a pizza stone in Naples.

"Oh." Tanner frowned. "Did you need something else?"

Need. Louise shuddered at the word. She had lived her entire life priding herself on not *needing* anything or anyone.

"Yes," Louise said, her eyes falling on her afternoon's worth of correspondence lying on the secretary. "Please take that stack of letters to the mailbox." She, of course, could take the cards herself—she didn't *need* Tanner to do it—but if the girl was going to be here, Louise thought, she may as well make use of her.

6

AT 7:00 A.M. on the dot Monday morning—her first waking up in Mrs. Wilt's house—Tanner's eyes popped open. She knew it was seven, because she counted the chimes of the grandfather clock, just as she had done when they woke her at four, five, and six. She had no idea how she'd slept through the midnight to 3:00 a.m. chimes—or how she hadn't noticed during daylight hours how shockingly loud the metallic strikes were. She couldn't possibly understand how the *neighbors* slept through it, much less Mrs. Wilt.

She grabbed the pillow beside her head, jammed it over her face, and screamed into it—the only recourse she could think of, aside from taking a hammer to the clock and hitting it repeatedly until it splintered into toothpicks, which, of course, was what she really wanted to do.

At home Tanner typically slept until at least ten, though eleven or twelve was preferable—but that was clearly not going to happen here. The trumpeting clock aside, the bed was wildly uncomfortable—hard, yet lumpy. And that was coming from someone who was used to sleeping on a pullout couch. Tanner sat up and rubbed her bleary eyes. She wanted a new mattress. And earplugs. And to not be living in this musty old house with a musty old woman.

But as none of those things seemed to be readily possible, she needed coffee. And lots of it. She briefly considered ordering Starbucks on Uber Eats, but quickly dismissed it after considering that all the fees and tip would quickly add up to an expensive cup of coffee. And she was already down twenty dollars for the pizza from the two hundred dollars her mom had given her to tide her over until her first paycheck. She'd have to search the kitchen cabinets and hope she got lucky—and that Louise wouldn't mind.

Tanner threw the blankets aside and stood, her leg humming with pain. Mornings were always the worst, particularly since she had stopped doing her strengthening band exercises recommended by Dr. Stephens (what was the point?). She crept down the hall, not wanting to disturb Mrs. Wilt. Not so much out of kindness, but because it was awkward enough being in a stranger's house and even more so being in the same room. Thank God she was able to zone out in her video games, though she would have much preferred to do it in privacy. She walked through the large room that served as a den, sitting area, and dining room, and into the kitchen. Her heart nearly stopped when she saw a person out of the corner of her eye, sitting at the table, directing a piece of toast to her mouth.

Mrs. Wilt.

"Oh!" Tanner said, putting a hand to her chest. "I didn't think you'd be up yet." And not only up, but fully dressed in a cardigan (lavender today), tan trousers, and orthopedic shoes, with perfectly coiffed hair and . . . Tanner looked closer. Pink lipstick! Who applied lipstick *before* eating breakfast?

"At seven fifteen?" Mrs. Wilt said, in that sharp, cutting way she had that clearly meant seven fifteen was the absolute middle of the day and Tanner was a good-for-nothing layabout for sleeping that late. But Tanner was too distracted by the smell of coffee to care.

She eyed the full pot. "Do you mind if I . . . I can go get more today. I just didn't bring any—" She was stammering, she knew, but she was desperate, and the woman made her uneasy.

Mrs. Wilt nodded and set down her half-eaten toast on her plate. "Mugs are in the cabinet above. I made extra, just in case."

"Oh," Tanner said, caught off guard by this kind gesture. "Thank you." Tanner poured herself a cup and, after adding the requisite amount of milk and sugar (read: a boatload), leaned back against the counter to take her first full sip. And just when the coffee flooded her with warmth, and Tanner was overcome with gratitude and felt that maybe she had been a little rushed in her judgment of Mrs. Wilt, she felt eyes on her. She glanced back over at the woman—who was glaring intently at her.

"Well, I guess I'll go back to . . ." Tanner paused. She wasn't sure if she should say *her* room or the guest room. Neither one felt accurate.

Mrs. Wilt nodded, dropping her gaze back to the paper. "Please be ready at nine to leave for my physical therapy appointment. I don't like to be late."

THE FIRST THREE days passed in a very *Groundhog Day* fashion. As promised, Tanner drove the woman to the appointed destinations on her calendar in Mrs. Wilt's fifteen-year-old Mercury Grand Marquis. (Tanner almost laughed when she saw it in the garage. Of *course* this was the car she would have to drive. It was the quintessential old lady boat. God forbid Mrs. Wilt have something fun.)

When they returned home, sometime in the afternoon, Tanner retrieved a slice of pizza from the fridge and then settled in on the couch to play *Horizon Zero Dawn* until Louise's cocktail hour, wherein Mrs. Wilt would sit in silence in the living room nursing a drink. At five, she turned on the local news for precisely one hour. From six to seven she ate dinner in the kitchen, and then she would return to the den and watch some legal or crime drama, the volume of which she turned to FULL, allowing Tanner to make out every single word, even with her door shut. Although Tanner was hard-pressed to say which was more irritating—the television volume or the near-constant trilling of the telephone. Who had a *landline* anymore? Tanner had taken to answering it sometimes, simply because she could reach the phone faster than Mrs. Wilt, thereby cutting off the obnoxious, piercing ring. (Which is how she quickly realized they were all junk calls, robotic voices offering zero percent credit card balance transfers, or accented English explaining that Louise's social security benefits had been suspended or, once, that she had won a free cruise.) At nine, the old woman trudged to her room and, presumably, to bed.

In other words, living with Mrs. Wilt was as predictable as the grandfather clock Tanner wanted to smash to bits.

Until it wasn't.

WEDNESDAY AFTERNOON, JUST as Tanner was gearing up to battle a Stormbird—one of the fiercest enemies in *Horizon Zero Dawn*—a loud pounding rattled the front door.

"I'll get it," Mrs. Wilt called, and slowly made her way down the hall, with the now-familiar step-thump of her walk. Tanner zoned back into her game, assuming it must be a delivery of some kind—until she half heard Mrs. Wilt greet someone warmly, which surprised her, as Mrs. Wilt hadn't done anything warmly in the short time she'd known her. A deep baritone responded, surprising Tanner even further, but if she looked, instead of disabling the lightning gun, she knew from experience she wouldn't survive the encounter.

"Shoot him in the eyes."

"What?" Tanner said, still unable take her eyes from the screen, where she was now pinning the Stormbird to the ground with her Ropecaster.

"Just do it."

There wasn't much Tanner hated more than being told what to do by some guy who thought he knew better (and in her experience, they *always* thought they knew better), so she ignored the directive, nailed the Stormbird's chest and both wings with the Tearblaster, and then used her freeze gun to kill it dead.

"Wow," the deep voice said, and at that, Tanner looked up smugly—and into the mahogany eyes of a man. A man that looked around her age, maybe a little older—twenty-three or twenty-four? A man in a work shirt casually unbuttoned at the collar, with an inky black outline of a tattoo peeking out the rolled-up sleeve on his right bicep. A man with mousy-brown, devil-may-care hair tucked behind his ears and brooding eyebrows that belied his affable gaze. And Tanner—though she would have sworn mere minutes earlier that she did not find anything remotely attractive about men with tattoos or long hair or . . . *broodiness*—found that she had trouble tearing her eyes from his.

"Tanner Quimby, this is August Wright. He lives up the street and helps me out with odd jobs from time to time. August, Tanner."

"Aw, they're not always odd, Miss Louise. Sometimes, they're pretty normal." He grinned, two deep smile lines bookending his lips.

Tanner's brow lifted. Miss *Louise*? She glanced at Mrs. Wilt, waiting, almost giddily, for her to put him squarely in his place.

Mrs. Wilt swatted his bicep with her hand. "Oh, stop." And Tanner wasn't sure what shocked her more—the ruggedly hot man standing in this room (like a majestic whale suddenly surfacing in a backyard swimming pool) or Mrs. Wilt's complete transformation into a coquettish schoolgirl. She was positively beaming.

Tanner would have been beaming as well, but she had completely sworn off hot men after Grant. They were nothing but trouble.

"Nice to meet you." August's gaze was steady. "And nice kill."

"Uh . . . thanks," Tanner said.

"But if you shoot 'em in the eyes, you get a huge damage bonus."

"You play *Horizon Zero Dawn*?"

"Yeah, it's only like—"

"The best game ever," they said at the exact same time.

That settled it. She was going to marry him and have eighteen babies.

Until she remembered what she looked like. Had she showered yesterday—or the day before? A lock of hair hung limply in front of her face, and Tanner quickly tucked it behind her ear. She smiled nervously, and then stopped when she couldn't remember if she had brushed her teeth after her slice of pizza at lunch. Or breakfast.

"Mrs. Wilt, you didn't tell me anyone was coming over. I would have changed into something more . . . appropriate."

"Oh," Mrs. Wilt said, her soft face sharpening so instantly when she turned from August to Tanner, it reminded Tanner of that optical illusion where the drawing looked like a young maiden until suddenly the lines of her hair turned into an old hag, and you forgot how to see the maiden. "I wasn't aware you owned anything appropriate."

August covered a smile with his hand, and Tanner felt heat crawl up her cheeks.

"So, what's going on with the car?" August said.

"Well, I thought it might be time for a good once-over," said Mrs. Wilt. "Make sure everything is tuned up properly."

"We just did that, remember? What, two months ago?" he said. "It's in great shape."

"Yes." Mrs. Wilt paused briefly. "Yes, of course you did. But better safe than sorry, no?"

August shrugged. "You're the boss." He clamped his jaw down on the piece of gum he was chewing and flashed one more grin at Tanner.

Tanner chose not to return it. She was sure this . . . August . . . was used to grinning and charming his way into everything. Plus, she was irritated. Mrs. Wilt hadn't expressed any concern about the car to her, which was just so tiresomely, predictably sexist. "Check the rod bearings," she said to August. "There's a slight click in the engine, and it's probably just a valve train slightly out of alignment, but—" She glanced at Mrs. Wilt. "Better safe than sorry."

August froze midchew. He narrowed his eyes at her, studying her as if she were now the whale cresting out of a swimming pool. Satisfied, she flitted her eyes back to the screen. "Yeah . . . I'll do that," he stuttered. "I'll . . . uh . . . grab my tools from the car."

When the door closed behind him, Tanner turned to Louise. "I could have done that, you know."

"Done what?" Mrs. Wilt asked innocently, as if she hadn't heard what Tanner had said.

"Checked your car for you. I'm good with that stuff. My dad taught me."

"Isn't that a modern skill to have," Mrs. Wilt said curtly. "Why didn't you?"

Tanner opened her mouth, but then promptly shut it. Mrs. Wilt had her there. A touch of guilt bloomed. Tanner hadn't brought up the click either, and she should have at least said something, if not checked it herself.

"Besides," Mrs. Wilt said. "Isn't it more . . . interesting for him to do it?" Her face remained passive, and Tanner blinked. Could it be? Was Mrs. Wilt alluding to August's . . . *hot*ness? Well, she'd have to be *blind* not to see it. But, hello, cougar! Maybe Mrs. Wilt was a little more interesting—a little less predictable—than Tanner had thought.

"Now, if you'll so kindly move. It's three minutes past my cocktail time."

Tanner's face fell. Or maybe not.

The front door opened and August walked back through the den carrying a rectangular gunmetal toolbox. As he strode to the sliding glass door and opened it, stepping out onto the back patio, Tanner kept her eyes glued to the screen. Then she set her controller on the coffee table and thought perhaps she would go take a shower. Not for any specific reason, of course. Certainly *not* because August would still be here when she got out and have a better first impression of her.

It wasn't until later, when August was long gone, Mrs. Wilt was on to the evening news, and Tanner, fresh and clean, was heating up yet another slice of pizza in the kitchen, that something strange occurred to her: August had come in and out the sliding glass door twice more in the hour he had been there, which led to the backyard.

But Mrs. Wilt's car sat in the garage.

• • • • •

AT MIDNIGHT WEDNESDAY night, Tanner lay awake in her dark room, lit only by the bright screen of her cell phone. She knew she should put down her phone and sleep, but (a) the bed was wildly uncomfortable and sleep was hard to come by, which meant (b) she would lie awake thinking about her life and how she'd ended up in this musty old-fashioned room with heinous wallpaper, and then the anger at the unfairness of it all would once again overwhelm her. Scrolling Instagram was easier. Well, not easier, but it allowed her to direct her hate at her friends' cheery, perfect lives, instead of at herself. But tonight, a memory from one year ago assaulted her first thing. She stiffened as she stared at the video of herself and her teammates. She remembered the moment so clearly—it was the fall season opener, the score was tied at one, and in the final two minutes of the game, Vee crossed the ball, and Tanner was in the perfect position. She booted the ball as hard as she could, and like a cannon, it shot past three defenders, directly to the upper ninety, just out of reach of the keeper's outstretched fingers. And then she watched as her teammates—Vee first—made a beeline to her, clobbering her with such enthusiasm and joy, she nearly had to look away. Instead, Tanner stared at herself, trying to remember the last time she'd felt so proud. So capable.

So *herself.*

She waited for the anger to rise up, but instead she found a tidal wave of something else: grief. She missed being good at something other than a stupid video game. She missed the camaraderie of the team. She missed her life, her *real* one. Not whatever this surreal day-to-day existence was that she was living in someone else's home.

She missed Vee.

And her dead-on Gwyneth Paltrow impression that she utilized at weird times ("I'm going to need you to consciously uncouple from that cheeseburger so I can eat it").

Their late-night conversations that ranged in seriousness from Vee's brush with death when she was thrown through the front windshield of a car at the age of five and Tanner's bizarre but persistent fear of the sun exploding (something she'd never admitted to anyone) to which celebrity they would most like to have sex with: Michael B. Jordan for Vee, to which Tanner replied, "Could you be any more unoriginal? Even my grandma wants to have sex with him"; and Timothée Chalamet for Tanner, to which Vee replied, "He looks like a hot drug addict."

Tanner had had friends before, of course—good friends—but from the moment she met Vee, when they happened to sit next to each other at freshman orientation's Wildcat Welcome and, during the cheesy icebreaker, serendipitously shouted the exact same favorite pizza topping (black olives), she knew this was different. And when they discovered they were not only both incoming freshmen on the soccer team but in rooms next door to each other, their sisterhood was cemented. *Soul mates*, they often joked over the past three years of friendship, but Tanner also knew it wasn't really a joke. One glance at Vee's face and she knew exactly what she was thinking or what she was going to say or do—which made them a powerhouse on the field and inseparable off it. Tanner and Vee knew that no matter what happened in the future—where their soccer careers took them, who they married, what states they lived in—they would be the constants in each other's lives.

But Tanner had gone and fucked that up, too.

Just as the wave of loneliness crested and self-pity threatened to wash over her, Tanner heard something. A sharp creak. She peered out into the dark silence of her room, even darker after staring at the bright screen. Convincing herself it was nothing more than the house settling or the wind bending a tree outside, she turned back to her phone—and then, she heard it again.

A creak, followed by the slow and eerie *eeeeeek* of an unoiled door hinge opening. Disoriented, she couldn't tell which direction it was coming from. Was someone in the house? Senses on high alert, she sat up straighter, heart racing a bit, until finally she heard Mrs. Wilt's familiar gait with her cane, albeit slower and more muted than usual, as if Mrs. Wilt was taking care not to wake Tanner. Relieved, she leaned back against her pillow. Mrs. Wilt was likely getting something from the kitchen—a glass of milk, a snack, maybe even a dram of the vodka she seemed to be so fond of. But a few minutes passed and Tanner didn't hear the fridge open, or a cabinet; she heard the unmistakable squeak and swoosh of the heavy door that led out to the garage. What could Mrs. Wilt possibly need from her garage in the middle of the night?

Tanner blinked. It wasn't any of her business what Louise needed from her garage—this was Louise's house, and she was welcome to go wherever she pleased at any time of the day or night. On the other hand, Tanner was technically her caretaker, and responsible if Mrs. Wilt fell down those four wooden steps onto the cement floor of the garage. And what if she was . . . sleepwalking or something?

Annoyed, Tanner growled softly and tossed her phone onto the pillow beside her, cursing herself for thinking this "job" wouldn't be anything more than an unusual living arrangement. A solution to her problem. It was starting to feel like more of a problem than a solution. She walked down the hallway, flipping on light switches as she went. When she got to the door that led out to the garage, she swung it open with more force than necessary and then stared into the dark abyss, letting her eyes adjust. At first she couldn't make out anything but the hulking shadow of the Mercury Grand Marquis. "Mrs. Wilt?" she called out just as the car roared to life, the gun of the engine filling the small space and startling Tanner.

She rushed to the passenger door and flung it open, causing the interior lights to flood the car. Mrs. Wilt sat at the wheel wearing a thin, short-sleeved, flower-patterned housedress, her typical puffed helmet of hair flattened in the back, her lips pale, bare of the pink lipstick. Tanner couldn't say what surprised her more—that Mrs. Wilt owned pajamas or the shock of her transformation. Out of her daily uniform, she looked diminished, somehow. Vulnerable. Frail. She looked . . . *old*.

"Mrs. Wilt," Tanner repeated. "What are you doing?"

She turned to look at Tanner and blinked slowly. "Huh?"

Tanner felt a pang of sympathy for the old woman. She seemed so out of it—as if she didn't know any more than Tanner why she was sitting in the front seat of her car.

"You're not supposed to be driving, remember?" Tanner said gently. "Your hip." She reached across the passenger seat and console and turned the key, killing the engine.

Mrs. Wilt blinked again and turned back to the steering wheel. "Where am I?"

"In your car," Tanner said. "I think you were sleepwalking." She didn't really think that, but it seemed a much nicer thing to say than *I think you're not firing on all cylinders*.

"Oh!" Mrs. Wilt gave a little laugh. "I haven't done that in years. Used to scare the heck out of Ken, though." She paused, and then: "Please don't mention it to Jules. It will only worry her."

"Um . . . OK." Tanner hadn't even thought of saying anything to Jules but now wondered if she should. "Let's go back inside . . . do you need help?"

"No," she spat. "I got all the way out here by myself, didn't I?"

And just like that, Mrs. Wilt was back.

After walking her to her room (well, following her at a safe distance in the hall, as Mrs. Wilt *didn't need help*), Tanner lay awake staring at the ceiling. Mostly because the bed was so uncomfortable, but also because she was growing worried about her charge. *Had* Mrs. Wilt been sleepwalking, or was it something else—maybe the beginning stages of dementia? She wasn't sure. But what she did know was this job was becoming much more of a responsibility than she'd thought it would be—or wanted.

7

ACCORDING TO THE wall calendar in the kitchen, Thursday morning was bridge. After she dropped Mrs. Wilt off a few streets over, Tanner would have the entire house to herself for two full hours to play her video game in peace. She craved being alone, even more so after the previous night—to get a break from the weight of responsibility for Mrs. Wilt's well-being.

She had watched the old woman like a hawk all morning, looking for signs of forgetfulness, but Mrs. Wilt didn't seem confused at all, just irritated. "Are you going to follow me into the bathroom, too?" she growled. "Or do I have permission to relieve myself in private?"

After dropping Mrs. Wilt off, Tanner navigated the tree-lined lane back to Mrs. Wilt's house. The neighborhood, like many suburban communities in Atlanta, was a healthy mix of 1960s brick ranches and 1970s midcentury-modern homes, most of which had been lovingly cared for, renovated, or completely torn down, leaving a McMansion sprouted in its place—save for one house on the street in a massive state of disrepair. Tanner had noticed it the first time she'd driven to Mrs. Wilt's for her interview. The house appeared abandoned, or as though someone had decided to remodel it, taking one half of the house down to its studs, and then quit midproject.

Today, though, there was a car in the driveway. An old Ford Bronco with extra-large tires, and some rust damage peeking out from the undercarriage. She shifted her gaze from the car to the house, or more specifically, to a man on a ladder leaned against the house. A man with devil-may-care-hair and a tattoo peeking out of his right shirtsleeve.

August.

Her heartbeat revved at the sight of his back, which only managed to irritate her. He was just a man, after all. She didn't realize she had slowed almost to a crawl until he turned and looked directly at her. His expression morphed into one of recognition, and then he smiled and waved. Heat flooding her face, Tanner pushed her foot on the gas and sped away five houses down to Mrs. Wilt's.

Once safely in the garage, she gripped the steering wheel and rested her forehead on the apex. What was wrong with her? Why didn't she just wave back? When she lifted her head, a movement in the rearview mirror caught her eye, and for a split second of terror and humiliation (and, she would have had to admit if under interrogation, excitement), she thought August had followed her home. But no, it wasn't a man standing behind the car at all—it was a woman. A tiny spit of a thing with a pink stripe in her otherwise blond hair and an angry look on her face. Had Tanner accidentally tapped a car parked on the side of the road and not noticed? Taken out a mailbox? She quickly ran back through the three hundred yards she had driven home, over the speed limit and nearly blinded by mortification.

She pushed the driver's side door open and stood, turning to face the woman while wondering the best way to greet her when she had no idea what she had done. Fortunately, the woman spoke first.

"Are you her granddaughter?"

"Whose granddaughter?"

"The batshit crazy woman who lives here. Louise? Is that her name?"

"Oh . . . um . . ." This woman seemed amped up and unnecessarily aggro. Sure, Mrs. Wilt had her . . . eccentricities, but *batshit crazy* was a little harsh. "No, I'm not her granddaughter. I'm her . . . I'm taking care of her. I just started this week. Who are you?"

"I'm her neighbor. I live right next door."

Tanner stood awkwardly gripping the keys, not sure what to say next. "Is there a . . . problem?"

She laughed, one quick exhale of *ha!* and then: "Yes. If you consider threatening my boyfriend's life a problem."

"Oh! Um . . ." Tanner didn't want to get in the middle of a neighbor spat, but she thought surely there must be some mistake. For the past four days, anytime Mrs. Wilt had left the house, Tanner had been with her. "When did she . . . when did this—"

"A few months ago. I wanted to call the cops, but Declan talked me down, said we should wait—try to speak to someone in the family. But nobody's been in or out of this house in weeks."

"She broke her hip a few months ago. She's been in recovery." Tanner didn't feel right telling Mrs. Wilt's business like that, but inexplicably, she felt a little protective of her. Or maybe she instinctively knew revealing a vulnerability would knock this woman down a few pegs, take the wind out of her very angry and self-righteous sails.

It worked. The woman's face changed, leaking her anger like a deflating balloon. "Oh. I didn't know that."

Tanner wasn't sure what to say next, so she went with something vague, hoping it would end the conversation. "Well, I'm sorry about . . . your boyfriend. I'm sure she didn't mean any harm."

The woman's eyes went hard again. "I don't know about that. The handgun seemed pretty convincing."

Tanner paused and then chuckled. "I'm sorry. It sounded like you said 'gun,' for a second."

"I did."

Tanner blinked. "Gun, as in, the *weapon*?"

"Pointed it right at Declan, no farther than where I'm standing from you. I'm telling you, that woman is certifiably insane. You know she's been in jail."

Tanner's eyes grew even bigger. "What? No, she hasn't." Tanner of course didn't know the first thing about Mrs. Wilt. Not really. But she felt confident that the old woman had never been to jail.

"Yes, she has."

Tanner narrowed her eyes, skeptically. "How do you know?"

"She said it! 'I'd gladly go *back to* jail.'"

If Tanner had a reply, it got lost somewhere between her brain and her mouth.

"You be sure to tell her, and her family, that next time we'll be calling the police." The woman turned on her heel, leaving Tanner standing open-mouthed in the garage.

Jail?

She tried to picture Mrs. Wilt in an orange jumpsuit and shackles, and the image was so absurd, she nearly laughed out loud.

And a *gun*? She couldn't imagine her even knowing how to hold one, much less *threatening* someone with it. But then she remembered Mrs. Wilt in the car the night before, not acting like herself. Maybe it was just one in a long string of episodes. Maybe Mrs. Wilt really did have a problem.

Still stunned from the exchange, Tanner walked inside and stood in the middle of the kitchen, and the silence that she had been looking forward to now felt foreboding. Eerie. The hairs on her arms pricked up. She eyed the many kitchen cabinets warily, as if they all suddenly knew things she didn't. Held things.

Like secrets.

Or a gun.

Tanner shivered. She hated guns. She'd never even seen one in real life and wasn't eager to change that anytime soon.

She slowly pulled open the drawer closest to her, half expecting a Beretta to jump out like a snake in a trick pop-top can. Instead, she spotted a pile of junk: innocuous chip clips and twist ties and matchbooks. But what if a gun was lying in wait somewhere in the house? If Mrs. Wilt really was showing signs of dementia, then being in close proximity to a firearm didn't bode well for anyone's safety.

Tanner didn't see any choice: she was going to have to say something to Jules. She slid her thumb across the screen of her cell and scrolled for Mrs. Wilt's daughter's number. Tanner preferred texting whenever possible but felt like this situation required a live conversation. It rang five times before Jules's voicemail picked up.

Tanner left a message and then walked into the den, growing

increasingly agitated as she eyed all the drawers and cabinets in this room as well that could be concealing a weapon. Suddenly feeling like a woman on a mission, she rushed the buffet, opening every drawer and door, rifling through the expected tablecloths for various seasons, and candlestick holders and serving platters.

No gun.

The secretary where Mrs. Wilt wrote her many cards and letters offered the same—typical stationery equipment like paper, pens, stamps—save for one small door with a keyhole and no key to be found. Tanner studied the roughly four-inch-square box and decided it was too small to hold a gun anyway.

Then she methodically made her way through the two smaller bedrooms and hallway, only to find two more locked closets—and locked not just by the handles but with dead bolts. She tried to picture the closet doors in her own house and felt sure the handles didn't even have keyholes, much less dead bolts. It occurred to her that perhaps Mrs. Wilt had added them as a security measure for just this reason—so Tanner couldn't rifle through her things. Anxiety began to envelop her like a sweater, reaching a fever pitch when she arrived at Mrs. Wilt's bedroom door. Snooping was wrong, of course, in any room of the house, but felt even more invasive in someone's bedroom. She hesitated, weighing the moral dilemma of snooping with her fear of living in a house with a handgun owned by a woman who likely had dementia.

She peered into the room and eyed the nightstand. That was the most likely place for a gun, wasn't it? Right near the bed, so one was prepared to fend off intruders at night? At least that's what every cop drama had led her to believe. She decided she would just check that one drawer, and if a gun wasn't there, she'd wait for Mrs. Wilt's daughter to call her back.

She crossed the room in three long strides and tugged the drawer knob. It didn't budge. And that's when she noticed the keyhole.

Locked.

Like the box in the secretary.

Like the closets in the bedroom and the hallway.

Like the fence she had scaled to the backyard on the day she'd moved in and the fire alarm had sounded.

Thinking, she slowly retraced her steps back to the den and glanced at the front door—then did a double take. The front door had a chain lock and three—*three*—dead bolts. How had she not noticed that before?

She turned toward the back of the room and closed the distance to the sliding glass door. Only one lock. It looked heavy-duty, but still—anyone could just break the glass if they wanted to . . . *Hammerglass.* Mrs. Wilt's words echoed in her head. *Chair wouldn't have worked, by the way.*

Heart pounding, Tanner stood holding on to the door handle, wondering why it suddenly felt like Mrs. Wilt's house was locked up tighter than Rikers Island.

Being safe was one thing, and then there was . . . *this.*

To be fair, Mrs. Wilt did watch a lot of crime shows. Maybe she was just a paranoid old lady. Scared of her own shadow. Or maybe there had a been a rash of break-ins in the neighborhood. Or maybe the house had come like this—with the shatterproof glass and all.

Or maybe Mrs. Wilt had something of value she was trying to protect.

The shed in the left corner of the backyard drew Tanner's eye. It, too, had a thick metal chain through the door handles, held together with a sturdy padlock. She slid open the sliding glass door and traversed the cement patio and then the grass until she was standing in front of the shed. She tugged on the lock. It held. She peered in the windows on either side of the door, but they were covered in grime and she couldn't see a thing.

She looked from the shed back to the sliding glass door and thought of August. Why had he come out here yesterday? The only way to the garage was either back through the house or through the fence to the driveway. But the fence was locked, too. She stood there, confounded, and then realized there was a simple way to get answers to at least one of her many questions. Before she could change her mind, she stormed back through the house and out the front door, the midday summer sun blinding her once again with its brightness as she marched the five house lengths down to where she had spotted August.

He was still perched atop the stepladder when she reached the yard, and she tried but failed not to notice how the fabric of his T-shirt stretched taut against the muscles of his back as he hammered a nail into a two-by-four.

"Hey," she said, and when he turned, most of the curiosity that had propelled her this far vanished in one fell swoop and was replaced by awkward embarrassment.

"Hey," he echoed, offering her that same full smile. God, why did he have to be so unnervingly attractive? It was irritating. "Did you come to apologize?"

"Apologize?"

"Yeah, for not waving to me. It hurt my feelings. That was you in Mrs. Wilt's car, right?"

"Yeah." She wasn't going to let him charm his way with her. "And that's what I came to talk to you about."

"Not waving?" He looked amused. Well, hot and amused, which

only further irritated Tanner. He began descending the ladder one step at a time.

"No. Mrs. Wilt's car. How was it yesterday?"

"You mean that engine click?"

"Yeah."

"Didn't even hear it. And the valve train was fine."

Tanner's forehead wrinkled. "Are you sure?"

"Are you hungry?" He stepped down from the last rung and was suddenly on level ground. The nearness of his body temporarily stunned Tanner—so much so that it took her a minute to comprehend what he had said. Even then, it didn't make sense.

"What?"

"I thought we could go grab a sandwich."

"What?" she repeated.

"You know, like two pieces of bread, generally with meat or cheese in the middle. I like mayo on mine. Not a fan of tomatoes, though. There's this great deli in that shopping center on the corner. They have a killer Reuben."

"I know what a sandwich is."

"Good. Do you want one?"

"No. I mean, I have to pick up Mrs. Wilt." She didn't know what time it was and likely had an hour or more before she had to get Mrs. Wilt, but this line of unexpected questioning was throwing her off balance.

"OK. Well, how about tomorrow? No, wait, Monday would actually be better."

"Monday," Tanner repeated. "As in, four days from now?"

August paused and then made a big show of mouthing the days and then counting them on his fingers. Finally, he grinned at her and said, "Yes."

"You want to know if I'm free Monday," Tanner said, still trying to understand exactly what was happening. "To eat sandwiches."

"Well, they have soup, too. Or whatever you want to order. You know, if sandwiches aren't your thing."

"I like sandwiches."

"Great." He grinned again, and Tanner wished he would stop, because the goddamned glow of it somehow scrambled her brain and made her forget simple things, like words. And how to put them together in a sentence. "So, Monday?"

"Um . . . yeah. I just . . . it would have to be around one, because Mrs. Wilt has her . . ." Tanner searched her brain for Mrs. Wilt's schedule, but couldn't immediately recall what Monday was, so she just said vaguely, "Appointments in the morning. And I have to drive her."

"OK. I'll pick you up at one."

"OK," Tanner said. August tossed the hammer he was holding into his open toolbox, shut and locked the lid, then stood and pulled a grease-stained cloth from the back of his jeans. He wiped his hands, stuffed it back into his pocket, and then nodded at Tanner, who was embarrassed to find she'd been watching his every movement like a National Geographic filmmaker observing the behavior of a rare species of penguin. "See you then."

"OK," she said again as he grabbed his toolbox with one hand and strode to the Bronco. Tanner turned to leave, confused as to how she'd come over for one thing and gotten something else entirely. Like the time she'd regrettably ordered a dress from one of those Instagram ads, and it ended up looking like it had been hand-stitched by a chimpanzee. It wasn't until she reached Mrs. Wilt's driveway that an unnerving thought occurred to her—had August just asked her out . . . on a *date*?

She thought that was something that only happened in movies. Like *High School Musical*. Or those old-fashioned nineties romantic teen comedies that her mom loved. It had certainly never happened to her. Unless you counted Grant's 2:00 a.m. requests for company, which she didn't.

Tanner glanced behind her, her gaze traveling down the sidewalk, as if to confirm she hadn't just dreamt up the entire episode, but even if he hadn't already driven off, the trees growing out of the five yards in between blocked her view. Slowly, she turned back to the open garage, the sight of Mrs. Wilt's Mercury Marquis causing her to remember the other shocking thing August had said—that he hadn't even *heard* the click. She blinked. The engine had definitely been clicking. Which meant August was either hard of hearing . . . or he was lying. And Tanner didn't think there was anything wrong with his ears.

She thought back through her strange morning—the angry neighbor, the search for a firearm, the locked-up-tight cabinets and doors, and the conversation with August that had really left her with more questions than answers (and, apparently, a lunch date). And Tanner thought perhaps it was time she found out more about the woman she was living with.

AFTER LIVING WITH her for a full week, Louise had to admit that Tanner wasn't as bad as she thought she would be.

She was worse.

For starters, she was a terrible driver. Not reckless or careless or a speed demon or overcome with road rage. Louise could have handled any of those. Would have understood it, appreciated it, even. But no . . . Tanner was slow and methodical, like a surgical resident performing brain surgery for the first time. It was painful to witness. *Just drive!* Louise wanted to shout, the same way she used to yell at a teenaged Charlie to "use a fork!" when he shoved supper in his mouth with both hands like he was a contestant in the Coney Island hot dog–eating competition.

Louise couldn't understand the overabundance of caution—particularly when the Mercury Grand Marquis Ken had insisted on buying, as if he'd been waiting his entire life to get one the way most men wait to buy a Corvette, was safer than a goddamned tank.

And the meddling! Louise had felt confident that Tanner was so self-involved, she would have no trouble minding her own business when she moved in. But lo and behold, the girl actually had to have a streak of concern, following Louise out to the garage when she was trying to test how painful pushing the gas pedal would be to her hip. (The conclusion? Very.) She hadn't planned to turn the key in the ignition, but God, she missed driving. The hum of the engine, the *freedom*.

And then Tanner had appeared.

Louise had had no choice but to pretend she was confused. And though she was used to pretending—to being something or someone that she wasn't—there was a specific indignity to being a certain age and pretending your mental faculties weren't up to par. Or maybe the indignity was that Tanner believed it so readily.

The girl relayed the entire episode to Jules, of course, even after she had *specifically* asked her not to—and then tattled about that little spat she had all but forgotten about with her neighbor. Though how Tanner even knew about that, she had no idea. That was a fun conversation, being reprimanded by her own daughter. Again.

"Mom, we've been over this. You can't go around threatening people at gunpoint."

Louise rolled her eyes. “I did not *threaten* him at gunpoint.” She had, technically speaking, but Jules had always been so dramatic. “It wasn’t even loaded.”

“I think the point remains,” Jules said curtly.

“Well, the man is an asshole.” Jules knew. The man had been an asshole for the two years he’d lived next door. A leopard doesn’t change his spots. And quite frankly, he needed a gun in his face, and Louise would have enjoyed nothing more than pulling the trigger. (Not that she *would* have. She wasn’t insane.)

“Be that as it may.”

Louise cleared her throat. “Listen, I’ve been thinking about taking a vacation shortly.”

“A vacation? To where?”

“Oh, I don’t know—I’ve always wanted to go back to Italy, travel around Europe. Your dad and I had always planned to.”

“What? You know you have to take a *plane* to get there, yes? You hate flying.”

“Well, I hate Metamucil, too, but it gets the job done.”

Louise could nearly hear her daughter’s eyes roll. How she had raised a child with no sense of humor, she had no idea.

“When were you thinking of going?”

“I’m not sure. Soon. Maybe next month.”

“Next *month*? You’re joking.”

“No, not at all.”

“Mom. You can’t up and go to Europe. What about physical therapy?”

“I’m sure they have physical therapists in Italy, dear.”

Jules exhaled loudly. “I’m worried about you. Does this have anything to do with—”

Louise cut her off. “You’re always worried about me.” Louise didn't avoid hard truths; she was a pragmatist, after all. She just didn't think there was any use dwelling upon them. "I'm fine."

"Did you call that support group that I sent you?"

"It's on my list to do this week." It absolutely was not on her list. "Darling, have you tried that dating app I sent you? Juanita's daughter just got engaged to a lovely man she met on there. Well, he's gainfully employed, anyway." Louise didn't care if Jules used the dating app or not (although companionship wouldn't be the worst thing in the world for her), but it was a surefire way to get her off the phone.

"Mom, I have to go."

"Of course, dear." And then, with more force than usual, she added, "I love you."

One never knew when it was the last time you'd get to say it.

8

TEXT EXCHANGE THE DAY AFTER LOUISE WILT WAS REPORTED MISSING TO THE POLICE

JULES: Are you there yet?

CHARLIE: Just walked in the door. Keep your pants on.

JULES: Is any furniture turned over? Does it look like a struggle?

CHARLIE: . . .

CHARLIE: Nope. Well, aside from all this blood.

JULES: 😐

LUCY: 😂😂😂

Two minutes later . . .

CHARLIE: Her suitcase isn't in the closet. I told you—she probably talked that nurse girl into driving her to the beach or something.

JULES: She's not a nurse.

LUCY: Mom does love the beach.

JULES: You know, she did say something a few days ago about wanting to take a trip.

CHARLIE: See! There you go.

JULES: But to Italy, not the beach. And she wouldn't just take off without telling us.

CHARLIE: I know this may come as a shock, Jules, but Mom is allowed to do things without your written consent.

JULES: What about the kitchen? Did she leave a note or anything? Check the table.

CHARLIE: Ah, yes! Here it is: I've gone to the beach with my nurse, Tanner. Be back on Friday.

JULES: . . .

LUCY:

One minute later . . .

CHARLIE: Huh.

JULES: What?

CHARLIE: Her car is still here.

JULES: You didn't check that first?

CHARLIE: No, I was looking for all the blood, remember?

LUCY: Maybe they flew?

JULES: Mom hates flying.

LUCY: Uber?

JULES: . . .

LUCY: I'm getting worried, guys.

CHARLIE: Yeah, something's not right.

JULES: OH, REALLY?

Thirty seconds later . . .

CHARLIE: Hold on. I hear ringing.

Charlie followed the sound of the ringing to the guest room, where he and his wife slept when they spent the night every other Thanksgiving. His wife, Jen, complained about the bed every time—that was it lumpy and uncomfortable, and couldn't they just drive the two and half hours in the morning, stay for the turkey, and then leave directly after? Charlie pushed open the already cracked door. He targeted the ringing to the tangled mess of bedsheets and dug around with his hand in the twisted heap until he finally latched on to the hard rectangle of a cell, the screen announcing MRS. W'S UPTIGHT DAUGHTER, and knew that could only be referring to one person.

He slid his thumb across the touch screen.

"Jules?"

"I guess we know why Tanner's not answering her cell phone," his big sister said. "Still think I'm overreacting?"

9

FOURTEEN LOUISE WILTS lived in the United States, according to Google.

Most of them were dead.

Tanner read through the first few obituaries with interest, only to find they all followed a similar pattern with certain details swapped out: Salem, Oregon, became Chicken Bristle, Illinois. Age ninety-four became eighty-three or eighty-nine or, once, an incredible one hundred six. The occupations ranged from school guidance counselor to librarian to church organist, but the Louise Wilts were all survived by loving family members.

None of them had been to jail, as far as Tanner could tell.

And none of them were the very much alive and breathing Louise Wilt who dwelled under the same roof as Tanner.

In fact, Tanner couldn't find *her* Louise Wilt online anywhere.

Was it even possible, in this day and age, to have no online footprint at all? Tanner wasn't sure.

The only thing she had become sure of in the four days since her strange conversation with the neighbor was that Mrs. Wilt did own a gun. Her daughter Jules had confirmed it when she returned Tanner's call.

"Where does she keep it?" Tanner had asked.

"Locked up in the nightstand beside her bed," Jules had said. At least that accounted for the contents of one of the locked drawers in the house, Tanner thought.

"She doesn't keep it loaded. But if it makes you more comfortable, I can ask her to give you the key?" Jules said. And then added in almost a mumble, "Though I don't know that she will."

It didn't make Tanner feel more comfortable.

Neither did the fact that her Louise Wilt wasn't anywhere to be found online. As if she didn't exist at all.

Regardless, after her fruitless Google search and her phone call with Jules, Tanner tried to put it all out of her mind. The locked doors, the gun, the neighbor. Yes, it was all a bit strange. But Mrs. Wilt was a bit strange. And really, it was none of Tanner's business. As long as she drove Mrs. Wilt to her appointments and continued to receive a paycheck for her efforts—that was all that mattered. The only thing that continued to stick in her craw was August and the engine click. She was sure there was a simple explanation, she just hadn't been able to come up with it.

But she'd be seeing him soon enough—she looked at the clock on the dashboard: one hour and twenty-three minutes, in fact, not that she was counting—and she'd be able to ask him in person and clear up the whole matter.

The passenger side door of Mrs. Wilt's car opened, and Tanner jumped out and hurried around the car to take Mrs. Wilt's cane and put it in the back seat. She did not offer Mrs. Wilt a hand to help her into the car, as she had made that mistake the first week only to be sharply rebuked with "I am *not* an invalid."

When Tanner returned to the driver's seat, Mrs. Wilt was struggling with her seat belt. She managed to pull it across herself fine, but it was the clicking in that seemed to vex her. Tanner patiently waited. After finally hearing the *click*, she started the car, ignoring the other clicking noise of the engine (that August allegedly didn't hear), and carefully reversed out of the parking spot.

"How was physical therapy?" Tanner asked, the same question she asked after every errand, changing out the event, just to fill the air between them.

"Torture," Mrs. Wilt said, the same response she had given to the same question last Monday and Wednesday. Tanner understood. She had been through her own share of torturous physical therapy, for whatever good it did her. She could have said as much to Mrs. Wilt, could have let her know how much she empathized with her, could have created a starting point for connection. She'd thought about it, last Monday and Wednesday and now, but always ended at the same conclusion: What was the point? So instead, she settled her hands at ten and two on the steering wheel, her mouth in a straight line, and drove.

BACK AT THE house, Tanner took her time getting ready for her lunch . . . thing. Not that she cared how she looked, of course. It was just nice to have a reason to wear jeans rather than athletic pants or pajamas (never shorts or a skirt—the scar on her knee was too shiny, large, and grotesque to reveal). She even blow-dried her typically wavy hair straight and swiped a shimmery nude gloss across her lips.

At 12:58 p.m., she appraised herself one last time in the mirror and, pleased with the result, went into the den and perched on the couch to wait.

At 1:13 p.m., Mrs. Wilt step-thumped through the room on her way to the kitchen. Tanner felt Mrs. Wilt's sharp gaze fall on her, but if the woman thought it strange that she was just sitting there, not playing video games (and surely she did), to her credit, she didn't say anything.

At 1:22 p.m., Tanner got up and went to the front door, peering out the blinds to the driveway. No Bronco. No August.

Maybe she'd gotten the day wrong? No, they'd definitely said Monday. She remembered him counting the days on his fingers. Maybe he'd forgotten the time. Or he'd gotten held up at his job—even though she wasn't sure what his job was. In fact, Tanner realized, she knew even less about him than she did about Mrs. Wilt. She would have scoured the Internet for him as well, like she did every guy she was interested in (not that she was interested in him!), but she couldn't even remember his last name. She knew Mrs. Wilt had said it when she introduced him, but she hadn't committed it to memory. And she had too much pride to ask Mrs. Wilt—or even to tell her that she was supposed to be seeing him. Especially now that it looked like she wouldn't be.

By 2:26 p.m., Tanner accepted the reality that August wasn't coming. There would be no sandwich eating. She was being stood up. And that old, faithful, familiar feeling of anger she had somehow kept at bay all morning crept back in.

Tanner flicked the button on her PlayStation and flopped back onto the sofa, stewing in her fury. Not to mention her embarrassment at her naive hopefulness. That she thought she had been asked on a *date*, and had been excited about it, despite her best efforts not to be. As she punched buttons on the controller, she tried to focus on August's faults—how his long hair had been pulled up into a man bun (a man bun!), how grease clung to the undersides of his fingernails like black half-moons, how irritatingly charming he was. A charming, slick, dirty-fingernailed, man-bunned liar. That's what he was. First lying about the car, and then saying he would show up somewhere on a specific date and time and not even bothering to. Who would want to go eat sandwiches with someone like that?

At four, when Mrs. Wilt came in to take over the living room for her cocktail hour, Tanner felt more irritable instead of less, and she just wanted to stay lost in the postapocalyptic world of *Horizon Zero Dawn*, which somehow felt cozier and more comforting than the real world.

She tossed her controller on the coffee table with more force than necessary, and it clattered to the ground. She huffed to go pick it up. She knew this was barely a step up from a child's tantrum but didn't really care. As she began to storm off, she heard Mrs. Wilt's voice behind her.

"Why don't you join me?"

Tanner turned to look at her. "Excuse me?"

"I suppose if we're going to be living together, we should make some effort to get to know each other."

Tanner nearly laughed out loud. They'd been living together for more than a week, and with all the silent car rides, there had been plenty of opportunity to "get to know each other," but Tanner had assumed Mrs. Wilt remained as uninterested in her life as Tanner was in Mrs. Wilt's.

"Besides, you look like you could use a cocktail."

Tanner cocked her head and crossed her arms. “I don’t drink.”

Mrs. Wilt stared back blankly. “I don’t understand.”

“I don’t really like it. The taste,” Tanner said, though she’d only ever had beer. Once. It had been bitter and lukewarm, and she didn’t understand how anyone could chug it, much less enjoy it.

Mrs. Wilt took a loud, deep breath, then waved her hand and muttered something in a language that did not sound like English.

“Huh?”

Mrs. Wilt repeated the phrase, louder this time: “Chi non beve in compagnia o è un ladro è una spia.”

“Is that . . . Spanish?”

“Italian.”

“What does it mean?”

“He who won’t drink in company is either a thief or a spy.” Louise raised an eyebrow. It was something Tanner had dealt with often at Northwestern—not the question of whether she was a thief or a spy, but the need to explain herself to her peers who immediately judged her as a teetotaler, a prude. (Not Vee, of course. Vee liked to party, but she never pressured Tanner or made her feel less than for not drinking. At parties, Vee would even go so far as to get Tanner a half-filled Solo cup of beer and switch it out every now and then so it looked like Tanner was drinking and she didn’t have to field the annoying questions about it.) Out of habit, Tanner continued with her rote explanation anyway.

“I play soccer—well, I *played*—and I didn’t want to interfere with training. Plus, getting caught with it was a surefire way to lose my scholarship.” She nearly chuckled at that. The irony. She’d lost it anyway, hadn’t she?

Mrs. Wilt didn’t respond, and Tanner stood there awkwardly, not sure what to do next. If this was supposed to be an opportunity for them to get to know each other better, Mrs. Wilt certainly didn't seem to be making much of an effort. Tanner could turn and carry on to her bedroom, leaving Mrs. Wilt to her cocktail hour, but she had to admit, she was a little curious about the old woman.

Tanner cleared her throat. "Are you Italian?"

"No."

Tanner waited for further explanation, if Mrs. Wilt actually knew Italian—her accent was quite good—or just that one phrase to showcase at dinner parties, like how her dad had a signature joke to break the ice ("I'm reading a book about antigravity. It's impossible to put down!"), but Mrs. Wilt offered none.

In the continued silence, Tanner wondered, really, why she didn't drink. It wasn't like she was ever going to play soccer again. And yes, the taste was horrific, but there was a reason so many people imbibed, despite that—it numbed feelings. And Tanner had quite a few feelings that could stand to be numbed. Rough edges sanded down. "Maybe I will have just a . . ."

Mrs. Wilt nodded, as though that was what she'd expected to happen all along. Tanner walked over to the buffet and helped herself to a small pour of the clear vodka in a short glass. She took the smallest sip and immediately regretted it. The warm liquid burned all the way down her throat. Her eyes watered.

"There's some tonic in the cabinet," Mrs. Wilt said.

Gratefully, Tanner retrieved the carbonated beverage and added it to her vodka. Then she sat down on the couch across from Mrs. Wilt, re-creating their exact same positioning from the first day she came to interview.

Clutching her lukewarm glass, Tanner looked at the sliding glass door, the dark reflective screen of the blank television, the delicate framed watercolor of cardinals on the far wall. And then her eye was drawn to the rhythmic tapping of Mrs. Wilt's wedding band on her ring finger on her own glass. Tanner wondered why Mrs. Wilt still wore her wedding band. Then she wondered how long they would sit in silence like this.

"Jules said you were quite good."

"At what?"

"Soccer."

"Oh. Right. Yeah, I was."

"What happened?"

Every muscle in Tanner's body tensed, causing her to grip her glass tighter. "She didn't tell you?"

"Oh, she made mention of an accident. She wasn't sure of all the details."

Tanner nodded slowly, trying to swallow down the scream building in her throat. She wondered when she'd ever be able to not feel like this.

"Are you planning to go back to school?"

Tanner clenched her teeth. "Not this year."

"Mm." Though Mrs. Wilt's response sounded noncommittal, Tanner heard it loud and clear. The judgment. And she wondered if Mrs. Wilt had been talking to her mother.

"Did you go to college?" she fired back.

"No."

Tanner sat smugly, point proven.

"My stepfather felt it was unnecessary for girls."

"Oh."

She wanted to change the subject. But she couldn't think of anything else to ask Mrs. Wilt, aside from why she had so many locked doors and cabinets in her house—which would be an outright confession of her snooping.

So they sat, the only sound the tinkling of ice melting in Mrs. Wilt's glass. Tanner wished she had ice in her glass. The warm tonic water had improved the taste of the vodka, but only slightly.

The grandfather clock bellowed and dinged five times, causing a rush of relief in Tanner, as if it were a school bell announcing the end of class. She sat, waiting to be dismissed to the sanctuary of her room.

Instead, Mrs. Wilt studied her, and Tanner feared she wasn't through with her interrogation about soccer and college. Finally, she spoke. "Do you know how to drive a manual transmission?"

Well. That was unexpected. "Like, a stick shift?"

Mrs. Wilt nodded.

"Yeah." Tanner flashed back to the Home Depot parking lot her father had made her drive around in after hours to practice changing gears. "Why?"

"Oh, just curious." Mrs. Wilt put her hand on her cane and pushed herself to standing. "If you'll excuse me, I need to go to the ladies'. Turn on the news, will you?"

Tanner stared after her for a beat and then reached for the remote and flicked on the local ABC station, where the anchors were in a frenzy over an early-in-the-season hurricane named Athena that was currently hitting the gulf coast of Florida and was expected to dump massive amounts of rain on Atlanta and its surrounding suburbs in the following twelve hours.

Then she stood and walked into the kitchen to dump out the rest of her drink in the sink. As she padded back into the den, the anchors had switched to a new headline. Tanner half listened as she spied the empty tonic water bottle and took it back into the kitchen to dispose of it.

New details in a forty-eight-year-old cold case from Ohio have led investigators here to Atlanta. One of the most notorious and largest jewelry heists—in which more than $3 million of cash and jewels, including the famous thirty-seven-carat Kinsey diamond, were stolen from the guest vault of the Copley Plaza, a luxury hotel in Boston, in 1975—ended without any arrests when the trail went cold in Akron, Ohio. The FBI has announced that, through new evidence, they have reason to believe Patricia Nichols is a suspect, if not the *criminal mastermind behind the heist—and that she may live in the Atlanta area, likely under an alias. Nichols has lived in various locales, including Morocco and Sardinia, Italy, and is fluent in at least three languages.*

Tanner reentered the den and strode to her room, only glancing at the television. What she saw stopped her in her tracks.

Thanks to age-progression software, police have released this photograph of what Patricia might look like now.

Tanner stared at the picture filling the screen, and then she barked with a sharp clap of laughter. It was the spitting image of Louise Wilt. She squinted. And then shook her head. It was a likeness, certainly—the same flock of crow's-feet, the same brownish-grayish-greenish eyes, the same thick, sturdy nose.

Patricia would be in her eighties, around five feet nine inches tall with hazel eyes. She's believed to be a known associate of notorious 1970s mobster Salvatore D'Amato, who originally went to prison for tax fraud in 1983 but is currently serving out a life term for bludgeoning a fellow inmate to death. The FBI is asking the public, if they have any information pertaining to the case or Nichols's whereabouts, to call the tip line at their local law enforcement agency.

Thank you, Linda. A train derailment is blocking part of a northwest Atlanta neighborhood . . .

"What'd I miss?" Mrs. Wilt's voice startled Tanner, and she glanced up at the woman standing at the door frame opening from the foyer into the den. Tanner realized she hadn't even heard the step-thump of her cane down the hall and wondered how long she'd been standing there.

"Nothing," she said, suddenly aware of her heart thudding against her rib cage. She studied Mrs. Wilt's in-the-flesh face and compared it to her memory of the computer-generated image that had been on the screen. It was uncanny, the resemblance. She kept her gaze locked on Mrs. Wilt's face and then her profile as she step-thumped past Tanner, and finally the back of her head as Mrs. Wilt reached the sofa. And then Tanner glanced back at the TV, now showing aerial footage of a train lying sideways halfway off its track.

Mrs. Wilt tsked as she slowly lowered herself onto the cushion. "How terrible. I certainly hope no one was injured."

"Mm-hmm," Tanner said, and then she turned and escaped to her room, laughing at the very absurd idea that Mrs. Wilt could be a—what was the term they used?—*criminal mastermind*. It was merely a coincidence. Aided by the fact that, in truth, all old white women were nearly indistinguishable from one another.

Weren't they?

• • • • •

ONE OF THE most irritating things about being eighty-four, Louise thought, was not how—without fail—her bladder woke her in the middle of the night, but how difficult it was to go back to sleep afterward. She lay in bed staring up at the ceiling, her mind still as wishy-washy as ever, that stupid eighties song "Should I Stay or Should I Go?" running on a loop in her brain. She couldn't name the band with a gun to her head, but she could picture Ken doing his awkward shoulder shimmy, goofy grin plastered on his face, bushy eyebrows wiggling—to the severe embarrassment of their children. He'd been the indecisive one in their relationship, not her. He would dither for hours over every single choice if she'd let him (which she didn't): Where to go for dinner? Ankle socks or midcalf? Romantic comedy or thriller? But now she wished he were here to tell *her* what to do for once. It was so unlike her to waver over anything, but she'd been chewing on this for days. Should she try to make a run for it? What was the point, really? She was old. And tired. And likely it was just her ego wanting her to go. The fact that she'd made it this far, this many years, and didn't want to give him the satisfaction of catching her.

She sighed and let the rock refrain play one more time in her head. She didn't need to decide tonight anyway. She still had time. A week at least. But maybe the fact that she hadn't gone anywhere yet *was* her decision.

The telephone on the nightstand trilled in her ear, jarring her out of her thoughts. She squinted at the clock. One thirty-four a.m. Who on earth would be calling at this time of the night? It rang again. She sat up gingerly and pulled the metal bead string of her lamp, flooding the room with light, before finally picking up the phone on its third ring.

"Hello?"

She thought she could make out someone breathing on the other end, but no words.

"Hello," she repeated, this time a vexed statement.

Nothing. Just when she was about to hang up, she heard it. So soft and low, she almost thought she made it up in her head. A whisper. But one that she would recognize anywhere. "Hey, kid."

Her breath caught in her throat, making her voice wonky as she croaked out the name: "George?"

It had been years since she'd heard it—the low rumble of that voice. But time vanished in a second. She was eighteen again, hearing it for the first time. Twenty-two. Twenty-seven. Time was immaterial.

I've missed you, she wanted to say, her dry eyes suddenly stinging with damp. Instead she cleared her throat. "You're not supposed to call," she said. "You can't be calling."

"They're coming for me."

"What?" She tensed, her entire body alert. Fight or flight. She kept her voice calm.

"George. They're not coming for you. It's me he wants, not you."

"No. They know where I am. And I can't leave. They've got this place under more surveillance than Chongqing, China."

Louise furrowed her brow. "What?"

"You know—the most heavily surveilled city in the world? They have a hundred and sixty-eight CCTV cameras for every thousand people. Or maybe it's a hundred and eighty-eight. Oh, the memory does go, doesn't it?"

Louise nearly smiled at how George hadn't changed one bit,

still harboring a trove of useless trivia and all, but then—ever pragmatic—she zeroed back in on the problem at hand. "OK, well. I'll come get you."

"Absolutely not, no, that's not what I . . ." George's voice waned and then suddenly came back in full force. "You save yourself, kid. I just . . . I wanted to hear your voice one more time. Take care."

"What? No! George—" She heard a click. "George? George!"

She sat, holding the receiver, panic stealing the breath from her lungs. And while her mind swirled with the shock of hearing George's voice after all this time, the swell of love and heartache and what-could-have-beens, the realization that George was in danger and it was all her fault, one thought blared through the melee like a fog-horn blasting out into the night: she was out of time.

10

TANNER WASN'T SURE what woke her in the middle of the night. Perhaps it was the rain falling down so hard outside the window it sounded like marbles being poured out of an endless bucket. Or was it the phone? She could have sworn she heard it ringing, but maybe it was just part of a weird dream. Or nightmare, more like, the way her heart was thudding in her chest, and with the pool of sweat it felt like she was lying in.

She shivered, the hair on her bare arms standing at attention. A loud crack of thunder startled her, and she swallowed a scream. She pressed a hand to her chest to calm her racing heart, nearly laughing at how on edge she was. It was late and dark and raining and she had just had a wicked nightmare, all of which added up to a major murder mystery vibe. Surely all of this would seem less frightening in the morning light. She took a deep, shaky breath and slowly blew it out, feeling better already.

Suddenly, the door to her room flung open. This time, Tanner did scream. A hulking shadow stood in the dark doorway, and Tanner flattened herself against the headboard, hoping it would swallow her whole. Then lightning flashed, throwing a split-second spotlight on the intruder, followed by an even louder explosion of thunder.

"Mrs. Wilt?"

"Get up, girlie," the woman said gruffly, step-thumping into the room and flipping the overhead light on. Tanner squinted against the blinding brightness.

"What? What are you—"

"Get your things. We're leaving."

"Leaving? Right now?"

"Yes."

Tanner sat there dumbly, heart still galloping, her brain a slush of questions and confusion.

"Chop-chop!" Mrs. Wilt barked, clapping her hands sharply. It was then that Tanner noticed Mrs. Wilt was fully dressed in her lime-green cardigan and tan slacks. "We have no time. They're coming."

Tanner stared at the woman. "Who's coming?"

"There's no time for questions!" Mrs. Wilt snapped, and it wasn't her harsh voice that struck Tanner, but the slight tremor she spotted in Mrs. Wilt's right hand, when Mrs. Wilt had never been anything less than composed. The old woman was scared, and Tanner knew she could no longer ignore the preponderance of evidence: the locked doors, the gun, the jail time, the carbon-copy photo of Mrs. Wilt on the news. "Oh my God," she breathed.

Mrs. Wilt hobbled over to the closet and pulled Tanner's suitcase out of it with one hand. "You have five minutes to pack."

"Pack? For what? No! I'm not going anywhere with you."

"You have to."

"No, I don't."

Mrs. Wilt turned toward Tanner and looked her dead in the eyes, where Tanner found nothing but raw determination. "Yes. You do. You're my driver."

Tanner nearly laughed out loud. "Uh . . . yes. I am. For things like your hair appointment. And bridge group. And physical therapy. Not for strange middle-of-the-night getaways to God knows where because you're on the run from God knows what."

Mrs. Wilt narrowed her eyes at Tanner and her nostrils flared, but when she spoke again her voice was calm, steady. "I'll pay you."

"What?"

"Five thousand dollars. Cash."

Tanner wavered. "No. That's ridiculous."

"Ten thousand."

Tanner laughed, and then stopped when she saw Mrs. Wilt's face. "Are you serious?"

"Yes."

Tanner paused, considering, and then countered, "Ten thousand, six hundred and ninety dollars."

Mrs. Wilt stared at her. "That's . . . oddly specific. But OK. Ten thousand six hundred and eighty dollars it is."

"Ninety."

"Yes, ninety, whatever. Let's go."

But instead of leaping to her feet, Tanner froze. Here it was, a way to get the money she needed to go back to Northwestern. Back to her *life*. Hers for the taking. But she couldn't, right? This was illegal. Or seemed to be. At the very least, it was super sketch. She shook her head. "I can't."

Mrs. Wilt rolled her eyes heavenward and made an exasperated grunting sound, and then just as quickly, her face recovered and she looked preternaturally calm. She exhaled. "Fine."

"Fine?"

"Yes, I expected nothing more, really. You can stay here."

Tanner hesitated. Mrs. Wilt's one-eighty from determined to instant capitulation was nearly as unnerving as the knowledge that she was a wanted criminal. "I can?"

"I mean, not here, of course. Because this is my house and you don't have permission to be in it any longer. But you can go back to your mother's and live in the basement and play your video games in your underthings and mope around about how pitiful your young life is."

Tanner's mouth dropped open, but no sound came out. Finally, she found words. "Ouch."

Thunder cracked so loudly this time, the noise filled the room, sucking up all the vacant space between them. Tanner couldn't be sure if it was her imagination or if just above the constant thick patter of raindrops, she heard the low blare of sirens in the distance.

They stared at each other.

"Now, whether you're coming or not, would you please GET. UP."

The second Tanner stood, Mrs. Wilt closed the gap to the bed and bent over, letting go of her cane to shove both hands between the mattress and the box spring. She came up with two fistfuls of stacked bills wrapped in plastic and dumped them on the bed and then went back in.

Tanner gaped. She couldn't have been more shocked had Mrs. Wilt been pulling out live, wing-flapping chickens—but it did explain why the bed was so lumpy.

She didn't mean to say it out loud, but the money was such damning evidence, she couldn't help herself. "You are a thief."

Mrs. Wilt's body went stiff as a board, and she stared hard at Tanner, making Tanner's blood run cold. "What did you just say?"

"Nothing . . . I—" Tanner tripped over her words, suddenly consumed with fear. If Mrs. Wilt was the wanted jewelry thief, there was no telling what else she had done—or would do—in her efforts to get away with it.

The sirens were definitely sirens now—still distant, but growing louder above the din of the rain—and Mrs. Wilt stiffened. Then she stuffed the money into the empty green reusable grocery bag that Tanner only just now noticed was slung on her shoulder. The old woman gripped her cane and looked at Tanner one last time.

"Enjoy your life of following the rules, my dear."

"Wait, you're leaving?" Tanner realized she had assumed that Mrs. Wilt wouldn't go without her. How would she drive?

"Yes, I told you. I have to go."

"You can't leave me here! What do I say to them?"

"To who?"

"The police!"

"Whatever you want! It's no longer my problem." And then Mrs. Wilt was gone and Tanner stood alone in the middle of the floral-wallpapered guest room in a white camisole and a pair of old Victoria's Secret sweatpants with the word PINK on the butt, even though the pants themselves were gray. A dichotomy that had always confounded Tanner.

She wasn't thinking about her pants right now, though. She wasn't thinking about the sirens that seemed to be growing louder by the second, or how she would have to move back into her parents' basement (as wildly unappealing as that was). She wasn't even thinking about all that money—or how ten thousand dollars would mean she could possibly start back at Northwestern as early as next quarter. She was thinking about what Mrs. Wilt had just said: *Enjoy your life of following the rules.*

She gritted her teeth. That was rich, coming from a *criminal*. But . . . the really annoying part? It was also true. Tanner *had* always followed the rules. And where had that gotten her? Exactly nowhere, that was where. Tanner worked her jaw.

"Shit!" she yelled. And it felt good, so she did it again. "Shit, shit, SHIT!"

And then, as if having an out-of-body experience, she grabbed her suitcase, stuffed a bunch of clothes in it from the dresser drawers, and charged out of the room, screaming, "Mrs. Wilt! Wait!"

Tanner rushed down the empty hall and into the den. She would have run right past the sliding glass door into the kitchen and then the garage, where she was hoping to catch the old woman before she took off into the night, but a bright light coming from the backyard stopped her in her tracks. She paused and squinted through the pouring rain—were those *headlights*? Coming from . . . the shed?

She flung open the sliding glass door, slid it closed behind her, and held her roller bag over her head, trying to keep the rain out of her face as she ran toward the lights. The barn doors of the shed were open, and sure enough, the two round beams of light emanated from a car that took up nearly the entire interior of the shed, leaving about two feet of space on either side.

But not just any car.

A mint-green Jaguar XKE. Convertible. Tanner wasn't sure of the year, but it had to be between 1961 and 1975 because those were the only years the car was manufactured.

She dropped the roller bag into the squish of grass at her feet and gaped.

"THANK THE LORD," Louise muttered when she saw the girl and her suitcase appear in the beams of the headlights. Her left hip had felt like it had cracked in half again when she pressed her foot on the clutch just to turn the car on. She had no idea how she was going to actually drive it out of the shed.

When Tanner didn't move, Louise rolled down the window and stuck her head out into the dry air.

"Are you coming, or are you just going to stand there like a drowned rat?"

"Is this . . . yours?" They were both shouting to be heard over the hammering rain and the hum of the engine.

Oh, for the love. Louise pushed open the door, put her cane down on the ground, pushed herself to standing, and then step-thumped around the back of the car and let herself in on the passenger side. She looked at Tanner again, who remained standing as still as a statue in the Trevi Fountain.

She leaned across the gearshift to the open window.

"Tanner!" The girl looked at her. "Would you get in the goddamned car?"

And, whether it was the surprise of Louise cursing or the fact that the sirens had grown so loud they both would swear the police cars were actually in the house, that's exactly what Tanner did.

* * * * *

WITH ADRENALINE PUMPING through her veins as fast as a fish on a waterslide, and water dripping down her forehead, Tanner threw the Jaguar into first gear and gunned it through the open gate that Mrs. Wilt must have unlocked before she opened the shed. She shifted to second, rounding the corner from the driveway to the road, and when they got to the end of the street, she looked up just in time to see a swarm of red-and-blue lights come barreling toward them and take a right just before they would have smashed into Tanner's side of the car.

"Oh my God," she breathed. She glanced in the rearview mirror to see if they were going to pull into Mrs. Wilt's driveway, but the back windshield was tiny and covered in rain, making the lights blur together like an abstract painting. Red brake lights illuminated, and Tanner squinted, but it was impossible to tell which house they were stopping in front of. It didn't matter—Tanner knew in her bones the person they were looking for was sitting directly beside her. Terror and anxiety flooded her system, scrambling her circuits. What was she *doing*? What had she done? Was she an accessory to a crime now? Could *she* go to jail? "*OhmyGodohmyGodohmyGod*."

"Please drive to 75 North," Mrs. Wilt said calmly.

Rain flooded the windshield. Tanner gripped the steering wheel and glanced in the rearview mirror again, shivering. Her wet hair dripped down her back, her drenched shirt clung to her chest, and she was chilled to the bone. They needed to go back. *She* needed to go back. Yes, that was it. She would get out of the car, walk back to the house, explain what had happened. That she wasn't in her right mind.

Except the prospect of facing those police officers somehow terrified her even more. So Tanner eased off the clutch and mashed the gas pedal, and the car shot off into the night. As she shifted gears and tried to put as much distance between them and the police as possible, Tanner wondered, Was this all it took? Had she always been one split-second decision from a life of crime?

Apparently.

And now what was done was done.

And it was all Mrs. Wilt's fault.

As Tanner revved the Jaguar down the on-ramp to 75 North, she replayed the events of the evening, leading up to this moment, trying to understand how she got here, in the driver's seat of a classic Jaguar (a *Jaguar*!), speeding away from law enforcement, and found she was easily able to pinpoint it to what had seemed at the time like an offhanded comment: *Enjoy your life of following the rules*. Tanner had the creeping feeling that Mrs. Wilt knew exactly what she had been doing to get Tanner to do what she wanted, and suddenly she felt like a marionette on strings, Mrs. Wilt the grand puppeteer. She glanced over at the woman, who was bent at the waist and digging for something in the bag at her feet. "That was very manipulative, you know," Tanner said, her voice shaky. Weak. "What you did back there."

Mrs. Wilt didn't respond.

"Mrs. Wilt?"

Silence. A Mack truck passed on the left, its massive tires sending a spray of water onto the already soaked windshield. Tanner groped for the handle and turned the wipers up a notch.

"Did you hear me? I said that was very manipulative—"

"Yes, I heard you."

Mrs. Wilt straightened her back, apparently having found what she had been looking for—some kind of book. She opened it and then clicked a pen, which turned out to be a small flashlight, in her right hand.

Tanner kept glancing from the road to the book, trying to determine what could possibly be so important that Mrs. Wilt needed to read it in the middle of the night. Was it a guide of some sort for being on the lam? Or maybe coded instructions for where to drop all that money.

She squinted, just barely making out a page illuminated by the penlight—and that was when she saw the tiny squares lined up like train boxcars.

"Are you doing a . . . *crossword puzzle*?"

"Trying to. This flashlight is just about good for nothing."

Tanner's hands were shaking. Her palms were clammy. It felt like a thousand moths were fighting to get closer to a streetlamp in her stomach. They were on the run from the police, for Pete's sake. And this woman was brooding over word games.

With her hands on the steering wheel at ten and two, Tanner turned her attention back to the road and concentrated on driving the speed limit, while glancing in the rearview every few seconds, sure she would see blue lights behind them at any moment.

After a few more miles, with the only sound Mrs. Wilt's pencil scratching the paper, Tanner broke the silence once more.

"Where are we going, anyway? Do you have like a, I don't know, a safe house or something?"

"Just stay on 75 North for a while."

"All the way to Tennessee?"

Mrs. Wilt paused. "A little farther."

"How much farther?"

Mrs. Wilt mumbled something in response.

"What? I couldn't hear you."

Mrs. Wilt cleared her throat and let the book fall to her lap. "California."

"CALIFORNIA?!"

The rain had finally begun to let up and was now more of a light mist on the windshield. Mrs. Wilt concentrated on her book, leaving Tanner to stew in her growing panic as the reality of her situation came into sharper and sharper relief. Mrs. Wilt was a wanted criminal (a *criminal*!), and they were on the run (the *run*!). From the police (the *police*!).

And that wasn't even the worst of it.

"Oh my God," she said, slamming her foot on the brake and swerving the Jaguar into the emergency lane.

"What on earth?" Mrs. Wilt said, grabbing the door handle.

Tanner, wide-eyed and breathing heavily, looked over at her companion. "I left it." Panic gripped her, even as she hoped what she was saying wasn't true. But she could picture it exactly where she'd left it, in the bed, likely tangled up in the sheets when she'd tossed them off to hurriedly pack and chase down Mrs. Wilt.

"Left what?"

"My cell phone."

Mrs. Wilt blinked. "Well, I should hope so."

"What do you mean?"

"They're quite trackable, cell phones. Or have you never seen an episode of *CSI*?"

"Why wouldn't we want to be tracked, *Mrs. Wilt*?" She emphasized the name because she wanted to hear her say it. Out loud. What they were doing.

Mrs. Wilt turned back to her crossword puzzle, humming lightly.

"My whole life is on that phone," Tanner mumbled, mostly to herself.

A bout of dizziness overwhelmed her, and she gripped the steering wheel, hoping the black dots in her vision would fade sooner rather than later. It wasn't just her cell phone she was driving away from. It was her entire life.

Her entire miserable, pathetic, awful life.

She flicked her blinker on, even though she saw no headlights coming up from behind in the side-view mirror—the highway was desolate. She slowly pulled the car back onto the road and exhaled.

She felt unmoored, off-balance, a little like something or someone had completely taken over her body and made the decisions that had brought her to this point.

But as Tanner shifted back up to fifth gear, the Jaguar's engine humming like a symphony of bees in perfect, beautiful unison, the dark road stretching out before her like an endless lane of possibility, she had to admit she felt something else, too, for the first time in ages.

Alive.

11

PHONE CALL THE DAY AFTER LOUISE WILT WAS REPORTED MISSING TO THE POLICE, AFTER CHARLIE AGREED WITH JULES THAT THERE MIGHT BE SOMETHING AMISS

"LET ME GET this straight—you're saying there are *two* people missing now?" Danny Shield had rather hoped to get off duty on time this evening to make it to his condo association's Craft Beer Book Club night. He didn't even like craft beer, to be honest, or the books they chose—usually something where a barrel-chested man (they were *always* barrel-chested) had to solve a crime that the police were either too inept to figure out, or too corrupt. Danny preferred nonfiction texts, but he did like having something to do—a reason to leave his one-bedroom apartment. He had tried other things, of course, like the local spinning gym, but quickly realized no one stood around to chat after and he was exerting a lot of effort for nothing—not to mention the crotch soreness. He envied those with a robust social calendar. Back in his small hometown of Blackshear, where he had lived for the first thirty-seven years he'd been alive, he'd had one, too. But since moving to just outside of Atlanta six months ago, he'd struggled. How did one make friends as an adult?

He shoved his fingers into his hair and took a deep breath as he tried to parse what Jules was saying. "This"—he squinted down at the chicken scratch of his notes—"Tanner Quimby . . . she's a health-care professional of some kind?"

"No. She's a . . . she's just a girl we hired to look after things. Look after my mom."

"She's not a nurse, then?"

"No!" The woman sounded exasperated.

"Did you do a background check before hiring her?"

"No."

"Wait. So you hired a gi—" Daniel caught himself just in time. Jules could call her a girl all she wanted, but Daniel had been reprimanded by his sister enough to know. He cleared his throat. "Young woman, a *stranger*, with no caretaking credentials, to live with your mother."

"She's not a stranger. She's the daughter of a . . . friend of the family."

"Oh." Daniel straightened his spine. That didn't seem nearly as nefarious. "And you think she's *kidnapped* your mother?"

"No! I don't know. I just—they're gone, OK? And look, Tanner's cell phone—"

"Yes, you said. She left it on her bed."

"Yes."

"Which leads you to believe—"

A deep-throated growl cut off Daniel's next words. "Do you know any twenty-one-year-old girls, Officer?"

"Of course."

The silence that followed allowed Daniel to hear his answer and how poorly it could be misconstrued.

"No! I mean . . . ah . . . what I mean to say is, my niece is around that age."

"Well, Officer Shield—"

"You can call me Danny."

"What?"

"My name. It's Danny." Danny knew he should be more formal—keep it professional—but back home everyone called him by his first name. And honestly, it sounded like this woman could use a friend, more than a police officer.

"Fine. I don't know about your niece, *Danny*, but when my daughter was that age, her phone appeared to be surgically implanted in her hand."

"I see your point."

"All I'm saying is, it's been more than twenty-four hours, so if you could open this as a missing persons case—"

"That's a myth."

"What?"

"The twenty-four-hours thing. It's not true. I filed the missing person report about your mother as soon as you called."

"Oh."

"And I'll add Tanner to the APB. You said the Mercury Marquis is in the garage, correct?"

"Yes."

"And there's no other vehicle she could possibly be in?"

"No. Unless she rented something."

"I'll look into it."

"Thank you."

"Have you been in touch with any of Tanner's family or friends?"

"Yes, my sister Lucy has called her mother."

"And I assume she hasn't heard from her daughter?"

"No."

"OK, well, if you could email me a recent photo of your mother and ask Tanner's mother for a recent picture of her daughter, that would be helpful."

"And then what?"

"Then I'll get this sent out and be in touch with any information."

"What about the phone?"

"What about it?"

"Don't you want it for . . . evidence or something? What if there's information on it?"

"Is it locked?"

"Yes."

"Do you have the pass code?"

"No."

"Then right now it's as good a use to us as it is to you."

"Oh. So . . . that's it?"

"Well, yes. And of course, if you think of anything else that might point to their whereabouts, or if anyone hears from them, let me know."

"And *that*'s it?"

"Yes. I'm sorry. There's not really much more we can do."

After hanging up, Danny navigated his mouse to the file folder on his computer screen that housed the missing person report for Louise Wilt. As he was filling out the new information, his email dinged, and he was unsurprised to find a message from Jules with the requested picture of her mother attached. He opened the attachment and found himself staring at a large photo of a woman that reminded him a bit of his own grandmother—her teased gray curls, slightly yellowed at the ends; the deep lines in her face a road map to a lifetime of emotions; kind but stern eyes.

"Can you STOP with the leg?"

Danny froze. He knew when he looked up, he'd be looking into the eyes (and not the breasts, *never* the breasts, though it took all the strength and will he ever hoped to possess) of Officer Rosa King.

He looked up.

Her dark brown eyes were narrowed, nostrils flared in irritation, arms crossed just below her perfect, heaving bosom (not that he was looking). Dear God, the woman was as intimidating as she was stunning. Which was to say—*very*.

"I'm sorry. I didn't realize—"

"I don't understand how you can't realize it! It shakes the entire desk. And the pencil cup! It's so loud."

From the time he was young, Danny had been a fidgeter, shouted at by numerous annoyed teachers and his mom, but unable to suppress the unconscious rapid jiggling of his left leg when seated.

"I'll try to control it," he said. And he would, too, do his very best. He would do *anything* for Rosa King. *I'd run into a burning building for you*, he thought, feeling swoony and light-headed. It was the reason he'd gotten into policing so many years ago. He wanted to be a hero. And since joining this precinct six months ago and first laying eyes on the tall, robust woman, he specifically wanted to be Rosa King's hero. Though he had a feeling that, if it ever came down to it, Rosa would be the one saving him from a burning building. She was just so . . . competent.

Rosa, seemingly unaware of his affections, or else aware and eager to ignore them, looked past Danny at his screen. "Who's that?"

Danny, who had momentarily blocked out everything save for

Rosa's presence, followed her gaze. "Oh, this missing woman. Well, her family hasn't heard from her in a few days; I don't know that she's missing, though. Seems like she just took a vacation without telling her kids. And after dealing with her daughter, I have to say, I'm not sure I blame her." He chuckled, but Rosa's lips remained a straight line.

"Huh." She stepped closer, which was to say her breasts moved nearer to his face. His heart rate increased exponentially, and he cursed whatever hormones insisted on turning him into a twelve-year-old boy whenever he was in her proximity.

"What?" he said, his mouth dry.

"Don't you think that lady looks just like the BOLO chain of command emailed out this week from the FBI? It's hanging up in the break room, too."

"Does it?" Danny didn't recall getting the email, and he rarely looked at that bulletin board in the break room. He tried to stay out of the break room as much as possible, in fact. It always smelled like days-old fish. But he didn't want to admit not paying attention to the current FBI's Be on the Lookout. "What's she wanted for again?"

"Robbery, I believe. A big jewel heist in Boston in the seventies."

"Huh," Danny said. "Interesting." And he made a mental note to search his email, or—if need be—look in the break room, if for nothing else than to have another reason to strike up a conversation with Rosa King and her perfect, perfect—

"Danny. My eyes are up here."

Damn it.

12

LOUISE WOKE WITH a start, the constant rumble of tires speeding over highway filling her ears, rudely reminding her she was sitting upright in a car, and not at home in her semi-comfortable bed ("semi" because when you got to Louise's age, nothing was ever fully comfortable). Instead of just the usual pain in her hip, every muscle in her body ached, like she had been beaten head to toe with a switch. That was only one of the myriad problems with old hot rods—the shocks were terrible. Not to mention the bucket seats. She had to give it to Ken—at least the Grand Marquis was comfortable on a road trip. She lifted her head and tried to gently stretch the crick out of her neck, stiff from having lolled about on her chest for God knew how many miles. She cursed herself for forgetting her airline pillow.

This was exactly what happened when one acted rashly, without a plan, Louise thought. You left behind essentials like airline pillows and brought along neurotic, unseasoned girls instead.

Not that she had had much of a choice in the matter.

She glanced over at Tanner, who was staring at the road ahead, either in a zombielike state of no sleep catching up with her or lost in her own thoughts, and she swallowed the slight pang of guilt for having to involve Tanner in her affairs at all.

Though, for someone who had never broken the law before, the girl certainly took to it like a duck to water. Louise recalled her surprise—and relief—at Tanner's sudden car-handling skills as she floored the Jaguar out of the shed and barely slowed to take the turn from the driveway onto the main road.

And then there were Tanner's words that kept replaying in her mind: *You're a thief.* How could the girl have possibly known? Her own *children* didn't even know. And suddenly this girl who'd been living with her for a week figured it all out? No. It was impossible. She must have drawn a conclusion based on the evidence before her—the stacks of cash, combined with the unfortunate arrival of the police. Louise could see how the circumstantial evidence would cause any reasonable person to infer the same.

Of course, Louise didn't believe the police had actually been coming for her.

Sirens had always raised her hackles over the years, but what were the odds that the police had finally caught up to her, after all this time? On the exact same night that George had called? Minuscule. It had to be a coincidence.

Regardless, the police were the very least of her concerns.

Louise needed to get to George.

Before Salvatore D'Amato could.

• • • • •

"WHERE ARE WE?" Mrs. Wilt asked, and Tanner startled. She must have been so deep in her thoughts, she hadn't realized the woman had woken up. Tanner may have acted rashly when she was half asleep at 1:00 a.m., but she was wide awake now and had had three and a half hours for good sense to take over. She'd never been on the lam before. Really, her only reference for what it was like was movies, but they all ended the same way. The people on the run got caught, eventually. "We just drove through Nashville," she said. In Chattanooga, Mrs. Wilt had told Tanner to follow the signs to 24 West and then promptly fallen asleep. Tanner hoped she hadn't missed a turn. "I'm going to jail, aren't I?"

"No. California." Mrs. Wilt tilted her head, considering. "Although the food's not much better. They juice everything."

"How are you making jokes? This isn't funny. I've never broken the law in my entire life."

"Well, that can't be true." Mrs. Wilt leaned two inches toward Tanner. "Technically, you're breaking the law right now." Tanner followed Mrs. Wilt's gaze to the odometer and saw that she was driving seventy-two in a seventy. She slowed down.

"Are you going to tell me what's going on?" Tanner felt fairly confident she knew exactly what was going on, but she wanted to hear Mrs. Wilt say it. That she was an international jewelry thief and had now put Tanner in the awkward and very rude position of being her getaway accomplice.

"What do you mean?"

"Why did we have to leave in the middle of the night?"

"Pull over at this next exit."

"What?" Tanner asked. "What for?"

"There's a Waffle House, and I'm hungry. Aren't you?"

Tanner was surprised to discover she was. Famished, really. Who knew breaking the law would take so much energy?

"I will not pull over until you answer the question."

"Which one?"

Tanner gritted her teeth, clenching her jaw. She envisioned driving the car into the guardrail and ending the misery right then and there. "Are you or are you not a wanted felon who is currently being hunted down by the police?"

Mrs. Wilt looked out the window as if the trees—the same tall pines that they'd been passing for miles—were suddenly fascinating.

"Mrs. Wilt?"

Finally, after what seemed like another interminable length of time, the woman spoke: "No."

Tanner felt a rush of relief, followed quickly by slight confusion. "You're not?" If Mrs. Wilt wasn't the jewelry thief, then why the sudden need to leave? And what about the police?

"No. Technically, a felon is someone who's been convicted of a crime. I've never been caught."

Tanner stared at the old woman, her jaw as unhinged as a python's before swallowing an antelope.

"I answered your question."

"Huh?"

"You're driving past the exit."

Tanner turned her gaze back to the road and indeed saw that the window of opportunity to get off was nearly gone. She jerked the steering wheel, swerving the Jaguar at the last possible second onto the exit ramp. Then she slammed the brakes, pulling the car to a sudden stop in the emergency lane. Still gripping the wheel, she collapsed forward, closed her eyes, and tried to slow her breaths, which were coming very rapidly.

"Oh my God. I'm going to jail. I'm going. To. Jail."

A sharp pain drew all her attention to the back of her upper arm.

"Ow!" She jerked her head up, realizing Mrs. Wilt had pinched her. Hard. "That really hurt! What'd you do that for?"

"You're spiraling."

Tanner rubbed her arm. "Yeah, I *am* spiraling. Yesterday, my biggest concern was being stood up for a lunch date. And today, I am—apparently—an *outlaw*."

"You had a date?" Tanner tried to ignore the tone, conveying Mrs. Wilt's great surprise that someone would deign to ask her out.

"No—that's not . . ."

"With who?"

Tanner paused, chewing her lip. Didn't they have more important things to discuss? But by the look on Mrs. Wilt's face, she wasn't going to let it go. Tanner grumbled August's name.

"*August?*" Mrs. Wilt's eyebrows shot skyward.

"Yes," Tanner said defiantly. "Is that so hard to believe?"

"He doesn't exactly seem like your type."

"How so?"

"He's . . ." Mrs. Wilt hesitated. "Well, it's not my place to tell you about his past, I suppose."

"His *past*?" Tanner's eyes narrowed. That sounded nefarious. Not that any of it mattered. Who was Louise to talk about someone else's past, anyway? "Can we please focus? On the part where the police are hunting us down, preferably. I mean, what is the plan here?"

Mrs. Wilt crossed her veined, clawlike hands over each other in her lap and set her jaw. "The plan is you are going to drive me to

California. I am going to pay you the sum we agreed upon, and then you are free to go wherever you like."

"And what about the police?"

"What about them?"

"What if they catch up to us before we make it to California?"

"They won't."

"How can you be so sure?"

"They haven't managed to find me in forty-some-odd years; I don't have high hopes for their success in the next five days—which is exactly how long we have to get to California."

"*If* I decide to take you," Tanner said.

Mrs. Wilt regarded her for a beat. "Yes," she said slowly. "If you decide to take me." Then she nodded her head at the glowing yellow Waffle House sign towering at the end of the exit ramp. "Do you think you could weigh your options over breakfast? Sitting here isn't getting either of us closer to where we want to be."

Tanner felt certain eating scattered hash browns wasn't going to change their status as fugitives or give her a better idea of what to do in this highly unusual situation—but she felt just as certain that continuing a conversation with Mrs. Wilt was equally futile. She sighed, and then reluctantly put the car into drive. After flicking the left turn signal and looking over her shoulder, she carefully pulled the Jaguar back onto the exit ramp.

In the parking lot of the Waffle House, Tanner turned the key to the off position for the second time in the past two minutes and took a deep breath. Mrs. Wilt unbuckled her seat belt and reached into her bag, withdrawing a canary-yellow scarf that she wrapped around her hair and tied in a knot under her chin. Then she flipped down the passenger sunshade and used the three-inch mirror to apply her customary pink lipstick.

Tanner watched in awe—was now really the time to care about one's appearance? And then it dawned on her—the scarf was for concealment. To be incognito. Although, if one didn't want to draw attention to oneself, bright yellow was perhaps not the ideal choice.

After capping her lipstick tube and dropping it back in her purse, Mrs. Wilt reached for the door handle.

"Wait."

Mrs. Wilt stilled. She turned her scarfed head to Tanner. "Yes?"

"Shouldn't I . . . have a disguise, too?"

"A disguise," Mrs. Wilt repeated.

"Yes, like—" Tanner pointed at Mrs. Wilt's wrap and then gestured to her own head.

Mrs. Wilt arched an eyebrow, then reached down, digging into the bag at her feet, and produced a worn navy-blue ball cap, with a visible sweat ring on the rim. "Knock yourself out," she said.

Tanner took it, suppressing an *ew*, and then fixed it onto her head and glanced in the rearview mirror. "Do you think it's enough? I mean, it's a little like when Superman puts on glasses and expects no one to recognize him."

But Mrs. Wilt was already halfway out of the car. Tanner jumped out and retrieved her shoulder bag and Mrs. Wilt's cane from the trunk (which was surprisingly spacious for a two-seater coupe, Tanner thought) as if they were merely at the hairdresser or Aldi. Her eyes landed on the green grocery bag of cash, and she briefly wondered how much was in it. She walked around to the passenger side and handed the cane to Mrs. Wilt, who Tanner noticed was even slower to stand up than usual.

"Is it OK to just leave the bag?"

"The bag?"

"Of cash."

"Oh," Mrs. Wilt said. "Yes, it should be fine."

"What if someone steals it?"

Mrs. Wilt blinked at Tanner. "That would be rude."

"You don't think we should bring it in?"

Mrs. Wilt looked around the mostly empty parking lot and then back at Tanner. "No. I don't." She turned and started walking toward the entrance. Tanner glanced at the green bag through the rear window once more and then followed Mrs. Wilt.

The restaurant had only one other patron in it, a man sitting on a stool at the counter, his back to the door. Tanner followed Mrs. Wilt to the far corner booth, eyeing the ceiling for cameras. There were none that she could tell. But then she wondered if she knew what a camera would look like. What if they hid them somehow?

She slid into one side of the booth, feeling exposed, like she had a big WANTED sign blinking in bright red above her head and every person in the Waffle House who glanced her way would instantly know.

"Look at that!" Mrs. Wilt said sharply, and Tanner startled, her heart jumping to her throat.

"What?" Her eyes darted to the parking lot. Had a police officer pulled in? Had a *line* of police cars pulled in? Were they surrounded? Seeing no flashing lights, she let her gaze fall back on Mrs. Wilt.

"They have a pecan waffle! That sounds delightful."

"Coffee?"

Tanner jumped again and looked up at the Waffle House waitress, a woman with deep hashtag wrinkles fanning from her thin lips and heavy mascara caked on her lashes. She turned the two white coffee mugs on the table right side up.

"Please," Tanner said, and then remembered she shouldn't show her face and quickly tilted her head at an angle so the brim of the ball cap obscured her face.

"I'll take mine over plenty of ice with cream and sugar," Mrs. Wilt said.

"You got it," the waitress said, pouring coffee into Tanner's mug. "Ready to order?"

Mrs. Wilt nodded. "I'll have two poached eggs and whole wheat toast. No butter on the toast. And half a grapefruit."

"We don't have grapefruit, ma'am."

"Oh. Well, whatever fruit is available."

"Sliced tomatoes?"

"That's fine."

Tanner eyed Mrs. Wilt. "I thought you were getting the pecan waffles."

"No, all that sugar. It's terrible for you."

"Ohhh-kay." Tanner pulled the brim of her hat down further and said, without looking up, "I'll have the All-Star Special with bacon *and* sausage. Coffee and orange juice. And hash browns, scattered, instead of grits. Actually, bring the grits, too."

When the waitress left, Tanner ripped open three sugar packets and dumped their contents into the coffee. She felt Mrs. Wilt's eyes on her. "What?"

"I didn't know you ate anything other than pizza."

"Oh. That's all I could afford."

"Mm."

"So," Tanner said, taking a small sip of the burning-hot coffee. And then she glanced around the small restaurant once more and lowered her voice to a near whisper. "Why shouldn't I just turn you in?" The thought had occurred to her multiple times as she was driving. It wasn't too late. And it was likely the most responsible thing to do. Not to mention the one that was most self-preserving.

Mrs. Wilt shrugged, nonplussed. "I guess you could. But then I wouldn't have a ride to California and you'd be out ten thousand dollars."

Right. The money. Tanner hated to admit how much she wanted that money, but she did. That money equaled a one-way ticket back to Northwestern. Tanner felt a buzz of excitement at her life—her *real* life—being within her grasp once again. Although, she pondered, it wouldn't be much of a life if she were inside a jail cell.

"Is the money . . . legal?"

Mrs. Wilt had the nerve to look offended. "Are you asking if I *stole* it?"

Tanner nodded.

"No. It's mine."

Tanner gnawed the inside of her cheek. She wasn't sure why she'd bothered asking. It wasn't like a thief would be honest. She decided, rather than belaboring the point, to move on. "What's in California?"

"A friend."

"Does your friend have a name?"

Mrs. Wilt hesitated. "George."

Tanner raised an eyebrow. A *male* friend. "And why are we going to see him?"

The waitress appeared suddenly with the plates of food, causing Tanner to duck her head again. After the waitress set them down, Mrs. Wilt busied herself arranging the eggs on the toast and cutting the tomatoes into six equal slices.

Tanner sat there not touching her own plates, waiting.

"Mrs. Wilt?"

"Hmm?"

Tanner suppressed a growl. Talking to this woman was like slamming her head repeatedly into a brick wall. "Why are we going to see George?"

Mrs. Wilt slowly chewed a slice of tomato and swallowed. "I think . . . the less you know, the better."

Tanner opened her mouth to protest, but Mrs. Wilt cut her off. "Look, you are making this more complicated than it needs to be. You drive me to California. If you drive fast enough, it's three days out of your life. You earn ten thousand dollars for your trouble."

"Ten thousand six hundred and ninety dollars," Tanner reminded her.

"Yes, right," Mrs. Wilt said, popping a piece of egg yolk–drenched toast into her mouth. After chewing and swallowing, she looked at Tanner again. "What's the money for?"

"Nothing," Tanner said.

Mrs. Wilt's eyes bored into Tanner's for a beat, and then she shrugged. "That's fine. Doesn't matter to me either way as long as I get to California. As I was saying, it's quite simple."

"Except for that whole getting-caught-by-the-police bit."

Mrs. Wilt shook her head. "This talking in circles—doesn't it exhaust you?" She gestured with her fork to Tanner's plate. "Eat your food before it gets cold."

Tanner nearly refused on principle, but her stomach growled, and she picked up her fork, mind reeling. Mrs. Wilt certainly seemed confident, but then again, what did she have to lose? She was a hundred and fifty years old. If she went to jail—*back* to jail, if her neighbor was to be believed—well, she was at the end of her life, anyway. But Tanner could be in there for years. Wasting her entire life wearing an orange jumpsuit, eating gruel, and getting tattooed with safety pins. She shuddered, then poured syrup over her waffle and took a hearty bite, savoring it in case it was her last real meal.

What she needed was more than Mrs. Wilt's confidence—she needed a guarantee. As she was chewing, an idea occurred to her. She swallowed and looked at Mrs. Wilt.

"OK."

"OK, what?"

"I'll drive you to California."

"Wonderful."

"On one condition."

"Yes?"

"If we get caught, you tell the police you kidnapped me."

Mrs. Wilt froze, her eyes as wide as saucers. "You want me to *lie*?"

Tanner's face mirrored Mrs. Wilt's. "Well . . . yeah. I thought—"

"Kidding," Mrs. Wilt said, her expression immediately relaxing. "It's a deal." She stabbed another square of yolk-soaked toast with her fork, and then pointed at the empty space next to Tanner. "You dropped something."

Tanner looked to her right, wondering what she could have possibly dropped. All she saw was her shoulder bag—and she hadn't taken anything out of it. "What?"

"Your sense of humor."

BACK IN THE car, Tanner spent the first few miles of highway settling into the idea that she had willingly agreed to transport a wanted felon across many, many state lines—likely breaking many, many state laws—to California. She first tried to comfort herself with what Mrs. Wilt had said: it's only three days, no big deal. Plus, Mrs. Wilt agreed to take the rap! When that didn't quell the anxiety, Tanner remembered something her dad had told her backstage at her first-ever sixth-grade orchestra performance. *It's not nerves—it's excitement! You're excited to perform!* It worked, too, up until the moment the curtains drew back and she saw the packed auditorium with hundreds of expectant parents, and promptly threw up on her cello.

But she was an adult now, and maybe this *could* be exciting—it was a road trip, after all, and aren't road trips, by nature, supposed to be fun? The snacks! The music! The stops to see roadside attractions!

"Do you know where America's biggest ball of yarn is?" Tanner asked.

"Is that a serious question?"

Tanner frowned. And then she thought of the police and frowned again. Maybe fun wasn't the answer—maybe it was best to employ the same tactic she used when her team fell behind in a soccer game: focus on the things she could control to mitigate the risk of the opponent scoring again. In other words: play smart.

"I think we should look for a drugstore," Tanner said.

"To buy yarn?"

"No. Hair dye, scissors. We need to change our appearance."

Mrs. Wilt didn't respond, and the silence pushed Tanner to elaborate, make her case.

"It's like, the first thing they do in every on-the-run movie ever." Tanner tried to think of a specific one to reference, but could only come up with one—Julia Stiles in *The Bourne Identity*, a film her father and Harley watched together every time it came on TBS. "Have you noticed how the girls always end up looking even prettier afterward?" Tanner said. "It's so annoying. When you hack off your hair with a pair of kitchen shears in real life, it's going to look like you hacked off your hair.

"Ooh!" She had another thought as the car reached its cruising speed of sixty-nine miles per hour. "Should we get burner phones?" She squinted, considering. Maybe that was just in *The Wire*. And that series was old. It was one of the ones she and Grant had binged over the last summer, thanks to a list they had found on BuzzFeed cataloging the top ten television shows of all time. Tanner wasn't sure it warranted a best nod—it was *so* depressing—but they had laughed at how dated the technology was. "I mean, I guess that's technically for drug dealers, which you're not." Her memory flashed to the stacks of bills Mrs. Wilt had pulled out of the mattress. "*Are* you? I know you said it was legal, but that was a *lot* of money. More than I've ever seen at one time in my life."

"Tanner."

"Yes?"

"Please stop talking."

Why am *I talking?* Tanner wondered as she flicked her turn signal to drive around a very slow Honda Civic. "I never talk this much."

"You have no idea how pleased I am to hear that."

"Maybe I'm in shock." Tanner flicked her gaze to the rearview mirror and studied her reflection.

"What are you doing?"

"Looking at my pupils. They dilate when you go into shock."

"I'd prefer you look at the road."

"Oh my God," she said. "I could have Stockholm syndrome. Does it happen this fast?"

Mrs. Wilt narrowed her eyes. "You are aware I didn't actually kidnap you, yes?"

"Yeah, but—"

Mrs. Wilt cut her off. "Did you happen to take a psychology course in college?"

Tanner brightened, puffing up a bit. "I did. How did you know?"

Mrs. Wilt nodded once and let her gaze drop back to her crossword. "You have just enough knowledge of the subject to be insufferable."

"Oh." Tanner sat back into her bucket seat and kept her thoughts to herself for the next few miles—until the silence in the car became overwhelming. This was a road trip! They needed music. She reached for the knob to turn the radio on, and a loud crackle of static blared out into the air between them.

"The antenna's broken," Mrs. Wilt said over the noise. "I never got it fixed."

Tanner sighed, wishing for the thousandth time that morning that she had her cell phone, with her Spotify playlist and unlimited Amazon Music selection. She stared out the windshield at yet another green exit sign, another government-built cement bridge, and found that the excitement she had felt briefly the night before, and even the anxiety she'd felt just moments earlier, had swiftly been replaced by a stifling sense of boredom, with no relief in sight.

It was going to be a very long three days.

13

TEXT EXCHANGE TWO DAYS AFTER LOUISE WAS REPORTED MISSING TO POLICE

JULES: Can everyone meet at Mom's house tomorrow?

CHARLIE: Why? Did they find her?

JULES: No. The FBI is coming. They have some questions for us.

CHARLIE: THE FBI! Jules, what did you say to them?

JULES: Nothing! $100 it's because of Tanner. No one cares when an old woman goes missing, but a fresh-faced 21-year-old blond girl? Well, call the National Guard.

CHARLIE: You mean, the FBI.

JULES: Whatever. When you were at the house, was the back shed open?

CHARLIE: The back shed?

JULIE: You know, where mom keeps all the stuff she buys from HSN?

CHARLIE: . . .

CHARLIE: I have no idea. Why?

JULES: Danny said something about tire tracks in the backyard. Coming from the shed.

CHARLIE: Who's Danny?

JULES: The cop.

CHARLIE: You're on a first-name basis with the cop?

JULES: Sorry, Officer Shield. Is that better?

CHARLIE: HIS LAST NAME IS SHIELD? OMG, is he a Marvel comic book character?

JULES: Charlie, please focus. And where's Lucy?

CHARLIE: I don't know where Lucy is. You said something about tire tracks?

JULES: Yeah, he asked if she owned another car.

CHARLIE: Besides the Marquis? Yeah, right.

JULES: That's what I told them. Why would she have two cars?

CHARLIE: Unless there was a deal too good to pass up on HSN.

JULES: *Laughed at "Unless there was a deal too good to pass up on HSN."*

JULES: So can you come tomorrow?

CHARLIE: Let me talk to Jen.

JULES: Lucy, you there?

25 minutes later . . .

LUCY: Sorry, was at vibrational sound healing. Catching up now. Are you guys talking about the Jaguar?

CHARLIE: . . .

JULES: . . .

CHARLIE: Vibrational who?

JULES: What Jaguar?

14

WHATEVER EXCITEMENT TANNER had felt in being behind the wheel of a 1968 Jaguar XKE quickly dulled when she realized it was missing one crucial component: air-conditioning. In the middle of the night, with her adrenaline pumping and the sky dark, it hadn't been an issue. But in the midmorning of a hot September day in Tennessee sitting on I-24 in a line of bumper-to-bumper cars that hadn't moved for twenty-three minutes, and no breeze to speak of coming through the open windows, she felt like she was sitting on the surface of the sun itself.

"August offered to fix it," Mrs. Wilt said, "but the kit he found online was going to cost more than two thousand dollars. I didn't see the point."

At the mention of August's name, Tanner's face got even hotter—which she hadn't thought was possible. She swallowed her embarrassment and anger, reminding herself everything was fine because she'd never have to see him again. "There's got to be a way around this," Tanner said, lifting her arms to try in vain to dry the massive pits of sweat on her shirt so it would no longer stick to her. She glanced over at Mrs. Wilt, who was now reading a thick paperback mystery. Although she had removed her headscarf once they got back in the car, her cardigan remained. A cardigan! And not even a faint sheen of sweat on the woman's brow or upper lip. "If only I had my phone," Tanner muttered.

Mrs. Wilt turned the page of her book and clicked her tongue, then murmured something.

"What?"

"Nothing."

"What did you say?" Tanner pinched the front of her T-shirt and shook it, hoping to create a breeze. "Tell me."

"I said it's a wonder you can even remember to breathe without it, that's all."

"Without what?"

"Your phone."

Tanner rolled her eyes, instantly irritated. "You know, that's so typical."

"What is?"

"I can live without my cell phone, thank you very much. It just so happens that it would be exceedingly convenient to have it right now."

"How so?"

"For starters, we would know what the holdup is up there."

"A dump truck tipped, spilling gravel all over the road."

Tanner jerked her head to look at the woman. "How do you know that?"

"I don't. But it seemed like an answer might make you feel better."

"Not just *any* answer," Tanner said. "I would like to know the truth."

"Why? What difference does it make if it's an accident or construction or a herd of buffalo crossing the street? The traffic will move when it moves."

"OK, but my phone would also give me an alternate route—maybe we could get off at the next exit and go around the traffic."

"Ah. So you want an atlas." She paused and ducked her chin at Tanner, causing her eyebrows to go skyward. "You do know what an atlas is, don't you?"

"Of course," Tanner said. "It's that statue of a man holding a globe. But I don't know how that could possibly help us now."

Mrs. Wilt's mouth dropped open.

Tanner waited a beat. "Kidding." She smirked, pleased she'd finally pulled one over on the smug woman.

Mrs. Wilt grunted and reached out for the latch on the glove box. Peering into it, she rifled around in it for a few seconds and then began pulling things out. "I know it's in here somewhere," she muttered. "Here, hold this."

Tanner stared at the piece of metal in Mrs. Wilt's hand as it took a few seconds to register what she was looking at. "Oh my God!" She flattened herself against the car door, to get as far away from it as possible. "You brought your *gun*?"

"Yes," Mrs. Wilt said calmly, and then wagged it a bit. "It's just a pistol. It's not gonna bite you."

Tanner flinched, the door handle digging even deeper into her spine.

"You're really scared of it?" Mrs. Wilt eyed Tanner curiously.

Tanner felt a flash of irritation, but her gaze remained glued to the gun. "*Sorry*, when you grow up doing active-shooter drills in school, a fear of guns is kind of ingrained."

"But you don't mind killing aliens with them."

"What?"

"On your video game thing."

"You mean the automatons?"

"Who?"

"They're more machine robots than aliens. And that is completely different than using a gun in real life."

"If you say so."

"I do say so." Tanner's back throbbed where the door handle was still digging into it, and she could already feel her shoulders getting sore from the tension. "Now could you please put that thing away?"

"Why? It's not dangerous."

Tanner scoffed. "Don't give me that 'it's not guns that kill people, it's people who kill people' bullshit."

"Well that's just idiotic." Mrs. Wilt said. "A gun can stop a man dead in his tracks. I've seen it happen."

Tanner's eyes went round. "You have?"

"Yes. But not guns without any bullets."

"What?"

"This gun isn't dangerous, because it's not loaded."

"Oh." That did make Tanner feel better. Slightly.

Mrs. Wilt tilted her head. "I don't think." Tanner gaped as Mrs. Wilt spun the barrel like she was freakin' John Wick himself and then eyed the chamber. "Oh, wait. Yep, there's one bullet in there."

Tanner pressed herself so hard into the door, she was surprised it still held. Her legs quivered, while the half-digested waffles threatened to make a reappearance. "Can you please just put it down?" she squeaked.

"OK, OK. No need to get all worked up." Mrs. Wilt bent over to set it on the floor.

"Not there!"

"Where would you like it?"

"I don't know, back in the glove box. And maybe unload it first?"

Mrs. Wilt removed the bullet from the gun and Tanner shuddered. Then Mrs. Wilt placed both the gun and the bullet back into the glove box.

"Wait!"

"Yes?"

"Don't . . . put them together."

Mrs. Wilt appraised her. "Are you afraid it's going to load itself?"

"It would just . . . make me feel more comfortable."

"Fine." Mrs. Wilt left the bullet in the glove box and then looked around the small interior of the car, finally settling on stashing the gun somewhere behind Tanner's seat in the trunk. Tanner didn't feel much more at ease with that, but she was glad she wasn't looking at it anymore.

The gun taken care of, Mrs. Wilt returned to her rummaging in the glove box. "Here it is," she said, producing a folded-up map, but before she had a chance to unfold it, the car in front of them started to move.

"Looks like we don't need it anyway. How about that."

"How about that," Tanner repeated, and she slowly eased her left foot off the clutch and pressed her right foot onto the gas.

For the next three hours, they drove in silence, Tanner grateful for the stiff breeze whipping in the half-open windows, and Louise slowly turning the pages of her book. Tanner studied the green highway signs and the horizon and played the license plate game she used to play with her sister, Marty, on family road trips to the beach, trying to see how many different states she could find. She was trying to remember if she had Idaho already when a yawning metal structure seemed to appear out of nowhere on the horizon, like something from an M. Night Shyamalan movie.

"Oh my gosh," Tanner said.

Mrs. Wilt looked up from the pages of her book. "What?"

"It's the arch!"

Mrs. Wilt blinked at Tanner, then the Gateway Arch on the horizon, and then looked back at her book.

"I totally forgot about that," Tanner murmured. She remembered learning about it in elementary school, likely during a social studies lesson on national monuments, and it was so iconic that it felt like something you'd seen in person before, even if you hadn't—like the Statue of Liberty or the Golden Gate Bridge.

But she hadn't seen any of those in person before. And she was surprised at her growing excitement. Now, this was a road trip! It wasn't the biggest ball of yarn—it was better.

"We have to stop."

"We just got gas after breakfast," Mrs. Wilt said without lifting her head.

"No, I mean at the arch." Tanner screwed her face up trying to remember what else she had learned about it in school. "I think they let you go all the way to the top. Imagine that view."

"We're not stopping."

"Why not?"

"We don't have time."

"C'mon. It'll take an hour, tops. When are we ever going to be back in St. Louis?"

"Never, if I can help it."

"Exactly."

THE BRAINCHILD OF Finnish American architect Eero Saarinen, the Gateway Arch in St. Louis, Missouri, was a 630-foot stainless steel monument—the tallest in North America—and cost $13 million to build in the early 1960s. Tanner didn't know any of that, of course, until she read the pamphlet while waiting in line at the ticket kiosk inside the glass-windowed atrium.

"Wow, says here the margin of error allowed was less than half a millimeter when they were constructing it—otherwise the whole thing would have failed. I wonder if that means crumpled to the ground? Crazy." Tanner pulled her ball cap lower over her eyes and glanced at Mrs. Wilt, who was wearing a deeper scowl than usual on her face.

"Are you OK?" The nearby parking decks had been full, but Tanner had managed to find an open spot on the street in front of a TGI Fridays, about four blocks from the entrance of the park. Still, it was hot, and Tanner wondered if the exertion—along with the headscarf, which Mrs. Wilt had promptly redonned, and the sweater—had been too much.

"Fine," she replied curtly.

When they got to the front of the line, Tanner ordered two adult tickets for the tram ride to the top of the arch, making sure to keep her chin lowered to conceal her face.

"Twenty-eight dollars," the man behind the plastic window said.

Tanner adjusted her own shoulder bag and looked expectantly at Mrs. Wilt.

"I'm paying for it?" Mrs. Wilt said. "I didn't even want to come."

"I believe it was me who didn't *want* to come," Tanner said, staring at Mrs. Wilt with purpose.

"Twenty-eight dollars for an elevator ride," Mrs. Wilt muttered as she reached into her handbag for her wallet. "Highway robbery, is what it is."

After they received their tickets, the cashier directed them to a winding security line on the opposite side of the atrium ("You picked a great day—the line is usually out the door!" he said jovially), and Tanner wasn't sure if it was her imagination or if Mrs. Wilt was walking even slower as they made their way toward it.

"Are you sure you're OK?"

"An hour, my ass," Mrs. Wilt grumbled. "That line alone will take forty-five minutes to get through."

The pace you're walking, it will take forty-five minutes to get to *the line*, Tanner wanted to say, but she bit her lip.

Once they were in line, it moved much quicker than either of them thought. In ten minutes, they were already halfway through the snaking ropes, and though Tanner thought this would have pleased Mrs. Wilt, she sensed the old woman getting tenser and tenser the closer they got to the front.

"Is that a metal detector? What is this, the airport?" And then Mrs. Wilt froze. "We should leave."

"What? Why?"

"Just turn around."

"No, we're almost there."

"Tanner. We need to go. Now."

"Why?"

Mrs. Wilt grabbed Tanner's arm with her clawed hand and leaned in close so she could speak in Tanner's ear. She whispered something in a low voice.

"What? I can't hear you."

"I said," Mrs. Wilt said though clenched teeth, "I put the gun in your bag."

"*What?*" Sweat broke out at Tanner's hairline and she felt panic grip her chest as she clutched the strap of her shoulder bag, which suddenly felt heavy with the weight of a concealed weapon. How had she not noticed that before?

A few people nearest them jerked their heads at her shout and then started shifting nervously, as though they were not eavesdropping, but they absolutely were.

"Why did you do that?" Tanner hissed, looking around wildly. There were only seven people between them and the metal detector. Tanner wasn't sure what the punishment for bringing a weapon onto federal grounds was—and she didn't want to find out. But the line was single-file, and about thirty people were already behind them—and they were confined by those black retractable belt barriers on either side.

"Oh my God," she breathed. "OK, let's go.

"Excuse me," she said sweetly to the family behind her. "We need to get out of line. It's an . . . emergency."

She repeated this shuffle dance with Mrs. Wilt behind her, winding her way back through the maze of barriers, to the great irritation of the many guests in line, until they finally reached the starting point. Just a few more steps until they would be out the glass doors. She tried to keep herself from breaking into a sprint to reach the relief of freedom—

"Excuse me."

Tanner nearly walked into the uniformed security guard who stepped in front of her, cutting off her path. He kept a hand on his belt—right near his holstered gun. Her heart hammered in her chest.

"Can I ask why you stepped out of line?"

Tanner's mouth went dry. "Oh, uh. We changed our minds."

He nodded once sharply. "I need to ask—do you have a weapon on your person?"

Tanner let out a high-pitched sound that was a mix between a laugh and a scream. "A weapon? Uh . . . why, why, why would you think that?" she stammered.

"Because it appeared that you got out of line when you saw the metal detector. It's my job to watch for suspicious activity."

The group of scattered tourists in the atrium had now stopped and were rubbernecking intently. Tanner felt heat flood her face and knew her ears were turning as red as her cheeks. She'd always flushed completely, like a cartoon character in love.

"Oh, for goodness' sake," Mrs. Wilt said. "I got tired of standing, if you must know, and my granddaughter is kindly escorting me to sit down."

Tanner tried not to gape when Mrs. Wilt said *granddaughter*, but the lie slipped so easily off her tongue and was so convincing, Tanner had to remind herself it wasn't true.

The guard's hardened face didn't soften at all as he let his gaze travel to Mrs. Wilt. "We have benches this way," he said, pointing the opposite direction from where they were going. "I'm happy to escort you." He reached out and put his hand on Mrs. Wilt's arm.

In a movement so fast, Tanner would have missed it if she blinked, Mrs. Wilt swatted the security guard with her handbag. "Get your hands off me."

The guard jerked his hand back, but straightened his spine and widened his stance. "I'm going to have to ask the both of you to come with me."

"What?" Tanner froze. Oh God, he knew. *Of course* he knew.

Headscarf or no, he recognized Mrs. Wilt from that police rendering making the rounds, and now they were going to jail. If Tanner thought she had been panicking before, she was mistaken. *Now* she was panicking.

"We will do no such thing," Mrs. Wilt said. "You know, you're lucky I don't report you to the Department of Justice—there is nothing compliant with the Americans with Disabilities Act about this . . . this tourist trap."

"You're welcome to file a complaint. After you come with me."

Tanner eyed Mrs. Wilt in terror. Her first thought: Surely she would say something else? Get them out of this somehow.

"Fine. I hope your office has chairs." Tanner's eyes bugged as big as half-dollars. This was it. She really was going to jail.

The floor may as well have been wet cement as Tanner followed the security guard and Mrs. Wilt, who she noticed was somehow walking at a normal pace—if not faster than usual. *Now*? Now was when the old woman chose not to drag her feet? Tanner's heartbeat thundered in her head, and she thought she might pass out from the crippling fear and anxiety—not only were they busted, but the security guard was going to find a gun in her bag, and didn't that kind of undermine the entire kidnapping ruse? Not only that, but she had *lied* to him. That surely was also against the law as well, wasn't it? Perjury or something. Or was that only if you lied in court? She glanced left and right for a trash can—anything to stash her bag in—but she knew it was pointless. There were surely cameras everywhere, and the guard would likely notice she had a bag at one point and then—miraculously, once in his office—did not.

The guard led them through a gray door off the atrium marked AUTHORIZED PERSONNEL ONLY, down a long hallway lit by glaring fluorescent lights, and into—to Tanner's small relief—a small, nondescript room with no windows. (Tanner wasn't sure what she had been expecting—a two-way mirror? An interrogation spotlight? Waterboarding?)

"Have a seat."

Mrs. Wilt made a big ordeal of leaning on her cane and slowly sitting in one of the two folding chairs shoved up against a beige wall. Tanner sat in the other one. The security guard remained standing. If this was for intimidation purposes, Tanner thought, it was working.

"Do you know it's against the law to strike a federal officer?"

"Oh please. I hardly *struck* you. Didn't your mother ever teach you to keep your hands to yourself?"

Tanner could see the man's jaw muscle working as he clenched his teeth. She knew the feeling.

"Where are you from?"

"Atlanta," Mrs. Wilt said. Tanner twitched at that. They were on the run—she didn't think now was the time to start being honest.

"And what are you doing here?"

"Is this not an open-to-the-public tourist destination?"

The man raised his eyebrows. "Please just answer the question."

"Going up to the top, like everyone else."

"Until you got tired."

"Until I got tired."

Tanner watched this exchange, wondering if the officer was just biding his time until backup arrived. Or maybe he was baiting Mrs. Wilt into saying something incriminating. He reached his hand out—careful not to touch Mrs. Wilt, Tanner noticed. "Please give me your bag."

Mrs. Wilt did as instructed, and Tanner gripped the strap of her own bag tighter. She fantasized about sprinting out the door. Pulling a fire alarm. Anything to end this nightmare. She nearly shouted, *I have a gun!* just to get it over with, but she could hardly move, much less speak, as the man set Mrs. Wilt's bag on the table to the right of him and rifled through its contents. Finding nothing, he handed it back to her.

"Now yours," he said, looking at Tanner.

She didn't move.

"Ma'am, please give me your bag."

"Tanner, give the man your bag."

Tanner did as she was told, but felt like the hand taking the strap off her shoulder, gripping the large canvas bag and shoving it into the guard's outstretched fingers, belonged to somebody else. Was this what an out-of-body experience felt like? The pounding in her head turned into a ringing in her ears, and she closed her eyes like she used to do during scary movies when the forewarning sinister music began, and she waited, her stomach all screwed up in knots. Would he arrest her right there? Would she get a phone call? Whom would she call? Certainly not her mother.

"Tanner?"

Coming back to herself, Tanner realized Mrs. Wilt had said her name a few times. She opened her eyes. "Yes?"

"Take your bag back."

Confused, Tanner looked from Mrs. Wilt to the security guard, who was holding her bag out to her. She took it. She scanned the table for the gun, but it was nowhere to be found.

"Now, I trust you two are leaving for the day, and we won't have any more trouble out of you?"

"Any *more*?" Mrs. Wilt said. "There wasn't any trouble to begin with until—"

"Yes, sir," Tanner said loudly, drowning Mrs. Wilt out. She didn't know why he was letting them leave, but she did know better than to question it or give him any more time to change his mind. "We'll be leaving."

Mrs. Wilt gripped the handle of her cane. "After I get my money back for these tickets," she said, pushing herself to stand. "Twenty-eight dollars. You'd think this was the Eiffel Tower."

FIFTEEN MINUTES LATER, Tanner and Mrs. Wilt stood squinting in the bright sunshine on the cement just outside of the arch's glass atrium, twenty-eight dollars in cash firmly in Mrs. Wilt's clutched hand. As she fumbled around trying to get it back into her wallet, Tanner tried to force steel back into her trembling appendages and understand what had just happened; why they were free, and not handcuffed and sitting in the back of a police car.

"Well," Mrs. Wilt said. "Let's carry on." The woman was unusually chipper—particularly for having come so close to being caught. Unless . . . she had known all along that they weren't actually close to being arrested.

"Why did you tell me you put the gun in my bag?"

"I thought I did," Mrs. Wilt said breezily. She started walking in the direction of the car.

The wheels of Tanner's brain spun as she remembered Mrs. Wilt's reticence to go to the arch from the very beginning. Her slow walk, the way she tensed up the closer they got. And it hit her. She hurried the few steps to catch up with Mrs. Wilt. "You didn't want to go."

"What?"

"Up in the arch. You're—you're afraid of heights." It was a shot in the dark, but as soon as she said it—and saw the look on Mrs. Wilt's face—she knew it was true.

"I'm not *afraid*," Mrs. Wilt tutted. "I just don't like them."

The confirmation momentarily scrambled Tanner's circuits. "So you *lied* to me? We could have been arrested!"

"By that mall cop? Hardly."

"Are you *kidding*? That's literally what happened back there."

Mrs. Wilt waved Tanner off with her free hand. "Nothing would have happened at all, if you hadn't been so adamant that we stop."

"You think this is *my* fault?" Tanner scoffed. "You are insane! Do you know that? Absolutely insane."

Mrs. Wilt started humming lightly, as if she hadn't even heard Tanner, making Tanner want to punch the trunk of a tree they were passing in the park. Mrs. Wilt didn't speak again until they reached the Jaguar, settled into the front seats, and were buckling their seat belts.

"No more unscheduled stops," she said. "We're driving straight through to California. I think we can agree we both would be better off once we're out of each other's company."

"Agreed," Tanner said tightly.

"Good."

"Fine."

The interior of the car was stifling. Sweat already pricked her hairline as she jammed her left foot on the clutch, her right on the brake, stuck the key in the ignition, and turned it.

Nothing happened.

She did it again.

Nothing.

She looked over at Mrs. Wilt and smiled sweetly. "Is your battery as old as the car?"

"Certainly not. August just put a new one in last year."

August.

Tanner nearly growled as she threw open the car door, the metal squeaking on its hinges, and popped the hood, while glancing at the cars blocking them in front and behind—they'd need to find someone who would kindly give them a jump so they could be on their way. But the overwhelming smell of gasoline that filled her nostrils the second the hood opened immediately told her the battery was the least of their concerns.

Tanner knew just enough about cars to know that smell likely meant the fuel pump was busted.

And they wouldn't be going anywhere, anytime soon.

15

TRANSCRIPT OF FBI INTERVIEW WITH LOUISE WILT'S CHILDREN (JULES WILT VAUGHN, CHARLIE WILT, AND LUCY WILT), THREE DAYS AFTER LOUISE WAS REPORTED MISSING TO THE POLICE

SPECIAL AGENT LORNA HUANG:
OK, we're recording.

JULES: Great. Now, are you going to explain why all this crime tape is here? Was a *crime* committed?

HUANG: We're investigating.

JULES: Oh, God, I knew it. Is Mom OK?

HUANG: We have no reason to believe she's in harm's way right now.

JULES: Then why the crime tape? Do you know where she is?

HUANG: Her last known whereabouts are in

St. Louis, Missouri, three days ago.

LUCY: What was Mom doing there?

HUANG: Apparently going to the arch.

CHARLIE: Going where?

HUANG: The St. Louis arch.

CHARLIE: I thought you said she wanted to go to Italy.

JULES: She did!

LUCY: Oh, I hope they went to the top—the view is supposed to be extraordinary.

JULES: For the thousandth time, Mom hates heights. This doesn't sound right.

HUANG: We have surveillance video, if you'd like to view it.

CHARLIE: Surveillance video?

HUANG: Yes. They had an . . . altercation with the security guard.

JULES: Well. That does sound like Mom.

LUCY: So where are they now? Have you found them?

HUANG: Not yet. The Jaguar apparently

broke down in St. Louis and they spent two nights there. But we have an APB out and feel confident we'll bring them in today. It's a fairly noticeable vehicle.

CHARLIE: Great! So why are we all here?

HUANG: I have a few . . . questions I'd like to ask about your mother that may help us find her.

JULES: Like what?

HUANG: Well, first I'd like to confirm her physical appearance. Had she made any changes recently? Dyed her hair, that sort of thing.

JULES: Not that I know of.

HUANG: So she still looks like this picture.

LUCY: Oh, Mom hates that picture.

JULES: She does?

LUCY: Yes, that was a week when her regular hairdresser was out of town—I think in the Keys—and she had a substitute.

CHARLIE: Her hair looks the same as it always does.

LUCY: Don't tell her that.

HUANG: Does she own any phones or computers, besides the ones we found here on the coffee table?

JULES: Wait, you searched the house?

HUANG: Yes, this is an active investigation.

JULES: She only owns the one laptop and cell phone. See, why didn't she take her cell phone? And Tanner, too. It doesn't make sense.

HUANG: Does your mother own any expensive jewelry?

JULES: I'm sorry?

HUANG: You know, heirloom pieces or rare gemstones, diamonds.

JULES: I'm not sure how this has anything to do with—

HUANG: Just protocol. Looking for anything she might be able to sell in order to have funds for her . . . trip. Her bank accounts and credit cards haven't been touched.

CHARLIE: You've looked at her bank accounts?

HUANG: Again, it's protocol.

LUCY: Mom didn't believe in banks. Her mother lived through the Depression and warned her against them. She kept all her cash stashed throughout the house.

HUANG: I see. [*clears throat*] And is there anything else . . . unusual about her?

JULES: [*audible snort*]

HUANG: Let me clarify. The Jaguar was registered to one James Byron.

CHARLIE: Who's that?

LUCY: Maybe someone she plays bridge with?

HUANG: He lived in Jacksonville, Florida.

CHARLIE: Where does he live now?

HUANG: Nowhere. He's dead.

[*PAUSE*]

LUCY: Why does Mom have a dead man's car?

HUANG: That's something we're trying to figure out.

JULES: What are you saying?

HUANG: I'm not saying anything, except that we're looking into it.

JULES: Do we need a lawyer?

CHARLIE: No! Of course not. Obviously there's been some kind of mix-up with paperwork. Maybe Mom forgot to get the title transferred.

HUANG: I just have to ask one more time, is there anything you can think of that would make your mother need to leave town suddenly, without warning?

JULES: No, absolutely nothing. This is ridiculous. I'm sure when we find her, we can clear all of this up.

CHARLIE: Not anything. I mean, Mom's no angel, but—*ow!* Jules, that hurt.

HUANG: And Ms. Wilt, you'd say the same? There's nothing you can think of from your mother's past—something that might be a clue that could help us find her now? [*pause*] Ms. Wilt, if there is something—

anything, no matter how small—
that could help us find your
mother . . .

JULES: Lucy?

CHARLIE: Luce?

LUCY: Well . . . there is one thing.

HUANG: Yes?

[*PAUSE*]

LUCY: I don't think Louise is Mom's
real name.

[*LONG PAUSE*]

CHARLIE: *WHAT?*

[*JUMBLE OF LOUD VOICES, UNCLEAR*]

CHARLIE: Why on earth would you say
something like that?

JULES: GODDAMN IT!

HUANG: If everyone could just calm—

JULES: I ALWAYS KNEW you were her
favorite.

16

AS IF THERE weren't enough reasons for Louise to dislike her, Tanner Quimby snored. Not a light, delicate wheezing, either, as might be befitting of her stature, but a full-on foghorn of a sound that after a scant five minutes of hearing was enough to grate the nerves quite severely. Between that and the motel room's window air-conditioning unit sounding like a 747 taking off every time it clicked on, Louise had been lying wide awake in her bed for three hours.

But really, Louise knew it wasn't either of those things keeping her awake. She could nod off sitting straight up in a chair (and had on many occasions). It was George.

Two days. TWO DAYS! That was how long the mechanic had said it would take to get and install a new fuel pump. "Car this old? That's a special order." Louise thought it had been lucky when a man driving a tow truck had pulled up beside them, no less than a minute after Tanner had popped the hood in downtown St. Louis, and asked if they needed help. Ten minutes later, the car was hitched up to his crank, and Louise and Tanner sat in the front seat of the cab—only to be driven twenty-two *miles* outside of St. Louis to the man's mechanic shop, situated on a two-lane road next to the Golden Village Motor Inn, a white brick bar named the Cobra Lounge, and not much else. And then to be told they would be stuck there—in the middle of nowhere—for *two days*. (Thank God for the bar, Louise had thought when she saw it.)

Which meant instead of the three days Louise had calculated they had left until she got to George, it was going to be five. Sunday.

The same day Salvatore D'Amato was being released from San Quentin.

That was cutting it close. Too close.

Louise didn't pray often—church was more of a social event for her than a spiritual one—but she closed her eyes and implored whatever gods would listen that she wouldn't let George down. Again.

In the opposite bed, Tanner inhaled, the repetition of her loud staccato snorts grating Louise's very last nerve.

She slowly pulled out the drawer of the side table where she had stashed the green grocery bag with the ninety thousand dollars in cash—the girl had been right; it could easily get stolen, and then what? Louise needed to figure out a better way to store it, but she'd deal with it tomorrow. For now, she groped in the dark, reaching underneath the bag, her hand landing on the Gideon Bible she knew would be there. She pulled it out and then lifted it in the air as high as she could between the beds and let it go.

THUD.

"Huh? Whuhwasthat?" Tanner's voice penetrated the darkness, thick with sleep.

"I don't know," Louise lied. Then she gently rolled onto the side of her good hip and closed her eyes, trying to fall asleep in the few blessed minutes of peace she knew she'd have before the snoring started up again.

THE NEXT MORNING, after a pitiful breakfast consisting of weak tea from the motel room coffeepot, a Nutri-Grain bar from the vending machine that tasted like it had been there since the motel had been built seventy years ago, and her handful of pills from the W section of her plastic pill case, Louise sat in the corner club chair trying to work on one of her crossword puzzles. Trying, because she was experiencing those annoying tremors in her right hand (why not the left hand? Why was it always the right?) and because it seemed every three seconds, Tanner was moving—from the bed to the floor. From the floor to the bathroom. From the bathroom to the desk. Opening and closing drawers as if she were going to find something other than a pad of paper and a pen. She drummed her fingers, sighed loudly numerous times, and then set her sights on the TV remote. Louise wasn't sure just how many television channels the motel cable had (at one point she glanced up and saw 643 on the top right of the screen), but Tanner methodically flipped through all of them no less than fourteen times, never landing on one for more than thirty seconds.

The girl was restless. Or maybe it was that her attention span—without that blasted video game to distract her—was roughly the length of a squirrel's.

After the next round of channel flipping—when Tanner landed once again on one of those god-awful panel shows where the women have such polarizing views, they talk over each other rather than to each other (and this is supposed to be entertainment)—Louise decided it was time to take matters into her own hands.

"Who did Faith Ford play in *Murphy Brown*? Five letters, starts with a *C*."

Tanner turned her head from the television screen to Louise and blinked, as if there were someone else in the room Louise might be speaking to besides her. "I don't know who any of those people are."

"You've never seen *Murphy Brown*?" Louise tutted. She wasn't prone to superlatives, but *Murphy Brown* was truly one of the best television programs ever, aside from *The Jeffersons*, which she and George had religiously watched together every Saturday night that first season in 1975. She never watched it again, of course, after that year. It reminded her too much. Of what she was missing.

"Candice Bergen was the lead. And Charles Kimbrough was Jim," Louise went on, if for no other reason than to give Tanner something else to pay attention to than the television. "And then there was Frank. Well, I can't remember who he was. But what in the devil was that woman's name?"

"If you had a phone, you could look it up," Tanner said.

"That would be cheating."

Tanner raised one eyebrow at her and then looked back to the screen, flipping the channel again, this time to some nature documentary with a British narrator.

Louise cleared her throat and set the crossword book on the end table beside her. "So. You're scared of guns. What else?"

Tanner didn't bother looking over this time. "What else am I scared of?"

"No. Or sure. Just tell me something else about you."

"Why?"

"This is called conversation. It's what we used to do before cell phones ruined it."

Tanner rolled her eyes. "I know how to have a conversation."

"Wonderful!"

She cut her eyes to Louise. "What do you want to know?"

"Are you an only child?"

"No. I have a younger sister, Marty. And a brother—"

"Marty?" Louise interrupted. "Is that short for Martha?"

"No."

"It's just Marty?"

"Yes."

"And you're Tanner. What's your brother's name—Jessica?"

Tanner's expression remained bored, as though she had heard it all, her entire life. "You know, I'm sure in your generation it was fine. But these days, it's common acceptance that gender norms"—Tanner made air quotes with the index and middle fingers on both hands—"are merely a social construct."

Louise stared at her for a beat. "Did you learn that in psychology, too?"

"No," Tanner shot back. And then: "Sociology. I'm just saying, what if my brother's name *was* Jessica?"

"Is it?"

Tanner hesitated. "No."

Louise nodded once. "Because that would be ridiculous."

"Whatever."

"So how did you and your sister end up with boy names?"

"They're not *boy* names. They're just . . . names."

"Fine. How did you end up with your 'just names'?"

Tanner sighed. "Right before I was born, my mom read in some magazine that girls with ambiguous gender names are more successful—it gives them an edge in the job market or something."

Louise paused, and then laughed so hard it caught in her throat and she started coughing, tears coming to her eyes. When she finally calmed: "Well, that worked out well. They must be pleased as punch."

Tanner flipped the channel once again, this time landing on a blond woman wearing heels and a skirt suit and a toothpaste-commercial smile, hawking cubic zirconia earrings on a home shopping channel.

"What's your sister do?" Louise asked.

"She's a freshman at Georgia Southern."

"What's her major?"

"Sorority life."

"Ah. Are you two close?"

"Not especially."

Louise waited a full minute for Tanner to elaborate, but she didn't. So she picked up her crossword puzzle and glanced at the *Murphy Brown* clue again. Her hand shook harder, and she cursed the medication that was supposed to control it, and stared at the *Murphy Brown* clue again, cursing her faulty memory even more. On her birthday every year when Louise lamented getting older, Ken used to say it was "better than the alternative," but now she wasn't so sure that was true.

DIMLY LIT AND hazy with the cigarette smoke that hung in the air, the Cobra Lounge looked exactly like every biker bar from every movie Tanner had ever seen, complete with the jukebox in the corner and the glazed mahogany bar top. The only difference? This bar had no actual bikers in it. In fact, there were only two other patrons in the entire establishment—one couple seated in the back corner sharing a plate of cheese fries and staring at their respective phones.

"Evening, ladies." The bartender, who looked as though he'd been working there since the bar opened (in 1923, if the sign on the door was to be believed), acknowledged Tanner and Mrs. Wilt as they slid onto their bar stools. Time had hunched his frail shoulders, and a shock of white-gray hair remained glued above each ear, leaving the top exposed to the elements. He wiped the bar counter in front of them with a dishrag and then turned his attention to Mrs. Wilt. "May I say, you're both looking very thirsty. How can I fix that?"

"Finlandia on the rocks. Two olives."

The man nodded, approving, and then looked at Tanner.

"I don't know. Coke's fine."

"She'll have a whiskey sour," Mrs. Wilt said.

Tanner stared at the old woman. Had she forgotten already that Tanner didn't drink?

Mrs. Wilt waved her hand. "It's mostly juice, girlie. Trust me, you'll like it."

The bartender nodded again. "Coming right up. If you need anything else, my name's Leonard." He paused. "If you don't need anything, name's still Leonard." Tanner glanced from the bartender to Mrs. Wilt, wondering if she thought he was as cheesy as she did, but her eyes grew wide as she saw Mrs. Wilt pat her headscarf coyly and offer the man a genuine grin. "Thank you, Leonard."

Was this how old people flirted? Ew.

As they were waiting for their drinks, Tanner toyed with a straw wrapper. "What'd you go to jail for?"

Mrs. Wilt turned her head slowly to look at Tanner. "How do you know I did?"

"Your neighbor told me."

"Declan? You met that asshat?"

"No, his girlfriend."

"Ah."

"So, why did you go?"

"What happened to your knee?"

Tanner raised an eyebrow.

"What? I'll answer yours if you answer mine."

"Fine. I fell from a two-story balcony."

The bartender set two highball glasses in front of them. "Drink responsibly, now," he said, and Tanner looked up just in time to see him wink again at Mrs. Wilt. "Don't spill it." Tanner eyed her curry-colored drink, garnished with an orange wedge and an unnaturally red cherry, and took a small sip, fully expecting to hate it. But it was surprisingly sweet, with the perfect amount of acidity for balance. It tasted like fruit juice. "Are you sure this has alcohol in it?"

"Yes. Was it your apartment? The balcony?"

"No. It was at a party I didn't even want to go to in the first place." A dark cloud passed over Tanner's face as she remembered Vee begging her to come to the party. Why hadn't she just said no, like the other three hundred times? She'd be back at school, going to practice, enjoying her senior year, living with Vee.

Vee.

Tanner cringed again as she remembered how she'd treated her best friend when she'd come to visit her in the hospital. The unforgivable things she had said—laying the blame for her accident squarely at Vee's feet.

"What happened?"

Tanner sighed. What happened. She had replayed what had happened so many times in her head. The hundreds of things she could have done differently from what she did. But she'd never told a soul what really caused her to fall, because she was too embarrassed. So it didn't make sense why she felt compelled to say it now. Maybe she'd been holding it in too long, or maybe she felt so far away from her real life, it didn't matter. It wasn't like Mrs. Wilt was going to tell anybody.

"The party was supposed to be small, but it got out of hand. There were hundreds of people in a two-bedroom apartment, and a lot of them were smoking weed, probably doing other stuff, too. I was worried about the secondhand smoke, getting drug tested, and losing my scholarship, so I went out to the balcony. It, too, was small, and I thought I was alone, but . . . this guy followed me out there."

Tanner had never seen him before—or since—but she could picture his face so clearly. The greasy pores on his nose, his stupid swoopy bangs—the exact same style that every frat boy wore even though they had to constantly push the hair out of their faces—his swimming, unfocused brown eyes. Her palms went a little clammy, and she grabbed a napkin from the bar top and started twisting it. "He was drunk, probably didn't even know his own name. But he was trying to hit on me, sloppily." She remembered his sour breath as he got closer, how even though he was only a few inches taller than her, he seemed to take up so much space. "He was so annoying. And gross. And I just wanted to get away, so I backed up as far as I could against the railing. And then . . . it gave way."

"Why didn't you kick him in the groin?" Mrs. Wilt said. "They don't teach you girls how to do that these days?"

And there it was. What Tanner had been chastising herself for these long five months. She *should* have kneed him. Or shouted in his face. Or just pushed by him with all her soccer-strength force.

She *had* been taught how to stand up for herself, how to fight back. Not only that, but she had been told her entire childhood ad nauseam how *powerful* she was, how girls were just as strong, smart, athletic as boys, if not more so. Wasn't that what all her girlhood T-shirts had said? Fierce. Brave. #GirlPower. She'd always thought—no, *known*—she would never be some . . . victim. So much so that when the #MeToo movement gained momentum when she was in high school, she was confused and honestly appalled. How could that many women let themselves get taken advantage of in that way? If she had been in a hotel room with that nasty, bloated Harvey Weinstein and he had demanded a blow job, she would have told him to fuck right off.

Turned out, she couldn't even say it to a drunk, stumbling college boy.

"I was . . . afraid," Tanner mumbled, and then quickly added, "Not of him. He was harmless, really. Just drunk. And it's not like he . . . touched me or anything." Tanner closed her eyes—he just kept coming. Forward, hulking. "I thought if I yelled or hit him, people would say I was overreacting." She'd seen it before. A hundred times. Girls being told they were too uptight, couldn't take a joke: *Oh, what, you're like a* feminist? Tanner only liked being the center of attention on a soccer field. She didn't want to make a scene.

"Hm," Mrs. Wilt said.

Not an overwhelming response to having bared her most embarrassing moment, but Tanner was grateful the woman didn't lie or say anything placating or patronizing like *You know it wasn't your fault*.

She also knew it hadn't been Vee's fault, either, of course. She could have left the party. She could have relaxed and not worried about the secondhand smoke. It wasn't like they were drug tested every week. And most obviously, as Mrs. Wilt had so kindly pointed out, she could have kicked the nameless asshole in the groin. But after the accident, she had been so furious and needed someone to blame other than herself, so she lashed out at her best friend.

But that wasn't even the worst of it.

When Coach Barry came to visit her in the hospital after the first surgery, he was trying to cheer her up with a stupid joke: "Well, the good news is, your drug test came back clean."

"Of course it did. I'm not Vee," Tanner replied. She regretted it the second it came out of her mouth. It was her jealousy talking. Her anger—not even at the drunk boy, but at herself. The anger felt so big and unwieldy that she couldn't bear the weight of it and had to thrust it on someone else, if even for a brief second. She channeled it into outrage at Vee. That Vee had made her go to the party. That Vee and their other teammates could drink and smoke and party with abandon and somehow *they* were still on the team, and Tanner would never play again.

Vee had been drug tested the next day. Suspended from the team indefinitely the next week. And she hadn't talked to Tanner since. Not that Tanner could blame Vee. What kind of person narced on a friend like that? Much less a purported *best* friend? Tanner knew she should have reached out immediately. Apologized, begged for forgiveness. But the more time that went by, the more embarrassed she became—and the more certain she was Vee wouldn't forgive her. Or even respond to a text.

Once she got back to Northwestern, Tanner knew she could make it right. She had to. But that wasn't the only reason she was so determined to get back there. She fantasized—often—about running into that guy again. About doing what she should have done that night.

"So that's why you're so angry," Mrs. Wilt said.

"Because my life was completely destroyed in a matter of seconds?" Tanner scoffed. "Yeah. That's why I'm so angry."

"Completely destroyed seems to be overstating it a bit, don't you think?"

"No, I don't. I lost my scholarship, had to move home, and will never play soccer at a competitive level again, which was only everything I'd been working for my entire life."

"Your entire life? You're what—twenty?"

"Twenty-one."

Mrs. Wilt shrugged. "So you pick something else. You've got plenty of time."

The woman's nonchalance only further angered Tanner. "I don't want to pick something else." She knew she sounded childish and stubborn, but it was true. She had only ever wanted to play soccer—first at the collegiate level, and then professionally.

Mrs. Wilt took a sip of her vodka and then leaned in close to Tanner. "You want to hear a secret?"

Tanner slurped down the rest of her whiskey sour and gestured to Leonard for another. "Not especially." She'd heard enough pep talks from her mother to last her three lifetimes. That whenever one door closes, another opens. That she had her whole life ahead of her. That she could be anything she wanted to be! Anything, except a senior at Northwestern playing soccer and being recruited by the top women's teams in the country. Anything, of course, except that.

Mrs. Wilt continued anyway. "Nothing in life goes according to plan. Nothing. And the sooner you accept that, the better off you'll be."

Tanner grunted. "Are you always so inspiring?"

"Watch Oprah if you want inspiring. I just tell the truth."

Leonard delivered her second drink and waited as Tanner picked it up and drained half of it in one gulp.

With both hands on the counter in front of him, Leonard eyed Tanner and then Mrs. Wilt. "Is this your daughter?"

Tanner rolled her eyes, while Mrs. Wilt chuckled, which made her roll her eyes even harder. "Granddaughter."

"No," he said in fake admonishment. "You must have been a child bride."

"And you must be looking for a bigger tip," Mrs. Wilt said, but she was smiling. "Do you have children?"

Leonard shook his head. "My wife, God rest her soul, never could. We talked about adopting, but it just . . . wasn't in the cards for us."

"Oh, I'm so sorry."

Tanner didn't know if she was sorry his wife died or that he didn't have children or both. She also found she didn't really care. She tossed back the second half of her drink and asked for a third.

Mrs. Wilt looked from the drink to Tanner, then to the bartender. "Leonard, do you have menus? We should order some food."

Two and a half hours later, Mrs. Wilt limped across the parking lot under the moonlight, as it was apparent Tanner needed her cane more than she did.

"I can feel my heartbeat in my eye," Tanner said, and then giggled. She felt like she was floating. And spinning. Was this why everyone drank? No wonder.

Was she drunk? She thought maybe so. And if so, wasn't this certainly a week of firsts for her? She was on the run from the law. She'd seen a gun *in person* for the first time. A gun!

With her free hand, she made a fake pistol out of her thumb and pointer finger and then pulled the fake trigger. "Pew-pew! Pew, pew." Then she collapsed into giggles again.

"C'mon, Annie Oakley," Mrs. Wilt said. But Tanner was struggling to put one foot in front of the other. She stared down at her sneakers as if her eyes were in control of making them move. And then she saw a large oil stain on the pavement. Seeing it reminded her of something. Something else she had wanted to do as a child, besides play soccer, and she brightened. "Iwannawushtucks."

"Excuse me?"

Tanner didn't understand why she was having such trouble forming words. She tried again. "I d'cided. WhudIwannnabe."

"That was fast."

This time Tanner concentrated on each syllable. "I want. To wash. Tucks."

Mrs. Wilt made a noncommittal murmuring sound as she pulled the old-fashioned key to the door of the motel room out of her pocket, and it angered Tanner.

"No! Thisisimportend. You know those adver . . . adver . . . adver—youknowwhatImean. Commercials! With the oil spills and the soap and the little duckies. Thassss what I wannado. Wushtheducks."

"Well. That is certainly ambitious." Mrs. Wilt unlocked the door and pushed it inward with her left hand. "After you, girlie."

Tanner stood rooted to the cement outside the door. "Ducky duck ducks. Duck duck GOOOOSE!" She patted Mrs. Wilt on her scarf-covered head and then howled with laughter. Her head swam with a wave of dizziness. Her stomach roiled. "Uh-oh," she said. And promptly threw up on the brick wall of the motel, to the right of the open door.

YEARS AGO, WHEN Charlie was in high school and he stumbled in the door after his midnight curfew, Ken helped him to bed and then came to Louise laughing. "Poor kid can't lie down without holding on." Louise smiled, knowing that was exactly what Ken would have said tonight had he been there to witness Tanner's state—though washing the vomit off the side of the motel with an ice bucket of water had been less than funny. As had the interminable groaning and whimpering once Louise got Tanner to bed, which had finally settled into a raucous snoring.

Louise let her thoughts remain on Ken for a bit longer, until her thoughts drifted to the barman at the Cobra Lounge. Despite his stooped shoulders, thinning hair, and liver-spotted hands, there was a certain manliness about him that Louise found quite appealing. Or familiar, anyway. His eyes reminded her of Ken. Not the color—an overcast blue compared to Ken's milky brown—but something about the mischievous way they crinkled when he smiled. Like the worst he'd ever hurt you was to lightheartedly poke fun and then apologize immediately after. Or maybe she just enjoyed his flirting. It had been months since Louise had been on the receiving end of a man's attentions (Ernie from bridge notwithstanding, as being the sole widower in a group of widows, he flirted with *everyone*), and she decided that was entirely too long.

"Mrs. Wilt." Tanner's voice cut through her thoughts, and Louise turned to peer at her through the dark.

"Yes?"

"You never tol' me whatyou wenna jail for." She was still slurring a bit, and Louise knew it was going to be a rough morning for her. And that she likely wouldn't remember much—if any—of this conversation anyhow.

"Mail theft," Louise said, remembering the incident from thirty-nine years earlier as if it were merely yesterday. How she couldn't help herself. The checks had been *right there*. For the taking. How shocked Ken was when he came to collect her from the county jail (not that it took much to shock him). And his displeasure months later, when she pleaded guilty and they had to pay a $500 fine. Nothing made Ken more irritable than having to part with money—not even his wife going to jail.

"Mail? Like letters?"

"Yes. Now go back to sleep." She did feel bad for the girl—and not just for the ferocious hangover she was likely to endure. She was so young. She had no idea how long life was. People always said life was short, but it wasn't. Not really. You could cram so many different lives into one. Be so many different people.

Louise would know. She'd been at least three.

17

AN EXPLANATION, OF SORTS, FROM LUCY TO THE FBI, BUT MOSTLY TO HER SIBLINGS, DIRECTLY AFTER HER ADMISSION THAT SHE DIDN'T THINK LOUISE WAS HER MOTHER'S REAL NAME

LUCY: It was back in high school. We were on a tour of Ohio State University.

JULES: Hold on. *You* were on a college tour? You didn't even want to go to college.

LUCY: I know. But I did want to go to a Garbage concert in Columbus, and that was the only way Mom would let me go. I had to look at the school—and she insisted on coming, too, to make sure I did.

CHARLIE: Good Lord, you had the worst taste in music.

JULES: Mom went to a *Garbage* concert?

LUCY: No. She stayed at the hotel.

HUANG: Can we please focus?

LUCY: Sorry.

JULES: Sorry.

CHARLIE: The worst. Remember when you were obsessed with that boy band and you locked yourself in your room and cried for like three days straight because you didn't get tickets to their concert?

LUCY: I was in the fifth grade.

HUANG: [*clears throat*]

LUCY: Anyway, we were walking on campus and this woman came up to Mom, all emotional-like, and kept calling her Patty. "Patty, is it really you?" Stuff like that. At first Mom kept telling her she was mistaken, and the woman became more adamant and hysterical. Finally, Mom relented and hugged her, and the woman cried all over her. It was kind of a spectacle.

JULES: And?

LUCY: That was it.

JULES: What did she say when you asked her?

LUCY: Asked her what?

JULES: WHY THE WOMAN WAS CALLING HER PATTY.

LUCY: Oh. I didn't.

JULES: Jesus H. Christ.

CHARLIE: That doesn't mean anything. Sounds like the lady was crazy. Mom was just trying to get rid of her.

JULES: Women can have emotions without being "crazy," Charlie.

CHARLIE: Not everything is a therapy session, Jules.

LUCY: No, Mom definitely knew her.

CHARLIE: How do you know? I swear, if you start talking about people's auras—

LUCY: She said so.

JULES: She did?

LUCY: Not in so many words. But when the woman left, Mom glanced at me and said, "That was another life. Ages ago."

JULES: And what did you say?

LUCY: Nothing.

JULES: Why on earth not?

CHARLIE: Same reason she saw a Jaguar in the shed four years ago and didn't say a word about it until yesterday.

LUCY: I just figured Mom has a right to her private life.

JULES: Ha! She absolutely does not! She's our mother.

HUANG: Did you say the woman called her Patty?

LUCY: Yes.

HUANG: OK, I think I have all I need here.

18

"UHHNNNNN," TANNER GROANED Thursday morning when she woke. It felt as though a bullet had lodged in her forehead right behind her eyes, the pain radiating out and spreading to her skull, throbbing in time with her pulse. She tried to swallow, but her mouth was sour and dry, like she'd been chewing cotton. She blinked, squinting at the dim motel room, confused, until the previous night came roaring back to her with the same vengeance as her headache. The whiskey sours. Projectile vomiting. Something about . . . ducks?

She groaned again and glanced at the digital clock on the nightstand: 10:37 a.m.

"Mrs. Wilt?" she said, her voice croaky. She tried to sit up, but her head throbbed in earnest, and she lay back down. Pride may have prevented her from asking her for help in typical circumstances, but currently she was not above begging for a glass of water if it would make one appear. Unfortunately, Mrs. Wilt did not respond.

From her supine position, she glanced around the room slowly, as if the old woman might suddenly materialize from thin air. The bed, neatly made, didn't even look slept in. The chair she had sat in the day before to do crosswords was empty. The only place left for her to be was in the bathroom.

"Mrs. Wilt," she said again, her voice even weaker this time. Her stomach churned. She tried to swallow again, hoping to keep her nausea at bay, and she couldn't believe that other people made themselves feel this way voluntarily. All she knew was that if she were to recover—and she wasn't quite sure that was a given—she would absolutely never drink again.

She closed her eyes, wishing her mom were there. Why was that? No matter how much she hated her at times, it was instinctual, this yearning for her mom's care. The way she would put a cool cloth on her brow when she was sick. Bring her flat Sprite. Rub her back until she fell asleep.

Now, she felt so . . . alone. She sat up then, ignoring the extra pounding of her head. *Was* she alone? She remained still, straining to listen for a noise from beyond the closed door of the bathroom.

"Mrs. Wilt?"

No response. She threw the covers off and stood, a wave of dizziness and nausea threatening to sit her back down, but somehow, she remained standing. And then hobbled to the bathroom door, knocking once before turning the handle. The bathroom was empty.

She glanced around the room once more, and this time the dizziness did force her back onto the edge of the bed. She put her hands on her knees. Where was Mrs. Wilt? She lay back, closing her eyes, which only made her head hurt worse. She groaned again. Maybe Mrs. Wilt was just out getting breakfast—she glanced at the clock again and saw it was close to eleven. Or lunch. But she knew the Cobra Lounge wasn't open yet, and it would only take ten minutes, tops, to get more ancient packaged snacks from the vending machines.

Tanner expected the door to the hotel room to open any second, for Mrs. Wilt to appear. But as seconds turned to minutes and minutes turned to fifteen and then thirty and then forty-five, Tanner grew increasingly concerned.

Where could the old woman have gone?

Tanner shivered. What if Mrs. Wilt *had* gone to the vending machines and . . . had a stroke? Or a heart attack. Or a brain aneurysm. Or some other old person health issue. And the front desk called an ambulance and she was in a hospital somewhere alone and no one knew to tell Tanner? Or what if no one had been at the front desk, and she was still lying on the dirty floor of the lobby?

That thought propelled Tanner to her feet. She ignored her waning-but-not-fast-enough headache and moved with purpose, out of her room, down the cement sidewalk, past the other few motel room doors, and through the smudged glass entrance to the small lobby. A teenaged girl with limp brown hair braided to the side and a pimple-riddled complexion looked up from the cell phone clutched in her hand. No greeting. No *how can I help?* Just a blank stare.

"I'm looking for . . ." Tanner faltered. How to explain to a stranger her relationship to Mrs. Wilt? The woman was very technically her charge, but that didn't exactly roll off the tongue. Maybe partner? No. That sounded . . . romantic. She could always lie and say *grandmother* the way Mrs. Wilt had been telling anyone who asked. It would certainly be easier. Tanner started over.

"Have you seen an elderly woman this morning? We checked in

two days ago. Room nine? She's about, well . . . about my height, likely wearing a cardigan and orthopedic shoes. Oh, and a bright yellow headscarf."

The girl stared at her, and Tanner couldn't read her blank expression. Finally, she responded: "Nope."

"Are you sure? Maybe even just walking by outside a couple hours ago?"

"Unh-uh." She looked back down at her phone.

"OK. Well . . . thanks."

Perplexed, and not just a little concerned, Tanner loped back to the room and sat on the edge of the club chair. Panning the small area for any clues she may have missed, her gaze landed on Mrs. Wilt's suitcase, zipped and parked on the floor next to the television bureau. (Tanner's was on the other side, unzipped, clothes flooding out of it, a mix of clean and dirty. She'd sort it later.) Mrs. Wilt's purse, Tanner noticed, was gone, which meant the gun was with her. And then she remembered the cash. She stood and went to the nightstand between the beds, where Mrs. Wilt had stashed it when they got to the hotel. A deep, gut instinct compelled her to open the drawer, and sure enough—it was empty.

Panic flooded her nervous system. Had they been robbed? Had Mrs. Wilt been taken against her will while Tanner lay unconscious in her drunken state? Or . . . had Mrs. Wilt left on her own? Tanner jerked her head in the direction of the car mechanic across the street, even though she couldn't see it through the curtained windows. She tore out of the room, and barely looked both ways as she sprinted across the very hot black tar of the two-lane road. Breathing hard, she banged open the door of the small shop, a few tinkling bells heralding her entrance. The owner—and as far as Tanner could tell, the only man who worked here, as he was the same man who had driven the tow truck on Tuesday—looked up, a half-smoked cigarette dangling from between his lips.

"You alright?" he said, his gaze traveling down her body, and then darting away as if to give her privacy. That was when Tanner realized what she must look like—wild, matted hair that may or may not have dried puke in it; the same sweatpants and camisole she'd had on last night. No bra. And no shoes—hence the scorching heat on her soles when she'd crossed the street. She folded her arms over her chest, suddenly aware that her nipples were likely visible through her top.

"Is she gone? Is the car gone?"

"Who?" He crinkled his forehead, keeping his eyes trained on her face. "You mean the Jaguar?"

"Yes, the Jaguar!"

"No." He gestured with his hand to the garage area beyond the door behind the counter. "Fuel pump should be in sometime this afternoon."

"Oh. OK."

"I'll call the motel when it's done, like I said I would. It'll be tomorrow 'fore lunch at the earliest."

"Right."

"You sure you're OK?"

"Yep," Tanner said. She turned and found her way back across the street, this time feeling every searing step and cursing herself for not at least putting on shoes.

In her room, she collapsed back in the club chair, her mind racing. Where was Mrs. Wilt? And how could Tanner possibly find her? It occurred to her, yet another problem in a myriad of problems when you're on the run with a wanted criminal: when you lost said criminal, it wasn't like you could call the police.

Her knee throbbed from her little jaunt across the street—matching her headache, which was back in earnest now—and Tanner cursed herself for pushing it too hard. She rubbed her leg with her thumbs and leaned her skull against the back of the chair and did the only thing she could do: she waited.

THREE HOURS LATER, Tanner heard the key slip into the lock on the door. She sat up and crossed her arms, both relieved and furious, ready to unleash on Mrs. Wilt—if it was, in fact, Mrs. Wilt on the other side.

Time stilled as Tanner endured a moment of panic—what if it was the *police*?—but she saw the familiar gnarled hand push the door in, and then the base of the cane followed. She took in the woman she'd briefly thought she may never lay eyes on again. Something was different about her, but Tanner didn't have time to discern what it was.

"Where have you been?" she growled.

"You're up," Mrs. Wilt said, shutting the door behind her. "How are you feeling?"

"Besides being worried to death?"

"Isn't that your natural state?"

Tanner ignored the barb. "Where *were* you?"

"I was getting my hair done."

Tanner paused. That was what was different. Instead of the canary-yellow scarf, Mrs. Wilt's hair was exposed and freshly curled and teased back to her original bouffant. "You're kidding."

"Not at all. I found a lovely woman in the yellow pages who runs a little operation out of her garage about two miles down the road."

Tanner narrowed her eyes, still disbelieving. They were on the run from the law, for Pete's sake. And Mrs. Wilt felt the need to go to a . . . *salon*? "How did you get there?"

"I walked."

"You walked. Two miles."

"Yes."

"In this heat." Tanner didn't have her phone to check, but it had to be nearly ninety degrees outside.

"Yes."

"With your bad hip. And your cane."

"Mm-hm."

"To get your *hair done*?"

"I think you're all caught up now."

"And where's the money?"

"What?"

"The cash. It's not in the nightstand."

"Why were you looking for it?" Mrs. Wilt gave Tanner a hard stare.

"Because I thought you left me! You could have written a note or something, you know."

Mrs. Wilt eyed Tanner, but her face was unreadable, and whether she agreed she should have left a note, Tanner would never know.

"Well, girlie, it appears you survived," Mrs. Wilt said nonchalantly.

And with that, Tanner snapped. Pure blind fury—no, *rage*—enveloped her, the same way she felt when she learned she'd never play soccer again, or when she realized her mom bought bread and butter pickles instead of dill.

"STOP FUCKING CALLING ME GIRLIE!" she roared.

Chest heaving with the exertion, Tanner stared at Mrs. Wilt with wide eyes, almost as surprised as the old woman looked at her in return. And, as usual, Tanner's anger slowly leaked out of her. She'd had enough of these Hulk-outs by now to know they were like fireworks—one big, brilliant explosion of anger, and then it was over. Spent.

Just like with the pickles, she regretted it instantly. But at least that had been directed toward her mom. Now she was screaming at old women, too? That didn't make her much better than those nursing home workers who abuse their charges, as Tanner had seen on an episode of *Dateline* once. She wanted to apologize, but stubbornness kept her from opening her mouth. Mrs. Wilt hadn't apologized for what she had done, and Tanner would be damned if she said she was sorry first. But the longer the silence stretched between them, the more a pit of anxiety grew in Tanner's stomach, where only seconds earlier anger had been. She'd already alienated every single person in her life with her uncontrollable outbursts—and now she was doing it to the only person she had left.

IN THE OVERWHELMING quiet after Tanner's exclamation (and what an exclamation it was!), Louise cocked her head, studying the girl. Reappraising her like a scientist reclassifying a species. She honestly hadn't known Tanner had it in her. She nearly wanted to give the girl a standing ovation—it was about time she stopped skulking around, sullenly pouting, talking in circles, dithering about, and actually put her foot down about something for once.

Up until this very point, there wasn't much Louise could understand about the girl. Soccer? Louise had been to a match in Italy once and thought the rules were overly complicated and the fans were loud and obnoxious. Video games? Who on earth could spend that much of their time glued to a screen? The girl didn't even *drink*, for Pete's sake! (Though Louise had thought, given time, she could fix that—and sure enough, she had.)

But anger.

Anger was something Louise understood intimately—particularly having been a young woman herself.

Anger at her mother for refusing to leave her abusive stepfather.

Anger that, though he had never laid a finger on her, his leering presence forced her to lock her bedroom door at night just to feel safe in her own house.

Anger that she felt so goddamned *powerless*. All the time. Unable to change her circumstances.

And if hadn't been for George, anger likely would have swallowed Louise up completely—and who knew what would have happened to her?

"Get up," she said to Tanner now, breaking the silence.

"What for?" The girl looked stricken. Scared.

"We're going somewhere."

Louise put her hand on the doorknob behind her, effectively letting the girl know she wasn't going to take no for an answer. Tanner made a big scene of pushing herself to standing—like a toddler dragging her feet to the bath—and grabbed the baseball hat off the top of the dresser. She paused and looked at Louise, as if she had just realized something.

"Aren't you going to put on your scarf?"

"There's no need. My hair is done."

Tanner's lower jaw dropped open. "*That's* why you were wearing it?"

"Of course."

"I thought it was your . . . disguise."

"I know you did," she said, unable to keep the small hint of amusement from her voice

Tanner stared at her a beat, then groaned and dropped the cap back on the dresser. "Let's go."

THE WOODS BEHIND the Golden Village Motor Inn were overgrown with thick brush and vines. At first, when she followed Mrs. Wilt out of the room, Tanner had thought she was being unceremoniously kicked out. Perhaps Mrs. Wilt was walking her to the front office to get her own room and then letting her find her own way from there. Of course, it didn't make sense, considering she had left her suitcase behind. But Tanner couldn't possibly understand where else they could be going, and now, staring at the woods—which appeared difficult to traverse for an able-bodied person, much less someone with a cane—she was even more confused. "You want to go on a hike?" She tilted her head, looking at the forest with concern as Mrs. Wilt barreled her way into the trees and disappeared.

"Come on." Mrs. Wilt's disembodied voice floated back out to Tanner, who looked longingly back at the run-down Bates-like motel that—compared to the forest—now seemed downright welcoming.

"Are we *trying* to get murdered?" Tanner asked as she pushed her way through a curtain of dead vines and went after Mrs. Wilt, if for no other reason than that she didn't want to be left to die alone.

Tanner walked slowly behind Mrs. Wilt, nausea still roiling her stomach, a mild headache still throbbing behind her eyes, and feeling ever more sheepish for how she'd spoken to Mrs. Wilt, as she pushed sharp pointy branches out of her face. She wondered if this was Mrs. Wilt's idea of a punishment. And then thought it must be, as she grew hot, sticky, and disgruntled, slapping at mosquitoes and remaining on high alert for snakes and poison ivy. "If you wanted fresh air, we could have walked along the road a lot easier," she muttered.

"Ah, here we are."

Tanner looked over Mrs. Wilt's shoulder and saw a small clearing, the ground littered with a few crumpled beer cans and the remnants of what might look to some like a bonfire, but to Tanner looked like a place where cult members sacrificed goats and worshipped the devil.

"Is this the part where you tell me you're Wiccan? How did you even know this was here?"

"I didn't. But it's perfect."

"For what?"

Mrs. Wilt reached into her handbag and pulled out her pistol.

"Oh my God!" Tanner squealed, putting her hands up. She had only been joking about the murder, but now it didn't seem so funny. "I'm sorry, I'm sorry! I didn't mean to yell at you!"

"Good Lord, child," Mrs. Wilt said, exasperated. "I'm not going to shoot you." And true to her word, instead of pointing the gun at her, Mrs. Wilt held it out to her like a gift, keeping the barrel trained on the ground. "Here. Take it."

Tanner straightened her spine, staring at the weapon. "No."

"Yes. You're going to learn how to shoot it."

"No, I'm not."

"Yes, you are. It's the only way to get over your fear."

"I don't want to get over my fear."

Mrs. Wilt ignored her. "You like psychology—think of it as exposure therapy."

"Exposure therapy," Tanner repeated.

"Like when someone is scared of snakes, and then they hold one and aren't scared anymore."

"I would never hold a snake."

"Take the gun."

Tanner eyed it. She knew she didn't *have* to take the gun, but she had to admit, part of her was intrigued. She'd never held one before, much less shot one. And when would she get the chance to do so again? Plus, the gun wasn't loaded, so it wasn't like it could actually hurt anything. But then again, they were in the middle of the woods, in the middle of nowhere, and what if someone happened by? She didn't know if there were laws about carrying a weapon in the woods, even unloaded ones. She frowned. "Are you sure this is legal?"

"Have you always worried this much?"

Tanner considered this, thinking back to her childhood, how her stomach used to stitch itself into knots the night before a big test, how she hated for her dad to leave for his weeklong car-sales conferences because she was sure his plane would get hijacked, he would wreck on the way to the hotel, he wouldn't come home. "Yes," she said.

Mrs. Wilt moved her hand holding the gun an inch closer to Tanner. "Come on," she said. "We're already out here. In for a penny, in for a pound."

Tanner hesitated for one more heartbeat and then gingerly took the gun from Mrs. Wilt. It felt surprisingly light in her hand.

"First rule is, you never point it at anybody unless you mean to use it."

Tanner frowned. "Didn't you point it at your neighbor?"

"Yes," Mrs. Wilt said matter-of-factly. She leaned over, picked up a crumpled beer can, then step-thumped over to a low branch of a tree, steadied the can on the limb, and walked back over to Tanner, who stood there holding the wood-grain handle in both hands, taking care to make sure the muzzle was pointed away from both herself and Mrs. Wilt and not to touch the trigger.

"Alright. Shoot the can."

Tanner looked at her dumbly. "How?" She had assumed she'd be getting a full lesson plus demonstration, like the time her mom taught her how to make hospital corners when making a bed.

"Point it. Cock the hammer. Pull the trigger. It's not rocket science."

"Right." She stared at the gun. "What's the hammer?"

Mrs. Wilt audibly exhaled. Still grasping the head of her cane in her left hand, she took the gun from Tanner with her right, and in the blink of an eye pulled back on the protruding metal piece with her thumb and shot a can on the ground less than ten feet from where they were standing. The report echoed through the air.

Tanner flinched and tried to cover her ears with her hands, but it was too late. "Oh my God! It's loaded?"

"Yes."

"I thought you took the bullet out."

"I put some back in."

"You had more?"

"Of course. What good is a gun with no bullets?"

Tanner's heart thundered in her chest as Mrs. Wilt offered the gun back to her. She swallowed, reminding herself that she had just held it in her hand and nothing bad had happened. With a trembling hand, she reached for it again. It felt heavier this time. Her head and legs felt lighter. Wobbly.

"Point it at the can."

Tanner did as she was told.

"Steady your right hand with your left."

She cupped her right hand with her left. She thought about fear. And hated herself for feeling it so often. She wished she could be more confident. More self-assured. More like . . . Mrs. Wilt. But then she remembered the arch. "Wait a minute. You're saying when someone is afraid of something, they should just suck it up and do it anyway."

"Yes."

"So, if someone was, say . . . afraid of heights, they should go to the top of a tall building, like, I don't know—the St. Louis arch."

"Be quiet. You need to concentrate."

Tanner grinned and then cocked back the hammer with her thumb, as she had seen Mrs. Wilt do. She lined up the can with the sight of the pistol. Then she closed her eyes and squeezed the trigger.

19

"HOLY SHIT! THAT was absolutely amazing!" Though it had been a full hour since Tanner had last fired the gun, she was still living on the high of the adrenaline coursing through her veins.

"You do realize you missed the can. Three times." Mrs. Wilt let go of her cane and eased herself up onto the same bar stool at the Cobra Lounge she had sat in the previous night, as Tanner took the one beside her.

"I would have gotten it on the fourth try, if you had let me try again."

"I couldn't let you use all the ammo. What if we need it?"

Tanner was about to ask what on earth they might need bullets in the gun for, when Mrs. Wilt spoke again.

"Money's in my suitcase, by the way," she said. "Most of it. The rest is in my purse."

"Oh." Tanner felt a little sheepish for not trusting Mrs. Wilt.

Even though she *shouldn't* trust her, because she was a jewelry thief. But still, she wanted to, which certainly *felt* like Stockholm syndrome, even if it wasn't the textbook definition.

"And I know you think it's stolen, but it's not. It's from Ken's life insurance policy."

"Oh," Tanner repeated, noticing a flash of sadness in Mrs. Wilt's eyes. Tanner felt a quick stab of empathy. Whether *that* was from Stockholm or not, Tanner felt compelled to offer an olive branch in return. "Your hair looks nice."

Mrs. Wilt laughed, one sharp "ha!" And then: "It looks like a football helmet."

"Er . . ." Tanner wasn't sure how to respond, because it did look like a football helmet, especially right after she got it done, all fluffed and frozen in place.

"I swore I'd never have old lady hair," she muttered, and Tanner couldn't tell if she was talking to her or herself. "But you'll see. It changes. Gets so thin and brittle you feel lucky to have any hair at all."

"I think your hair looks lovely." It was the same ancient bartender from the evening before. Liam or Nelson or whatever his name was. In fact, everything about the Cobra Lounge looked the exact same as the night before, down to the same couple in the corner staring at their phones.

Tanner waited for Mrs. Wilt to snap at him, explaining why her hair wasn't *lovely*, but instead Mrs. Wilt eyed him coquettishly—the same way she'd looked at August that day in her living room. "Thank you, Leonard."

Tanner rolled her eyes, but also felt a flash of what . . . pride? Admiration? Old people flirting was still gross, of course.

"Vodka on the rocks and a whiskey sour this evening?"

"Just Coke for me," Tanner said.

Leonard nodded. "Give me just one minute. I need to get more ice from the back."

"Take your time," Mrs. Wilt said.

Tanner toyed with a cardboard coaster advertising a light beer, and then she glanced at Mrs. Wilt. "I'm sorry I yelled at you earlier."

Mrs. Wilt shrugged as if people screamed *fuck* at her on a daily basis. "It's fine."

"Really?"

"Yeah. Angry women don't bother me. It's the ones who aren't furious that I worry about."

"What?" Tanner asked, confused. "Why?"

"Means they aren't paying attention."

Tanner snorted. "Pretty sure you stole that. It's on, like, every third poster and T-shirt at every pussy-hatted women's march ever."

"Doesn't mean it isn't true."

"Well, I don't feel so furious anymore." As it turned out, shooting guns was quite therapeutic. Mrs. Wilt offered a slight nod, as if she'd known that would be the case all along, and Tanner started to realize the woman might be a bit smarter than she gave her credit for.

"You know what else you could use?" Mrs. Wilt said.

"I'm *not* having a drink." Just the thought of it made Tanner's stomach lurch. Leonard returned and set the Coke down in front of Tanner and the vodka in front of Mrs. Wilt.

"Anything to eat?" he asked.

"The grilled chicken salad. Italian dressing on the side," Mrs. Wilt said.

Leonard nodded and looked at Tanner.

"I'll have an order of wings. And fries. Ooh! And mozzarella sticks."

Leonard stared at her for a beat, as if waiting to make sure she wasn't going to add a fourth item, and then said: "Coming right up."

"Dear God, you eat like my son, Charlie," Mrs. Wilt said after Leonard turned back toward the kitchen.

"That's so sexist."

"What? Because I made an observation that you eat like someone I know?"

"No. Because you said I eat like a man."

"No. I said you eat like my son, Charlie. Who happens to be a man."

"Same difference."

"No. It's not. And you know that's the problem."

"What problem?"

"With your generation. Everything is black and white. A person makes one mistake—or one perceived mistake—and suddenly they're . . . what do you call it? Terminated."

"Terminated?" Tanner laughed, taking a pull of her Coke from the straw. "I think you mean canceled."

"Yes, that's it. There's no discussion anymore, no nuance."

"I didn't realize sexism was nuanced."

"You're twisting my words. That's something else your generation is good at."

"Are you done?"

"For now."

"Good. What were you going to say?"

"About what?"

"You said, 'You know what else you could use?'"

"Oh right. That." Mrs. Wilt took a sip of her vodka. Put the glass down. "You need a lover."

Tanner sputtered, spraying Coke onto the bar top.

"Someone older," Mrs. Wilt continued.

"What, like him?" Tanner joked, nodding toward Leonard, who was at the far back of the bar, washing glasses in the sink and whistling.

"Don't be ridiculous," Mrs. Wilt said. "He's for me."

Tanner sat, stunned for a beat. "You're kidding, right?"

"Not a bit."

"You're going to . . . you know."

"Have carnal relations? Certainly. If the man is willing. I've found most of them are."

"Please don't say 'carnal relations.'"

"OK. Sex, then."

"Please don't say that, either."

"Oh, I know you think it's only for lithe twenty-year-olds. I did, too, when I was your age. But if I recall, it wasn't all that good. I do hope boys have gotten better at it."

Tanner thought about Grant. The sweating and grunting. How the anticipation was often so much better than the actual act. How she was left wanting every time he finished, tossed her his discarded T-shirt, and then kissed her on the nose and rolled over to start snoring.

"They haven't."

"Pity," Mrs. Wilt said. "Good news is, they get much better with age. Some of them, anyway. Not the good-looking ones, of course. Steer clear of them."

"I know, I know. Because they're jerks."

"No. Well, yes. Sometimes. But they're also terrible lovers. They don't have to work for it. Fair-to-average-looking men are perfect. They're like goldendoodles."

"Goldendoodles?"

"You know, eager to please. Grateful for the attention." She grinned. "They slobber a bit."

"Ew," Tanner said. "Can we talk about something else now, please?"

The food arrived, and Tanner, ravenous, mowed down eight french fries, one after another, pausing just long enough to wash them down with a long pull of fizzy, sweet Coke. She began to feel much more like herself.

They ate in silence, and at the end of the meal, Mrs. Wilt took three twenties out of her purse, placed them on the check that Leonard had left, and then placed the metal room key on top of the cash.

Tanner gaped at her. "What are you doing?" She had not fully believed that Mrs. Wilt was actually serious about sleeping with this . . . old man (*ew!*), and furthermore, she hadn't considered where she was planning to do it. In their *shared* room, apparently.

"Giving Leonard a key."

"To *our* room? Where am I supposed to sleep?"

"Relax. I booked a second room when I returned from the beauty parlor."

Tanner gaped at her. Not only was Mrs. Wilt going to do it, she had *planned* it. Ahead of time. Given it forethought.

"What if he hadn't been working tonight?"

"Then I would have had a lovely evening to myself—away from your snoring."

"I don't snore!"

"Yes. You do. Like a truck driver."

Leonard appeared then, and paused when he saw the room key on top of the cash. "Do you need change?" he asked Mrs. Wilt.

"No."

He picked up the key and looked at it, then looked at Mrs. Wilt. Tanner wanted to crawl under the bar and die a little bit, but she also was wildly curious how this was going to play out.

"What time do you get off this evening?" Mrs. Wilt asked.

"Eleven."

"Could you possibly return that key to me then? Room fifteen."

Leonard nodded deeply, almost a bow. "I'd be delighted to."

Tanner had to admit, it was pretty damn smooth. For an eightysomething-year-old, anyway.

FOR MONTHS AFTER Ken died, Louise often got caught unawares with the thought of something banal she'd never get to do again now that he was gone. Like hear him laugh at a ribald joke; or yell at him for making a wild bid in couples bridge; or taste his spaghetti carbonara, which he had perfected when she was pregnant with Lucy and craved it constantly. (It wasn't until years later that experts said raw eggs were bad for growing fetuses, but Lucy had turned out just fine, hadn't she? Well, mostly fine.)

Or have sex. It wasn't so much the physical act she missed (though she *did* miss it) as it was the closeness, the short balm to loneliness that being intimate with someone provided. She didn't even know she missed it until one Sunday at church, when Bernie Hubertson asked her out for coffee the same way he had for the past four Sundays (the same way he asked *every* widow out for coffee—and because women talked, Louise knew it wasn't really coffee he wanted to have), but this time he touched her arm, ever so briefly, gently running his thumb over her skin. And—God help her—she felt a flash of desire. For Bernie Hubertson. Who smelled like an undesirable mix of Bengay and stale coffee and mothballs. She wished Ken had been alive just so she could tell him, and they would laugh and laugh and laugh together at how pathetically widow desperate she had become. But Ken wasn't there, and if that wasn't just the most unfair thing—that Ken was gone, and Bernie Hubertson was not—she didn't know what was. She did not, for the record, have sex with Bernie Hubertson, but she did begin to seek out more discreet opportunities for male companionship from time to time—and she quickly realized they were not that difficult to find.

Now, Louise stood in the center of a motel room that was an exact replica of the one she had slept in the previous two nights—same worn, mottled carpet that was more a noncolor than any specific one. Same orange-and-brown-paisley bedspreads. Her right hand trembled as she attempted to unbutton her cardigan. If Leonard noticed, he didn't say. He simply put his hand over hers and took over the chore naturally, as though it were a routine they'd perfected over many years together. She wondered how long he'd been married for. How his wife had died. Louise found even if Leonard hadn't said anything, she could somehow tell a widower from miles away. They were like those tables in restaurants that wobbled, unsteady on their feet. Missing the matchbook or stack of coasters that held them upright, stable.

When he finished unbuttoning her cardigan, Leonard carefully helped her out of it and draped it neatly on the bed that was nearest to them. Then he leaned in and gently kissed her in the soft spot where her jaw met her earlobe. She closed her eyes and concentrated on the sensation, the warmth that radiated through her. A flicker of anticipation fluttered her stomach. She opened her eyes.

"I have a bad hip," she said into Leonard's ear. "My right one, so take care."

Leonard lifted his head and allowed a few inches of space between them. He grunted. "I have a bad everything."

"Everything?" Louise popped an eyebrow.

He grinned that sweet-Ken mischievous grin, and Louise's heart squeezed. She could see something of the boy Leonard used to be. A boy who had learned to rely on his wit and charm to woo a girl, rather than overt good looks. In other words, the very best kind. Like her Ken. She felt simultaneously warm and sad.

"Well, not everything," he said.

"Thank God," she said, and reached for the hem of her cotton blouse, slowly lifting it up and over her head—careful not to muss her hair—and added it to the cardigan on the bed.

The actual sex part was fine, if not a bit mechanical, the consequence of Louise knowing her body well enough that she moved Leonard's hands where she wanted them, gently directing with words when necessary. Though it went on a bit longer than Louise would have preferred. Those darn little blue pills that Ken used to pop—and she was confident Leonard had also taken—were a double-edged sword as far as she was concerned. Still, it scratched an itch.

Afterward, she lay in the bed, in that glowing state of relaxation, her fingers threaded through Leonard's sparse gray chest hairs, his arms gently but firmly around her shoulders. "That was lovely," Leonard said.

Louise pretended she didn't hear his voice break on the word *lovely*. She knew he was thinking of his wife. She also knew it wouldn't do to ask about her. Or try to comfort him with words. When it came to grief, words, she found, were always lacking.

She simply said, "It was."

She put her head next to her hand on his chest.

She closed her eyes and tried not to think about Ken. She tried not to think about George. She tried not to think about Salvatore D'Amato.

She tried to revel in the moment, in his body heat, in the masculine scent of his skin, in how good it felt to be held.

Because she knew—it very likely would be the last time she ever was.

20

A CONVERSATION BETWEEN TANNER'S PARENTS, THREE DAYS AFTER LOUISE WAS REPORTED MISSING TO THE POLICE

"DO YOU THINK I was too hard on her?" Candace sat at the kitchen table, wringing her hands as she looked at her husband for absolution. They had just gotten off the phone with an FBI agent—the *FBI*!—and Candace didn't know whether she was going to throw up or faint, but her mind flooded with the images of every missing child on the news that had filled her with dread from the moment she became a mother. Elizabeth Smart. Madeleine McCann. Jaycee Dugard. She knew their names by heart, their faces, their parents' faces, because she pored over the details of the cases the way only a fellow mother can—as if searching for clues to keep her daughters from meeting the same fate.

And now.

"No, I don't think you were too hard on her—"

"This is my fault," Candace cut her husband off, feeling

undeserving of the absolution that she was looking for him to offer. "That she's out there. God only knows where."

"You think everything is your fault."

"Everything *is* my fault! You're the dad—the sun rises and sets on you! You wouldn't understand. I should never have kicked her out."

Candace cringed thinking of it. They had planned to sit Tanner down calmly that evening, explain to her that they loved her, but it was time for her to move on with her life. But then, the pickles. She'd been Tanner's punching bag for months—well, *years*, really, if you counted back to high school. She knew kids, daughters especially, took all the anger, frustration, world-weariness out on their mothers because they could. Because mothers would always love them—even at their worst. But even the best mothers had a breaking point.

"It was a joint decision, if I recall. She needed a nudge. She was drowning here, remember?"

"And now she's missing!" Candace knew she was reeling, but really, what mother wouldn't be?

"Look," Jim said in his preternaturally calm, logical way. "She's with an eighty-year-old woman who uses a cane to walk. They're not exactly going to party it up in Cancún. And the FBI have their best people on it. They're going to find her."

"How do you *know*?"

"I just do. It's all going to be OK. Trust me. Plus, if the FBI was worried they'd been kidnapped or . . . worse, the questions would have been completely different. It's clear Tanner and Louise took off of their own volition."

Candace looked at him hopefully. His rationality had often irritated her to no end over the years, but in times of crisis, she had to admit, she found it soothing. "I did think some of their questions were a bit strange."

"Yes, particularly when they asked if she'd ever been involved in any criminal activity," Jim said. "Imagine it! Our Tanner! But they have to cover all their bases, I suppose. Protocol and all."

"Do you think we need a lawyer? They always think it's the parents when a kid goes missing."

"Honey, she's not a kid anymore."

Candace knew that. She did. Except Tanner would always be a kid to her. Her *baby*. She had sworn from the first moment she held Tanner in her arms that she would be different. The kind of mother that Tanner could turn to—would *want* to turn to. That they wouldn't scream at each other, the way she had with her own mother. And for years, it was exactly how she'd imagined it. Tanner loved her wholly, completely, throwing herself into Candace's arms with such fervor every chance she got, smothering her with wet little-kid kisses.

She couldn't pinpoint when exactly things changed. Was it the first time Tanner rolled her eyes at Candace? Or when Tanner hissed at her to roll up her windows in the sixth grade when she was picking her up from soccer practice because her music was "soooooo embarrassing"? Or the first time Tanner shouted "I hate you!" because Candace wouldn't let her attend the sleepover of a school friend whose parents she had never met? Candace, of course, knew these little moments were normal—healthy, even. The natural order of things. But that certainly didn't make them hurt any less. Tears sprang to Candace's eyes as she thought of the last five months Tanner had spent at home, wallowing over the tough curveball life had thrown her recently. All Candace wanted was to wrap her arms around her daughter. To take away Tanner's pain as easily as she had kissed her skinned knees when she was little. But holding a porcupine would have been easier than holding her own daughter.

Jim put his warm hand over hers, stopping her from tearing a paper napkin that she hadn't even noticed she was holding to shreds.

"She's a smart girl. She's our Safety Director, remember?"

Candace half smiled at the nickname they had given their firstborn when she was five, because she was such a rule follower—and wanted to make sure everyone else was following the rules, too, going as far as announcing from the back seat when the car odometer edged even slightly past the posted speed limit of whatever road they were on. And though it seemed like a parent's greatest relief to have a kid so conscious of right and wrong, Candace, of course, worried about that, too, hoping Tanner would still be able to cut loose and have fun. Not be so rigid and anxious all the time. She had plenty of time to be anxious later. When she was a mother.

The phone trilled again, startling them both. Candace snatched it up, hoping for news, while at the same time fearing it.

"Hi, Mom."

"Marty, sweetheart," Candace said, immediately recognizing her second-born's voice. At least Marty didn't hate her. Not all the time, anyway.

"Any news?"

"No, nothing yet."

"Mom, what if something happened to her?" Marty burst into tears.

And though it was precisely what Candace had been worrying about, she did the only thing a mother could in this situation. She lied. "Oh, honey. I'm sure she's OK."

"I'm coming home," Marty said, sniffling.

"No, Marty. You just started the semester. You shouldn't miss your classes. And there's nothing you can do here anyway."

"The professors post everything online these days, Mom. It's fine. Besides, I don't want to be here, not knowing anything, while she's . . . out there. She's my *sister.*"

"I know," Candace said, because she did. Marty and Tanner may have grown apart over the years, but the love of a sister was as constant as the sun. You might not feel its rays every day, but it was always there. "Hey, do you know Tanner's phone pass code, by chance? She left her phone at Mrs. Wilt's house, and the FBI agent said it could be helpful to try to reach out to some of her friends, see if they've heard from her."

"Of course. It's 7719—the date the US women's team won their fourth World Cup."

"That was her pass code in high school, wasn't it? You don't think she's changed it?"

"No. Tanner's pretty predictable."

"Mm," Candace murmured. She may have thought that at one time about her daughter, too, but now . . . she wasn't so sure.

21

CAREFUL WHAT YOU *wish for.* Tanner could hear her mother's grating singsongy voice in her head as she drove the Jaguar west on I-70 toward Kansas City. She'd spent two full days wishing the car could be fixed so she wouldn't have to spend another minute in that desperate, paisley-clad motel room, only to remember just an hour into the trip how miserably oppressive the car was. At least the motel had air-conditioning. Mrs. Wilt sat beside her in her ridiculous oversized sunglasses that fit over her regular glasses, her yellow scarf firmly back in place. If one squinted, Tanner supposed she looked like some kind of fifties movie star, with the content smile that curved her pink-painted lips upward.

Tanner assumed the smile was from Mrs. Wilt's . . . evening. She shuddered trying to once again scrub the image of Mrs. Wilt in flagrante delicto from her brain, while at the same time feeling a modicum of respect for the old woman. The confident way she decided what she wanted and did something about it. It reminded her of Vee. How she wasn't scared of anything. How she dripped confidence as easily as Tanner dripped sweat after a three-hour soccer practice. Tanner didn't think she could ever behave so boldly toward a man—a *stranger.* But then, she wondered—why not? She hadn't thought she'd ever be on the run from the police, either. Or fire a gun. Or get drunk. In fact, Tanner had surprised herself more in the past four days than she ever had before—admittedly in some ways better than others. Tanner felt something blossom in her chest. Something that felt an awful lot like hope—or at least something different from the anger she had been submerged in for months, anyway. (Admittedly, it could have also been heartburn from the three cups of that awful motel room coffee she had downed in quick succession that morning before they hit the road.)

As morning melted into afternoon, it was as though Mrs. Wilt started leaking her short-lived joy like helium from a balloon and Tanner was inhaling it from the air between them. In fact, the more Tanner's mood buoyed, it seemed, the more Mrs. Wilt's declined. It started about an hour after they left St. Louis, when Mrs. Wilt looked up from her crossword and said, "Think you could step on it a bit? I've seen sloths that move faster."

"I'm going the speed limit."

"Precisely," Mrs. Wilt muttered.

A few minutes later, she looked up again. "You know, it's a well-known fact you can go up to nine miles *above* the speed limit without the cops stopping you."

Tanner frowned. "I don't think that's true."

Mrs. Wilt emitted a low growl and turned back to her crossword.

When they reached Kansas City around 1:00 p.m., Tanner pulled off at a gas station, filled up, and walked inside to pay with the cash

Mrs. Wilt handed her, glad to be free of the increasing hostility in the car, if even just for a few minutes. She hoped maybe eating would improve Mrs. Wilt's mood.

"Guess where we're going for lunch?" she said with as much joviality as she could muster when she slid back into the front seat of the Jaguar. Mrs. Wilt shot her a look that told her in no uncertain terms that she was not going to guess. Tanner was not deterred. "The cashier told me about this amazing barbecue joint a few miles away—at another gas station. She said it was on the Food Network and everything."

"No."

"No?"

"If you're hungry, go back in and get some chips. We have to go."

"We do?"

"Yes. We lost a lot of hours—*days*—what with the car breaking down and your ridiculous stop at the arch."

Tanner ignored the barb and narrowed her eyes, trying to understand where this sudden pressure was coming from. "Well sure, but we still need to eat—"

"GEORGE'S GOING TO DIE!" Mrs. Wilt roared, her voice filling up the small space between them in the front of the Jaguar. "FOR THE LOVE OF GOD, CAN YOU JUST DRIVE?"

LOUISE TRIED TO adjust her position in the bucket seat, but instead of the brief moment of respite she hoped for, the pain in her hip radiated outward, staking its claim. Louise grimaced. She had known she was going to pay for that walk to the salon one way or another, and though she used to harp on Ken for the exact same thing when he would try to play basketball with the kids at Thanksgiving or put the ladder against the house to clean the gutters ("You're not as young as you think you are!"), she just couldn't seem to accept that fact, either. Nobody wanted to believe their body was failing them, even when the evidence was as plain as the nose on one's face.

The pain, combined with her rising anxiety about making it to George in time, had turned her bright mood that morning considerably sour—which was the only explanation she could come up with for her unexpected and dramatic surge of emotion. Louise felt bad for yelling at the girl, she did. But honestly, what did Tanner know about life and death? Or loyalty, for that matter.

Louise kept her gaze on the windshield, trying to ignore Tanner's stare—her eyes wide and round as marbles. The girl looked at her for one more beat and then silently put the key in the ignition and drove.

For the next few miles, Louise waffled between feeling contrite for her uncharacteristic outburst and fuming, directing her anger at Tanner, though she knew it wasn't Tanner she was really angry at.

She was about to say as much when Tanner opened her mouth. "I didn't know about George." She took a deep breath. "I know you're paying me to do this and you keep saying the less I know the better, but seeing as how I'm on the run from the police—*for you*—and we do have to be stuck in this car together, the least you could do is be nice to me."

Louise reset her jaw, glad the girl had saved her from apologizing—one of Louise's least favorite activities. She sighed and offered Tanner something else instead: "We're not on the run from the police."

Tanner jerked her head toward Louise and then back at the road, her brow crinkled. "We're not?"

"No," Louise said. It had served its purpose, allowing Tanner to believe they were, but seeing as how it didn't actually make the girl drive faster, she didn't see any reason not to tell her the truth. "Those sirens the night we left? I imagine they were for my next-door neighbor."

"The asshat?"

Louise nodded. "The asshat's girlfriend, anyway. She calls the cops on him at least once a month. Sometimes twice."

"What for?"

Louise pursed her lips. "What do you think? Domestic disturbance, or whatever they call it these days."

"Why isn't he in jail?"

"She won't press charges. Even after two black eyes, a dislocated elbow—and that's what I could *see*. She takes him back, no matter what."

"Geez," Tanner breathed. "That's crazy."

Louise shrugged. She had seen worse. So much worse. "Tale as old as time."

Silence enveloped them for the next few miles, and then Tanner spoke. "Hold on, so if the police are not chasing us—why couldn't I bring my cell phone?"

"It's not the police I'm worried about tracking us."

"Who are you worried about tracking us?"

Louise paused. There was no need for the girl to know *everything*. As if reading her mind, Tanner said, "So what's . . . going on with George? Is he sick?"

Louise sighed. It was her own fault for not being able to keep her mouth shut. Before she could reply to Tanner's query, Tanner spoke again. "And that's why we have to get there so fast—because he's . . . *dying*?"

Louise nodded. It wasn't technically the truth, but George *could* die if Louise didn't get there in time, so it was close enough.

"Wow. I'm so sorry. Is he like, an ex-boyfriend or something?"

Louise nearly chuckled. *Ex-boyfriend.* It really was none of Tanner's business, but she hadn't talked about George—or that night—out loud with anyone. Ever. Not even Ken. Maybe it would feel good to finally get it off her chest. Like a deathbed confession—which was exactly what it might end up being, all things considered. She took a deep breath.

"George is my . . . well, *was*, I suppose . . ." Her what? Whole world. Other half. Soul mate. Though it was true, it all sounded so ridiculous. Juvenile. "Business partner," she settled on, because that was true as well. Even if the business they had been conducting was illegal. "Years ago. And I did something . . . made a decision that George didn't agree with."

Louise closed her eyes and realized then the other reason why she hadn't talked about that night in forty-eight years. And it wasn't just because she didn't want to get caught. It was because talking about it brought every detail screaming back to her in sharp focus: the cold winter night breeze coming in from the open window raising goose bumps on her skin, George shouting, the gunshots. The blood so thick and dark in the rays of the moonlight it looked like chocolate syrup. Louise had nearly convinced herself it was. Nearly.

"What was the decision?" Tanner prompted.

Louise shook her head. "It doesn't matter. It was so long ago. The point is, I made a mistake. A big one. And now I have to set things right." She thought of Salvatore and tried to keep the fear from her voice. "Before it's too late."

"Oh," Tanner said, soft-like, her eyes wide and glassy, a look of pure—what? Pity?—on her face. There weren't many things Louise hated more than being pitied, but when Tanner gripped the steering wheel and slowly pushed her foot down harder on the gas, bringing the car up to exactly nine miles over the speed limit, a little grin curved the corners of Louise's lips. Sometimes pity could work in your favor.

TANNER HAD A thousand questions running through her mind, starting with the obvious: If they weren't actually running from the police, then what was with that news story? Tanner wondered if it was all just some big mistake—a coincidence. She had seen a mug shot that *looked* like Mrs. Wilt, and then extenuating circumstances—the middle of the night wake-up; the cold, hard cash; the actual *getaway car* stowed in the backyard shed; the police sirens—had caused her to connect all the dots incorrectly. It made sense, actually, because Mrs. Wilt certainly didn't behave like someone on the run from the law. She clearly didn't care about disguising herself (except when her hair wasn't coiffed), and it wasn't as if she was trying to lie low like a criminal might, or remain unmemorable to passersby. (Tanner was certain *Leonard* was going to remember her, anyway. Ew.) Still, it had been on the tip of her tongue to ask. To confront her about the news, the mug shot, the jewel heist; to look in her eyes and make sure it was all a big misunderstanding. But then, how could she?

George was dying. And Mrs. Wilt may have said *business partner*, but it was so clear the way she talked about him—that wistful look in her eyes—that he was so much more. A first love? An unrequited love? A long-lost love? Tanner wasn't sure, but she was positive there was love involved. And though she had never been overly starry-eyed when it came to love—mainly because she had been so let down by it in her short life—Tanner couldn't help but be swept away by the romance of it all. Mrs. Wilt running to the *love of her life*—Tanner was sure of it now—to make amends for a decision she regretted.

Regret. Now that was a feeling Tanner was wildly intimate with. Regret for going to that party, for sure, and for how she had been treating everyone ever since, and for snitching on Vee and getting her suspended from the team. Regret for stepping backward instead of forward on that balcony. For making herself smaller. Yes, Tanner knew how it felt to make a mistake, to want to set things right before it was too late. And though it may have been too late for Tanner, it wasn't for Mrs. Wilt.

Tanner felt a sudden flush of empathy and understanding for the old woman that she had not experienced up to this point. If Mrs. Wilt needed to get to George before he kicked the bucket, then by God, Tanner was going to get her there. Who knew how much time he had left?

She drove for the rest of the afternoon and into the evening with purpose, stopping only for gas and quick bathroom breaks, loading up on chips and snack mix and gas station hot dogs to keep her hunger at bay. Each mile that ticked by filled her with a sense of accomplishment, and the small wave of hope she had felt that morning only grew—aided by the massive relief Tanner felt by no longer worrying about being on the wrong side of the law. She nearly laughed at how wrong she had gotten it all, until she remembered that George was at death's door.

They made it as far as North Platte, Nebraska, when Mrs. Wilt finally said in a resigned but firm voice, "That's enough. Let's stop here for the night."

Tanner glanced at the round analog clock in the dash—its thin white hands pointing to eight twenty-five. "Are you sure? I've still got a few more hours in me," Tanner said.

"Yes, but I don't."

"Oh. OK," she said, somewhat disappointed, as Tanner felt with her newfound energy, she could probably make it all the way to California without stopping.

She pulled off at the next exit, which had a road sign offering three hotels. "Which one?"

"Doesn't matter," Mrs. Wilt said, waving her hand. "Whichever is closest."

Tanner pulled into the Holiday Inn Express because the marquee announced free breakfast, which would save them time in the morning and get them back on the road faster.

As she was unloading their suitcases from the back of the Jaguar into the ground-floor room Tanner had paid for with cash in the lobby, she noticed Mrs. Wilt leaning very heavily onto her cane and walking with a more-evident-than-usual hitch in her step.

"Mrs. Wilt," Tanner said. "Are you OK?"

"I'm fine," she growled.

Tanner frowned, trying to think what Mrs. Wilt had done differently to possibly exacerbate her hip soreness. She gasped dramatically. "*Mrs. Wilt.* Did you get a . . . *sex* injury?"

The woman paused in her tracks and looked back at Tanner with one of her classic long, hard stares. "Don't be such a child. It's from sitting in the car for so long."

"And from that eight-hundred-mile walk yesterday," Tanner chided.

Mrs. Wilt ignored her.

Later, after they got settled (which of course consisted of Mrs. Wilt hanging every single article of clothing up in the closet, even though she was hurting and they would be there for less than twelve hours), Mrs. Wilt let out a groan of pain as she rolled in her supine position to turn the lamp off beside her bed.

Tanner sat up and turned the light back on. "Alright. Let me see."

"Let you see what?"

"Your hip."

Mrs. Wilt's body went rigid. "Absolutely not."

Tanner sighed. Naturally Mrs. Wilt was going to be difficult about it. "Come on. I think I can help. At least a little."

Mrs. Wilt eyed her dubiously, but Tanner stood anyway and retrieved the small complimentary lotion from the bathroom counter. After a brief standoff, Tanner looming at the edge of the bed, Mrs. Wilt clutching the sheets to her chin, she finally relented and allowed Tanner to gently pull the sheets down. After another brief pause, Mrs. Wilt rolled her eyes and lifted her nightdress to reveal her leg, the skin hanging loose and accordion-like, and then her hip, covered in a large swath of nude underwear—literal granny panties.

Tanner rubbed a dollop of lotion between her hands and very lightly began smoothing it on Mrs. Wilt's loose crepe-papery skin, working her fingers beneath the elastic of the underwear, gently massaging the tissue on and around the ten-inch straight line of scar peeking out from beneath it. Body tense, Mrs. Wilt sucked air through her teeth at the initial touch and then slowly, over time, relaxed into it.

"Where did you learn this?"

"Soccer," Tanner said. "Our trainer taught me some things." Tanner knew she was good at it—Vee used to beg for leg massages at night when they were watching trash TV, throwing her legs into Tanner's lap, cuing Grant (when he was there) to make his obnoxious lesbian jokes.

Her mom was good at it, too. Tanner thought of the multiple times her mom determinedly massaged her knee and leg in the months after the surgery, the way the nurse had shown her in order to increase blood flow and circulation, and to relieve the muscle tightening that naturally occurred around an injury. They both knew what she was really doing was hoping for a miracle. "Doctors have been wrong before, Tanner. I'm just saying, let's not give up all hope yet."

Tears unexpectedly sprang to her eyes as she thought of her mom's cool touch, her soothing voice. Why was she such a bitch to her all the time? She didn't mean to be. It wasn't her mom's fault that the balcony railing had collapsed when she leaned against it. Or Vee's, either.

She bit her lip, refusing to let actual tears fall, and continued rubbing Mrs. Wilt's hip. She registered the intimacy of the act—as well as the fact that she was not repulsed by her puckered, wrinkled skin, as she once might have been. Maybe she was just overly emotional and sympathetic—given what Mrs. Wilt had confided in her about a few hours earlier—but she felt nothing but tender affection for the old woman, so much so that it struck her as silly that she still referred to her in such a formal way.

"Mrs. Wilt," Tanner said, gingerly tugging the woman's nightdress down over her hip and pulling the sheets and blanket back over her rail-thin body, as a mom would tuck in a child for the night. "Given the . . . circumstances, don't you think we should be on a first-name basis?"

Mrs. Wilt opened her eyes, and Tanner stared into the bright greenish brown of them, sure Mrs. Wilt was having her own epiphany. A bond was growing between them—partly situational, sure, but also one of mutual respect and, dare she say . . . fondness? Tanner was overwhelmed by it, the feeling jarring into sharp relief just how *alone* she had felt these past months. Mrs. Wilt blinked, and then her lips, which had ever-so-slightly been curving upward, set themselves in a straight line.

"No. I do not."

Then she reached up, turned off the light, and rolled over onto her good hip in one fell swoop, leaving Tanner standing there in the dark, her hands sweet smelling and sticky with cheap lotion.

"Thank you for the massage," Mrs. Wilt said, her voice muffled a bit by the pillow. "Good night."

Tanner stared at the back of the woman for a second and then crawled into her bed and eventually fell asleep.

Until sometime during the night, when a high-pitched scream shattered the silence of the room, bolting Tanner directly out of her slumber.

22

HER HEART WAS pounding in her ears so loud, Tanner felt like she was underwater—unable to see or hear and move as fast as she wanted. She fumbled with the lamp, trying to find the switch to turn it on.

"Mrs. Wilt?" she said, the room finally flooding with light.

The woman was sitting straight up, too, staring directly at Tanner.

"Did you hear that?" Tanner asked. A ridiculous question. How could anyone *not* have heard the ear-piercing shriek that still rang in Tanner's ears? She glanced around wildly, half expecting someone else to be standing there. She was still half-asleep, but her synapses were all firing in fight-or-flight mode, and she couldn't make sense of what was happening. Mrs. Wilt didn't respond, and when Tanner turned back to her, she noticed the woman wasn't looking at her, per se. She was looking in her direction, but her eyes were unfocused. Unseeing. Then Mrs. Wilt's face screwed up in what

Tanner could only describe as abject terror, and her hands shot up to her face as she screamed again, this time in words: "No! No. Get off me! Get off!"

Tanner jumped up and closed the three steps between them, wrapping her arm around Mrs. Wilt's shoulder. "Mrs. Wilt! Stop it," she said, shaking her lightly. "Stop!"

Finally, Mrs. Wilt's hands stilled, and she turned to look at Tanner and blinked. She blinked again. "What are you doing here?"

"What do you mean? You were acting crazy. Screaming and moving your hands."

"Oh. I must have been having a nightmare."

"A nightmare?!"

"Yes," she said sharply, coming back to herself. "You've never had a nightmare before?"

Tanner, her heart still beating rapidly even though the initial fright had diminished, scoffed in disbelief. That was *more* than a nightmare.

"Could you kindly take your hands off me?"

Tanner realized she was still clutching Mrs. Wilt's shoulders—and rather tightly—which was how she noticed the vibration coursing through the woman's right arm. She let go, but not before glancing down at Mrs. Wilt's hand.

"You're shaking," she said.

Mrs. Wilt ignored her and yawned. "Turn off the light." She leaned back until her head rested on the pillow once more.

Tanner didn't move. "Are you serious? How am I supposed to sleep after that?"

"Try lying down and closing your eyes. Works wonders."

"Mrs. Wilt," Tanner said sternly. "What is going on? Why are you shaking?"

The woman didn't open her eyes. She just lay there, unmoving, but Tanner was determined not to back down. She remained seated beside Mrs. Wilt, willing to wait her out. Finally, after about a minute of silence, Mrs. Wilt opened one eye as if to say, *You're still here?*

"Fine." Mrs. Wilt let out a light sigh and opened the other eye. "If you must know, the nightmares are called a parasomnia, according to my doctor. Like a sleep terror, but worse. I get them about once a month. Or more."

"And they're so scary that you actually tremble in fear?"

"No. That and the nightmares are due to the Parkinson's."

"What?" The words shot out of Tanner's mouth like a bullet. "You have *Parkinson's*?"

"I do."

Tanner's jaw went slack. When she found words, she said, "Why didn't you tell me?"

"What for?"

"I'm your *caretaker.* Seems like something I should be aware of."

"You're my driver," Mrs. Wilt corrected. "I'm fine. I take some medication that helps with the hand tremors, and I deal with a few nightmares."

Tanner cocked her head. She didn't know much about the condition, except that some famous actor from the eighties had had it—and that it was incurable.

"Will you be . . . OK?"

Mrs. Wilt shrugged. "It's degenerative, so it's only downhill from here. The tremors will get worse. At some point, I likely won't be able to walk at all. I'll have hallucinations, dementia. Sounds like a real picnic."

"Aren't you scared?" Tanner asked, immediately cringing that she said it out loud. But she couldn't help it—Mrs. Wilt was being so flippant about everything, so matter-of-fact, as if all she had was a common cold.

Mrs. Wilt's eyes rounded in surprise, but she ignored the question. "Can you move? You're looming over me like you're trying to sell me a used car. It's unnerving."

"I'm sorry," Tanner said. "I just thought you might want to talk about it."

"Why? Does talking about it make it go away?"

"No. But neither does *not* talking about it."

Mrs. Wilt frowned. "Now you sound like Jules. She wanted me to go to some support group."

It was Tanner's turn to frown. Jules was the last person she wanted to sound like.

"Tanner, you're still looming. Go lie down. And turn out the light."

Tanner considered Mrs. Wilt for another beat and then stood, pulling the chain on the light before crawling back into her own bed. She turned until she was lying on her back and stared up into the pitch dark of the room. Parkinson's. Hallucinations. Dementia. It was all so . . . much. Lost in her own thoughts, she almost didn't hear Mrs. Wilt when she said in a low, quiet voice, "Yes."

Tanner froze, unsure at first that Mrs. Wilt had spoken at all.

"What?"

"I am scared."

Stunned by the admission, Tanner held her breath, mostly because she wasn't sure how to respond. Mrs. Wilt had never been anything less than invulnerable. Tanner didn't think she could possibly be scared of *anything* (aside from heights, of course)—but she also knew Mrs. Wilt enough to know that was exactly what she wanted everyone to think. And she knew how much it probably cost the woman to say it out loud.

Tanner wanted to console her in some way. But she knew from her own experience there was nothing she could say to Mrs. Wilt that wouldn't either be a lie or sound patronizing. Instead, Tanner did the only thing she could—match Mrs. Wilt's vulnerability in kind.

"You know what I'm scared of?" she whispered.

Mrs. Wilt didn't respond.

Tanner swallowed. "I'm scared soccer was the only thing I'm really, really good at." She knew it sounded a little ridiculous. Inferior in gravity compared to Mrs. Wilt's condition. Tanner wasn't *dying*, after all. But she was grieving, too—the loss of the future she thought she was going to have. An ability she had counted on and drawn confidence and—more importantly—her identity from. Without soccer, who was she? But that wasn't all she was scared of. Or even the biggest thing.

She took a deep breath, and then said in an even smaller voice, "I think I'm broken. Like I don't even know how to be a person anymore. How to be . . . anything." Like water circling the drain, her words crept close to the truth, but she couldn't bring herself to say her biggest fear aloud: that she had been so awful to everyone in her life—what she had done to Vee, how she had been treating her mom and the rest of her family—she thought maybe she was actually a bad person. Deep down where it mattered. And that she deserved to be lonely. To be alone. Her stomach felt cold and hollow. Weightless, but not in the good, airy way people usually mean.

Still, Mrs. Wilt didn't respond, and the dark air between them grew thick with silence. Tanner strained to listen for the woman's steady breathing and wondered if she had fallen back asleep already. Or maybe she was secretly rolling her eyes.

"Mrs. Wilt?" Tanner whispered.

"Hush," came the old woman's sharp reply. "I'm trying to think of something else you're good at."

Tanner paused, as it took her brain a second longer than it should have to catch up. "Ha, ha," she said dryly, but found she couldn't keep the smile from creeping onto her lips. And then a genuine laugh escaped.

"For what it's worth," Mrs. Wilt said, "I don't think you're broken."

Tanner felt her eyes sting once again, her nose tingle.

"You don't?"

"No," she said. "You're just human like the rest of us."

Tanner let out a slow and quiet exhale as Mrs. Wilt said softly, mostly under her breath, "Aren't we a pair?"

It was a throwaway line, Tanner knew. Something people just said. But she clung on to the *we* like a drowning person to a life vest, taking solace in how it made her feel—like maybe she wasn't so alone after all.

WITH THE ADDITION of six metal serving urns on a counter running the length of the room, the lobby of the Holiday Inn Express the next morning transformed into a breakfast buffet. Louise sat at a square table in an uncomfortable faux wooden chair, waiting for Tanner to get back with her plate. Louise had no idea what had gotten into the girl—why or how she had turned into a bona fide Florence Nightingale. It was a touch overbearing, but it was also a little nice. And she had to admit the ministrations to her hip really did make it feel better. Why couldn't they do *that* in physical therapy, rather than all those torturous exercises? She had told Jules PT was nothing but a racket, and this just proved her right.

Furthermore—and this didn't surprise anyone more than herself—she felt lighter this morning somehow, and thought it could, *possibly*, be in part due to sharing her diagnosis with Tanner. Talking about it. Not that she would admit it to anyone, least of all Jules. She had been surprised by the ease with which she admitted her fear to Tanner, and wondered if the girl was easy to talk to because she was a good listener or because she was so busy pitying herself, Mrs. Wilt didn't have to worry about the girl pitying her. She suspected it was the latter. But still, Louise had to admit that against all odds, there was something about the girl she liked.

"They didn't have poached eggs, so this was the best I could do," Tanner said, sliding a flimsy white foam plate in front of Louise, along with plastic-wrapped silverware. Louise eyed the hard-boiled egg, wheat toast, and mix of chunk cantaloupe and honeydew, and then looked at Tanner's own, piled high with pancakes, syrup, and four link sausages. She had no idea how the girl stayed so skinny. She could never have eaten like that—even in her twenties.

A young man with a few wiry mustache hairs above his lip and a belly straining against his white button-up shirt stopped at their table. "More coffee?" he asked.

"Please," Tanner said, pushing her cup toward him.

Louise pulled out the road map from the bag and set it on the table. "It looks like we have two options today. We can stay on 80 through Wyoming, or we can pick up 76 and then 70 through Colorado. The distance is roughly the same, but if I recall, Wyoming is a bit prettier of a drive."

She looked from the map to Tanner, but Tanner was staring past her, frozen in place like someone had pressed pause on a remote control, a fork held midway to her mouth, a sliver of pancake stuck on the end, syrup dripping off of it into a sticky pool on the table. "Tanner? You are making a mess. What in the world?" Louise turned to see what had captivated Tanner's attention so, when she spied a television mounted in the corner of the room where the wall met the ceiling. The volume was off, and she was about to comment on the child's clear addiction to screens when she realized what exactly she was looking at: a photo of herself, alongside one of Tanner with the words MISSING—CALL WITH ANY INFORMATION underneath.

"Oh for Pete's sake," Louise said under her breath. "Jules knows I hate that picture." It was the one from the church directory two years ago, when her stylist, Keely, had been on vacation in the Florida Keys.

"Why do they think we're missing?" Tanner asked in a tight, low, unnaturally calm voice.

"It's my daughter, I'm sure," Louise said. "She always goes worst-case scenario."

"Really?" Tanner asked. "And how do you explain that?"

Louise glanced back at the screen, where the words underneath their photos had changed to WANTED FOR QUESTIONING IN 1975 COLD CASE. Louise cocked her head, her stomach dropping. To make matters worse, the next picture plastered on the screen was of the 1968 mint-green Jaguar—not Louise's car specifically, but nearly an exact replica. Louise's heart nearly stopped completely. How *on earth* did they know about the car? Before she could begin to sort what it all meant, Tanner spoke, her voice so low Louise almost couldn't hear her: "It *was* you."

She turned to the girl, crinkling her brow. "What was me?"

"On the news!"

"*What* was on the news?" Louise wished the girl would just speak plainly instead of this cryptic guessing game.

"You were," Tanner hissed, her eyes darting from side to side. "The day we left. They put up some computer-generated mug shot and said you were wanted by the FBI. Well, I wasn't exactly sure it was you, but then you came in my room that night—"

"What?" But the word came out like a breath. A hard exhale. It didn't make sense. Nothing Louise had seen on the television or anything Tanner was saying made sense. She leaned forward, her heart now beating so hard, she thought it might vibrate the table. "Tell me exactly what they said."

"That you stole jewels!" Tanner now had a hand on either side of her face, covering herself from any onlookers, even though the other three people in the makeshift dining room were busily eating their overprocessed breakfasts, not concerned at all with what was on the television *or* the two women having an intense whispered back-and-forth. "From some hotel."

Louise's entire world narrowed and shifted, as if the earth had been knocked out of orbit and was in free fall in space. "Oh my God."

"They said a lot of other stuff, too! I don't remember it all. Something about how you were likely living under an alias and, and, and . . . that you had lived in Italy and some other places."

Shit! Shit, shit, shit. Louise closed her eyes, her mind spinning as fast as those teacups Charlie had made the whole family go on at Disney World on a family trip years ago. All this time, she thought for sure she'd gotten away with it—not with Salvatore, of course, but with the law, anyway. Sure, she got spooked by police sirens now and then, but she hadn't actually believed they would ever find out. For starters, besides George, Salvatore was the only person who knew what she had done, and Salvatore would *never* talk to the police. Ever. That much she knew, and that was what she had secretly been counting on all these years. So, *how did they know*?

It didn't matter how, Louise quickly decided, her pragmatic side busting in and taking over. She needed to figure out what to do, and fast. So they didn't catch her before she could get to George. And the most immediate problem was that despite her never having transferred the title over from James when she bought the car, somehow the FBI knew about the Jaguar. The very noticeable, very rare mint-green Jaguar that was sitting wide open in the parking lot not fifty yards from Louise right this second. An idea came to her fast as a lightning bolt, and she opened her eyes, intending to look for the young man who had offered them coffee. But the first thing she saw was Tanner, staring at her pointedly, her eyes wild as an untamed horse about to be roped and ridden.

"So it's true?" Tanner whispered. "It's all true? We *are* on the run from the police?"

Louise opened her mouth, unsure of how to respond. "Yes, but I didn't know. Until now."

"Is George really dying?"

"Yes," Louise said, thrown by the question. She had braced herself for the girl's ire, panic—a complete downward spiral to rival the one from the first night they fled. What she got was something different.

"OK," Tanner said, her gaze hardening, resolute. Then she arched an eyebrow. "Do you think we should get disguises *now*?"

23

CONVERSATION IN THE FBI'S ATLANTA FIELD OFFICE, FOUR DAYS AFTER LOUISE WAS REPORTED MISSING TO THE POLICE, AT LUNCHTIME

"MOTHER FUUU . . . ARFERGNÜGEN!" Lorna picked up the unwieldy roller chair and slammed it down onto the industrial carpeted floor with an unsatisfying thud, the metal wheels squeaking. This was the reason she hated working out of field offices other than her own in Boston—or more specifically, hated working with teams other than her own. Her team would never—*never*—have made a mistake as colossal as this one.

"Jamal," Lorna said through clenched teeth. "I remember specifically saying to distribute this BOLO internally and to NOT leak it to the press for THIS EXACT FLUFFING REASON." For most of her adult life, swearing had been a staple in Lorna's vocabulary—as common as pepperoni on pizza. Recently, at the behest of her nine-year-old son, Philip (who had somehow been born with such a sense of propriety that if Lorna hadn't been there when she pushed his overly large head out of her overly small vagina, she would question if he was really hers), she had been trying to tone down her language. But this fresh-out-of-Quantico (and straight off the turnip truck, if you asked Lorna) noob was certainly testing Lorna's resolve.

"Yes, ma'am. I'm sorry, ma'am."

"Enough with the DOGGONE *ma'am*." That was another thing about these southern field offices—the old-fashioned manners were enough to grate Lorna's very last nerve. "I'm not your goddamned grandmother." Oops, it slipped. Well, Philip wasn't here. What he didn't know wouldn't hurt him.

"Yes ma'—Mrs. . . . I mean, Special Agent Huang. It was a mistake."

"Well, your mistake caused our POI to ditch her very recognizable car—the one advantage we had in finding her." Lorna had just gotten the call that police officers in North Platte, Nebraska, had pulled over a seventeen-year-old kid who was given the keys to a Jaguar that morning as a "tip" by "some old lady" while he was working the breakfast shift at the Holiday Inn Express. "She said she didn't have any cash," he said, by way of explanation. As if people offered their cars in lieu of gratuity on a regular basis. Poor kid probably thought he had won the lottery until he saw the flashing blue lights behind him. Naturally, when police got to the hotel, Patricia was gone, without a trace. Lorna pinched the bridge of her nose, attempting to ward off the headache she felt coming on.

"Now, please get out of my office and do your job. *Better* than you have been doing it. You can start with getting me that file I asked for on Louise Wilt." She looked at him pointedly. "*Yesterday.*"

"Yes, ma'am." Jamal's eyes went wild. "I mean, Special Agent ma'am, er . . . Huang. I'm almost finished with it." He nearly tripped over his own two feet trying to get out the office door.

Good Lord, where did they get these children from? Lorna could swear the new agent trainees got younger every year. That one looked nearly as young as Philip—who would do a much better job of it, Lorna was sure.

Lorna took a deep breath and exhaled, reminding herself it wasn't Jamal's fault *completely* that she was agitated. She was the one who spooked Patricia in the first place, releasing the age-progressed image to the Atlanta media, causing the woman to run. She hadn't really believed Patricia would still *be* in Atlanta; she was just hoping for another lead. But on the plus side, it let her know her gut instinct had been right.

Lorna drummed her fingers on the desk. *Where are you going, Patricia?*

She picked up her cell and called Baskers in her home office.

"Whatcha need, Lorna?" She adored working with Baskers for many reasons, two of which were that she could count on him to do his job and he didn't waste time with small talk.

"Phone records for the Holiday Inn Express in North Platte, Nebraska, for the last twenty-four hours. Outgoing calls only." She knew it was likely to be too much information to be helpful, but perhaps they'd find an anomaly that they could pinpoint to Patricia.

"You got it."

"Thanks."

While waiting for her next move to come to her, Lorna flipped through the thick case file on her desk, staring at the black-and-white photos of a svelte and well-dressed Patricia Nichols a few footsteps behind Salvatore D'Amato on the streets of Brooklyn in the weeks leading up to the robbery (D'Amato was always being tailed by the FBI for something or other). She reread the front-page newspaper clipping in the file from the *Boston Globe*.

January 2, 1976, Boston, MA—In the early morning hours of New Year's Day, when revelers were dropping into bed at the Copley Plaza hotel from resplendent parties, two armed men dressed in clown wigs and play glasses with fake noses handcuffed the skeleton crew of a staff at the hotel's front desk, held the security guard at gunpoint, retrieved the master key set, and methodically unlocked 52 safety deposit boxes in the hotel's vault for guests.

No one was injured, but the thieves made off with more than $3 million of jewels and cash, including the famous 37-carat Kinsey diamond, fashioned into a ring by the renowned jeweler Gustavo Trifari in the early nineteenth century and worn mere hours earlier to a New Year's Eve fete by screen siren Penny Wyman.

"The robbers certainly knew what they were doing," said Boston Police Sergeant Carl Yewl. "We believe they had intel that Ms. Wyman planned to stay at the hotel and return her ring to the vault after wearing it to her evening celebration."

The seven staff members detained agreed the two thieves were polite to a fault, one going so far as to apologize for confining them. Before departing, the bandits gave a $50 bill to each hotel staff member they held captive and left at approximately 6:15 a.m., just before the 7:00 a.m. shift arrived.

While Yewl says they are following up on a few strong leads, including looking into New York Mafia kingpin Salvatore D'Amato, no arrests have been made, and the stolen goods have yet to be recovered.

The Copley Plaza Heist file officially became a cold case in 1981, five years after the crime, with no viable leads and in accordance with the statute of limitations—meaning even if an agent were to find the perpetrators in connection with the armed robbery, no arrests could likely be made, unless there were extenuating circumstances, like proof of racketeering or falsifying identification or murder. But due to the high-profile nature of the lead suspect, Salvatore D'Amato, and the publicity surrounding the case, agents continued to poke around in the file every few years—it would be a huge coup to any field agent to recover the Kinsey Diamond, whether an arrest was made or not. Lorna was the fourth agent to inherit it. But she was the first female. Maybe that's why when she was going through the list of leads and associates of Salvatore D'Amato, Patricia Nichols stuck out like a sore thumb. According to the original detective, Patricia had been a "girlfriend" of D'Amato for a few weeks prior to the robbery. They had searched for her in vain, hoping she may have some inside information due to her proximity to D'Amato in the weeks leading up to the crime, but she had vanished as thoroughly as the Kinsey diamond. And while she was just a footnote in the case file—not even a person of interest—Lorna found it all a little too convenient.

Since the beginning of time, women had often been underestimated for their abilities. Ignored. Looked over. As she had been twice for promotion the past five years. Or, if one needed a second example, her dad's favorite (a historian, he volunteered at the Fort Laurens museum in Ohio and knew more about the American Revolution than was necessary for anyone to know, which meant Lorna knew more than was necessary for anyone to know as well)—Sybil Ludington, the daughter of Colonel Henry Ludington, who got on her horse to warn colonial forces of British advancement—riding twice the distance of her male counterpart Paul Revere, and getting none of the renown.

And it didn't take a rocket scientist in this case to see that Patricia Nichols had a perfect opportunity to make off with more than $3 million worth of jewels from her Mafia boyfriend.

It just took a woman.

Deeper in the file, Lorna had found the detail that set the current chain of events into motion. Special Agent Kristoff Herman, the third detective to research this cold case, had gone as far as to release the photos of Patricia to the news—a common practice in cold cases to reignite the public's interest and hopefully drum up new clues—in her hometown of Akron, Ohio, ten years earlier. According to his notes, Kristoff hadn't thought her a suspect, either, but was hoping to find her for questioning about Salvatore (seeing as how several federal agents had visited him in San Quentin over the years, and received exactly zero information in return). And Kristoff got one good lead: a woman who preferred to remain anonymous, but had last seen Patty while she had been on a college visit with her daughter to Ohio State sometime in the late nineties.

Lorna let her eyes graze over the transcript of that call, a chill running up her spine as she remembered the conversation with Patricia's kids that confirmed this interaction:

ANONYMOUS TIPSTER:

I do hope she's OK. Patty saved my life. If there's anything I can do to return the favor—

HERMAN: Where did she say she was living at the time?

TIPSTER: She didn't.

[*PAUSE*]

TIPSTER: Although . . . now that I think about it, I do remember her daughter complaining about the cold and saying it never got that cold in Atlanta. Or was it Alabama? One of those places.

Kristoff had then repeated the process, running the pictures of Patricia on the news, focusing on Atlanta and Alabama, to no avail.

All Lorna did was take that a step further, reasoning that Patricia likely looked a lot different now than she had in 1975. Using age-progression software and a tech artist, she released the new image to Atlanta media and . . . bingo. A phone call from Officer Shield saying her FBI photo looked an awful lot like his missing person Louise Wilt. Sometimes in cold cases, all you needed was a lucky break.

A knock at her door jerked Lorna's head up.

"Mrs. . . . er, I mean . . . Special Agent Huang?"

"Yes, Jamal?"

"I'm done with the report. On Louise Wilt."

She held one hand out, taking the papers he offered, and shooed him away with her other. Once he shut the door, she glanced at the first page, unsurprised Louise's social security popped up not only for herself but for an eight-year-old girl named Maylene Winters, who'd died in 1963. It was a common enough practice before the age of the Internet and national databases for criminals to buy new identities, including social security numbers, on the black market—and they most often were numbers belonging to dead people.

She scanned the rest of the pages, finding nothing else of note—until she reached the criminal background check. Lorna paused, her brow lifting in surprise. A gun to her head, she would have sworn Patricia had made sure to play it straight living life as Louise Wilt in order to avoid getting caught. And she did, mostly, save for one incident in 1984, when Louise Wilt pleaded guilty to theft. More intriguing, the amount stolen in question was $532 in personal checks. What would a woman with $3 million in jewels—$27 million in today's money—need with such a paltry sum? And why would she risk it?

But having worked theft and robbery cases for most of her career, Lorna found she knew the answer before she even asked the question. For criminals like Patricia Nichols, the thrill of the risk was more often the reward in itself.

Or, as Lorna's nǎi nai used to say: A fox may grow gray, but never good.

24

TANNER COULDN'T EXPLAIN what came over her when she saw her picture on the morning news in the Holiday Inn Express. Or when she realized (again) that Mrs. Wilt was, in fact, the wanted jewel thief. It wasn't shock or panic, as one might expect. It was a sense of . . . calm. Maybe because she had known all along, deep down, who Mrs. Wilt was, ever since seeing the rendering of her on the five o'clock news—and this simply confirmed it.

Or maybe it was the look in Mrs. Wilt's eyes when she said she didn't know they had actually been on the lam. Tanner believed her.

Or maybe it was the simple, and admittedly pathetic, fact that Louise had called them a pair. And Tanner wanted so desperately to be part of a team once again—even if the other half of that team was a wanted felon—that she took it to heart.

Regardless of the reason, while she knew she should be scared that they were being pursued in a national manhunt—*terrified*, really—she was now more determined than ever to get Mrs. Wilt to George. To finish what she'd started.

"What's the plan here?" Tanner asked, after they made it safely back to their room. Clearly, Mrs. Wilt *had* a plan and was currently acting on it, which had started with handing their server the keys to the Jaguar as a tip—a *tip*!—but only after borrowing his cell phone. Mrs. Wilt retreated to a corner of the lobby, and Tanner just watched as the woman made a series of phone calls and then returned to the table; handed the cell back to the kid with the shit-eating grin, along with the keys; and then said calmly to Tanner, "I need to go pack."

Back in the hotel room, Mrs. Wilt didn't bother looking up from the pair of pants she was carefully removing from the hanger and folding in the yawning suitcase on the bed.

"Mrs. Wilt?" Tanner prompted again.

The woman step-thumped over to the bathroom counter, where she proceeded to apply her pink lipstick before methodically tucking it and the rest of her toiletries into her zippered makeup bag.

The phone trilled.

"Would you get that?" Mrs. Wilt said.

"What?" Tanner asked, frustrated that she wasn't getting any answers, as it rang again.

"Answer the phone."

Tanner strode to the landline on the nightstand between the two beds and lifted the receiver to her ear, heart pounding as the brief thought entered her mind that the hotel was already surrounded by a SWAT team and helicopters, and on the other end of the line was a hostage negotiator.

"Hello?"

"Ma'am?" said a gruff voice.

"Yes?" she said weakly.

"You ordered a taxi? I'm out front."

Tanner paused and then swallowed her fear, letting relief take its place. She knew Mrs. Wilt had a plan. "Thank you." She hung up and looked at the woman. "We're taking a taxi?"

"I'm taking a taxi, yes."

"What do you mean?"

"A taxi? It's transportation for people who don't have a car."

"No, you said *I*," Tanner said, and she realized it was the second time Mrs. Wilt had used the singular pronoun. "Are you . . . are you *leaving* me?"

"I think it would be best for us to part ways here, yes."

"No!" Tanner nearly shouted.

Mrs. Wilt eyed her. "I'll pay you the money, if that's what you're worried about."

"No, that's not . . . how are you going to . . ." Flustered, Tanner stumbled over her words.

Mrs. Wilt was back by her suitcase, zipping it and hefting it up and onto the floor. "You can call the local police when I'm gone—they'll get in touch with the FBI—but please give me a few hours' head start."

"What?" Tanner was reeling now. "No! You *need* me." But as she said the words, it became apparent the truth was the other way around. Tanner needed Mrs. Wilt. Or needed to be needed, anyway. It occurred to her that was what had felt so good yesterday—having an objective, a goal. Something she'd been sorely lacking the last six months of her life. Something her mom kept harping on like a broken record. "You just need to find a new purpose in life, that's all," her mom said, chirpily and often, as if Tanner should just go to Target and toss a new purpose in her cart along with a throw pillow.

Tanner's entire spine would tighten, her fists clenching. "I *had* a purpose," she'd spit in return.

But now she knew her mom had been right (not that she would ever admit that out loud). She did need to get out of the house. To stop all her navel-gazing and wallowing. To find a new purpose.

And now that she had found one (albeit with a woman on the run from the law, which was likely *not* what her mom had hoped for), she was scared. Not just of facing the FBI by herself and answering all their questions (a prospect she found distressing, at best)—but of losing that feeling that she had just finally recaptured, of having a reason to get up in the morning. She was terrified that alone, without Mrs. Wilt, she'd find herself just floating along in the current again, instead of paddling with intent.

"I needed you to drive and you did, and I do appreciate that," Mrs. Wilt said. "But I've called a friend and I can take it from here." She reached into her purse, and Tanner knew it was for the money.

"Stop!" Tanner said. She knew it was nonsensical, begging a wanted felon to let her come with. But strangely, it also seemed to be the only thing that actually made sense. "I'm coming. I'm making sure you get to George. And I won't take no for an answer."

Mrs. Wilt cocked her head, studying her, and Tanner wasn't sure if it was her imagination, or if she saw the slightest hint of a smile on the old woman's face.

"In for a penny, in for a pound, right?" she added.

Mrs. Wilt's expression remained stern, and then—ever so slowly—she did smile, not wide enough for Tanner to see the metal fillings in her back teeth or anything, but enough. "OK," Mrs. Wilt said. "Get your things."

A whoosh of relief flooded her system, and Tanner scrambled to where her suitcase was on the floor, clothes falling out of it in disarray.

She stuffed them all in, zipped it up, and then stood, following Mrs. Wilt out the door into the bright sunshine where a black Ford Escape with a taxi marquee on its roof sat idling in the parking lot.

"Wait," Tanner said, grabbing Mrs. Wilt's arm to slow her before they reached the car.

"Yes?"

"You still have to tell them you kidnapped me, if we get caught."

Tanner may have been acting rashly, but she wasn't stupid.

"SO, WHAT'S THE plan?" Tanner asked for the second time in as many hours. After getting their bags out of the back and accepting the cash from Mrs. Wilt's hand, the taxi driver departed, leaving them standing in the parking lot of a large brick Catholic church, abutting an even larger cemetery in Fort Morgan, Colorado.

She turned to look at Mrs. Wilt, but the woman was no longer beside her. She was step-thumping her way to the front of the church. Tanner rushed after her and caught up in time to slip into the door behind her. As her eyes adjusted to the dim light, she followed Mrs. Wilt through the vestibule and then into the grand nave with a tall vaulted ceiling, and stunning stained-glass windows on either side filtering the sun's rays. A few people were scattered among the pews, heads bowed.

Mrs. Wilt crossed herself, and Tanner furrowed her brow. "I thought you were Methodist," she whispered.

"Raised Catholic," Mrs. Wilt replied. "Old habits."

"What are we doing here?"

"We're waiting." Mrs. Wilt slipped into the back pew, and Tanner sat beside her, taking in the scenery, starting with the very large and intimidating true-to-life sculpture of Jesus on the cross at the front of the church above the pulpit, and she remembered her neighbor growing up, Mrs. Danbury, who made excellent thumbprint cookies to entice the neighborhood children to her house so she could share the gospel with them. "You have a friend in Jesus," she would say, while crumbs cascaded down Tanner and Marty's shirts. Tanner didn't remember much else, except that the woman would end every sentence with "Mm-hmm, amen."

Tanner got a sinking feeling in her stomach. "The friend you called," she whispered to Mrs. Wilt. "It's not *God*, is it?" She respected people's beliefs, but thought they might need a little more than faith to get out of the situation they were currently in.

"Shh," Mrs. Wilt hushed her again, more sharply this time, and Tanner closed her mouth. Mrs. Wilt checked her wristwatch, and then readjusted her body, settling into the hard pew. In a few minutes, she was nodding off, lightly snoring, her head slowly falling toward her chest.

"Mrs. Wilt!"

"Huh?"

"You're sleeping."

"Not anymore," she said, her voice low. "*Someone* keeps talking."

Tanner crossed her arms. "Are you going to tell me what we're doing here?"

Mrs. Wilt grunted. "Just wake me when you see the priest."

FORTY-FIVE MINUTES TICKED by before Tanner finally nudged Louise, who startled, opened her eyes, and found Tanner staring at her. It took her a second to remember where she was, and then it all came flooding back—the news, the taxi ride. And while she felt a twinge of guilt for allowing Tanner to stay the course, she also had to admit she was glad the girl had stuck around. Perhaps she was getting soft in her old age.

"The priest," Tanner said, nodding her head to the front of the church toward a man striding past the prayer candles. The spitting image of Ronald Kepoe, save for his mother's blue eyes (though she couldn't see them from where she was sitting), Tony (or *Father* Tony, she supposed) was in his black cassock, clutching a Bible and making his way to the confession booth. Louise waited until he disappeared into his side of it, and then pushed herself to stand.

"Oh my God, are you going to confession?" Tanner hissed, sitting up. "You could have just done that back in Nebraska rather than making us drive all the way out here."

"Wait here," Louise said, ignoring the barb, and made her way to the front of the church, slipping into the other side of the confessional, closing the door behind her, and sitting down on the hard bench in the semidarkness.

"Bless me, Father, for I have sinned," she said automatically, surprised at how rote the words were from her childhood.

"How many days since your last confession?" His voice was low and soothing. Kind. So nothing like Ronald Kepoe, after all.

"Sixty-six . . ." Louise paused, trying to multiply the numbers in her head. She stared at the ceiling of the booth. "Years. Which would be twenty-four thousand days, give or take?"

Father Tony didn't respond right away. He cleared his throat. "Welcome back," he said.

"I'm not actually here to confess," she admitted. "I knew your mother." She paused, but when Tony didn't respond, she carried on. "I didn't receive a Christmas card from her this year, so I assume she's passed."

"She did," he said quietly. "It'll be a year next month."

"I'm sorry to hear that. She was very proud of you, you should know, even if she didn't understand your . . . calling. To be fair, when she named you Anthony, I told her you'd either be a priest or the owner of a pizzeria."

Louise heard a chuckle and then a light sniffle, and she remained quiet, giving the man his space for remembering. "What are you here for," he said finally, "if not to confess?"

"Well, I helped your mother some time ago, and I'm in the position where I could use some help now, and I was hoping you might oblige."

"What kind of help do you need?"

"Just a place to stay—for a few hours, max, until a friend meets me there."

"All are welcome in God's church," he said.

"Thank you, but I need somewhere more . . . secluded."

He paused. "Are you . . . in danger?" She could hear the scrutiny in his voice—she could nearly hear the wheels in his brain turning, trying to piece together what she *wasn't* saying.

"You could say that."

Another pause. "And how did you know my mother?"

There it was. The million-dollar question. Louise wasn't sure Irene had ever told her kids about her life . . . before. And if not, it wasn't Louise's place to break that news to him—but he also would be much less inclined to help her if he didn't know. She closed her eyes, praying—they were in a church, after all—that Irene had told him. "Like I said," she said weakly. "I helped her once."

Silence. Seconds ticked by, but to Louise it felt like hours. Finally he spoke, so softly Louise put her ear up to the divider. "Patty," he said. "Is that you?"

"Yes," she said, relief rushing through her. "Oh, thank God." She paused. "Er . . . *gosh*. I wasn't sure she had told you."

"*Told* us—you were like a deity in our house," he paused. "Sorry, Father."

Louise grinned.

"You said you need a place to stay?"

"Yes. Five to six hours, max."

"My sister Rosie lives just outside of town. I can drive you."

"That's very kind, but the thing is, Tony . . . *Father* . . . that it's possible some people may come here looking for me. Soon." Louise had to assume the taxi driver would see their wanted photos at some point and call the authorities when he put two and two together. She hoped she had at least his four hour-drive back to Kearney to make it out of the church and somewhere safe before that happened. An hour of that cushion was already gone. "I can't ask you to lie and say you haven't seen me."

"But I haven't seen you," Father Tony replied.

"Exactly."

"Ah," he said, everything clicking at once. "I forgot you've done this before."

"Asked a priest to cover for me? No. This is a first."

"Mm," he said.

"I kind of wish you'd gone with the pizzeria."

"You and my mother both." She could hear the smile in his voice. "Do you have something to write with?"

Louise reached into her bag for a pencil and her crossword book. She scribbled the numbers he gave her on the inside cover. "There's a phone in the church office. You can call her from there."

"Will she know?"

"Who you are? Without a doubt."

"Thank you so much," Louise said, pushing herself to stand.

"No, Patty. Thank you," he said, and she could hear the emotion once again in his voice. "Go with God."

Louise paused. She was pretty sure God wasn't on the side of thieves.

Or murderers.

"I will," she said, because priest or not—what was one more lie?

TANNER HAD NO idea what had happened in that confessional, but it had all begun to feel very *Da Vinci Code* (a book she'd had to read in Intro to Symbolism in Art when she was a freshman), and it didn't take much for Tanner to become convinced that Mrs. Wilt had tapped into some underground network of criminals that was going to help them get to George undetected—and possibly uncover stolen paintings while they were at it.

"Wait here," she said when she step-thumped her way back to Tanner after fifteen minutes in the booth. "I've got to make a phone call."

"Another one?"

Fifteen minutes after that, they were standing back in the parking lot, the afternoon sun bright in the sky, a light breeze ruffling the wisps of hair that had snuck out of Tanner's ponytail. Mrs. Wilt checked her wristwatch.

"Now are you going to tell me what we're doing?"

"Waiting for a friend."

"The one you called from that waiter's cell phone?"

"No, the one I called from the church office. She'll pick us up and we'll wait at her house for the friend I called from the waiter's cell phone. And he'll drive us the rest of the way to George."

"Oh." Simple enough. Although for being on the run, there was a lot of standing around and waiting involved. Tanner had rather thought it might be more . . . *exciting.*

"Is your friend's house a safe house?"

"It's a house that's safe, yes."

"Mm," Tanner said.

A few more seconds passed.

"I still think we should at least change our hair."

"I'm sure Rosie has scissors at her house."

"Really?"

Tanner brightened at the prospect.

"Don't cut bangs, though."

"Why not?" Tanner wondered if that was some amateur criminal move—maybe the first thing police looked for in a change of appearance was a new fringe.

"You'd look terrible with bangs. You don't have the right-shaped face."

"Oh."

FIVE HOURS LATER, Tanner sat on a floral couch in a living room, peering out the window at the driveway, waiting some more. She'd never been in a safe house before, but had hoped it would be a little cooler—sleek and modern with a closetful of displayed weapons that opened behind a hidden wall at the touch of a button. Not like a suburban house that looked very similar to her mom and dad's place, down to the eclectic mix of antique furniture, microfiber couches, and Ikea rugs and curtain panels. And the home's owner, Rosie, didn't exactly seem like a hardened criminal, the way she hugged Mrs. Wilt so tight when she got out of her car in the church parking lot, her eyes welling up while she repeated, "I wish Mom was here."

Then again, Tanner never would have suspected Mrs. Wilt for a wanted felon, either, which perhaps was what had helped her get away with it for so long. Until now, anyway.

Tanner adjusted her position, tucking her good leg beneath her, keeping her body turned so she could continue looking over the back of the couch, giving her the best vantage point of the driveway. She felt like a sitting duck, anxiety slowly oozing through her veins, even though Mrs. Wilt had assured her they'd be fine. That if the taxi driver did see their photos and called the police to tell them he'd transported them to the church, there was no way authorities would know where they'd gone from there. Regardless, Tanner wanted to be on the move, wanted to feel the breeze in her hair on the open road, wanted to recapture that sense of purpose that was slowly fading and being replaced by a low but insistent voice in her head saying, ARE YOU INSANE? THIS IS BADBADBAD.

Her stomach growled, even though Rosie had fed them a lunch of ham sandwiches and carrot sticks, and then offered a plate of pita chips, hummus, and grapes not an hour ago, which Tanner had mowed down half of. In fact, that seemed to be what Rosie was most concerned with—being a consummate hostess, rather than the fact that she was harboring wanted criminals in her house. She didn't ask any questions of Mrs. Wilt, save for: Are you hungry? What else can I get you? Would you like to take a rest? The latter of which Mrs. Wilt availed herself of, retreating to the guest bedroom after the hummus, while Rosie left to pick up her son from baseball practice.

Which left Tanner alone in the living room with her thoughts—and her rising anxiety. Couldn't the police trace the phone number

Mrs. Wilt had called from the church? Or what if there had been a street camera somewhere, and it had picked up Rosie's license plate—and the FBI was on their way here right now? Or what if—

Before she had a chance to conjure up another worst-case scenario, a movement in the driveway caught Tanner's eye. A gray minivan slowly pulled in and came to a stop. She squinted but couldn't see the driver through the afternoon sun's glare on the windshield. Her entire body tensed.

"Mrs. Wilt?" she shouted.

A beat of silence. "What?" came her disembodied voice from the back bedroom.

"Someone's here." Tanner thought her heart might hammer out of her chest for fear. How was she to know if this was the friend they were waiting for or the first to arrive of an entire SWAT team?

"Well, let him in."

"What if it's the cops? I can't tell who it is."

"Do you see flashing lights?"

"No."

"Then it's not the cops."

Tanner rolled her eyes and then watched as the door to the minivan slowly creaked open and a man stepped out into the driveway. A man she recognized immediately. She closed her eyes hard, certain they were playing tricks on her. But when she opened them again, it was still him. Her body went cold and hot at the same time. She gripped the back of the sofa so hard her knuckles were white.

"Mrs. Wilt!" she yelled again. When Mrs. Wilt didn't answer, she screamed her name a second time, louder.

"You don't have to shout, I'm right here," Mrs. Wilt said calmly from where she stood, gripping her cane in the opening of the hallway to the living room.

Tanner turned to her slowly and said through clenched teeth, "What is *he* doing here?"

Mrs. Wilt blinked and then peered out the large window at the man striding up the front walk.

"Who, August?" she said. "He's driving us to George."

25

A BREAKTHROUGH IN THE FBI'S ATLANTA FIELD OFFICE, FOUR DAYS AFTER LOUISE WAS REPORTED MISSING TO THE POLICE, AT DINNERTIME

LORNA BLEW ON the spoonful of red-orange microwaved tomato soup and then took a careful sip. It burned her mouth anyway, and tasted as awful as the plastic tub it came in. She sighed, trying to remember when she'd last had a home-cooked meal instead of something store-bought and on the go, and knew it had to be more than four months ago, before Rahul moved out. He loved cooking—whipping up culinary delights like pad thai, or lamb ragù over fresh pappardelle. Even his simple roast chicken was to die for. Lorna's mouth started watering and, disgusted with her current repast, she dropped the spoon back in the plastic canister, accidentally sending a spray of orange across the papers on her desk. She tried not to think about Rahul, or how custody of Philip would pan out in the impending divorce—which really meant she tried not to think about how, if Philip got to choose, he would probably choose his father.

Lorna shook her head to rid it of her myriad personal issues and picked up the case file detailing Louise Wilt's 1984 criminal arrest and prosecution, which had unfortunately received the worst of the soup splash. She plucked a tissue from the box on her desk and started dabbing at the stain, and then sat back in her chair, rereading the charges (theft by taking) and the specifics (six incidents of mail theft, the letters in question including personal checks totaling $532, written by one Dorothy Hipps).

For the fifth time that day, she scanned the court reporter's transcript and the judge's notes. It was an open-and-shut case. Louise Wilt pleaded guilty, and the judge reduced the penalty from a felony to a misdemeanor, ordering a fine of $500 and forty hours of community service, a light sentence likely due in part to Louise never having cashed the checks. That detail didn't bother Lorna, as it fit with her theory that Louise had stolen the checks for the mere thrill of stealing, rather than because she wanted the money. What bothered Lorna was the excuse Louise had given the judge for stealing in the first place.

JUDGE: Ms. Hipps is your neighbor, isn't she?

DEFENDANT: She is.

JUDGE: And I understand you help care for her at times, or at least have driven her to doctor appointments, taken her dinner, neighborly things such as that?

DEFENDANT: Yes, sir.

JUDGE: Well, I just have to ask. Why would you steal her mail, her *money*?

DEFENDANT: Because it was the right thing to do.

JUDGE: I'm sorry? How so?

DEFENDANT: Have you heard of Jimmy and Tammy Faye Bakker?

JUDGE: Of course. The televangelists.

DEFENDANT: Do you know how much money they have?

JUDGE: I don't. Though I imagine it's in the neighborhood of millions.

DEFENDANT: Do you know how much money Dorothy has?

JUDGE: No.

DEFENDANT: $514 a month. That's the amount of her social security check.

JUDGE: I see. And your point?

DEFENDANT: If anything, Jimmy and Tammy Faye should be sending money to her, not the other way around.

If Louise was to be believed, she stole the checks that Dorothy had been writing to the televangelists in order to keep her from getting taken advantage of. It was a brilliant excuse, clever to position herself as a kind neighborly savior rather than a coldhearted thief. But the problem was, when Louise offered this excuse, the judge had already given his sentence. He asked the question as an *afterthought* in the transcript. There was no need to lie. Or say anything at all.

And it was that detail Lorna had been chewing on all afternoon. She had to admit that, of all the things Louise could have stolen, mail wouldn't have been that big a thrill. A woman who had pulled off one of the biggest jewelry heists in history would likely need a bigger challenge to satiate her desire, rather than snatching a few envelopes out of her neighbor's mailbox. And maybe she did steal other things—slipping brooches or bracelets up her sleeve while at dinner parties. Who knew?

Or maybe she didn't. Lorna had to acknowledge the possibility that Louise was telling the truth. Lorna had seen a lot in her career—people leading double lives wasn't new—but she didn't think she'd ever seen a crook with such a devotion to . . . morality. Then again, she knew, too, that people found all kinds of ways to justify their bad behavior. Maybe Louise/Patty believed she was doing some kind of favor to the world—stealing from the rich but helping the poor.

A knock jerked her head toward the door.

Jamal was leaning into her makeshift office, his upper body visible, his lower half out of sight, as if he was protecting it from her ire.

"Hey—the police who interviewed that kid?"

"Yeah?"

"Said the woman borrowed his phone."

Lorna perked up. "Who'd she call?"

"They don't know yet. Apparently, she deleted the number or numbers before she gave it back to him—every call in his history was one the kid had remembered making."

"Who's his cell company?" *Please be AT&T. Please be AT&T. Please be AT&T,* Lorna mentally crossed her fingers. If it was AT&T, she had a guy there who would give her the phone records *before* the court order—which could take a day or two at the least.

"Verizon."

"SHIIIIIIIITake mushrooms." Not only would they have to wait for the court order, but Verizon's legal department was notoriously slow—sometimes taking up to two or three weeks to respond to a court order. And Lorna couldn't claim exigent circumstances, because though Louise was on the run—and it was *possible* she had taken the girl, Tanner, against her will—there was no evidence anyone's life was in danger.

Jamal hesitated, unsure how to respond to her outburst. "Do you want me to get the order?"

"*Yes,*" Lorna said, annoyed, his question reaffirming his inexperience. She was about to explain how you never leave any stone unturned in an investigation, but her cell rang, interrupting her. She held a finger up to Jamal and, with her other hand, swiped a thumb across the screen and put the phone to her ear.

"Agent Lorna Huang speaking," she said. And then her eyes grew wide, the corners of her lips turning up. Maybe they wouldn't need that phone number after all.

When she hung up, she looked back to Jamal, who still hadn't let his entire body enter the space.

"Jamal, book me a flight to Colorado."

"What happened?"

"Authorities in Nebraska say a taxi driver drove two women fitting the description of Tanner and Louise to a Catholic church in Fort Morgan this morning."

"For real?" he said, and then added just as quickly, "Can I come?"

Lorna stared at him dispassionately, weighing the pros and cons. The kid hadn't exactly proven himself to be an indispensable asset. But then she remembered her own early days at the bureau—how eager she was to just be given a chance.

"Fine," she said, and glanced at the pitiful tomato soup on her desk and briefly thought of Rahul, her heart pinching. Then she remembered this was exactly why he was calling it quits, because she *always put work first*. She rolled her eyes, irritated at the circular argument they'd been having for months before he finally packed a bag and made good on his promise to leave if nothing changed. As the breadwinner, she wasn't sure what exactly he had expected to happen. "Call in an order to go somewhere for dinner. We'll pick it up on the way," she yelled after Jamal. "I'm starving."

26

THE RAP-RAP-RAP ON the front door echoed throughout the house, but Tanner didn't move—or couldn't.

"Why him?" she hissed at Mrs. Wilt.

"With our pictures plastered everywhere, we couldn't exactly waltz into a Hertz and rent a car," she said calmly.

"And out of the hundreds of people you know, *he's* the only one who could? What about Rosie? Or the *priest*?"

"I wouldn't put either of them in that position. They've already done enough."

August rapped on the front door again, more insistently this time.

"But you *would* put August in that position?"

"I didn't *want* to," Mrs. Wilt said. "But he's dependable. And he owed me a favor."

Tanner opened her mouth to ask what that meant, but Mrs. Wilt cut her off. "Get the door. We're on the clock, here."

Tanner gawked at the woman for a second and then forced steel into her limbs and walked toward the foyer. Yes, she was embarrassed to see him after he'd stood her up, but he didn't have to know that. She could just pretend she didn't even notice. That's what she would do. Be politely terse, uncaring. "Cool as a cucumber," as her dad would say (which as a phrase was, admittedly, anything but cool).

She took a deep breath, fixed her face into one of disinterest, grabbed the door handle, and opened it, revealing August in all his man-bunned, tight-T-shirt glory. Dear God, was it possible that he was *better* looking than her memory? His eyes widened behind his aviators (because *of course* he was wearing aviators).

"What are you doing here?" he asked, and Tanner could tell he was genuinely surprised to see her. Leave it to Mrs. Wilt to withhold pertinent information from someone.

"Funny. I was just going to ask you the same thing." Good. Cool. Maybe a touch on the bitter side. Tanner made a note to reel it in a bit.

"You cut your hair," he said. She reached up and put her hands in her newly shorn, chin-length locks, having momentarily forgotten the hack job she'd done in Rosie's bathroom a few hours earlier. Heat rose to her face.

"Yeah."

He let his gaze slide over it and then down her figure. She tried not to squirm, tried not to care that she was wearing a ribbed racerback tank so old the bottom hem was frayed and there was a hole in the top left just above her breast. He looked back up at her with the verdict: "Badass."

Her cheeks grew hotter.

"C'mon," she said, turning away from the door, mostly so he

couldn't see her decidedly uncool expression. "Mrs. Wilt is in here, and we need to leave."

FIFTEEN MINUTES LATER, the three of them were in the minivan along with their belongings, August in the driver's seat, Mrs. Wilt beside him, and Tanner in the first row of seats behind August, feeling very much like a third wheel. August moved the gearshift into reverse and started backing out of the driveway. Tanner caught his eye in the rearview mirror and looked away. "Was this the only car left at the rental place?" she asked, needing to let her irritation out somehow.

"Miss Louise said to get something inconspicuous."

"And you chose this?" she said.

"Yeah. Every suburban mother in this country owns a gray Honda Odyssey."

Well, that was true. Tanner couldn't think of a comeback.

"Alright—where am I going?" August half turned to Mrs. Wilt.

"Redding, California," she replied, and started digging in her bag at her feet for her atlas. In the time it took her to pull it out and open it, August already had a route showing on the screen of the cell phone in his palm.

"Will this work?" he asked.

Mrs. Wilt looked up. "Oh, yes. Thank you." She took the phone from him and started studying the route, while Tanner balked.

"WHAT?" she roared, surprised at the force in her voice.

Mrs. Wilt ignored her. "Looks like you need to take 76 west to 80 north."

"Why does *he* get to have a cell phone?"

"No one knows he's with us," Mrs. Wilt said calmly.

Tanner crossed her arms and pouted, feeling very much the child she knew she was behaving like. But this mission to get Mrs. Wilt to George had gone downhill fast. It felt like she and Mrs. Wilt had finally found their groove together. They were a team—a *pair*—until August had to show up and ruin it all. In fact, she felt like she wasn't needed at all, now that August had arrived. Instead of being grateful they were on the road again, she resented the way he had swooped in like some goddamned superhero. They were doing just *fine* on their own (they were not) and didn't need some *man* to save them (gender aside, they absolutely did). As if on cue, August glanced back at her again in the rearview and flashed his ridiculously charming and handsome grin, but Tanner was not going to be so easily won over. She growled and turned her gaze out the window, deciding she would ask to be let off at the next stop. She nodded, cementing the decision, and told herself she'd be glad to be rid of Mrs. Wilt—and August—for good.

But the first place they stopped was at a rest area thirty minutes into the drive for Mrs. Wilt to go to the bathroom, and Tanner didn't think it made a lot of sense to get out there.

A few hours later, around 10:00 p.m., Mrs. Wilt directed August to pull over, much in the same way she had always directed Tanner, and Tanner knew this was it. They were going to stop at a hotel, and that was where Tanner would politely break the news. She'd ask for the cash from Mrs. Wilt, get her own room, and then figure out what to do in the morning, fresh eyed and—more importantly—free.

"Stop here for gas," Mrs. Wilt said, pointing to an Exxon. "Tanner, I need you to run in and get me a neck pillow. We have to drive through the night."

"We do?" Tanner and August said at the same time.

"Yes, I need to be in California by tomorrow evening, and we still have at least eighteen hours to go. With stops, we'll be lucky to make it."

"But . . ." Tanner said weakly.

August turned around in his seat after parking the van next to a pump. "Do you mind grabbing me an energy drink? Looks like I'm gonna need it."

"Uh . . . I guess."

"Thanks," August said, jumping out of the car.

Mrs. Wilt shoved a hand clutching two twenties back toward Tanner. "Don't get one of those inflatable pieces of crap, either. Memory foam would be preferable."

"OK," Tanner said, her head nearly spinning from how quickly her plan had been turned upside down. Even with her newly shorn do, Tanner shoved on the blue baseball hat and walked into the gas station with her head down and hands stuffed in her pockets. It was the first time she'd been in a store since the news that morning, and she half expected everyone to point at her, screaming, *Halt, thief!*

Her heart raced as she quickly picked out a can of Monster from the refrigerated section, along with a Coke for herself, and a blue travel pillow off a wire carousel display. Tanner doubted very much it was memory foam, but it wasn't an inflatable one, either, so it would have to do. She also grabbed a package of gummy worms, a bag of Doritos, some kind of snack mix, and a tube of beef jerky.

She paid without incident, keeping her head down the entire time, and when she got back to the car, beneath the bright fluorescent lights, she saw that Mrs. Wilt was no longer in the front seat. August was hanging out the driver's side, his arm resting on the half-open door, and grinning at her. "Looks like you're riding shotgun. Miss Louise wants her beauty sleep."

Tanner frowned. Being in the same car with August was one thing. Sitting right next to him? That was something else altogether.

THE FIRST HOUR of traveling on the dark highway was silent, save for the crinkle of plastic bags and intermittent crunching of chips. It felt like Tanner was holding her breath, waiting for something—though she wasn't sure what. The air was tense, thick, and she was hyperaware of every movement, as if she were acting on a stage and August sat in the audience. Not that he was looking at her. He didn't seem to even remember she was there at all, having not spoken to her since she first slid into the front seat and dumped all the snacks on the console between them, when he said, "Sweet. You sharing?"

It wasn't until they heard the light wheeze-snoring of Mrs. Wilt that August turned to her and spoke again, in a low voice, as if all he'd been waiting for was privacy. The thought of it was so intimate, it raised the hairs on Tanner's arm.

"Hey, I'm sorry about lunch that day."

Tanner stiffened. "Oh, I totally forgot about that," she said, a little too quickly, her voice an octave higher than usual.

"You did? Well, I felt really bad. I came by the next day to explain, but no one was home. I guess you guys had already left."

She consciously tried to relax every muscle in her body and face—play the part of the cool girl she so desperately wanted to be, even as she loathed caring what August thought of her. "Seriously, it's no big deal."

"OK. Well, cool. But I still want to explain." He bit into one end of a gummy worm and pulled until the other snapped off. Chewed. "I have a kid."

"Oh!" Tanner said, trying to cover her surprise. Babies seemed like such a futuristic concept to her. Like flying cars. She'd probably have one someday, but it was hard to really imagine. And she wondered if that was what Mrs. Wilt had meant when she said August didn't seem like her type.

"An eight-year-old son. Brayden."

"*Eight?!*" Tanner repeated. Her eyes bugged. That was more than surprising. That was downright shocking. "How old are you?" Holy shit. Tanner had been certain August was her age, or close to it. Did she have the hots for a bona fide DILF?

"Twenty-five."

She quickly did the math in her head. "Wow."

"Yeah, it was a high school girlfriend. Anyway, that's why I missed our lunch. She called and asked if I could take him to a doctor appointment at the last minute because she had a work conflict and her mother wasn't available. She has full custody, and I don't get to see him nearly enough, so when she asks, I drop everything to go."

"Oh," Tanner repeated. As excuses go, she had to admit that was a pretty solid one.

A few more miles went by. August messed with the radio, poking the touch screen to scan through the stations, which all seemed to be playing a version of the same country song. And then he said, apropos of nothing as far as Tanner could tell, "Can you not drive?"

"What? What do you mean?"

"I'm more than happy to help," he continued. "I really do owe her . . . a lot. But I'm just trying to understand."

Tanner's brow crinkled. "Understand what?"

"Well, if you're here, I'm not sure what she needed me for. Unless you can't drive. But I've seen you drive, so that doesn't really make sense." It seemed as though he was talking to himself more than her, trying to puzzle something out.

"Yes, I can drive," Tanner said slowly.

"I thought so."

Tanner's jaw dropped an inch. No. It wasn't possible. Surely August knew what they were doing? Who Mrs. Wilt really was? Tanner assumed he'd known way before she had—he knew about the Jaguar, anyway, which meant Mrs. Wilt clearly trusted him. "What exactly did Mrs. Wilt tell you?" she asked, keeping her voice low to match his.

"That the Jaguar broke down and she needed to get to California. But she didn't tell me you were with her."

"The Jaguar did break down," Tanner affirmed. "Back in St. Louis. We got it fixed, though."

"And then what happened?"

"She really didn't tell you?"

"Tell me what?"

Tanner glanced back at Mrs. Wilt. Her head lolled a bit on the neck pillow with the motion of the car; her lips were parted. She was sleeping soundly. Tanner felt a pang of guilt—as though she were betraying Mrs. Wilt's confidence—but she also strongly felt that August had a right to know. "Mrs. Wilt is a wanted felon. There's a national manhunt out for her—and me, too—right this second."

August stared at her for a beat—long enough for Tanner to feel the heat from his gaze. And then he threw his head back, laughing. "Good one," he said. "Seriously, you almost had me there for a minute."

Tanner's expression didn't change. "I'm not kidding."

He glanced at her once more and then back at the road. "Yeah, right." He chuckled some more, relaxing a bit into it, propping his left elbow up where the window met the door, his right wrist casually draped over the top of the steering wheel. Tanner continued staring at him, until finally he felt the weight of her stare and had no choice but to look at her once again.

He blinked. Did a double take. "Wait. Are you being serious?"

She nodded.

"Miss *Louise*?" he said, as if there were another Mrs. Wilt who Tanner was referring to, and she was the one wanted by police.

Tanner nodded again.

"What's she wanted for?"

"Some big jewelry heist back in the seventies. Apparently she stole like three million dollars' worth of jewels and cash from a hotel safe or something. And she's been living undercover ever since." Tanner paused and then added, "You really didn't know."

He pointed an index finger at his chin. "Does this look like the face of somebody who knew that?"

Tanner shrugged. "I thought with you taking care of the Jaguar and everything that you were maybe in cahoots with her."

His eyes grew bigger as he looked at her once more. "Cahoots? *Cahoots?*"

"What? I did."

"Yes, but are you from the 1940s?" His eyes shone as a small grin played on his lips, and then, adopting an affected voice, he said, "Aww, geewillikers, everything's aces, see?"

"OK," Tanner said, rolling her eyes. "You know what I mean."

"No, I'm clearly not in *cahoots* with Mrs. Wilt. I'm glad to know you think so highly of me, though."

A few more miles passed by in silence, August shaking his head every now and then, as if the new information about Mrs. Wilt was dawning on him all over again.

"You know, it's actually badass. I mean, she just seems like someone's sweet grandma, but she's . . . *gangster.*"

Tanner jerked her head at him, trying to ignore the pang that he had used the same adjective to describe her haircut and now it didn't feel special. Or that she *wanted* to feel special. To him. God, lust was annoying. "Sweet?" she said, arching an eyebrow.

A smile pulled at the right side of his mouth. "You're right. But still . . ."

"So, you're not . . . worried? Or mad? I mean, now, like it or not, you *are* in cahoots with her, and she didn't really give you a choice."

"True," he said, and then shrugged. "But even if I had known . . . I probably still would have come."

Tanner furrowed her brow. "Did she save you from a burning building or something? Give you a kidney? I mean, you're acting like you owe her your life. What'd she do?"

August shifted uncomfortably in his seat. And then rubbed the back of his neck with his big masculine hand (not that Tanner was noticing). "She, um . . . she helped me get a job."

"A job," Tanner repeated, thinking that didn't seem like nearly big enough a favor to then ask someone to drop everything, fly to Colorado, and be your getaway driver on the lam in return—without even telling him that's what he's doing. "What do you do?"

"I'm a line cook for the Stadium Grill—it's this twenty-four-hour diner in downtown Atlanta. Miss Louise knew the owner and she called him up." He half smiled, like he was remembering something. "She actually lied to him—told him I was an excellent chef and had all kinds of experience, when I barely knew how to make a piece of toast."

"They didn't realize that as soon as you started?"

"Nope. On my first day, the head chef said, 'Everything you think you know about cooking? Forget it. Here, you do things my way.'" He flashed a full grin at Tanner. "That was easy enough."

Tanner reflexively smiled back, like Pavlov's dog, once again disarmed by the sum of the features on his face. *It's just a face!* she reminded herself, inwardly scowling at her lack of self-control.

Tanner stared out the window into the darkness beyond, barely able to make out the flat desert stretching out from either side of the road. She yawned and then tried to stifle it with her hand.

"You can go to sleep," August said. "I'll be alright for a few hours. Then maybe you can take a turn?"

Tanner nodded and leaned her head back on the headrest, closing her eyes, even though she didn't feel all that tired. Every nerve in her body was like the end of a live wire, adrenaline coursing through her veins, which she told herself was due to the anxiety of being pursued by the police, though she knew it was partly due to the excitement of being so close to a man who looked like August.

"Hey, wait," he said, and she opened her eyes without moving her head, cutting her gaze at him sideways.

"What did she do for you?"

"Huh?"

"Miss Louise—why are you helping her? I assume she did something for you, too."

Tanner paused, considering the question, replaying the past few days she had spent in multiple confined quarters with the woman; how far they had come on their own. "No. Nothing," she said, even as she knew deep down that wasn't really true at all.

AS UTAH MELTED into Nevada—not that anyone could tell without signage, as the clusters of sagebrush on the flatlands appeared indistinguishable from state to state—August and Tanner continued taking turns at the helm, but otherwise the hours seemed to blend into each other, each rest area or gas station they stopped at as unmemorable as the one before. They hoped they were unmemorable as well, Tanner and Mrs. Wilt taking care to never go in anywhere together, Mrs. Wilt donning a scarf and sunglasses, Tanner the baseball cap she had adopted that she now considered hers.

In the morning, the mood in the car was downright jovial, whether it was because everyone was punch-drunk from a lack of sleep or because the sunrise painted everything—including the breathtaking vistas of the Sierra mountains as they finally entered California—with a bright glow that made it impossible to feel cynical. They passed the time with Mrs. Wilt calling out crossword clues and Tanner and August trying to guess the answers. It turned out August had every bit of the competitive drive that Tanner did, and she got a jolt of pride every time she beat him to the punch with a correct word. Then they moved on to the license plate game, which August dove into with equal gusto, becoming downright giddy when he spotted Hawaii at a rest stop, a notoriously hard one to get. "I should get extra points for that one," he said.

"There are no points," Tanner said. "We're working together."

"So you think. I'm keeping track in my head."

As the afternoon wore on, the air turned decidedly more somber, like coming down from a sugar high—exhaustion beginning to set in, and for Mrs. Wilt, Tanner could tell pain was as well, the way she grimaced and caught her breath sometimes when she shifted her seated position. Or maybe it was the closer they got to their final destination, the more they were collectively holding their breath—at least Tanner was—expecting blue lights to flash behind them at any time, or a tire to blow. Anything to prove Murphy's Law was in effect, and they would not so easily reach their goal.

But aside from an agonizing two-hour traffic delay due to road construction, the trip went smoothly, and at 5:36 p.m., Tanner pulled the minivan into the parking lot of the Shasta Senior Assisted Living Center, maneuvered into an open space near the front entrance, and put the gearshift into park.

"We're here," she announced, for lack of anything more eloquent or less obvious. She waited to be overcome with a sense of accomplishment, but it felt so . . . anticlimactic. She wondered if climbers felt this way at the top of Mount Everest, or Neil and Buzz when they planted the flag in the moondust.

Or maybe it was because they hadn't completed the mission yet. Maybe she'd feel it once they got to George.

Without preamble, Mrs. Wilt opened her door, and August jumped out of the back to give her his arm and help her down from her seat. He set the cane on the ground for her to grasp, and then Mrs. Wilt set off toward the door, August following, leaving Tanner gripping the steering wheel, alone.

Tanner knew she should stay in the car, that it was safer for her and Mrs. Wilt to not be seen together, but they'd come this far, and Tanner would be damned if she didn't see it all the way through. She scrambled out of the front seat and caught up to them a few paces from the automatic sliding glass doors of the entrance.

The first thing she saw when they entered was a security guard at the opposite end of the room standing in front of an elevator bank, his feet hip-width apart, hands folded in front of his crotch. Guarding. If he was attempting to be intimidating, it was working. Tanner ducked her head and tried to shield his view of her by stepping behind August.

The check-in desk was on the left, a large plexiglass shield separating the admin from the guests.

"Welcome to Shasta Senior Living," she said, without smiling or any real warmth in her voice. "Can I help you?"

"We're here to see George Dixon."

"Are you family?"

Tanner felt Mrs. Wilt hesitate. "No."

The woman nodded, as if it was neither here nor there, and clacked her long pointy blue glitter nails on the keyboard in front of her. She frowned.

"I'm sorry, George Dixon appears to be in the memory care unit, and visiting hours are over for the day."

"What do you mean they're *over*?" Tanner said, poking her head out from behind August's shoulder. "It's not even dark."

"In memory care, family can stay until 9:00 p.m., but for all other guests it's a strict eight-to-five policy. It's in the best interest of the patients."

"Oh," Mrs. Wilt said. And Tanner looked at her, waiting for her to say more—to push back with her patented, no-nonsense, things-are-going-to-go-my-way-because-I-said-so attitude, but Mrs. Wilt remained quiet.

Tanner tilted her head. She'd never seen Mrs. Wilt go quiet when someone stood in direct opposition to what she wanted, but it couldn't be a good sign. She glanced at the plexiglass, suddenly grateful it was there. For the admin's sake.

August stepped forward, flashing the admin a smile that could have stopped the Ice Age in its tracks. "The thing is, George is expecting us, and we've driven quite some way," August said, his baritone voice dropping deeper and coming out smooth and syrupy like he was hosting a goddamned radio show. "Do you think you could just call the room to say we're here?"

"Sorry," the woman said in a way that made it seem she wasn't actually sorry at all. Was she made of stone? "The rules are the rules."

Out of the corner of her eye, Tanner saw the security guard not move toward them exactly, but ready himself to do so, his gaze hard and serious. Not wanting to chance a repeat of their St. Louis arch experience, Tanner gently took Mrs. Wilt's arm.

"Let's go," Tanner said. "We'll come back first thing. Eight a.m. It'll be here before you know it."

"Mondays it's nine. Staff meeting's at eight," the woman interjected, and Tanner turned slowly toward her, glaring. But the woman barely looked up from her screen, where Tanner was sure she was playing *Hay Day* or shopping for an extra supply of the sticks that she clearly stuck straight up her ass.

"Nine, then," Tanner said, as menacingly as she could without actually pissing the woman off—the last thing they needed was this gatekeeper to not let them in at all.

Tanner didn't realize she was holding her breath until Mrs. Wilt said "Fine" in a meek voice and—even more surprisingly—allowed Tanner to lead her back out the way they had come, with August in tow. If Tanner hadn't been so eager to get away from the security guard, she may have given more thought to how deferential Mrs. Wilt was acting, how very *un*–Mrs. Wilt.

But as it stood, she was just relieved to be getting out of the building without Mrs. Wilt having accosted anyone—and away from the prying eyes of the security guard.

27

MEMORY CARE.

The two words hit her like a prizefighter's punch to the head, complete with the ringing in her ears after. *Memory care.*

George.

Aside from cancer, it had been Louise's biggest fear when it came to the inevitability of aging. "I don't care what happens to my body, as long as my mind doesn't go," she said often to Ken, the kids, anyone who would listen. "If my mind goes, just take me out back like Old Yeller." As it turned out, once she got the Parkinson's diagnosis, she realized she preferred to keep both her mind *and* body intact, but beggars/choosers and all.

At her age, Louise had had enough peers succumb to dementia and Alzheimer's—two sides of the same coin as far as she was concerned—to know that when one had to enter *care* for it, it was likely at an advanced stage.

But George had sounded so . . . *with it* on that phone call. So clear minded.

Louise turned it over and over in her head while Tanner drove them away from the assisted living center. What if George *wasn't* clear minded? She tried to recall everything that was said, but she had been so caught off guard—and the irony wasn't lost on her that her own memory of the phone conversation was spotty at best. And the letter! Oh, now she wished she hadn't burned it. But she felt sure it, too, had been straightforward, the handwriting neat and legible, the information lucid and understandable—not the ramblings of a senile person.

Still, Louise's heart squeezed at the idea that George's sharp brain was misfiring—that perhaps they had waited too long for this reunion, missed too much. Would George even remember her? Know who she was? But another niggling thought kept pushing its way to the surface. What if this were all a figment of George's addled brain, the past memories mixing with the present, causing George to believe they were in trouble all over again? Was this entire journey based on . . . a delusion?

"August," she said, looking up to notice Tanner was pulling the minivan into another parking lot, this time of a motel—a squat pink stucco building with a giant marquee out front that announced in big block letters: THE THUNDERBIRD LODGE. "May I borrow your cell phone, please?"

"Sure."

In exchange, she handed him a wad of cash. "Why don't you go in and get the rooms?"

Her left hand shook as she tried to tap the name into the search bar, but the darned letters were so small on the screen—how was anyone supposed to work one of these damned things?

"Can I help?" Tanner's voice came quiet from beside her.

"They make these things for children, I swear," Louise growled, handing it over to Tanner.

The girl took the phone gently and palmed it. "What are you trying to type in?"

"A name. Salvatore D'Amato."

Tanner stilled, then tilted her head like a parrot. "Why does that name sound familiar?"

Louise narrowed her eyes. The girl had surprised her on multiple occasions, knowing more than Louise had given her credit for.

Tanner shook her head slowly and tapped the name out on the screen. Her eyes moved swiftly left to right, reading the results, and then went wide with recognition. "A mobster! That's right—they said on the news that you were an associate of his or something." Her excitement at remembering quickly veered into alarm. "*Are* you? It says here he . . . *killed* a man." She looked square into Louise's eyes. "In prison."

"Give me that," Louise said, ignoring Tanner's question. She scanned the entries, clicking on the second news story, and sure enough, she found exactly what she was looking for.

EX–MOB BOSS TO BE RELEASED FROM PRISON EARLY

An ex–mob boss best known in the New York crime scene of the mid-to-late 1970s, who went to jail for tax fraud and then subsequently killed a man behind bars, effectively earning a life sentence, has been granted early release from prison due to health reasons.

The attorneys for Salvatore D'Amato, 76, argued for compassionate release for the man who was recently

> diagnosed with stage 4 pancreatic cancer—and who, according to his lawyers, was receiving inadequate medical care at San Quentin.
>
> "Not only has he shown exemplary behavior, becoming a spiritual leader of sorts and mentor to others in prison, but he has been denied the basic human right of seeing a doctor or receiving any treatment for his condition."
>
> The Federal Bureau of Prisons did not specify a release date, but sources say it could be as early as this weekend.

Louise's thumb scrolled back to the date of the article—it had been written Tuesday, just five days earlier, which meant Sal could already be out, for all she knew. She felt simultaneously relieved that George's intel was correct and not the work of some kind of Alzheimer's-induced fever dream, and a heart-pumping horror that Sal could be . . . anywhere.

The door of the minivan jerked open, and Louise startled.

"Got the rooms," August said, flashing two key cards.

Louise pressed her décolletage with her palm, trying to slow her heart. "You scared me."

"Sorry, Miss Louise," he said, clicking his heels together and holding up his elbow like a footman on *Downton Abbey*. "Can I help you out?" He set her cane upright, and she clutched his arm with one hand and the head of the cane with the other, slowly easing herself down from her seat.

"Wait, should we be worried about that guy?" Tanner said, jumping out of the car and grabbing the two suitcases out of the back. August had his travel bag already slung over his shoulder.

"What guy?" August asked as they walked at a snail's pace toward the first-floor bank of exterior rooms.

"Oh, just some murderer Mrs. Wilt is friends with."

Louise cut her eyes to Tanner. "Want to say that a little louder? I don't think they heard you in Oregon."

"Sounds like a nice dude," August deadpanned. "Is he coming to visit?"

"I don't know, Mrs. Wilt, *is* he?"

Louise stopped walking and pinched the bridge of her nose with her free hand. "Could you two kindly *shut up*?"

August and Tanner stared at her.

"Now, I'm going to go in this room," she said, gesturing to the door they were in front of. "And I'm going to run a bath and have a cup of tea and get a good night's sleep, and I don't want to be bothered. By either of you."

"OK," Tanner said. "I'll be quiet. I'm exhausted anyway."

"No."

"What do you mean, no?"

"I'm not sharing with you. You snore."

"At least I don't scream bloody murder in the middle of the night, scaring everyone half to death," Tanner retorted.

"Fine," Louise nodded. "Then you agree we shouldn't share a room."

"No! I don't agree with that."

"I'll sleep with her," August piped up, and Tanner and Louise both turned to him with wide eyes. His face blanched. "I mean—*wow*! No, that came out wrong. What I'm trying to say is, I'm happy to share. Separate beds, of course."

"So you *don't* want to sleep with me?" Louise jerked her gaze back to Tanner, who was wearing a sly smile. Where had *that* come from? She felt a surge of pride for the girl—especially when she saw how flustered August was. She had the feeling August wasn't a man who often found himself caught flat-footed.

"That feels like a trick question," August said, and then pointed his thumb in the direction of the parking lot. "How about I sleep in the car?"

Louise rolled her eyes, having had quite enough. "Whenever you two are done with this very painful mating ritual, could I have the key, please? My hip is not getting any better standing around here. I'm not as young as the two of you." Then she eyed them both. "Or as stupid."

THE DOOR CLOSED behind Mrs. Wilt, and Tanner stood staring at it for a beat. Then she looked at her shoes, her suitcase, anywhere but at August. Her confidence left as quickly as it had come. Her words replayed on a loop in her head: *So you* don't *want to sleep with me?* Who *said* something like that? To a near *stranger*? "I can go get another room," August said, breaking the silence. "She gave me plenty of cash."

"No, that's silly," Tanner said quickly. She didn't want him to think she cared either way. "We're just sleeping."

"Of course. Right," August said. He reached for the handle of her bag at the same time Tanner did, and their hands touched. Tanner felt a pulse of electricity course through her entire body and jerked her hand back. August gave her a look that she couldn't decipher, and another bolt shot through her.

"I've got your bag," he said.

"OK, thanks." She fell into step with him to the room three doors down, inwardly cringing—and irritated—at her obvious attraction to him. But she couldn't help it. Her stomach was in knots at the prospect of spending an entire night alone with him. She knew she had so many other things to worry about—Mrs. Wilt, getting to George, and whoever this Salvatore murderer guy was. But for some reason, all her brain could concentrate on was the spare few inches separating them as they walked, the heat she could swear was radiating off his body, the muscles flexing in his arm as he carried her roller bag. He'd stood her up, for Pete's sake! But maybe that was why she liked him. If her track record with Grant was anything to go by, clearly she was a walking jerk-magnet. Although August didn't really seem like a jerk. Then again, Grant hadn't at first, either. Maybe this was a bad idea. It wasn't too late to speak up, get another hotel room. But if she was being honest, she didn't want another hotel room.

"I'm starving," August said, setting her roller bag down so he could slip the key in the door and open it. "Think this place has room service?"

"Absolutely. If by room service, you mean that McDonald's across the street and you have to go pick it up yourself."

August grinned at her, and her insides went warm and gooey, like the middle of an underbaked cake.

Mrs. Wilt had been right. She really was stupid.

"OK, BEST ELEVEN out of twenty," August said.

Tanner laughed, her cheeks sore. "I don't think that's a thing." She was lying on her bed, propped up by pillows, and August was on his. A wastebasket on the far side of the room sat as their target. The impromptu game of crumpled-paper basketball had started when Tanner tossed her cheeseburger wrapper across the room and into the trash can. August, not to be outdone, followed suit. Then Tanner did the same with the empty french fry box. When they were out of fast-food refuse, August found a pad of paper with the Thunderbird Lodge logo and began ripping sheets off of it to scrunch up into balls.

The first few minutes alone in the room had been decidedly awkward, both of them retreating to their respective sides and setting down their bags. Tanner immediately flipped on the TV to counteract the silence, not even paying attention to what it was, until August said, "Big fan of golf?" She looked up, and sure enough it was the Golf Channel, some white man in a polo taking a swing at a little ball on a vast green lawn.

"Yeah, but only when there's nothing on QVC."

That earned a laugh, and Tanner relaxed a bit. "I thought you were going to get us room service," she said, and he grinned again.

He asked her questions as they ate—where she grew up, what other video games she liked to play besides *Horizon Zero Dawn*, how she came to live with Mrs. Wilt. The conversation flowed easily. So easily, in fact, that Tanner forgot to be self-conscious about what she said, telling August everything—well, almost everything. She left out the boy on the balcony and what had happened with Vee. But as she recounted the rest—the fall that ended her soccer career and her multiple surgeries—she was surprised to find it hurt a bit less. A bruise that wasn't quite as tender when pressed. And even more surprisingly, when she told him her plans to return to Northwestern, she couldn't quite place what was so urgent about it.

"Bet you've got a badass scar," August said, which Tanner was slowly realizing was his favorite adjective. August hadn't been quite so forthcoming when she asked questions in return, but Tanner shrugged it off. Maybe he just liked to keep his cards close to the chest.

When they ran out of paper to play basketball, Tanner sat up and stretched, catching a whiff of her underarm and realizing it had been two days since she'd last bathed.

"I need to take a shower," she said. "I'm disgusting."

"Me too," August said, and just like that, a sliver of awkwardness worked its way back between them. Or maybe it was just Tanner's fear that her brief thought of them in the shower together was all over her face.

"You go first," he said. "I'll find a good show for us on the Golf Channel. Or QVC."

Tanner laughed again and crossed the room to her suitcase. She unzipped it and lifted the top flap, and then let out a startled squeal.

August jumped from the bed. "Are you OK? What happened?"

Tanner clutched her T-shirt. "Sorry, I'm fine. Mrs. Wilt put her gun in my suitcase for some reason, and I didn't know it was here."

August peered over her shoulder, and Tanner tried not to notice how close he was standing. How if she leaned back just an inch, her shoulder would touch his chest. His eyes widened when he saw the pistol lying on top of her clothes. "Oh my God."

"Right? *Thank* you." Even though the gun didn't terrify her as much now that she knew how to use it, she felt validated she wasn't the only person shocked at the sight of a weapon.

"Is that an antique?"

"What?" Tanner furrowed her brow.

He stepped next to Tanner and reached across her, picking up the gun and turning it over in his hand. "Does it even shoot anymore?"

"Yes, it shoots," Tanner said indignantly.

"It seriously looks like something out of a John Wayne movie, like a literal six-shooter." He spun the barrel the same way Mrs. Wilt had in the car, and Tanner tensed.

"Can you please put that down? It's loaded."

"Oh, sorry," he said, setting it on the dresser. "You scared of guns?"

"A little," she said, though she found that emotion had lessened as well now that she had handled one. "You're obviously not."

"Nah, I grew up with them. Hunting with my dad, target practice, stuff like that."

"You hunt?"

"Not anymore. I killed a deer once when I was eleven, and I cried so hard we had to leave the woods, because Dad said I scared off anything else within a hundred miles."

Of course he had, Tanner thought. Of *course* on top of being hot and manly and funny and good-naturedly competitive, August was *sensitive*, too. She looked at his face, his full grin. She watched as his lips slowly fell into a straight line, his eyes studying her face. Her heartbeat revved to a gallop, and she wondered if the thumping of it was visible on the outside of her shirt. Was he going to *kiss* her?

His hand reached up and his eyes narrowed. She felt like she was watching a horror film—terrified and exhilarated, she wanted to close her eyes, but at the same time didn't want to miss anything.

"Is that—I think you've got . . . ketchup? In your hair." His hand passed her face as he reached for a lock of hair. "How'd you manage that?" he asked, the grin returning to his face.

"Oh," Tanner said, feeling her face turn eight shades past beet red. She stepped back before he could touch her hair, and grabbed a clean change of clothes from the top of the suitcase. "I better get in the shower, then."

She darted toward the bathroom and wondered if her humiliation would wash off as easily as the ketchup.

After a long, hot shower, she was pulling on a fresh tank top and yoga pants, the steam still clinging to the mirror in the form of fog, her newly short hair still dripping rivulets down the back of her neck, when a knock at the door startled her.

"Sorry," she called out. "I'm almost done."

The knock came again: *Thud-thud-thud.* Tanner stared at the door. Maybe he couldn't hear her. Or maybe—her heartbeat picked up speed once again—it wasn't . . . "August?"

She put her hand on the knob and turned, unsure what she was going to find when she opened it. She peeked through the crack and felt a rush of relief when she saw his familiar visage. He stood there, filling the entire opening of the door, his muscled arm above his head, holding on to the frame. "Sorry, I know I took forever," she said. She stared at him, waiting for him to say something in reply, but he just looked back at her, his dark eyes brooding more than usual.

"Are you OK?" she asked.

He shook his head once, and then in one swift motion removed his hand from the door frame and brought it directly to her face, palming her cheek and rubbing the corner of her lips with his thumb—setting everywhere he touched aflame. Like he was King Midas but turned everything to fire instead of gold. Tanner thought she might be dreaming, that her legs might give out, that she would die if she didn't feel his mouth on hers. Without thinking, she closed the inches between them and tilted her face toward his—and finally, *finally*, their lips met and Tanner had to keep herself from sighing. He kissed her long, soulfully, *expertly* even, and when he finally pulled back to look at her, Tanner thought it was a good thing his arms were around her holding her upright, because otherwise she would have melted into the floor.

"What was that for?" she asked.

He shrugged, bit his lip. "I chickened out earlier. Missed my chance," he said. "I didn't want to miss it again."

If there were a swooning couch available, Tanner would have made use of it. Instead, she pressed her mouth to his once more, pressed the entire length of her body against his. After a few minutes (or hours, or years; time had become completely irrelevant to Tanner—she just knew it wasn't long enough), August pulled back again, rubbing her shoulders with his hands.

"So," he said. "I guess I need to tell you something."

"What, do you have another kid?" she laughed. But the serious expression on August's face cut it off abruptly. A gnawing unease took up residence in her gut where pure want had just been. She nearly suggested they just keep kissing. Whatever he had to say could wait—especially if it was going to ruin the future chances of them kissing some more. But he led her by the hand to the bed and sat down, gesturing for her to sit beside him.

He took a deep breath and scratched the back of his head, scrunching his face and squeezing one eye shut, as if bracing himself for a hit. "I have a record."

Tanner eyed him. "Like . . . the kind you play on a turntable?"

"Like the kind you get when you go to jail."

Tanner stared at him a beat, waiting for the shock to hit her (the shock he so clearly thought she was going to experience), but all she felt was . . . annoyed. "Oh my God. Has everybody been to jail except me? Is that just a rite of passage that I missed?"

August tilted his head back, appraising her. And then he knocked into her shoulder with his own. "You're young. There's still time."

"So, what'd you do?" she asked.

"I lured young women into hotel rooms and killed them."

"What?" Tanner's breath left her.

"Sorry," he said, ducking his head. "Oh shit. That was awful. Why did I say that? It was really funny in my head. Like, *really* funny."

"Not so funny out loud."

"No. Terrible. Am scratching that one from the stand-up comic set pronto."

"Probably smart," Tanner said, though she couldn't help a small grin at his extreme self-flagellating. "What'd you really do?"

August sighed. "I got busted with weed in my car when I was a senior in high school. It was three ounces, which in Georgia equals a felony. My parents couldn't afford a lawyer, and half the time my public defender didn't even bother to call us back. I think I got a bad judge, too, or at least one that wanted to make an example of me. He gave me three years."

"You were in jail for three *years*?"

He nodded. "Anyway, that's why I owe Miss Louise."

"How do you mean?"

"It's not exactly easy to get a job when you have to tick that box on applications that you're a convicted felon."

Tanner sat with the avalanche of information August had deposited at her feet. Yes, it was a lot. No, she never imagined she'd be hooking up with a convicted felon (or a *dad*, for that matter), but, she reasoned, she also never imagined she'd be on the lam with an eighty-four-year-old woman who had perpetrated one of the largest jewelry heists in history. Yet here she was.

"Do you think Mrs. Wilt's OK?" she said, given it was the first time she had thought of the woman all evening, and felt a pang of guilt—that she was somehow shirking her responsibility, even though Mrs. Wilt had made clear she wanted to be alone. She felt something else, too, besides the guilt. Not that she *missed* her or anything, but after being with the woman nonstop for the past five days, Tanner found it was strange to be away from her.

"Yeah," August said. "I took her a burger. She was getting ready for bed."

Tanner wondered if August knew Mrs. Wilt had Parkinson's, and almost said something, but felt like it wasn't her right to tell if he didn't. What if she had one of those nightmares and Tanner wasn't there? She frowned, and August's face fell. "Is this the part where you make an excuse to leave?"

"No, I really just wondered if we should check on her," Tanner said, and then grinned. "So I don't feel guilty about it while we're making out later."

August's eyes brightened. He leaned his face toward hers, kissing her gently at first, and then more deeply, one hand sliding from her hip to the skin beneath her shirt. She sucked in her breath, and he stopped.

"You OK?" he asked. They were both breathing heavily, their foreheads pressed together, like they couldn't stand for at least a part of their bodies to not be touching for a second.

"Mm-hmm." She nodded. "But I'm not going to sleep with you." She thought if she laid down the ground rules now, she had a much better chance of actually adhering to them. As hot as August was and as much as she wanted him, she was also determined to not make the same mistake she had with Grant. She wanted to let her head rule her hormones this time.

"That's fine."

"It is?"

"I mean, obviously I'd prefer if we did," he said with a half grin. "But I understand." He paused. "I have to ask, though—is it because of the whole I've-been-in-jail thing? Or the whole I-have-a-kid thing?"

"Neither," Tanner said truthfully. Six months ago, Tanner would likely have been put off by both. But she'd realized Mrs. Wilt was right—nothing in life goes according to plan. Everyone has their shit. And August telling her the truth about his only made him more appealing. She smiled and added, "It was that awful young girl–serial killer joke. I can't sleep with someone who can't read a room."

He laughed, his breath warm on her face. "Wait! I've got other material. Let me try to make up for it."

"No," Tanner said, climbing on top of his lap. "I think you should stop talking completely."

28

A PHONE CONVERSATION IN SAN QUENTIN PRISON, FIVE DAYS AFTER LOUISE WENT MISSING AND HER DAUGHTER CALLED THE POLICE

"THIS IS IT, brother. How many times I tell you, keep the faith, we see each other again, we hug each other, eh? How many times? And now, today is the day."

Salvatore D'Amato held the prison pay phone receiver to his ear, listening to Guy's familiar deep Bronx-accented voice ramble on, for once not feeling the need to cut his brother off. It was the last time he'd use this phone, the last time he'd have to stare at the dingy cinder-block wall in front of him, listen to the yammering of the men behind him, impatiently waiting for their turn.

"Get off the fuckin' phone, cunt!" the inmate directly behind him yelled, as if on cue. "Your time's up!" Sal tensed, trying to let the anger roll off his back, the way he'd learned years ago from a prison chaplain who'd taken special interest in trying to "rehabilitate" him. Sal didn't know if it had worked, but he'd done his best to convince the right people over the years that it had. Not that it had done him any good. Who knew it would take a death sentence to get him out of his life sentence?

"What time are they letting you go?" his brother asked.

"Midnight," Salvatore said. "You'll be here." It wasn't a question but a directive, the same way he'd been commanding his brother—and everyone, really—their entire lives since they were orphaned in New York at the ages of fifteen and thirteen. You never *asked* for things, never gave people a chance to say no—that was how you made it in this world. By taking what was yours. Demanding it.

He'd had no idea how Guy had made it on the outside for so long without him.

"Wouldn't miss it for the world. I'll be there at one thirty. You'll see. Ah, if only Ma were still here. She'd make a whole pot of her gravy, eh? You remember her gravy, Sal? It was the best. On the whole of the Eastern Seaboard. I bet you could eat an entire pot right now. What they been serving you in there? Probably not fit to feed a horse."

"Listen, Guy. Not a minute later than two. I got somewhere to be, something to do, and I can't be late."

Guy paused. "Wait a minute, Sal, it's not illegal, is it? What you gotta do? I got out of that game a long time ago."

"No, it's not illegal, Guy. Jesus." Sal had heard rumors the higher-ups recorded all the phone calls now. He wasn't sure if that was true, but he didn't want to take any chances. "I'm just seeing an . . . old friend."

"OK, OK, just making sure, brother. I'll drive you wherever you need to go. Course I will."

"Tonight, then," Sal said, and pressed the hook switch with his pointer finger, effectively ending the call. He passed the receiver back to the man who'd been cursing in his ear, and brushed past him. Twenty years ago, Sal might have jabbed the guy discreetly with two stiff fingers right in his kidney. Hard. Or, depending on his mood and level of boredom, he might have bided his time, cornered him in the yard, and taken his anger and frustration out with his fists. But Salvatore was no longer the volatile kid of his youth. He was a changed man. And he didn't need revenge. Not anymore.

He just wanted what any reasonable person wanted—what belonged to him. What that conniving bitch Patricia had stolen so many years ago, right out from under his nose.

And he would do whatever it took to get it back.

29

"WELL?" MRS. WILT said, giving Tanner a look when they were alone in the front seat of the minivan the next morning. August was inside the motel office returning the room keys.

"Well what?"

"Are you going to make me spell it out? You're sitting there like the cat who got the canary."

Tanner was feeling pretty smug. And glowy. And exhausted from the hours-long marathon make-out session she had participated in with the hottest man she'd ever seen in her life. They hadn't gone to sleep until at least 4:00 a.m. Still, she pretend balked at Mrs. Wilt. "I didn't have sex with him, if that's what you're asking."

"Whyever not?"

This time, she balked for real. "Wait, *you're* the one who said not to do it with the hot ones. That they're German shepherds!" Or no, were the not-good-looking ones the dogs in the metaphor? Tanner couldn't remember.

"Dear God, child. Some rules are made to be broken."

"Oh, and why'd you put the gun in my suitcase?" Never mind *when*. Tanner couldn't even figure out when Mrs. Wilt had had time to slip it in, but the woman was nothing if not stealthy.

"For protection."

"From *August*? I thought you trusted him."

"You never know. He seems like a nice guy, but I've known plenty of men who seem like nice guys, if you know what I mean." She looked off into space, her eyes glazing over for a bit, as if lost in a memory. "My mom always kept a leg of lamb in the freezer. She never used it, though my stepfather gave her plenty of reasons to."

Tanner stared at her, unblinking. "What on *earth* are you talking about?"

Mrs. Wilt shrugged. "Just that it never hurts for a woman to have a backup plan is all."

"Well, I didn't need it, thank you. He was a perfect gentleman."

They both spotted August coming out of the office door at the same time, his jeans tight on his hips, the outline of his hard chest visible through his baby-blue T-shirt. He brushed a lock of hair out of his face, and his bicep tightened. Mrs. Wilt tutted. "That is entirely too bad."

AT 9:00 A.M. sharp, the motley threesome once again walked through the entrance of the Shasta Senior Assisted Living Center. Tanner was relieved to see the security guard was no longer at his post, but disappointed to find Sheila, the same sour-faced woman, behind the front desk. She glanced up when Tanner approached, but if she remembered them, her face didn't betray it.

"Welcome to the Shasta Senior Center," she said. "How can I help you?"

"We're here to see her friend," Tanner said. "George Dixon."

The woman click-clacked the keys once again and then held up a white card reader that looked almost like a credit card machine. She slipped it through the three-inch gap between the plexiglass and the desk. "Insert your IDs one at a time."

Tanner glanced at Mrs. Wilt with wide eyes. Could they actually chance inputting their real IDs? What if an alert went directly to the FBI as soon as the computer read their names? Or worse, what if an alarm went off, shutting the entire place down into a Code Red? Tanner had no idea how technology actually worked; she had only grown up with it. But Mrs. Wilt was already reaching into her handbag for her wallet. August slid his driver's license in first, and Sheila rewarded him with a guest pass—a sticker that had his name and image to affix to his T-shirt. Mrs. Wilt followed suit, and though nothing happened when she inserted her card—no SWAT team came out of the ceiling or anything—Tanner still held her breath when it was her turn. The machine beeped the same way it had for August and Mrs. Wilt, and then all three of them had their guest passes.

"Do you know where you're going?" Sheila asked.

"No," Tanner said.

Sheila pointed at the elevator bank with her pointy fingernail. "You're gonna take the hallway to your right all the way down until you see the sign that says MEMORY CARE UNIT. You'll need to scan one of your passes to unlock the door, and then it will automatically shut behind you. Room 273."

• • • • •

LOUISE DIDN'T SAY anything as they made their way down the hall. She couldn't tell if it was her natural slow-moving cane pace or the anticipation of seeing George mixed with the dread of whatever condition she'd find George in that made the walk feel as long as an airport runway, as distressing as a march to the gallows; but it was. When they reached the memory care unit, Tanner scanned her pass and a loud click came from the door. Once inside, they had to show their passes once again to a woman at another desk, a security guard standing sentry, and a few of George's words floated back to Louise from that phone call: "They've got this place under more surveillance than Chongqing, China."

She glanced up, and that was when she saw the cameras in nearly every corner of the room. She supposed in memory care, it made sense. You couldn't have one of your patients float out the front door, never to be seen again. But it was going to make absconding with one of them a touch difficult.

Down another hallway, they finally came to room 273, and Louise took a deep breath before knocking.

"Who is it?" The deep, scratchy voice was muted by the door, but Louise would recognize it anywhere. George. Her chest went tight, and she couldn't wait for an invitation. She opened the door, and her eyes fell on a figure on the other side of the room in a wheelchair, its back to the door. A woman, whose thin, bony shoulders fell slightly inward, toward her chin. Tufts of grayish-white hair stuck out haphazardly from her scalp like a mad scientist. Despite the effect of time and age to her appearance, Louise would recognize her anywhere. Even from behind.

"Emelda, is that you? I asked for an applesauce an hour ago."

George's face was turned, but not far enough to actually see who had entered the room. Far enough for Louise to see the many fine lines carving through her cheek, betraying the number of years that had passed between the women.

"No. It's me," Louise said.

"Who's me?" George said gruffly, grabbing the wheels of the chair with her hands, pushing them back and then forward again, executing a slow two-point turn until she could see Louise's face.

She blinked, as though she couldn't quite trust her eyesight. Louise held her breath. George blinked again.

"Patty?"

Louise's eyesight blurred, her head woozy with relief, not only at George recognizing her, but hearing her name—her real name—from her best friend's lips. She had forgotten what it felt like. To be known. Her grip tightened on her cane.

"Is it really you?"

"Well, I'm not the tooth fairy."

George blinked a third time. "I would like to say you haven't aged a bit, but I'm not a liar."

Louise arched an eyebrow. "You are a liar, you're just not a very good one."

George squinted past her at Tanner and August, who Louise had nearly forgotten were there. "Who'd you bring with you?" Her sparse eyebrows popped up. "Well, isn't he a *snack*. Why's the other one looking like she could catch flies?"

Louise glanced at Tanner, who indeed had her mouth hanging wide open.

Tanner moved it just then, searching for words. "She didn't tell me you were . . . you were . . ."

"Black?" George supplied.

"No."

"In a wheelchair?"

"No . . ." Tanner said, frustrated. "I thought you were a . . . *man*."

"Not the last time I checked."

Tanner turned to Louise, who shrugged. "I never said she was a man, you just assumed, which is interesting because I thought gender norms were a—what did you call it? *Social construct*."

Louise looked back at George. "Do you need an applesauce?"

George waved her hand. "No, I need you to sit your scrawny butt down and tell me what you've been doing for the last forty-eight years."

Louise step-thumped over to the edge of the bed and slowly lowered herself onto it. Her right hand was shaking something terrible. "Tanner, get me a glass of water."

"Oh, Patty," George said, eyeing her hand. "Parkinson's?"

Reaching into her bag, Louise paused, wondering if it was possible their connection still remained that strong after so many years. "How'd you know?"

"I live in a nursing home. Three people on this *floor* have it."

Louise swallowed a pill from her bag with the water Tanner supplied, and said, "What about you? Is it Alzheimer's?"

"Nah. Just my short term. They put me in here because I turned the kettle on for tea when I lived in a room in the independent living area and forgot about it. Nearly burned the whole place down." She pointed at Tanner and August. "Don't bother telling me their names, I'll never remember them."

"And Jermaine?" Louise asked, her voice going soft.

"Seven years ago next month. Emphysema," she chuckled, a faraway look in her eyes. "Would have died with a cigarette hanging out of his mouth, if they'd have let him."

Louise nodded, knowing George didn't have any use for her pity. "So . . . you know why I'm here?" she asked, still wary.

"Because you never listen to a blessed word I say. I told you not to come."

Louise let out a breath, her chest loosening a bit.

George tilted her head slightly, as if something had just occurred to her. "What day is it?"

Louise frowned. "You don't know what day it is?"

"I *told* you I have short-term memory issues. You never were good at listening."

"It's Monday."

"Monday?" George's eyes went wide. "Is he here?"

"I don't know."

"Is he out?"

"I don't know."

"Who's *he*?" August asked.

"That Salvatore guy," Tanner whispered. "The murderer."

"Glad to know you haven't changed a bit," George said, ignoring them both. "Still cutting it close, even when my life hangs in the balance. *Especially* when my life hangs in the balance, some might say."

"Oh, here we go," Louise said, rolling her eyes. "I knew you'd never really forgive me."

"Oh, I forgave you, I just won't ever forget. Faulty memory or no, when your best friend nearly has you killed, it's hard *not* to recollect."

"We're wasting time," Louise said, standing up and moving over to the window, pushing up on the frame. "Does this thing open?"

"Are you hot, too? They keep it ninety degrees in here, winter or summer. God knows why."

"No, I'm trying to figure out how best to get you out of here."

"That's something else you're good for—doing everything the hard way. What's wrong with the front door?"

"I thought you said security was too tight."

"Yes, for me to leave by myself. I'm in the *memory care unit*. They don't just let us wander off on our own. But they do allow day passes. You can pretend you're my friend."

"George," Louise said in a monotone. "I am your friend."

"So you say."

"Tell me what you need to take with you, we'll put it in my bag."

Louise set Tanner and August—who had been standing like two bumps on a log, watching Louise and George's exchange—to work, gathering the few things George dictated: a framed black-and-white photo of Jermaine in his military uniform (young and fresh-faced, the way Louise remembered him), a few pieces of sentimental jewelry, three changes of clothing, and enough pill bottles to rival Louise's own collection.

When it was all secured in Louise's bag, weighing it down, she handed it to Tanner to carry, and then nodded. "We ready?" she said to the room, and then, before waiting for a response: "August, get the wheelchair."

George eyed him as he walked around her, taking his position behind the chair and grabbing the handles. "Patty," she tsked. "You always did like 'em young."

August's eyes went wide as Tanner snorted.

"Don't laugh," Louise said sharply. "It only encourages her."

IT WAS SURPRISINGLY easy to check George out of the assisted living center for the day. Too easy, Tanner thought, after everything that had gone awry on this trip. But there they were, the four of them, in the minivan, the wheelchair now folded up and added to Mrs. Wilt's cane in the trunk, and August at the wheel.

"Where to?" he said.

"As far away from this place as you can get," George said.

"Miss Louise?" he said, looking at her reflection in the rearview mirror. But Mrs. Wilt didn't respond.

"Louise? Why's he calling you that?" George asked, and then she answered her own question. "*That's* the name you picked?"

"Of course," Louise said, studying the parking lot.

"Oh, Patty! That's fabulous."

"What's fabulous?" Tanner asked.

"*The Jeffersons.* Although you were always more of the George, with your harebrained schemes."

"Well, that name was already taken."

Tanner watched the two women continue to exchange barbs, the way they had been ever since they entered George's room, and she was surprised they'd hadn't seen each other in so long. Seemed like they picked up right where they left off—in the way that only best friends can. She was also surprised to find that in watching them she felt a little . . . jealous. Mrs. Wilt was *her* friend. Or at least her companion. And she missed having her attention all to herself. Or maybe it was that watching them reminded her of Vee, and she started missing her own best friend all over again.

She thought maybe it was time—past time—she did something about it.

"August, can I see your phone?"

He raised his thighs a few inches off the front seat and dug into his back pocket for his phone, holding his thumb on the sensory pad to unlock it before handing it to Tanner.

"Does that Cadillac look suspicious to you?" Mrs. Wilt said, studying the parking lot.

It wasn't clear whom she was asking, but Tanner turned her head and saw no less than seven various models of Cadillacs in the parking lot. "Which one?"

"Never mind."

Tanner began typing into the web browser of August's phone.

"You know, I haven't seen the coast in years," George said. "It's my dying wish."

"You're not dying, George," Mrs. Wilt said.

This jerked Tanner's gaze up from the screen. "Wait . . . she's *not* dying?" She was still sore that Mrs. Wilt had purposefully let her believe George was a man, but this was a bridge too far. "Have you ever told the truth about *anything*?"

Mrs. Wilt locked eyes with her, and Tanner was surprised to see in them not only shock but hurt. She opened her mouth to say something, but George cut her off.

"You told her I was dying?"

"Tectonic plates move faster than she drives," Mrs. Wilt said. "I had to tell her something. Besides, it wasn't a lie—" With that, she looked purposefully at Tanner once more. "You would be dying if Sal had got to you before we did."

"Oh Lordy, don't you go polishing the armor you're wearing over your white savior complex. I told you I didn't need you to come. He'd have had a tough time getting in after I put him on the Not Welcome Guest List."

"I don't think a lack of invitation ever stopped Salvatore D'Amato."

"Can we please stop saying his name?" Tanner said, shuddering. "It's giving me the creeps." Tanner still wasn't clear exactly what was going on, but from what she could gather, a murderer was going to be or had been released from jail and was hell-bent on finding George. She glanced around the parking lot once again. "And we should probably get out of here."

"So . . . to the coast?" August asked tentatively.

"What the hell," Mrs. Wilt said. "To the coast."

August put the car in drive, and Tanner entered her log-in information, pulling up her email. With her thumbs, she began typing to her best friend something she should have written months ago—an apology.

30

THE SILVERSIDE MOTEL on the coast of Northern California sat exactly three miles south of Eureka and three miles east of Humboldt Bay. It was kitschy, the tiny front office walls draped with old fishing nets and framed sea charts yellowed at the edges, the shelves stuffed to the gills with old shells, miniature lighthouses, and glass bottles—lest you forget you were at the beach. But it was off the beaten path, unassuming, and suited their needs perfectly for the one night they'd be there.

The man at the front desk offered Louise two connecting rooms—she didn't think Tanner and August would balk at sharing this time—and she was pleasantly surprised to find the rooms were clean, if small. After August deposited both George in her wheelchair and their luggage in the room, Louise took her time carefully hanging both her and George's clothing up in the tiny closet.

Laughter radiated from next door. Louise rolled her eyes. Thin walls—that could prove to be a problem later.

"You remember being young and in love like that?" George piped up. It was the first thing she'd said since they'd been in the room—and Louise had been surprised, but also not, at how easily the women fell into a comfortable silence with each other.

"Tanner's not in love," Louise said. "She's in lust."

"Oh, God. That's even better."

Louise chortled. She was happy for the girl. Tanner deserved some joy. Louise finished hanging the last blouse and then gripped her cane and step-thumped over to the small table and chair in the corner of the room. She sat down, her mind racing a mile a minute with everything she needed to think through. As promised, she would send Tanner and August on their way tomorrow with the money she owed Tanner. And then what?

"What do you think about Canada?" she said, giving voice to her train of thought. "We could probably find someone to sneak us across the border. I think Ellen still lives in Portland. Do you remember her?"

George didn't respond. She had maneuvered her wheelchair to the one window in the room, beside the front door. She was looking out it, much in the same position she'd been in when Louise entered her room at the nursing home.

"George?"

"This view is terrible."

"It's a parking lot."

"I wanted to see the ocean."

Louise stared at her a beat, wondering if she should push coming up with a plan. But she also knew when George got something in her head, she was single-minded in her need to see it through. Kind of like Louise. George was also, like most humans, more receptive when she was content—and nothing made her friend content like being near the water. "OK," Louise said. "Let's go."

AFTER A QUICK lunch of clam chowder and sandwiches from a small diner, August drove the unlikely foursome down a street that dead-ended at Humboldt Bay, a fourteen-mile expanse of deep water. That and a small strip of land on the other side of it were the only things between them and the Pacific.

"I said I wanted to see the ocean," George grumbled as August maneuvered her wheelchair over the mix of weeds and gritty sand to the left of where they'd parked the van.

"Close enough," Louise said. August set up the white plastic chair he had swiped from the pair that sat in front of the motel room, and then stepped back, allowing Louise to sit next to her friend.

August turned to Tanner. "Want to explore the coastline?"

The girl beamed bright enough to compete with the sun's rays glittering off the bay.

"Sure," she said, though Louise knew August could have asked her if she wanted to chew nails and the response would have been the same.

After the two lustbirds took off, George and Louise sat in silence for a minute, looking at the bay, the water gently lapping up against the shoreline, a warm breeze dancing on their skin.

"You know, I almost tore up your address and phone number when I got it."

Louise remembered the day, years ago, when she'd decided to search for her old friend on the Internet and found her home address within seconds. She couldn't believe George would be so cavalier. She sent her a letter berating her for her recklessness.

"Pretty ironic you were mad at me for my carelessness, while letting me know exactly where you were."

Louise grunted. "Well it was a good thing I sent it, wasn't it?" She'd done it under the pretense of safety, that it was important for George to warn Louise if Salvatore was getting out of prison, or if his people ever showed up. In reality, Louise just couldn't tolerate the idea she'd never see her friend again.

"Did you ever marry?" George asked.

Louise nodded. "Ken. Forty-three years we were together."

George raised her eyebrows in question.

"Heart attack. Textbook. Died in his sleep five years ago."

George put her veined hand over Louise's and squeezed. "So you met him right after . . ."

"I did."

"And he didn't care?"

Louise hesitated. "Well, I didn't tell him . . . everything."

George nodded.

"Did Jermaine ever forgive me?"

George watched a seabird glide across the sky parallel to the water, its wings still. "I think so," she said finally. "You know Jermaine. He was always so by the rules. He hated the position you put him in. Us."

"And you?" Louise asked. It was the question she dreaded the most—or the answer. That George had never truly been able to forgive her for what she'd done.

George turned to look at her then. "I *was* mad at you. I told you I didn't agree with what you were doing—that it wasn't gonna end well."

"I know, but I just couldn't—"

George let go of Louise's hand and held hers up, effectively cutting Louise off. "But I understood—better than Jermaine—why you had to do it; why *we* had to do it. You know, women didn't have as many choices back then as they do now. Sometimes you had to do the wrong thing to do the right thing."

Louise inhaled a lungful of sea air, the fresh tang of it cleansing her very soul, and then she slowly exhaled, feeling lighter by the second.

"Remember when we used to sneak into that movie theater?" George said with a mischievous smile.

"Well, that wasn't helping anybody but ourselves." Louise laughed, remembering how George had concocted the entire plot when they were twelve. Neither one of them could afford the twenty-five-cent entry fee, so Louise would run up to the box office and tell the ticket taker that she'd left her glasses inside and that her mama was gonna beat her black and blue if she didn't come home with them. Once she got in, she'd run to the back door and open it, where George would be standing, a huge grin on her face. "Do you really think things are better now? For women, I mean."

"Better than they were. Maybe not in Georgia. But in California, at least. No question. Why, you don't?"

Louise thought about her asshat neighbor Declan and his girlfriend, and how many women she'd seen just like her over her many years of living. She thought about her daughters and how she had worried over them constantly as teenagers—whether their skirts were too short, their shirts too tight. How she taught them to not take drinks from strangers, not drink too much, stay in groups, never walk home alone. How she harped on their need to be independent, take care of themselves—and how those conversations weren't much different from the ones her own mother had with her and that Jules had with her own daughter. And she thought of Tanner, who, when cornered by a leering drunk boy, instead of kneeing him in the groin or pushing him away or screaming in his face, capitulated to the long-suffering societal pressure to be polite, to be "good"—and fell off a goddamned balcony.

"I don't know," Louise said. "Sometimes it just feels like we still spend so much time trying to teach the house not to catch on fire, instead of teaching the arsonist not to light it."

THEY RETURNED TO the motel when the sun was halfway down the other side of the sky. Tanner and August had been making such mooneyes at each other in the car that as soon as August lifted George from the seat and gently settled her into the wheelchair, Louise waved them off. "Go on, we can manage from here."

"I can push it to the room," he said. "I don't mind."

"I mind," Louise said. "Looking at you two is giving me a cavity."

August shrugged. "OK. I'll go pick something up for dinner in an hour or two—is there anything special you want?"

"Nothing fried," George said. "It gives me gas."

"Yes, ma'am," August said, saluting, and he sauntered off with Tanner skipping by his side.

Louise sighed and laid her cane across George's lap. "Hold this," she said. Then she took the handles of the chair and slowly pushed it toward their door.

"You never said what you thought about Canada," Louise said as she inserted the key into the lock and turned.

"I think it's very clean," George said. "And cold."

Louise pushed her friend over the threshold into the dark room and closed the door behind them, already looking forward to taking her shoes off, lying on the bed to rest. When she turned on the light, she gasped. Sitting in the chair in the far corner of the room was a man.

Louise's heart revved and her hands went clammy. "Salvatore." She reached into the bag hanging on her shoulder, palm open to grasp the handle of her gun, and then froze when she realized she'd never gotten it back from Tanner.

"Uh-uh-uh," Salvatore tsked, waving a hand stuck in his jacket pocket at her, where a bulge suspiciously in the shape of a pistol resided. "Show of hands please." Louise slowly pulled her hand out of her bag and waved it at him.

"Don't think about trying to run, either," he said. "I'm not in the mood to continue this game of chase."

"You can rest assured I will not be running anywhere," George said.

Salvatore raised one eyebrow. "George, I presume. A pleasure to finally meet you."

"Wish I could say the same."

"If this is a social visit, can I sit?" Louise asked, not without a little annoyance. "My legs are tired."

"Be my guest," Salvatore responded.

Louise pushed George over to the bed and then took a seat beside the wheelchair so they were both facing him. A little closer now, she studied him, surprised that his face remained mostly unlined, his hair, though streaked with gray, still full and combed away from his face with gel.

"Is it just me," George said out of the side of her mouth, "or does he look a little like that guy—oh, what's his name? See? The memory. Gone."

Louise stared at her. "Do you remember the movie?"

"*The Usual Suspects*. He also played that Che Guevara guy. That was an excellent film."

"Benicio del Toro?"

"Yes! That's it," George said. "Why do men get better looking as they age? I'll never get over the unfairness of it."

"Are you two quite done?" Salvatore asked.

"Yes," George said, waving her hand. "Carry on."

"How did you find us?" Louise asked. Whether it was from George's wisecracks, or the fact that Salvatore hadn't killed them right away, or the relief that the one thing she'd feared for most of the past forty-eight years—Salvatore finding them—had finally happened and it couldn't possibly live up to the terror of her imagination, or the mere fact that maybe she really was too old to give a damn anymore, Louise's heartbeat slowed and she felt eerily calm.

He pointed a knobby index finger at Louise. "You—I could never find." He turned his finger, stabbing it at George. "This one was on the front page of every paper in the nineties, trying this case or that, putting people behind bars. Taunting me, it felt like." He tsked, wagging a finger. "Not a very low profile you were keeping."

"I told you to change your name, George," Louise hissed.

"Jermaine wouldn't hear of it! Leaving town and moving to California was all the running he was going to do."

"It was simple, really," Sal continued. "I knew if you thought George was in trouble, you'd come running. You never could mind your own business. Especially when it came to my wife."

A flash of anger burned though Louise. "Don't you talk about Betsy. You have no right."

"No!" Salvatore yelled sharply, hitting the table with his fist for emphasis. Louise startled. She'd nearly forgotten what a monster he transformed into when he was angry, how his face contorted, his eyes going dark. Her heartbeat picked up speed once more. "That is rich," he spat. "You, to talk about rights." He steepled his fingers, elbows resting on the arms of the chair. "You had no right to take what was mine, did you? But here we are."

"WAIT," TANNER SAID, sitting up, her hair sticking out in all directions, her shirt pushed up around her neck, one cup of her bra hanging down, revealing her naked breast.

"What?" August said. "I wasn't gonna take the bra off completely."

"No," Tanner said. "Do you hear that?"

"Hear what? Why are you whispering?"

"It's a voice. A man's voice. Coming from—" Tanner pointed at the inside door connecting their room to Louise and George's.

"Oh, I do hear that." August said, and leaned back down to plant a trail of kisses on Tanner's neck. "They probably ordered more towels or something."

Tanner pushed him off. "No, I don't think that's . . . what if it's that Salvatore guy?" She sat up straighter.

"I really don't think he could—"

"NO!"

They both jumped at the word coming through the wall and the pounding that accompanied it.

"Maybe he's out of towels?" August whispered.

Tanner leapt to her feet, pulling her shirt back down and running to her suitcase.

"What are you doing?"

"I've got the gun," Tanner said. "Mrs. Wilt never took it back!"

She unzipped her luggage and grabbed the pistol, holding it out in front of her with both hands and cocking it as she tiptoed to the door connecting the two rooms.

"What's the plan here?" August whispered, right behind her.

"I don't know," Tanner admitted. But she did know, in her gut, that Mrs. Wilt was in trouble. And she couldn't stand by and do nothing. "Open the door as quietly as you can."

August put his hand on the knob and turned it, slowly pulling the door open to reveal . . . another door.

"Shit!" Tanner said. She had forgotten that the adjoining room would have its own door. She heard another shout that sounded like Mrs. Wilt, and without thinking, she lifted her good leg and slammed her foot into the second door, kicking it down and taking some of the doorframe with it.

Heart beating wildly, she stepped across the threshold and waved the gun around the room, blind with fear. "Freeze!" she said, even though she couldn't see whom she was talking to, or if they were indeed moving. She wasn't even sure why she said it, except wasn't that what the good guy with the gun always said in the movies?

She felt August step up behind her, his arm coming into view next to hers, and then he gently took her hand and guided the gun to the right, to point it directly at a man sitting in the corner of the room. A man who kind of had an older Nick Jonas thing going for him.

"Thank you," Tanner said, and then she glanced at Mrs. Wilt and George, who both had their hands straight up in the air in a literal *don't shoot* motion and were staring at her wide-eyed.

"Yes, thank you," Mrs. Wilt said to August, lowering her hands.

"Sorry about that," Tanner said, ducking her head sheepishly. She trained her eyes back on the Jonas Brothers guy. "Are you Salvatore?"

"I am," he said. "And you are?"

"Tanner," she said, and then nodded at August. "This is—" She paused, not quite sure what to say next. Boyfriend? No, they certainly weren't serious. Lover? Gross. Only old people said that.

"Did you forget my name?" August hissed.

"No! This is August."

Mrs. Wilt spoke next, her voice level: "Well, now that we're all acquainted—"

Salvatore began to stand up.

"I said *don't move*," Tanner screeched.

He stilled midair, and then a slow grin spread across his lips. "Do you even know how to work that thing?" he said, his voice dripping with condescension. He said it in the way boys had been talking to her for her entire life, like she was an adorable baby panda. How *cute* that she thought she knew how to play soccer or video games or knew a little about engines in cars, but they clearly knew more or played better. And when she blinked, for a split second, she could have sworn that Salvatore's face had been replaced by that drunk, leering boy who she'd backed away from, instead of stepping toward. Instead of claiming her space on that balcony. In this world.

And then Tanner saw nothing at all but red. Driven by pure rage and fury, she squeezed the trigger as hard as she could.

BANG!

In the silence that followed, Tanner, her hands shaking as they still gripped the gun, opened one eye and then the other, half expecting the gruesome sight of a bloodied head in front of her. But Salvatore remained intact, his eyes and mouth large round Os of surprise.

The lamp beside him, however, hadn't fared so well.

"Good Lord, you're a terrible shot," Mrs. Wilt muttered, just as the door to the motel room burst open and everyone turned, startled by the commotion. A woman rushed into the room, gun drawn, two people flanking her with their guns drawn as well. "FBI!" she yelled. "Nobody move."

Tanner panicked. She was holding a gun! She had just tried to *shoot* someone! And the cops were here!

"You," the woman said, pointing her barrel directly at Tanner. "Drop your weapon."

Tanner set it on the dresser to her right.

"No! On the floor. Kick it over to me."

"Are you sure that's safe?"

The woman gave an exasperated look. "Please do as I say."

It took Tanner three tries to kick the gun to the woman, because she was afraid to kick it too hard, and the first two attempts were more like light taps.

The FBI agent then looked at Salvatore. "Are you armed?"

His hands were in the air. "No."

"Check his pockets," Mrs. Wilt said.

The FBI agent glanced at Mrs. Wilt and then nodded her head to the man on her right. "Check his pockets."

The man walked over to Salvatore, asked him to stand, and patted him down. "He's clean," he said.

Mrs. Wilt balked. "I knew that wasn't a gun!"

"Sue me," Salvatore retorted, and then nodded his head at Tanner. "At least I didn't call the police."

"*I* didn't call the police!" Tanner protested.

"Quiet!" the FBI woman said. "I'll be the one asking the questions here." She took what Tanner felt was an unnecessarily dramatic pause, considering everyone's eyes were already on her, waiting.

"Now, can somebody please tell me exactly where the money and jewels are?"

"I don't know about any money, but the second part is what I came to find out as well—where is my daughter?"

The FBI agent swung her head at Salvatore, her brow furrowed. "What?"

"My daughter Jules," he said calmly. He pointed at Mrs. Wilt. "She stole her from me forty-eight years ago, and I haven't seen her since."

31

JANUARY 1975, FORTY-EIGHT YEARS BEFORE LOUISE WENT MISSING AND JULES CALLED THE POLICE

A LOUD CRASH woke George immediately. It was just before midnight, January 1, not even a full twenty-four hours into the New Year. She sat up in bed, fully alert. Her husband, Jermaine, was a pilot for Ace Air Cargo Express, and though she typically appreciated the independence his work hours gave her, at that moment, scared and alone, she wished he were there beside her to help ward off whatever dangers lurked in the backyard—though she knew deep down she had probably brought them on herself.

She quietly slid her Ruger out of the drawer of her nightstand, and, clad only in a nightgown, tiptoed to the back door, where all the racket had come from. Holding the pistol firmly in one hand, she flipped on the light and carefully peered out the one square of window in the middle of the door. When she saw who was on the back porch, relief rushed through her and she quickly slid the chain off the door, unlocked the dead bolt, and opened the door.

Patty stood there, shivering, in nothing but a polyester shirtdress fitted at the waist and kitten heels, holding a blue blanket bundled in her arms. George wondered why she didn't have it open and pulled tight around her shoulders, given the thirty-six-degree weather—and that was when she heard the blanket offer a very tiny but unmistakably humanlike gurgle. Her eyes jumped from the bundle up to her best friend's face, and her stomach dropped to her toes.

"Oh, Patty," George said. "What have you done?"

Patty looked up at her, terror in her eyes. "There's something else you should know."

ONE COULD POSIT that everything leading up to the moment on George's back porch—*and* leading up to the events in room nineteen of the Silverside Motel some forty-eight years later—could all be traced back to one very specific kiss beneath an umbrella on the corner of Seventy-First Street and Thirteenth Avenue in Brooklyn, New York, in 1968.

Betsy Blau knew she shouldn't have kissed him—just like she knew she shouldn't allow him to walk her from the bus stop to her house every day. But, Betsy reasoned, her father didn't return home from the wharf until 6:00 p.m., like clockwork, and her bus dropped her off at 4:30 p.m. and Sal only walked her to the corner of her street, so her mother wouldn't know, and who was it really hurting, this simple act of *walking*?

To complicate matters, she was nineteen years old and had never been much farther than Bensonhurst. While Salvatore D'Amato, the man who had taken to showing up at her bus stop, waiting for her every afternoon, was twenty-four and so . . . *worldly*. Perhaps more importantly—if you squinted, he looked a little bit like Tony Curtis minus the blue eyes, and his Brut cologne was like a drug, the spicy tang of it overwhelming her senses and making her think a hundred different things—ninety-nine of which a nice Jewish girl like herself was absolutely *not* supposed to be thinking.

So honestly, it couldn't be helped. When Sal leaned down to kiss her, her body gave her no choice but to respond in kind, the sparks firing off every single nerve ending in her skin (and places she didn't even know she *had* nerve endings, truth be told), obliterating what she knew in her brain she *ought* to do—lean back when he leaned forward. Walk home alone. Tell him to stop meeting her. And she would. She would! But each day when she went to say the words, they melted in the back of her throat before she could push them out.

And then he kissed her.

She walked the rest of the way to her family's brownstone alone, in a fugue state of sorts, not noticing the raindrops soaking her hair, the fabric of her dress, feeling more like she was floating than like her feet were actually touching the ground. But then she made it up to her room half-drunk with giddiness, the other half of her filled with terror at the sinking realization of what she had done. It was irresponsible, kissing him in broad daylight like that. Downright dangerous, really. Her father would kill them both if he ever knew—which he *absolutely* would not—and there was nothing she feared more as a nineteen-year-old than her father's wrath.

She would end it tomorrow.

Except she never got the chance. When her father came home that night at 6:00 p.m. on the dot, he thundered through the door, calling her name in a rage. As fate would have it, a colleague of his happened to be driving by the corner at precisely the same time Betsy Blau was experiencing her first kiss, recognizing both his coworker's daughter and Salvatore D'Amato (nearly everyone in Bensonhurst recognized Salvatore D'Amato, his having made quite a name for himself as a leader of the Bath Avenue Crew, known for their particularly ruthless sort of bookmaking, loan-sharking, and gambling).

Though it was the 1960s and much of New York was experiencing a cultural revolution of sorts, Betsy's father retained a lot of old-school ideas—mainly that no Jewish daughter of his was to fraternize with a wop, particularly one the likes of Salvatore D'Amato, and that a girl was only as good as her reputation, which Betsy had all but thrown away. There were tears and screaming and a slap that cracked Betsy's face so hard the neighbors heard it, pausing ever so briefly as they ate their dinner. By the end of it all, Betsy had been unceremoniously deposited on her front stoop with a suitcase of her belongings, and nowhere to go but straight into the arms of Salvatore.

They were married a week later at St. Dominic Catholic Church.

He beat her for the first time two weeks after that.

At first Betsy tried to rationalize it. Sal worked so hard, he was under so much pressure, and really she *had* undercooked the roast, or overcooked the pasta, or not put enough ice in his gin. And it really didn't happen all that often. And he was always so apologetic the next day, surprising her with large bouquets of fresh flowers, sparkly new necklaces, bracelets, or earrings, tickets to the latest Broadway show (Broadway! She loved Broadway). She set herself to becoming a better cook, a better wife, but she always seemed to mess up somehow. Still, she loved him—even though a whiff of his Brut cologne sometimes nauseated her more than it turned her on—and she accepted it as her lot in life, the consequences of being married to a man like Sal, same as she accepted that it wasn't in the cards for her to be a mother. Years passed, and no matter what tips she tried out of *Ladies' Home Journal* (elevate your legs with a pillow after sex! Drink a teaspoon of Robitussin every day! Wear rose quartz jewelry!), her period came every month—and though lonely, eventually she started to think it was probably for the best.

Until 1974. When she got pregnant with their first child. While her life with Sal was a choice she had resigned herself to, the more the baby grew inside of her, the more she realized she couldn't resign her child to the same fate.

BETSY BLAU D'AMATO found George Dixon through a friend of a friend—the way most women throughout the Northeast had found Patty and George in their unassuming Ohio town over the fifteen years they'd been working together. It was a whisper network, before whisper networks were a thing, before women's shelters were prevalent, when women in abusive relationships had nowhere else to turn except back toward the men who pummeled them one minute and groveled their apologies the next.

When the call came through, George would have said no immediately. But Patty happened to be over at her house, watching the new sitcom they loved, *The Jeffersons*, chain-smoking a pack of Winstons, leg hung over the arm of the easy chair in a very unladylike position—and sitting closest to the phone. Patty raised her eyebrows at George as she talked to Betsy in her soothing but pragmatic way, wrote some information and a phone number on the back of the cigarette box, and said she'd call her back.

The problem was, George never could say no to Patty.

"She has a child coming," Patty pleaded. "You and I both know what it's like to be raised in that environment. We can't *not* do it."

"We have rules, too, Patty. For good reason. No police wives, no gangsters." Though Lord knew they got enough phone calls from both.

In the end, Patty won, and they spent three long months carefully formulating a plan, Patty traveling back and forth to New York to meet secretively with Betsy and prepare her for the night she'd be leaving and the new life she'd be entering. They often spent weeks with each client, not just because it took their document falsifier that long to come up with the new identities for the women, but because they had to plot the escape down to every last detail, making sure that no hiccup—a husband returning unexpectedly, a neighbor spotting them, a dog barking—would foil their mission.

Finally, a week before Betsy's due date, they were ready. George wasn't thrilled with the prospect of secreting a heavily pregnant woman out of Brooklyn, New York, but Patty (rightly) reasoned it was easier than translocating a woman and her crying newborn. But when Patty, dressed in black from head to toe, quietly knocked on the basement window of the D'Amato brownstone at 2:00 a.m. the night she had agreed upon with Betsy, no one answered. Sadly, it wasn't unusual in Patty's line of work. A woman getting cold feet. Changing her mind.

In Betsy's case it was neither. At dinner that night, Sal had poked her in the side. Said she was getting fat. That no man would want her. It was nothing new—Sal had been saying cruel things to Betsy for years, but whether it was the straw that broke the camel's back or pregnancy hormones or some kind of twisted fear of leaving, Betsy flew into a blind rage. Told Sal she was leaving him, that she'd been planning it for months. Sal returned this news with his fists, and by the time Patty tapped on the basement window in the early hours of the morning, Betsy lay across town at the Brooklyn Women's Hospital on life support, having delivered a healthy baby girl from her broken body.

She died two days later.

That should have been the end of George and Patty's connection to Betsy Blau D'Amato, save for one itsy-bitsy promise Patty had made in passing during one of the many hours she had spent with Betsy over the previous three months. "If anything happens to me before I get out, please save my baby. Don't leave him with Sal." (Though prescient about her impending death, Betsy had been sure her child was going to be a boy.)

"It's not our problem," George said.

"It's too dangerous," George said.

"What are we going to do with a baby?" George said. "Jermaine and I certainly can't take her. And you're not exactly the motherly sort."

Patty had to agree that George's analysis was spot-on, because it was. And George thought that was the end of that.

Until two months later, when Patty showed up a little before midnight on January 1, 1975, in George's backyard with Betsy and Salvatore D'Amato's baby, Jules, squawking in her arms.

32

ALL SEVEN PAIRS of eyes in the room turned and pinned their gaze on Louise.

"I'm sorry. You kidnapped his *daughter*?" the FBI agent said.

"I did," Louise nodded. "And I . . . I killed a man." She blurted it out before she could stop herself. It felt so good to confess, to push the weight she'd been carrying for so long off her chest. There was so much she would take back if she could. Not taking Jules, of course, but going to George's house. She thought they'd be safe there, at least while she figured out what to do.

Until the phone rang.

George and Patty were in the middle of frantic negotiations—trying to figure out how Patty could get new identification at the eleventh hour, when it typically took weeks to process. The logistics of where and how she would disappear with a baby who did not belong to her, hiding from a man who would surely never stop hunting—not because he cared about his daughter as much as because you didn't take anything from Salvatore D'Amato and live to tell about it.

They both stared at the shrieking handset. Finally, Patty picked it up and put the receiver to her ear.

"Georgia Dixon, I presume," came Sal's smooth deep voice. "Is that you? Or maybe it's your business partner . . . Patty."

Patty swallowed. How did he know her real name?

"Or Roxy, as she introduced herself to me."

That was the part Patty had chosen to play, a New York nanny who swooped in to care for Sal's motherless daughter. She had promised George she wouldn't take the girl. But she hadn't promised she wouldn't try to make sure Jules was OK. Taken care of. Loved and protected. It was easy, really, as Sal wanted nothing to do with fatherhood and hired Patty on the spot. Maybe it was too easy, Patty thought now.

"Yes, I knew it was you helping Betsy run off. You think I didn't keep track of her movements, her phone calls? What kind of husband would I be if I did not remain interested in my wife's new friends? Or trace her phone records . . ."

The mention of Betsy shot fire though Patty's veins. Whether she wanted to or not, she had befriended the woman in the months they had spent together. "How *dare* you. You killed her, you bastard."

"I have no idea what you're talking about. My poor Betsy fell down the stairs. But *you*—you have taken something from me. And if you give her back to the nice gentleman who followed you there, I won't report it to the police."

Patty's eyes went wild, clutching Jules, and searching the dark night beyond the windows for any sign of an intruder.

"There's one thing I can't make heads or tails of, though. I knew who you were when I hired you—but why did you take so long to steal her? You had every opportunity in the two months you were in my employ."

Patty didn't respond.

"No matter. Rest assured, if I ever see you again, you will meet the same fate as my dearly departed wife."

A click in her ear and the line went dead.

"I SHOT HIM, Louise," George said now. "I don't know how many times we have to fight about that."

It was true that when the man burst in through the back door, both George and Louise raised their pistols and pulled their respective triggers. It was all such a blur, neither one knew for sure which bullet had missed, hitting the Sheetrock in the wall behind him, and which one struck him in the face, crumpling his body to the ground and sending a thick spray of blood across the room.

And then they ran, grabbing a few of their belongings and only stopping at the airport to intercept Jermaine, who was so hotly furious when they told him what they had done, Patty thought he would never speak to her again. Not that it mattered, since they parted ways an hour later, vowing to never speak, never see each other again, for the safety of everyone, dropping Patty at a bus station, headed for North Carolina, where she stepped off hours later as a woman named Louise, who had adopted her best friend's baby.

"Let me get this straight. You're confessing to a kidnapping *and* a murder?" the FBI agent said.

"She didn't kill him," George said, exasperated.

"I did," Louise said, because whether it had been her bullet or not, she wouldn't let her friend take the fall. Not after everything she'd already put her through.

"No, you didn't," George said. "When we got back to the house, the body was gone."

"What?" Louise snapped her head so fast she nearly got whiplash. "You went back?"

"Jermaine insisted. In case he was alive and we could save him."

"But you were supposed to leave, like I did! So you wouldn't—"

"I know," George cut her off. "And we did shortly thereafter. We cleaned up the blood. Packed our things and set out for California. Had a friend in real estate who sold the house and sent us our money."

"OK," the FBI agent said emphatically while she put one hand on her hip and the other up in the air, palm facing the room in a universal *stop* motion. "Can we just back up here? I don't know anything about a kidnapping—but we'll get to that. I want to know where the money and the jewelry and the *Kinsey diamond* are that you stole from the Copley Plaza hotel."

"This again?" Sal snorted. "You FBI agents have been sniffing around me for years, and I don't know how many times I have to tell you, that was not me."

"I know it wasn't," the agent said. "I'm talking to her."

All eyes turned in the direction the FBI agent was looking.

"*Me?*" Louise said. "The only thing I stole was a baby. I thought that was why you were looking for me." She turned to Tanner. "That's what you said they said on the news—that I stole Jules."

Tanner stared at her hard, her brow furrowed. "No . . ." she said slowly. "I said they said you stole . . . jewels." She put her hand to her mouth. "Oh my God. I did say that. This whole time I thought you were some mastermind jewelry thief."

August looked from Tanner to Louise and then to the FBI agent in disbelief. "You're telling me we're all in this room together based on a . . . homophone?"

George let out a long, slow whistle, exaggeratively clapping her knobby hands together twice. "And here I thought you were just good-looking. Brains *and* brawn? Tanner, you may wanna keep him."

"OK, I've had enough," the agent in charge said. "You're all coming with me for questioning, and we're gonna get to the bottom of this before the day is over."

"I'm not going anywhere," Sal erupted. "I just got out of the clink and I haven't done anything to violate my parole."

"Breaking and entering into this hotel room doesn't count?" the FBI agent said. The man who patted Sal down now stood him up, cuffed him, and walked him out of the room first. But when they were passing Louise, Sal stopped in his tracks and held her gaze. "Look," he said. "I'm old. And I'm tired. And I've made a good many mistakes in my life. I'm not saying I regret most of them, or that I'm some changed man or anything. It's just that when someone looks you in the eye and tells you you're dying, you tend to take stock of your life and what you're leaving behind. And like it or not, Jules is part of me. I came all this way because I want to meet her. I want to see my legacy."

Louise gave him a hard stare. She wanted to say he should have thought of all that before he killed Betsy. Before he ever laid a hand on her in the first place. She wanted to say that Jules wasn't any more part of him than Louise herself was part of the royal family in England (which was to say, not at all), that Jules didn't have a mean bone in her body (irritating, yes, but not mean). But Louise wasn't completely coldhearted. She knew Sal didn't deserve it, but she also knew it wasn't up to her. It was up to Jules, whom Louise would finally tell the entire truth about the circumstances of her not-quite-legal adoption, and then let her decide.

It was what any good mother would do.

NEXT TO A Logan's Roadhouse, the FBI field office in Redding, California, looked like someone had taken the Atlanta field office, cut it in half, and shrunk it by two stories.

Lorna Huang sat in a corner office, a near-identical match to the one she'd used in Atlanta, shaking two Excedrin Migraine tablets into her hand, popping them in her mouth, and swallowing them without the benefit of water. Then she squeezed the bridge of her nose with her pointer finger and thumb, willing the medicine to work faster.

What a day. And night. Lorna glanced at her cell phone: 1:38 a.m. She sighed.

After hours of questioning each person separately and trying to piece together the full story, all Lorna had was a forty-eight-year-old kidnapping case that she couldn't—or wouldn't—move forward with because the father in question didn't want to press charges, and the girl in question, by all accounts, had a much better life with the woman her biological mother had asked to raise her.

And Lorna was no closer to figuring out who had knocked off the Copley Plaza hotel or where the Kinsey diamond might be (though many experts agreed whoever had stolen it had likely cut it into smaller diamonds in order to sell it on the black market, and Lorna had to admit that was probably true).

The only thing she knew for sure was that she had been wrong. About everything.

A knock at her open door lifted her head.

Jamal was looking at her.

"Mrs. Dixon is safely back at the Shasta Senior Center. And Mrs. Wilt—or Nichols, I guess—and Tanner and August are at the Sheraton. I've scheduled a private jet for 10:30 a.m. tomorrow to transport them—and us—back to Atlanta."

"Thank you, Jamal," she said. She had to hand it to him. They'd still be in Fort Morgan, Colorado, with their thumbs up their asses and a priest who was clearly lying—or withholding the truth, anyway—if it hadn't been for Jamal's quick thinking. He'd had the (dumb, in Lorna's opinion) idea to try and question Salvatore D'Amato one more time, and had found out that the man was set to be released from prison. Jamal had asked for the phone records for D'Amato, which was how he'd found D'Amato had placed a phone call to a nursing home in Redding, California, just days earlier. It seemed like a long shot, but it also seemed like a strong possibility that that was where Tanner and Mrs. Wilt's cross-country journey might be taking them.

Lorna had put a team on watch at the nursing home, and she and Jamal took the first flight out to Redding. Sure enough, who should show up Sunday evening in the Shasta Senior Center parking lot but Louise/Patricia, Tanner, and an unknown young man in a minivan. Lorna made the call to hold off apprehending them, in the hopes that they would lead them to where the jewels were stashed. But instead they'd led them to that kitschy motel and—to Lorna's great surprise—Salvatore D'Amato.

She nodded now at Jamal's report. "Good work."

"Thanks," he said, his face brightening.

Lorna really did think Jamal had a future ahead of him in the FBI; she just wasn't so sure she did anymore. She missed her son. She missed her *husband*. And most importantly, she couldn't remember why she spent so much time working. It wasn't just that this case had so spectacularly blown up in her face. For a long time, she'd wondered if she threw herself into her work so hard because she still truly loved it, like she had in the beginning, or if that feeling had slowly morphed into having something to prove. *Look at me! I have it all!* But the truth was she didn't have it all—unless "it all" was a crumbling marriage and a job that had flatlined for the past five years because, no matter how much she threw herself into her work, casting aside everything else in her life, she couldn't quite figure out how to get that next promotion. And now she wasn't sure that she wanted it.

"I'm gonna get an Uber to the hotel," Jamal said. "Meet you downstairs in five?"

She shook her head.

"No?" Jamal asked, surprised.

"Nope," she said. "I think I'm gonna head back to the coast. Get a room at that motel for a few days."

"The *Silverside*?"

"Yep."

"Ohh . . . kay." He hesitated at the door, then narrowed his eyes. "You sure you're alright, boss?"

"Yep, Jamal, I'm good."

And she was. For the first time in a long time. She needed a break. She *deserved* a break. She picked up the phone, dialing her husband's number. He and Philip were going to love it there.

33

TANNER PEERED AT her seatmate out of the corner of her eye. Mrs. Wilt's clawlike hands gripped the armrests so hard her knuckles were white. Her body pressed back into the seat as if she hoped it would swallow her whole. Her eyes were closed, not peacefully as though she were sleeping, but clenched the way a toddler might close them, convinced there was a monster in their closet in the middle of the night and not wanting to lay eyes on it. Tanner grinned, a warm feeling washing over her that felt an awful lot like fondness for this woman whose very presence, a mere seven days earlier, had made her want to throttle someone. Life was funny sometimes.

"You *do* know it's safer to fly in a plane than it is to ride in a car, don't you?" Tanner said.

Mrs. Wilt opened one of her eyes and found Tanner with it, leaving the other one squeezed shut.

"You do know guns can't load themselves in glove compartments, don't you?"

Tanner grinned wider. "Whatever." She looked past Mrs. Wilt out the airplane window at the puffy clouds beneath them, her brain swimming with all the information she'd learned about her cross-country companion over the past twelve hours. Mrs. Wilt may not have been the jewelry thief, but she had stolen a baby! From a murderous gangster! And Tanner had to admit she was a bit in awe of the life Mrs. Wilt had led. The way she'd thrown caution to the wind, bucked convention, broken the *law*, all to help those women. And one woman in particular—Betsy. Tanner felt a bloom of jealousy, wishing she could be more like Mrs. Wilt. That she wasn't so scared all the time. So fixated on the rules.

But then again . . . in the past week, she'd been on the run from the police. Broken the speed limit. Made out with an inappropriately hot man. Shot a gun!

Maybe she was a bit more like Mrs. Wilt than she thought.

"So, there's one thing I'm not clear on—does Jules know she was adopted?" Tanner asked, not solely because she was curious, but also in an attempt to keep Mrs. Wilt's mind off her fear.

"She's always known," Mrs. Wilt said, opening both eyes this time, but not loosening her grip on the armrests. "I told her as much truth as I could—that my good friend was her mother and that she died right after giving birth to her and wanted me to have her."

"And she never asked about her father?"

"Well, him I lied about. I figure thinking your biological father was dead was a sight better than knowing he was an abusive gangster that killed your biological mother and was serving time in prison for tax fraud, and eventually murder."

Put that way, Tanner thought she might be right. The captain turned off the FASTEN SEAT BELT sign and announced it was safe to move about the cabin.

"Let me ask you something." Mrs. Wilt cast a sidelong look at Tanner. "What were you thinking, running into the room half-cocked like that?"

"I wasn't thinking!" Tanner said, her eyes wide. She still couldn't believe she had done it, either. In the hours since firing the gun, all she could think was thank *God* she hadn't hit anyone. Even if Salvatore deserved it. She would never have been able to live with herself. She shook her head with a half laugh. "But I knew you were in danger, and I couldn't just stand there and do nothing."

"Well, at least we found something you're good at."

"What, gun handling?" Tanner asked, still laughing.

Mrs. Wilt cackled. "God, no. Salvatore's lucky you couldn't hit the broad side of a barn," she said, which made Tanner laugh even harder.

When they caught their breath, Tanner crinkled her brow. "Then what am I good at?"

Mrs. Wilt took a long pull from a plastic water bottle and recapped it. Then she glanced at Tanner and said purposefully, "Being a friend."

Tanner stiffened. She tried to swallow, but found it was hard with the sudden lump in her throat. Mrs. Wilt reached out and took Tanner's hand in her own. She squeezed. And Tanner realized in that moment, she didn't want to go back to Atlanta. She didn't want to go back to her life, to who she was *before*. Or maybe she just didn't want to leave the one person in her life that she hadn't pushed away with her anger and outrage—a person who seemed to genuinely like her. Or at least not mind her being around.

She tried to swallow again, but her throat was dry. "I sometimes feel like you're the only person in this whole world who . . . understands me."

Mrs. Wilt squeezed her hand once more and sighed. "Oh, Tanner. I just understand what it's like to be a woman."

Four hours later, when the pilot announced the plane was going to be landing soon, Tanner's chest got tight.

"I'm going to miss you." Tanner didn't even realize she had said it out loud until Mrs. Wilt turned to her with big eyes. She was a little embarrassed at her own earnestness, but it was true. Or close enough to the truth. She didn't know how to explain what she really felt. What Mrs. Wilt meant to her. How she had somehow, in the span of six days, completely changed her life.

"You are? Where are you going?"

"Well, I know George is coming to live with you." Tanner had overheard the two women talking before George was transported back to the nursing home the night before. "And you'll need to hire a real nurse to help with all the medical stuff."

Mrs. Wilt didn't respond. Not right away. Tanner wasn't even sure the woman had heard her. The plane started to nose-dive a bit in its descent. Mrs. Wilt clutched the armrest tighter and then spoke.

"I owe you some money, don't I?"

"Oh," Tanner said. "You don't have to—"

Mrs. Wilt cut her off. "I don't have it on me. The FBI confiscated the cash until I can send them the paperwork to prove it's Ken's life insurance. So you'll just have to visit me to come get it, you hear?"

Tanner nodded, understanding. "I'll visit you," she said. Cars on the highway below began to grow bigger than ants. Tanner could see pools in suburban backyards. She thought about the money and found that while she wanted to go back to school, finish her degree—it didn't seem so important to do that at Northwestern anymore.

Once, it had seemed like her only option. Like life was only supposed to go one way. Like there was one road on a map she was expected to follow, and when she got knocked off it, she'd scrambled so hard to try and get back on it, she couldn't see all the other routes available to her.

"So are you going to start going by Patty again?"

"No, I don't think so," Mrs. Wilt said. "That woman existed a lifetime ago."

"I have to ask—is that why you wouldn't let me call you Louise?"

"Because it's not my real name?"

Tanner nodded.

"No, it's because I prefer Mrs. Wilt."

"Why?" Tanner pressed.

"It's Ken's name. Makes me feel closer to him."

"Oh," Tanner said, and then narrowed her eyes. "So why do you let August call you Miss Louise?"

Louise cut her gaze sideways at Tanner. "I should think you'd know by now."

"Know what?"

"Men who look like August can be forgiven a whole manner of sins."

Tanner raised her eyebrows and then glanced behind her, where August was sitting three rows back. She could only see the top of his head, the side of his arm, but it was enough to flood her stomach—and lower—with warmth.

Didn't she know it.

ON A PRIVATE airstrip ten miles north of Atlanta, a group of people gathered together, all eager for Louise Wilt to step off the plane.

"Don't everybody rush her at once!" Jules directed. "She's been through enough."

"Stop telling us what to do. She's not even your real mother," Charlie said, a joke he'd worn out long ago, if anyone asked Jules. Which no one did.

"I told you all she was fine," Lucy said. "I don't know why no one ever listens to me."

"Because half the things you say don't make a lick of sense," Charlie retorted.

"Charlie," his wife, Jen, chided him, giving him that look that said, *Be nice to your sister, especially in front of your children*, and then she added, in case the look wasn't enough, "Be nice to your sister."

Tanner watched awkwardly from a few paces back as Mrs. Wilt got bum-rushed on the tarmac by a gaggle of people, all clamoring to touch her and fuss over her, tiny grandchildren throwing themselves at her legs. Tanner even thought she spotted an older granddaughter, about her own age, engulfing Mrs. Wilt in a huge hug.

And just like that, she was alone.

It was inevitable—and her own fault—but it didn't make it hurt any less. As she stood watching the grand reunion of Mrs. Wilt and her family, Tanner felt happy for her, yet jealous at the same time. She was losing yet another friend—the only one she had left. Suddenly, all of those big feelings she'd had for months that only came out as anger overwhelmed her, and after holding them back for so long, finally, *finally* the tears that filled her eyes spilled over onto her cheeks. It was pitiful, really, Tanner standing there feeling sorry for everything, but sorry for herself most of all.

And then out of the corner of her eye, she saw something. Or some*body*, to be more specific. A familiar figure coming from an outbuilding on the tarmac. It looked like her mom for a split second, but it couldn't be, because the figure was rushing toward her. Running, really. And she couldn't remember the last time she'd ever seen her mother run. If her mother even *could* run.

Tanner squinted, the familiar faces of Marty and Harley and her dad in tow behind the running woman, who Tanner still wasn't convinced *was* her mother—until Candace was standing right in front of her, throwing her arms around Tanner's neck, sobbing and sighing and squeezing her tight and repeating *My baby my baby my baby*, over and over.

If someone was watching, perhaps they wouldn't think much of it. After all, mothers and daughters have been hugging each other—have been fighting and making up—since the beginning of time. But for Candace, who had held Tanner in her arms a thousand times or more—from the first moment she came wailing into the world and the many moments since, doing her best to assuage all her hurts, to absorb them like a sponge the way only mothers can—it was nothing short of miraculous. The way the smallest and most inexplicable moments of motherhood are. Primal. She nearly collapsed in relief at the scent of her daughter's hair, her skin, the tangible weight of her body, and mostly the way Tanner squeezed her back—a full, active participant in the hug, rather than the passive way she'd been letting Candace envelop her for years, as though she were barely tolerating it.

"You're OK?" Candace said, leaning back and palming her daughter's face in her hands to look at her, to make sure with her own two eyes.

"I'm OK." Tanner nodded.

"Don't ever do that to me again."

"I won't."

They both knew it was a lie. Not that Tanner would abscond with an eighty-four-year-old suspected jewelry thief being chased by the FBI again—in fact, she would try very hard to prevent herself from being in that predicament for a second time. But Tanner, of course, like most daughters, would make many more choices throughout her life that Candace would likely not agree with, causing a fair amount of stress and anxiety, which her mother would then naturally reabsorb and view as her own shortcoming somehow.

"Your hair!" her mom said, putting her hands up on either side of Tanner's sheared locks. Tanner allowed her mom to study her and waited for the inevitable criticism—the furrowing of the brow, the frown, the utter disappointment.

"It suits you," her mom pronounced, cupping Tanner's shoulders with a gentle squeeze.

Tanner's sister, Marty, squeezed her body into the fray, throwing her arms around Tanner's waist, and then Harley and her dad piled on. Tanner couldn't remember the last time she'd been in a family hug, much less the center of one. She smiled through her tears, not caring for once who saw her crying.

When they finally let go and stepped back to give her space, Marty slipped a familiar rectangular shape into Tanner's hand.

Tanner gripped it, looking up at her sister. "Why do you have my phone?"

"The FBI gave it to Mom so she could try and contact your friends and see if anyone had heard from you," Marty said.

Tanner gaped, the thought of her mother seeing her messages momentarily rendering her silent.

"Don't worry. I went into it, not her." She leaned closer to Tanner's ear. "I hope you didn't like that Grant guy, by the way."

Tanner's eyes widened further, her stomach dropping at the thought of her sister seeing their sext messages—though it was determinedly better than her mom reading them. "Why?"

"I told him exactly what he could do with those disgusting dick pics."

A mere week ago, Tanner would have been furious at her sister for invading her privacy, but now a smile slowly spread across her face. And then she laughed. "Good," she said, slipping her arms around her sister once more and squeezing her tight. Tanner inhaled the familiar scent of her sister's shampoo.

She had so much to say to her, wanting to tell her all the things that had been for too long unsaid between them—*I love you. I've missed you. I'm sorry.*

But Marty opened her mouth first, and Tanner felt her sister's breath hot against her ear, releasing three other, unexpected words: "Who is *that*?"

Tanner and the rest of her family turned to see who Marty was looking at, in time to watch August Wright slowly trot down the stairs from the airplane, his chest muscles flexing beneath his shirt, his tattoos proudly on display in the glow of the evening sun, his bicep popping and stretching his already taut shirtsleeve as he reached up to gently jam his fingers in his long, loose hair, pushing it back from where it was determined to fall in his face.

Tanner grinned, Marty ogled, and Candace experienced a bad feeling in the pit of her stomach—that the man, whoever he was, was already going to be one of those decisions her daughter would make that she would completely not agree with—and was also very much out of her control.

34

ONE AND A HALF YEARS AFTER LOUISE WENT MISSING AND JULES CALLED THE POLICE

"TANNER, COME QUICK! I think this is it."

Tanner stood in a hairnet and rubber gloves, spraying dried scrambled eggs off a plate in the middle of the industrial kitchen before loading it into the dishwasher three times the size of the one in her apartment.

Mrs. Wilt had gotten her the job in food service at the Vinings River Retirement Village. Not by lying, the way she had gotten August a job, but by telling the truth: that Tanner was loyal and a hard worker, and she'd be a great addition to the hourly, minimum-wage staff. Tanner didn't think Mr. Trumbull, the head of the cafeteria, cared much about the loyal or hardworking part, but a high school student who had been working there for two months hadn't shown up for her last two shifts, so it was good timing.

Instead of hiring a live-in nurse, Mrs. Wilt and George decided it would be best to move into a new facility in Atlanta together, as neither of their conditions—George's memory loss and Mrs. Wilt's Parkinson's—were going to get better, and in fact were most definitely going to get worse. And it was best to be somewhere where they could be cared for properly.

And Tanner was pleased to get a job where she had an excuse to regularly visit her good friend Mrs. Wilt, in between her jaunts all over the globe. Tanner hadn't gone back to Northwestern with her money. Instead, she'd started traveling. First, to go see Vee and apologize in person. Her best friend forgave her, perhaps more easily than Tanner deserved—but they were best friends, after all. Tanner stayed for a soccer game—Vee had been let back on the team after a probationary period—and though it was bittersweet to not be on the field with her, Tanner was still the loudest fan in the stands.

Then she branched out, venturing to other cities, starting with a trip back to St. Louis to actually go up into the arch. August went with her on that one, laughing at her recounting of not making it past security and Mrs. Wilt's fear of heights. But the rest she took alone. She was young—and though August was undeniably hot, she didn't want to be tied down just when she'd found her wings.

Her most recent trip—two weeks in Italy—had been her favorite so far, thanks to Mrs. Wilt's suggestions of where to stay and what to do. Tanner sent her pictures every day, even after Mrs. Wilt admonished her to "put down your damn phone and enjoy it." Tanner planned to finish school, eventually—probably at a community college—and get her master's degree in sports science. Hopefully, one day, she'd be working at Vinings Village—or a nursing home like it—as a physical therapist for seniors. But for now, there was too much to see. Too much living to do.

And for right now, she had dish duty.

"*What's* it?" Tanner asked Beverly, one of the nurses on staff, who was Mrs. Wilt's favorite and one Tanner had quickly befriended when she started working there.

"Mrs. Wilt," Beverly said, and with one glance in her eyes, Tanner didn't have any more questions. She dropped the dish and raced out of the kitchen, through the dining hall, and down the long corridor toward the room she had spent so much time in for the past eighteen months.

Mrs. Wilt lay supine on her twin bed, eyes closed, body frail, a blanket pulled up to her chest and tucked beneath her arms. Her mouth was slack, her breathing nearly inaudible.

"She's been like this most of the morning. I called her family a few hours ago. They're driving in."

"Why didn't you come get me earlier?"

"I tried. You were in the middle of breakfast rush, and Trumbull wouldn't let me through," Beverly said apologetically. "I'll leave you with her for a minute. Let me know if you need anything."

Tanner stared at the woman, who looked so unlike the Mrs. Wilt she had first met, who was old, yes, but vibrant, full of life, healthy. Now her skin was pasty, wrinkled like a raisin in the sun, her veins more prominent. She reached out for the woman's hand, gently held it in her own, running her thumb over the raised ligaments, the blue veins, the papery skin, and recalled the one time Mrs. Wilt had talked about death, prompted by George's unexpected passing in her sleep just a few months after they'd both taken up residence at Vinings Village.

"That's the way to go," she said. "In your sleep, when you don't even know what's happening." And then she added, in a quieter voice, "I just don't want to be alone when it happens."

It was an oddly vulnerable thing for Mrs. Wilt to admit, and it made Tanner all the more determined to make sure that she wasn't.

Her breathing was nearly inaudible, and Tanner leaned closer, wondering if she was breathing at all. Then a big gasp of an inhale filled Mrs. Wilt's chest and rattled in the back of her throat, startling Tanner. She stared at her, expecting Mrs. Wilt to wake up any second, but the woman's eyes remained closed, her breathing returning to shallow.

After a few minutes of standing there, unsure what to do, Tanner gently sat on the edge of the bed, and then, without thinking, lay down on her side in the strip of mattress available, putting her head gently on Mrs. Wilt's shoulder. She wrapped her other arm across the woman's frail body, lightly stroking Mrs. Wilt's far arm with her fingers.

"I'm here," Tanner whispered. She looked up at Mrs. Wilt's face, so close she could see the fine hairs on her upper lip, her chin. She stared at the woman's lips, a nearly unrecognizable sallow beige without their typical coating of pink lipstick. She remembered all the times Mrs. Wilt had applied it, could picture her exact expression in the mirror, her lips forming an O, then pressing together in a line. Tanner smiled, though her eyesight was becoming blurry as she remembered Mrs. Wilt telling her offhandedly one day, "*Don't let them put me in the ground without my lipstick.*" She sat up, suddenly on a mission. She couldn't do much, but she could apply lipstick.

A tear slipped from her eye as she plucked the tube of lipstick from Mrs. Wilt's dresser and uncapped it. A few steps back to the bed and she twisted the tube up, reaching forward with the extended stick of color. As soon as she touched it to Mrs. Wilt's lips, the woman's eyelids popped open and her gaze shifted left toward Tanner.

Tanner screamed and dropped the lipstick, which left a streak of pink on the white sheets as it fell to the ground.

"What are you doing?" Mrs. Wilt asked, her voice croaky.

"Putting lipstick on you!" Tanner said defensively. "What are you doing?"

Mrs. Wilt struggled to sit up, and Tanner helped her, rearranging pillows behind her to support her neck and back. "What do you mean, what am I doing? I was sleeping until I felt you hovering over me. Touching my lips like that."

"We . . . they said you were . . . dying."

Mrs. Wilt waved a bony hand. "You people always think I'm dying. I haven't even had my breakfast yet." She arched one eyebrow at Tanner. "Have I?"

Her mind had been wandering a lot more lately, forgetting whole swaths of time, hallucinating people from her past. She told entire stories about Ken and George as though she had just spoken to them. Maybe she had, Tanner thought. Who knew?

Once Tanner stopped in to ask how her day was, and Mrs. Wilt said, "Oh, wonderful! I toured a submarine," and it was difficult to tell if she was being sarcastic or if she thought she'd actually been on an underwater vessel. The doctors said it was partly her Parkinson's advancing into the stages of dementia, and the cocktail of medication she was on to try to control the trembling, the dizziness, to preserve her ability to walk and talk—two skills that had been deteriorating over time.

Tanner smiled. "No, you haven't had your breakfast yet. I'll see if I can get you your poached eggs and toast."

Mrs. Wilt reached out, grabbing Tanner's arm with her hand. "Are there any pecan waffles back there?"

"Pecan waffles? I don't know. I can check the freezer. Why?"

"I want some."

"For breakfast?"

"Unless it's dinnertime."

"No, it's just . . . you always eat a poached egg and toast."

"Well, I'm not getting any younger, am I?" She pointed at the wall behind Tanner. "Take those cookies with you. The ones in the blue tin."

There were no cookies, in a blue tin or otherwise.

"OK, Mrs. Wilt. I'll get them," Tanner said. The doctors had advised it was easier and harmless to just go along with the hallucinations instead of fighting them, that it was less confusing to Mrs. Wilt that way. Tanner sometimes gently corrected her. But pretending there were cookies on a shelf? Well, that she could do. Tanner turned to go.

"Wait! I have one more thing to give you."

"What?" Tanner asked.

"Look in the bottom shelf of my dresser, beneath the sweaters down there."

Tanner did as she was told, pulling the drawer out.

"Should be an envelope. Has your name on it. You can open it later."

Tanner readied herself to pretend again, but was surprised to see that what Mrs. Wilt was saying this time was true. There was a manila envelope, smaller than document size, bigger than a letter, with *Tanner* scrawled across the front in Mrs. Wilt's handwriting. Tanner pulled it out and shut the drawer, standing up to her full height.

"What is it?" she asked, seeing a bulge the size of an acorn in the middle of the envelope.

Mrs. Wilt didn't say anything for what felt like a full minute, her eyes glazing over, and when she looked back at Tanner, it was with a one-thousand-yard-stare, which was to say, she wasn't really looking *at* Tanner. "A leg of lamb," she said. "Always good to have one in the freezer. In case you ever need it."

Tanner knew the lucid moment Mrs. Wilt had been having was gone, that the nonsensical mutterings had returned. She was about to open her mouth to say thank you anyway, but the door opened, and Mrs. Wilt's family began pouring in, Jules leading the pack. At seeing her conscious and sitting up, they all started shouting at once.

"Mom, you're alive! Oh, thank God. You gave us a fright!"

"Don't do that to us, Mom! I've been crying all morning."

"What? They said you were dying! I left an important meeting to be here." That was Charlie. "I mean, I'm glad you're not, of course."

As they circled around her, the younger grandkids shyly filling in the spaces around her bed (Poppy only coming in as far as the dresser, her face stuck in her phone), Tanner got squeezed to the edges of the room.

She turned to leave and had one foot out the door when she heard it, above the din. "Hey! Girlie!"

She turned and locked eyes with Mrs. Wilt, who offered her a grin and a wink. Tanner smiled, a laugh bubbling to the surface, her eyes brimming once more. She held Mrs. Wilt's gaze for another second and then two, savoring the moment.

Then she slipped out the door and started toward the kitchen to look for the pecan waffles, shoving the envelope in her bag in the break room on the way.

It wasn't until later that evening, alone at her apartment, that Tanner remembered it. Standing in her bedroom in a tank top and flannel pajama pants, she turned the envelope over, unclasped the metal brackets, and lifted the flap, gently dumping its contents into the palm of her hand.

She let out a small gasp.

It was smaller than she imagined—about the size of half a walnut, minus the shell—set in a thin silver band, eight tiny pointy prongs holding it in place. Still, in her disbelief, she knew exactly what she was looking at: the Kinsey diamond.

LOUISE WATCHED THE girl slip out, wondering if it was the last time she'd see her. She knew she was dying. She'd known it for weeks; she just didn't know when.

"Did I ever tell you George and I robbed the Copley Plaza?" she said, to no one in particular. "It was one of the biggest jewelry heists in history."

"Yeah, Mom. You told us. Right after you told us about that submarine tour, remember?" Jules said.

Louise had been trying to tell them for weeks what she had done—maybe it was the imminence of death and wanting to make sure everything was right with her soul. (She wasn't sure she believed in God, but it was never a bad idea to dot your i's and cross your t's just in case.) She knew her kids didn't believe her. The first time she'd said it, Jules had patiently explained (in the same manner one might tell a toddler where babies come from) that because she'd been wrongly accused of the Copley Plaza heist, her brain was mixed up, making her think that she *had* actually done it. They didn't believe she'd seen Ken, either. Sometimes he'd come into the room, sit on her bed, and hold her hand for a while. Sometimes his back was to her, arms crossed, like he was angry with her. It was the drugs, they said. For her Parkinson's. But she knew better.

He was waiting for her.

George would've believed her. George believed *in* her, no matter what. In life, there were two kinds of friends: friends who would wish you well on your journey to battle, and friends who would jump in the trenches with you. The latter were much more difficult to come by, but George belonged in that group. Which was how she had known, when she'd asked so many years ago, that George would rob the Copley Plaza with her.

She stumbled on the idea quite by accident when she was at Betsy D'Amato's one day, searching Sal's library for cash she could start to skim each week to finance Betsy's escape. Sal came home unexpectedly, and she had to dive in the room's one closet and hope no one found her. It was the most terrifying thirty-two minutes of Louise's life, but also ended up being the most lucrative, even though she didn't know it at the time. Sal went through the plans in detail to rob the hotel—two men, wearing masks, would go at 4:00 a.m. New Year's Day, when revelers were tucked in their beds, staff and security were light, and all the jewels worn to the party and the money of the hotel guests would be snug in their safe-deposit boxes until banks opened the next day.

It was a solid plan, Louise had to admit, but she didn't think another thing of it, until Betsy died. Until she posed as a nanny to take care of Jules. Until she overheard Sal on the phone saying the Copley was off. Their man who had hired them for the job had changed his mind, and Sal thought it was no longer worth the risk.

And that was when the wheels of Louise's brain started turning. She and George needed money. Or, that was to say, some of the women they'd relocated needed money. Every other day, they fielded calls from desperate women with mouths to feed, no husbands to care for them, no skills to speak of to get a job and earn a decent wage. Or the ones who did have skills had to leave their children alone all hours of the day so they could work full-time, make enough money to make ends meet. George and Louise wanted to help the women, but how? Their paltry funds were spent on getting women out, procuring new identification, travel expenses, and the like.

And now Louise had a way to score—what had Sal said in his office that day—$100,000 or more in cash alone? And the plan sounded so easy, so foolproof; the more she thought about it, the more convinced she became they could do it.

George wasn't as easy to sway. But in the end, she could never say no to Patty, and agreed on one condition—that they pose as men.

"I don't know. Do you really think we could pull it off?" Louise asked, unsure.

"With my voice and your height? Absolutely," George said.

And she was right, even if Louise thought all the apologizing George did to the staff as they were tying them up was surely going to get them caught. In her experience, men rarely said they were sorry for anything.

It was easier than either of them had anticipated. Louise asked for New Year's Eve off work, leaving Jules in the care of Salvatore's housekeeper. And George and Louise executed Sal's plan at the Copley Plaza down to the last detail. When they left the hotel in the wee hours of the morning, ripping their masks off and letting their hair out of their clown wigs before getting to the main street, they looked at each other for one exhilarating split second of *did we really just do that?* Then Louise took the train back to New York, and George took the loot with her back to Ohio. The plan was for George to distribute the cash to the women who needed it most, setting aside any surplus for future missions, while Louise lay low in the New York brownstone.

But nothing in life goes according to plan.

Sal told her, when he stopped in for dinner and a change of clothes, that he wouldn't be needing her services anymore. Tomorrow was her last day with Jules. And Louise made the decision right then. She'd take the girl and run.

To complicate matters, it wasn't until the evening paper came out that Louise realized what she and George had done: stolen one of the world's most famous diamonds. They had been pulling everything out of the safe-deposit boxes so fast, they hadn't stopped to see what was in them—and likely would have thought a diamond that big to be costume, anyway. Now, between the baby and the diamond, they were really in trouble.

In good news, at least they had cash with which to flee.

Though they'd no longer be able to continue their fifteen-year trade of helping women get out of abusive situations, Louise did disburse most of the money to the women who needed it, and continued to keep in touch with them over the years via letters and cards. George, for her part, went back to school in California, first working as a paralegal, and then a lawyer, eventually becoming a prominent attorney working some of the most high-profile cases involving women's rights.

After marrying Ken and moving to Atlanta, Louise stuffed the Kinsey diamond in an envelope in her locked nightstand drawer along with her pistol and never looked at it again. She thought of it sometimes, thought about trying to return it—what use did she have for a thirty-seven-carat diamond?—but where would she return it to? And how would she explain how she came into possession of it?

Diamond or not, what they had done was very illegal, and she had her children to think about.

But now, she was dying, and as all humans do, she was taking stock of her life, her possessions, and deciding whom best to pass them on to. She could, of course, have given the diamond to one of her children, but it didn't feel right. They had been part of her third life, her life *after*, and honestly, she just didn't think they'd understand. To them, she was a mother, and once a mother, you're never quite a fully formed person in the eyes of your children.

Tanner, on the other hand, had told her once that she felt like Louise understood her in a way not many people did. Louise had brushed her off, said something flippant like "I just understand what it is to be a woman in this world." But the truth was, she did feel a level of understanding with the girl, a kinship that perhaps was created under forced circumstances, but flourished beyond Louise's imagination. And it had all started in a Holiday Inn when Tanner realized they were on the lam and made the decision with fortitude that she would see Louise to her destination, come hell or high water.

It surprised Louise, and not many people did. Because it was something Louise herself would have done, and had done over the many years of her life—created her own rules, her own sense of right and wrong; forged her own path, regardless of what the world would have you do, who it would have you be.

Louise knew, without a shadow of a doubt, the diamond belonged to Tanner. What she didn't know was what the girl would do with it: maybe send it to Agent Huang anonymously, turn it in in person along with the truth, sell it on the black market and buy a yacht to sail around the world taking lovers in every port (Louise found this option brought her the most joy to imagine), or keep it locked away in a drawer, maybe confessing to a future granddaughter one day the whole sordid tale.

In the end, it didn't really matter to Louise what Tanner did. The ring wasn't hers to worry about anymore. Louise had made her choices in life.

Now, it was Tanner's turn.

Acknowledgments

As always, first and foremost I'd like to thank my readers—both the ones who have championed my books from the very beginning and the new readers who have joined along the way. I'd also like to thank all of the hardworking and amazing booksellers, librarians, and Bookstagrammers who help spread the word about my books and often physically put them in new readers' hands. It is because of you that I get to continue to make up stories for a living, and I am forever grateful.

And thank you to the following people:

My agent, Stephanie Rostan, who not only entertains my story ideas no matter how bizarre but also enthusiastically encourages me to write them. You are the absolute best in the business, and I am so impossibly lucky to get to work with you. Thank you for finding a home for my books in the publishing industry and beyond.

My editor, Kerry Donovan, who constantly pushes me to dig deeper. My stories and my writing craft are better for it.

The rest of my large and talented publishing crew at Berkley, including Christine Ball, Ivan Held, Claire Zion, Craig Burke (and his unrivaled enthusiasm for the *Jeffersons* theme song), Jeanne-Marie Hudson, Jin Yu, Tina Joell, Mary Baker, Kate Whitman, and the rest of the sales, marketing, and publicity teams. Thank you for all of your hard work shepherding my books into the world and getting them in the hands of readers.

My copy editor, Angelina Krahn. You had your work cut out for you with this one! Thank you for your close attention to detail.

My publicist, Kathleen Carter. You are a force, and I'm so grateful to work with you.

My film agent, Sally Wilcox. Thank you for loving Tanner and Louise and for creating such excitement for their story in Hollywood. Fingers crossed we'll get to see them on the big screen one day!

Chris Seltman, for sharing your knowledge of police work and investigations (and Anita LeBeau, for putting me in touch with your wonderful son-in-law).

Jeff Brown, for answering all of my questions about GBI protocol. Go Greer High Yellow Jackets!

Thomas Lyman, for your input on Georgia law and putting up with my numerous bizarre text messages about mail theft, crimes in the 1970s, and statutes of limitations.

Any mistakes or inaccuracies regarding police/FBI work in this book are solely due to my own mistakes and/or artistic license.

Dr. Brent Stephens, for once again sharing your expertise on my various characters' maladies. Who knew your medical degree would come in so handy?

Melinda Servick and her wonderful mother, ZZ, for sharing their hilarious family stories with me—some of which may or may not have inspired a few of Louise's antics. Melinda, your mom was truly one of a kind, and I like to think this book would have made her laugh.

My dad, Bill Oakley, for being the greatest writing retreat host ever. Thank you for all of the omelets, coffee, dinners, and running commentary on the ducks on the lake, and the offer to teach me how to open a padlock when you've forgotten the code. You are a trove of both useful and useless information, and I love you so much.

My beta readers, who I'm also lucky to call the very best of friends: Kristy Barrett, Caley Bowman, Jessica Chamlee, Brooke Hight, Megan Lobe, Kelly Marages, Laurie Rowland, and Jaime Sarrio.

My fellow writers who have become a much-needed and beloved community in this wild roller coaster of an industry, including Mary Kay Andrews, Nicole Blades, Karma Brown, Emily Giffin, Kristin Harmel, Kristy Woodson Harvey, Patti Callahan Henry, Kimmery Martin, Aimee Molloy, Kirsten Palladino, Amy Reichert, and Taylor Jenkins Reid.

My four children and the reason my heart beats: Henry, Sorella, Olivia, and Everett.

My husband, Fred. No one ever claimed it was easy to be married to a writer—and I don't think you would either. Thank you for loving me anyway.

Finally, thank you to the women for whom this book is dedicated: My late grandmother, Marion Oakley, who taught me the importance of never missing cocktail hour. My nana, Penny Wyman, who taught me how to be in charge while letting everyone else think they're in charge. My sister, Megan Oakley, who taught me to be my own person, even when all I wanted to be was her. And my mother, Kathy Oakley, who taught me—and continues to teach me—everything else.

THE *Mostly* TRUE STORY OF TANNER & LOUISE

COLLEEN OAKLEY

READERS GUIDE

Discussion Questions

1. When Tanner and Louise first meet, they make a lot of assumptions about each other. Have you ever gotten a negative first impression of someone that turned out to be wrong (or right) as you got to know them?

2. When we first meet her, Tanner is hell-bent on getting back to Northwestern, even though she can't play soccer. Why do you think she's struggling so much to accept the curveball life has thrown her?

3. Given their age difference, what do you see as the toughest disconnect between Tanner and Mrs. Wilt when they start living together?

4. Do you have a favorite person in Louise's family? What do you enjoy most about the character?

5. When Tanner started to pick up on several suspicious things around Mrs. Wilt's house, did you agree with her? Or did you assume she had an overactive imagination?

6. When Louise burst into Tanner's room demanding they leave immediately, what did you think was the real reason she needed to leave? Were you right or wrong?

7. If you could pick the getaway car of your dreams, what would it be?

8. What was the most memorable pit stop along the road trip for you as you read? Have you been to any of the places Tanner and Louise went?

9. Louise muses: "People always said life was short, but it wasn't. Not really. You could cram so many different lives into one. Be so many different people." Do you think that's true? Do you feel like you've lived different lives or been a different person at different times in your life?

10. Did you see a point where Tanner's mindset about aging begins to change from what she thought early on, that "all old white women were nearly indistinguishable from one another"? Did you agree or disagree with her there?

11. There are so many strong female friendships in this novel—Tanner and Vee; Louise and George; and then, of course, Tanner and Louise. How do these relationships differ, and how are they similar? Do any of them remind you of your own friendships? How so?

12. When George and Louise are catching up after being reunited, Louise asks George, "Do you really think things are better now? For women, I mean." What do you think? Are things better or worse for women in America now than, say, fifty years ago?

13. What would you say is the biggest life lesson Tanner learns from her friendship with Louise? And does Louise learn anything from having Tanner in her life?

14. The author was inspired to write this novel because of her close relationship with her grandmother and everything her grandmother taught her. Have you ever had the experience of learning from an older generation? What was the most valuable thing they shared with you?

Don't miss Colleen Oakley's

THE INVISIBLE HUSBAND OF FRICK ISLAND

available now!

THE STORM

At first, when Piper scanned the docks and didn't see the familiar rickety white-pine-and-fir fisherman's trawler, she thought nothing of it. Tom, like most Chesapeake Bay watermen, tried to beat the sun's rays onto the water every morning during crab season, squeezing in every minute of the government-allotted eight hours of crabbing per day. That put him back in the harbor just after lunch most afternoons, with plenty of time for his onshore duties—icing his catch, checking his floats, tending to the boat. But inevitably some mornings there was a delay—a net needing mending, the buy boat running late. On those days, Tom's deadrise would come puffing into the harbor later than the others, when the sun was halfway down the other side of the sky. But whether it was two, three, or four in the afternoon, it didn't much matter. Time on Frick Island had always been more of a theoretical concept measured in *jiffies* or *awhiles* or *later ons*.

Still, even though there was no telling on any given day when Tom would return, every afternoon when the Blue Point market closed at three, Piper flew through her closing responsibilities moving the packaged deli meats, cheeses, and any unsold fresh crab cakes from the display cooler to the back refrigerator, mopping the cracked linoleum floors, hanging up her apron on the hook in the office, and slipping her card in the punch time clock (even though she had never seen Mr. Garrison so much as look at them)—and rushed over to the docks.

Most days Tom was already there, helping tie off boats or diagnosing an outboard engine problem or simply standing around with other watermen, grumbling about the day's haul or the sharp drop in the market price of oysters.

And sometimes, on those days, the breath would catch in Piper's throat. And she'd stop and stare at him for a beat in wide wonder that of all the places in the world, God had found it fitting to put Tom Parrish on the same tiny spit of land that she, too, inhabited. And even more miraculous, that though he could have had his pick of mainland girls at the high school they once ferried over to before the sun woke every weekday, Tom chose her.

Fire. That was what Piper remembered when she thought of those early days on the ferry with Tom. There was a heat to those mornings, even in the dead of winter, when they could see their breath float out into the cold air in great big puffs, as if they were exhaling cigarette smoke. She'd never forget the way the clouds would suddenly blush pink at the first kiss of sunlight and how her face followed suit whenever she caught Tom looking at her. Or the way when Tom, two years her senior, first sat next to her on the boat when there were at least ten other empty spots he could have chosen, and his thigh burned so hot against hers, even through their jeans, that it warmed her entire body from the inside out. And she thought she might die from the sheer pleasure of it.

And she'd been dying a thousand tiny pleasurable deaths every day, ever since. Like the first time he clumsily kissed her, behind his dad's crab shack sophomore year, catching just the corner of her mouth and a few locks of her hair. And the second time, a week later, when he didn't miss at all. Or when he would leave notes for her in the pocket of her jacket, tucked in schoolbooks, or affixed to the outside corner of her bedroom window, and she wouldn't find them until hours later, running her thumb over the tiny block letters of his handwriting, her heart fit to burst. Or when, just a year earlier, they had been lying in the bottom of the very boat she was now scanning the horizon for, and—looking at the moon—he had whispered the words she realized she'd been waiting to hear from him since she was fourteen: *We should get married.*

She agreed immediately, because after seven years, she still felt the same way she did those mornings on the ferry—that when he looked at her, she was alive. And when she was away from him, she counted down the seconds until he would be near again.

But on this breezy April afternoon, Piper would have to count for a little while longer, it seemed. She slunk over to the bench, swiping the beads of water off of it with her bare hand. There had a been a storm that morning when they woke, a spring squall angering the seas, creating choppy waters that slowed even the most experienced boat captains. But watermen didn't stop for weather. As BobDan Gibbons, the official Frick Island ferry boat captain, often explained to the boatloads of tourists visiting from the mainland: *The crabs don't know it's rainin'.*

So Piper sat on the wooden bench, the dampness seeping through the back of her khaki slacks, and pulled a book out of her satchel, cracking the worn spine. Piper and Tom both loved to read, but whereas Piper enjoyed mostly mass-market mysteries, bodice-ripping romances, and even heart-pumping horror, Tom preferred higher-brow literature. For years, Tom tried giving her some of his favorite classics as gifts: *Moby-Dick, A Tale of Two Cities, Frankenstein.* And to please him, she would try to muddle through, even if it meant reading the same paragraph over and over, while her mind drifted to other things. It wasn't that Piper wasn't smart—she was. (Science-minded like her mother, though she was drawn to entomology over ecology. Could tell you the species, genus, family, all the way up to the domain of a number of insects that crawled the earth.) It was just that when it came to reading, she liked what she liked.

And so far, she only liked one of the books Tom had given her, *Their Eyes Were Watching God*, and she was currently rereading it for the ninth time. The first time she read it, it drew her in from the very first paragraph: the idea that for some men, their dreams sail forever on the horizon, resigned that they will never reach them. She thought that perfectly described Tom in a way she might never have put into words. Literally, at times, when she would catch him staring out into the ocean, as if he were looking at another life he could have lived. But Tom was a Parrish. And while some island watermen's families saw the writing on the wall—the marine life in the bay was dying off from pollution and overfishing, and the sea levels were rising, swallowing up their island with it, inch by inch—and encouraged their kids to leave for government jobs on the mainland, join the military, go to college even, Tom's family were stalwarts of the community. Tom's daddy and his granddaddy and his granddaddy before him were watermen. And even though Tom's father was no longer around to see if his son kept up the tradition, or maybe *because* he was no longer around to see it, Tom felt duty bound to take his place at the helm of the trawler when his time came.

It wasn't just that sentiment in the book that reminded her of Tom, though, or really why she loved the book as much as she did. It was, of course, the love story. Maybe she was too young, or didn't have enough life experience, to truly appreciate the deeper themes of independence and feminism, but she wasn't too young to understand the burning desires of love. And she believed with her entire being, the way maybe only young people can, that she was the earth and Tom, her sun, moon, and stars. Tom was her Tea Cake and she loved him in the same way she breathed—effortlessly and as if it were the only thing that kept her alive.

So that was what Piper was doing—sitting on a bench, lost in the love story of Janie and Tea Cake, when a shadow fell over her pages. She looked up with her well-known smile, ready to greet whomever it was standing over her.

"Hey there, Pipes," BobDan Gibbons said. His face was weathered, in the way boat captains' faces are, as if their skin were competing to match the wood on the decks of their ships.

"BobDan," Piper said, the dimples in both her cheeks still on display.

"I don't know how to tell you this," he said, taking his baseball cap off his head and curving the worn bill in the palm of his hand. "I'm sure everything will be fine, of course, but Tom . . . well, he's gone missing."

Even though the words didn't immediately register with Piper, they did pull the corners of her lips back into a straight line. She cocked her head. "What do you mean, missing?"

He cleared his throat, a sound like a race car engine gunning on the starter block. "Apparently he radioed out for help this morning, during that little rain shower we had. Old Mr. Waverly got the call. Said he was taking on water, but the connection was bad and it went out 'fore Waverly could get the coordinates. Coast Guard's been looking for him since, and we've got some of the guys out there, too. Like I said, I'm sure we'll find him 'fore long and everything'll be fine." He twisted the bill of his cap one more time, and Piper wasn't sure if it was that movement or the grim look in BobDan's eyes that caused her stomach to go hollow.

And then Piper remembered the *Teredo navalis*. Three months earlier, Tom had spotted damaged wood on the hull of his trawler—a few drill-size holes, as if someone had shot a BB gun clear through the wood. Upon further inspection, he discovered he had shipworms, a parasite that fed on docks and boats and had been wreaking havoc at marinas for centuries—there was even a mention of them in *Moby-Dick*. To kill them, Tom had the boat pulled out of the water and sprayed it down with a hose, and after a few days without saltwater, the worms curled up and died, their carcasses like little circles of copper wire. (Piper, of course, took one home to study under her microscope.) The boards needed replacing, but by that time, they had already run through most of their winter savings—and the little bit they had left needed to go to new crab traps for the season. Tom hoped, until he could scrape the money together, that any water that came in through the tiny holes could be handled by the bilge pump.

Piper wasn't sure why she was thinking of the worms, except that Tom was an experienced boater and maybe she was searching for what could have possibly gone wrong. But she quickly dismissed the thought, because speculation wasn't going to get her anywhere, not to mention it ran counter to the only thing BobDan said that she wanted to believe—that everything was going to be fine.

"I believe I might join the search effort, if you want to tag along," he said. "Shirlene is gonna man the marina, in case anyone calls with news."

Piper considered this offer, but decided she wanted to be there, on the dock, when Tom's boat came chugging into the harbor, his mouth bursting to tell the wild story of his day's adventure on the sea. And so she waited, on the bench, not noticing the growl of her stomach when suppertime came and went, and trying not to notice the other watermen that came in to dock one by one, their hats in their hands like BobDan's, their heads bent toward the ground, their eyes avoiding Piper's at all costs.

Four days later, the boat was recovered by a diver at the bottom of the sea.

Tom's body was not.

While the rest of the town knew the worst had happened, Piper held out hope. Maybe Tom got disoriented and swam in the wrong direction, washed up on a deserted island, and was currently eating coconuts and writing messages in palm fronds for passing airplanes. Or maybe a ship of Somali pirates picked him up and he was being held against his will, unable to negotiate his release due to the language barrier. Or a whale swallowed him whole and he was contemplating his escape from the depths of its belly. Each of her theories was more outlandish than the next, but to Piper, none were as ridiculous as what the rest of the town believed—that Tom was gone. That she would never lay eyes on him again.

In the days following the Coast Guard's announcement that they were calling off the search for Tom, Piper found herself growing increasingly intolerant. And not just with the rescue teams who were, in her view, prematurely giving up. She couldn't stand the way people started looking at her, their eyes filled with pity. She couldn't abide the way they began referring to Tom in past tense. But the final straw was when the members of the island's Methodist (and only) church—where the Parrish family had been attending for as long as the church had been on the island, and where Tom and Piper had exchanged vows and thin gold bands—started planning a memorial service for Tom. Upon receiving that news, Piper locked herself in her one-bedroom carriage house behind the Oleckis' bed-and-breakfast. She didn't answer the phone, or the door, not even when Lady Judy stopped by with enough smoked ham and beaten biscuits and peach cobbler to feed half the island. She left the food on Piper's stoop and it sat there all afternoon until the sun set. Until Mrs. Olecki retrieved it and set it out in the main house's toile-covered living room for her current boarders to enjoy for supper.

Piper missed the memorial service altogether, where Tom's mother, glassy-eyed and catatonic, stood propped up by her brother Frank on one side and her nephew Steve on the other and the Valium that had been pumping through her veins daily since her husband's aptly named heart attack—the Widow Maker—had made good on its promise. Where Tom's cousin Steve's newborn interrupted the reverend with her insistent squalls, eyes screwed shut tight, giving voice to the pain the watermen were too stoic to show. Everyone asked after Piper, murmuring their condolences to every Parrish in attendance. *Poor girl*, they said, shaking their heads, offering various superlatives: too young, most in love, the worst.

But Piper couldn't hear them. She was in her bedroom, staring at the dent Tom's head had left on his pillow when his alarm clock prompted him to get up at 4:30 a.m. two weeks earlier. Piper didn't dare touch it—not even to try to inhale his scent that surely remained on the floral cover. Nor did she touch Tom's near-empty mug of coffee sitting in the sink, a film of mold growing on the top layer of liquid still left in the cup. Or the book—*Middlesex*, by Jeffrey Eugenides—splayed open, pages facedown, on top of the two wooden crates they stacked in the corner to use as a side table in their tiny den. It was as if all of these things, Tom's things, suddenly sprouted magical properties, transformed into talismans beckoning Tom back to where he belonged—to his bed to sleep, to the kitchen to wash out his coffee mug and hang it on the hook next to the sink, to the threadbare easy chair in the den to find out what happens to the characters of his current novel. They weren't just reminders of Tom, they were promises. He was going to come home. Of that one thing, Piper was sure.

And then one morning, just like that, he did.

Author photo by Sarah Dorio

COLLEEN OAKLEY is the *USA Today* bestselling author of *The Invisible Husband of Frick Island*, *You Were There Too*, *Close Enough to Touch*, *and Before I Go*. Her books have been translated into more than twenty languages around the world and have won multiple awards including Georgia Author of the Year and the French Reader's Prize. A former magazine editor for *Women's Health & Fitness* and *Marie Claire*, Colleen lives in Atlanta with her husband, four children, three chickens, and a mutt named Baxter.

VISIT COLLEEN OAKLEY ONLINE

ColleenOakley.com

WriterColleenOakley

OakleyColleen

WriterColleenOakley

Ready to find
your next great read?

Let us help.

Visit prh.com/nextread

Penguin
Random
House